# simply *from* scratch

# simply *from* scratch

## Alicia Bessette

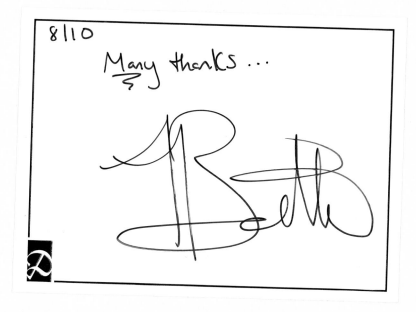

8/10

Many thanks ...

DUTTON

DUTTON
Published by Penguin Group (USA) Inc.
375 Hudson Street, New York, New York 10014, U.S.A.
Penguin Group (Canada), 90 Eglinton Avenue East, Suite 700, Toronto, Ontario M4P 2Y3,
Canada (a division of Pearson Penguin Canada Inc.); Penguin Books Ltd, 80 Strand, London
WC2R 0RL, England; Penguin Ireland, 25 St. Stephen's Green, Dublin 2, Ireland (a division
of Penguin Books Ltd); Penguin Group (Australia), 250 Camberwell Road, Camberwell,
Victoria 3124, Australia (a division of Pearson Australia Group Pty Ltd); Penguin Books
India Pvt Ltd, 11 Community Centre, Panchsheel Park, New Delhi—110 017, India; Penguin
Group (NZ), 67 Apollo Drive, Rosedale, North Shore 0632, New Zealand (a division of
Pearson New Zealand Ltd); Penguin Books (South Africa) (Pty) Ltd, 24 Sturdee Avenue,
Rosebank, Johannesburg 2196, South Africa

Penguin Books Ltd, Registered Offices: 80 Strand, London WC2R 0RL, England

Published by Dutton, a member of Penguin Group (USA) Inc.

First printing, August 2010
10  9  8  7  6  5  4  3  2  1

REGISTERED TRADEMARK—MARCA REGISTRADA

LIBRARY OF CONGRESS CATALOGING-IN-PUBLICATION DATA

Bessette, Alicia.
   Simply from scratch / by Alicia Bessette.
     p.  cm.
   ISBN 978-0-525-95182-7 (hardcover)
   1. Windows—Fiction.   2. Grief—Fiction.   3. Girls—Fiction.   4. Baking—Fiction.
5. Single fathers—Fiction.   6. Friendship—Fiction.   7. Families—Fiction.   I. Title.
   PS3602.E783S56 2010
   813'.6—dc22                                                              2010008894

Printed in the United States of America
Set in Sabon
Designed by Leonard Telesca

*This book is dedicated
to the friends who grew me up.*

# 1

## Zell

*I* KNOT NICK'S CAMOUFLAGE APRON under my boobs, unable to remember the last time I wore a bra, or preheated the oven. That's my widow style.

The brown sugar's as hard as a cinder block, so I hack at it with a knife. But after that the preparation's pretty easy, and I stir my improvised ingredients into a smooth cookie batter. That's when I smell smoke, which is jarring because there's nothing in the oven.

Or is there?

I flick the oven light switch, but the bulb's dead. All I can make out through the little window is a dark object on the top rack. It shouldn't be there; that much I know. Maybe I was supposed to check for foreign objects before preheating.

"Shall I let it burn, Captain?" I kneel, and Captain Ahab joins me. Gently I tug his velvet triangle ear. He snort-sighs, like the snuffle sound that horses make. He's unaware of the unidentified flammable object in the oven, which, any second now, will be swallowed in flames. Or maybe Ahab *is* aware of the impending disaster and simply takes it in stride. He's Zen that way; it's his greyhound style.

"Aye," I say in Captain Ahab Voice—that of a sloshed but kindly pirate. "Let it burn. Yer a saucy wench, Rose-Ellen."

I pull *Meals in a Cinch with Polly Pinch* down from the counter and let Ahab sniff the magazine's special pullout section, where Polly's electric white smile and tanned, peachy skin shine. She's shown winking, her arms crossed, her head tipped coquettishly.

The winner of Polly's Desserts That Warm the Soul baking contest receives twenty thousand dollars. Twenty thousand. The exact amount Nick mentioned in his e-mail when he told me about the money he wanted to raise for the people of New Orleans as they rebuild after the hurricane and the floods.

"Now, tell me that's not fate. Yarr." I kiss Ahab between his eyes.

An alarm screeches. A smoke alarm. A fire alarm. A saucy-wench-trying-to-bake alarm.

Balls.

The object in the oven is officially on fire. Its azure and orange wings shoot up as if inflated, as if ready for takeoff.

Minutes later, still on my knees, I yank open the oven door. Rolling, oily smoke engulfs me and Ahab. Something grips my shoulder, and I look up at a hulk of boots and helmet and axe.

"Get out of here, Zell!" It's Chief Kent. I recognize his gravelly voice. He hooks his thumbs under my armpits and hefts me to my feet. He pushes me through the now-roiling smoke into his second in command, either EJ or Russ; through the smoke, in their bulky black fireproof suits, they both look the same.

Here they are, Wippamunk's finest beer-gutted volunteer superheroes, extinguishing a fire at 111 High Street, the home of Rose-Ellen Roy (née Carmichael): Zell—me, the woman whose husband,

Nick, died on their watch, in another world, another lifetime. Do they think I've done myself in? Torched my house intentionally? Do they think my head burst into flames?

"Get her out of here!" bellows this second rescuer. He shoves me into a third rescuer, who drags me through the kitchen, through the living room, out to the front porch, and down the cement steps. I scream, "Ahab! Ahab!" the whole way.

Somehow I slip and land belly up on my yard's thin, hard crust of snow. My attic, with its one boarded-up window, seems church white against the blue, blue sky. The attic I will not—cannot—enter.

Russ SHEDS HIS FIREFIGHTER COAT, revealing spindly arms, a wife-beater undershirt, and reflective suspenders that flash in the sunlight. He kneels on the icy sidewalk that leads to my front porch. Shoveling was Nick's chore, along with car maintenance and—big surprise—cooking. I refuse to perform these tasks. I'll get to them later, I tell myself. For more than a year now, I've manually pumped my broken turn signal when turning left, eaten microwavable Polly Pinch meals for dinner, and stomped down two tire-width tracks in my driveway after every snowfall.

Russ holds a snout-shaped oxygen mask over Ahab's long nose. Ahab seems to think nothing unusual is happening, as if he's not breathing pure oxygen from a mask specifically designed for dogs that may have inhaled smoke. From time to time, he blinks.

I sit on the porch steps wrapped in a blanket from Engine 1747—incidentally, the year Wippamunk was incorporated as a Massachusetts town. Engine 1747 grumbles away in front of the house.

It's so cold, I can't really tell whether my nose is runny. I wipe it with the blanket anyway.

"Dogs dig me," Russ tells Ahab. "That's why I carry the mail. In my real job, I mean." With his free hand he gives Ahab a thumbs-up sign, then smacks his flank so hard that Ahab stumbles.

"You okay, Zell?" Russ asks.

"Well, is Ahab okay?"

"Right as rain." He grins and gives Ahab another flank smack.

"Then so am I, I guess. Right as rain."

"Zell? Got a present for ya," says Chief Kent. "Literally." He groans as he eases down next to me on the steps. Chief is older-gentleman sexy, in the way of many park rangers, bagpipers, and commercial airline pilots. But right now his face somehow reminds me of an old brick, his silver hair pokes out crazily, and his boots dwarf my bare feet. He's lived in this town his whole life, and he's been the fire chief since the year I was born.

In Chief Kent's huge hands is the object from the oven: a charred box the size of a human head, apparently made of hard plastic. The cube is deformed from heat. It looks like hardened lava coated with residue from the fire extinguisher. Its lid is sealed shut.

Chief Kent tosses it at me. I let it land, dense and heavy in my lap. I can tell right away there's something inside.

It's a present from beyond the grave. A present from Nick.

I always wondered where Nick hid his gifts for me. Several times a year, before Valentine's Day or my birthday or Christmas, I snooped around the house. Invariably I inspected the same places: behind the coats in the closet, the unusable fireplace, the clothes hamper. Nick followed me from room to room on these hunts. "You'll never find it!" he said, smiling with his mouth open.

Come to think of it, all his gifts—the small ones, anyway—emitted a certain odd, unfamiliar scent when first opened. A vaguely chemical, greasy, cavelike smell. The smell—I now know—of oven.

G.d. oven, Nick would have said. His father never allowed Nick to say "goddamn," but he preferred the abbreviation anyway, and the habit stuck.

"Zell!" Dennis trots up the sidewalk, waving his steno book. His J.Crew barn jacket has to be twenty years old, and a *Wippamunker* press pass flaps from the frayed pocket. The press pass is purely for show, because he's the only press person here.

He stops at the porch steps. His face is ruddy with cold and adrenaline. He and Nick worked at the paper together for ten years. They were about as close as two coworkers can be.

"Zell, thank God you're all right," Dennis says. "When I heard the street address over the scanner, when I realized it was your house, I—" He blows air through his lips, puffing out his cheeks.

"I'm okay, Dennis," I say. "I'm just the world's worst cook. That's all."

"Anyway." He licks the tip of his pencil; he always uses a pencil in winter because ink freezes. "Chief, cause of fire?"

Chief Kent pats my knee. "Ask Zell here."

"Cause of fire?" Dennis repeats.

"*Meals in a Cinch with Polly Pinch*," I say.

"Polly Pinch?" Dennis scribbles. "The celebrity chef?"

"That's off the record," says Chief.

The new guy pulls up and parks. He darts around the yard, snapping photographs, twisting his camera in all different angles. He peeks in my windows, then hurries over to Ahab, and the shutter clicks a few times in Ahab's face as Russ kisses him through the oxygen mask. The new guy photographs Chief, who, as everyone in Wippamunk knows, hates being photographed. And he gets a few shots of barefoot, braless me, slouched on the steps with a singed plastic cube in my lap. I'm wearing a camouflage apron and a neon orange blanket.

I watch him spaz around. He's got it all wrong, and that's why he's still, in my mind, the new guy, even though he took Nick's place at *The Wippamunker* more than a year ago. The contrast between his style and Nick's is glaring. Nick always strolled around casually before he took his camera out of his bag. He observed the scene, introduced himself, and asked for the homeowner's permission to take some photographs. "Let's not take ourselves too seriously," he was fond of saying. "Wippamunkers aren't Nixon, and I'm not Woodward and Bernstein."

The new guy bounds up the porch steps—Chief leans into me to avoid his swiftly moving knee—and continues snapping photographs inside. I hear him talk with EJ, who's in my kitchen, doing firefighter stuff, I suppose.

A moment later the new guy descends the steps. "No damage in there at all," he says.

"Wow, really?" I say, trying to sound cheery. "That's good news for me. Disappointing for you, I suppose, though."

He shrugs, fits the lens cap back on his camera, and walks to his car. I wonder what he knows about me. About Nick. And EJ.

A Wippamunk police cruiser pulls up to the house. France gets out, climbs the porch steps, and raps on my new neighbors' door.

"Hey, Zell," she says over the metal railing that divides the porch. Acne scars pock her thin face. Her eyes bulge slightly, and red ears poke out from under a low-slung cop hat. "You hurt?" she asks.

Before I can answer, the neighbors' door swings open. France shakes the hand of a tall man with close-cropped hair, hazel eyes, and cocoa skin. "Officer Frances Hogan," she says.

"Garrett Knox," says the man. "My daughter, Ingrid, and I moved here from the other side of town last month."

France reassures him that everything's okay; it was just an accidental cooking fire, and our shared house is no worse for wear.

"Glad to hear it," Garrett says. "Thanks." He waves to me—a quick flick of wrist—and flashes a warm smile before heading back inside.

My house is really half a house, a twin. During today's regular mail route, Russ accidentally slipped the Knoxes' copy of *Meals in a Cinch with Polly Pinch* into my mailbox. An understandable mistake, seeing as our mailboxes are side by side, epoxied to the vinyl between our doors.

Ahab and I were returning from a walk when I spotted *Meals in a Cinch* sticking out of my box. The headline promised to lift my spirits, so naturally I grasped the magazine and pulled it out, and saw Polly Pinch, midlaugh, surrounded by clean-cut teens all happily munching on carrots, apples, and a few other fiber-packed and wholesome after-school snacks. I read the teasers: PERK UP THE SPIRITS OF EVERYONE AROUND YOU! ENTER POLLY'S FIRST-EVER BAKING CONTEST AND WIN $20,000!

It was that dollar amount—Nick's same dollar amount—that did it. I headed inside, locked myself in the little powder room under the stairs, and read *Meals in a Cinch with Polly Pinch* cover to cover.

Garrett's daughter, Ingrid, comes outside now, clomping across the porch in knee-high Uggs. She grips the railing and does some pliés. A too-big red ski hat caps her long auburn braids. She's nine or ten, and her skin is lighter than Garrett's, the color of sunlight on oak floors. "What were you cooking?" she asks.

"Good question," Dennis mutters, licking the tip of his pencil.

"Flourless peanut butter cookies," I say.

Dennis scribbles.

"Why?" Ingrid leaps off the porch, clearing all four steps and landing with a crunch in the snow.

"I was making them for you," I say. It isn't exactly true, although

I might have brought over a dozen, if they turned out all right. After all, I would've had to test my contest entry on someone.

"I'm allergic to peanuts," she says. She smacks her gum.

Russ releases Ahab to me and shoves the doggie oxygen mask back into its case. "Ahab should be back to normal in no time," he says.

I look around and realize that I'm surrounded by the people who went on The Trip with Nick. There are Russ and Dennis on the sidewalk a few feet away, Chief Kent sitting right next to me, Officer Frances leaning against the porch railing, and inside, EJ, whom I can hear rummaging around because, to rid the kitchen of smoke, someone propped open the front door.

Ahab takes a few careful steps toward me but stops when the girl throws her arms around him and kisses his forehead.

"Ahab likes you," Russ tells her. "You should deliver the mail when you grow up. Like me."

"I'm going to be a chef on TV," she says.

This cracks Russ up. He laughs like a doofus and yanks his suspenders and lets them slap against his puny chest. "Well, I'll be back tomorrow with your mail, Zell," he says once he's collected himself. "Hey," he adds. "Tomorrow's Friday."

"Our standing lunch date," I say. Russ has been bringing me lunch every Friday since Nick's memorial service. He's a few years older than me and he's always been big brotherly; in grade school he designated himself my "bus buddy," sitting next to me even when his friends called him to the back of the bus.

"What do you want to eat?" he asks.

I try to smile, but I don't quite succeed. I mean, I used my oven for the first time in years, and I ended up with firefighters in my kitchen, a cop on my porch, and a reporter on my lawn. Granted, I've known most of these people for years. But still.

"Surprise me," I say to Russ, even though I expect nothing other than Orbit Pizza or leftovers generously donated by his wife. Which is fine by me, because otherwise I'd probably just skip lunch, like every other day.

Russ nods. "I'm full of surprises," he says, and galumphs to Engine 1747.

The radio at France's hip squawks. She turns the volume down and sighs. "Gotta go, Zell," she says. "I'll call ya later, okay?"

"Okay. See ya."

She tips her cop hat to Chief and Dennis, trots to the cruiser, and drives off.

"Thank you, Officer Frances," Ingrid yells after her. She scratches Ahab's back. Her fingernails are chewed and sparkly with old nail polish. Ahab sidles up against her; his back meets the level of her waist.

Her eyes fling wide. "He's leaning on me."

"Greyhounds do that," I say. "It's his way of giving you a hug."

Ahab's big for a grey: ninety pounds. But he's so gentle that she hardly even sways at his touch.

Chief Kent chuckles. "Nice hat, kiddo."

She shoves the hat, which slipped to the bridge of her nose, up toward the crown of her head. "Thank you." Then to me she says, "Do you like to cook?"

"I love to cook." It's a lie, of course. What I love is the thought of winning twenty thousand dollars. For Nick. For New Orleans. I never met those hurricane survivors, but he did. And because of them, he was a changed man. Maybe even a better man.

"You like Polly Pinch?" she asks.

I think of the impossible-to-avoid Polly Pinch. Her glowing face decorates cracker boxes in grocery stores all over America; she "pinches" a cracker between thumb and forefinger, holding it teasingly above her open mouth. In her most recent Big Yum Donuts television commercial, her breakfast in bed arrives on a silver tray and consists of only a foamy latte. With a sleepy half smile, she blows the steam, swallows, and moans her approval.

Polly Pinch is about the furthest thing you can imagine from the bifocaled, orthopedic-shoed Ye Olde Home Ec Witch—Mrs. Chaffin, who taught home economics at Wippamunk High School eighteen years ago. And until today—as I pored over the magazine and learned all about this dessert contest—I never knew how much I liked her. Polly Pinch, that is.

"I adore Polly Pinch," I say.

"You gonna open your present?" Ingrid asks. She points at the hard cube in my lap—the present from Nick that apparently was hidden in my oven for at least a year and three months.

I don't answer.

"Come on," she says. "Don't you want to know what's in the box?"

"Oh, there's nothing in it," I say.

Chief and Dennis exchange glances, which I pretend not to notice.

She skips over to me; Ahab, who was leaning against her, shuffles on the ice.

"There is too something in it," she says. Playfully she snatches the cube from my lap, holds it to her ear, and gives it a shake. It makes a solid knocking sound, like a toddler's toy, or wooden spoons.

"Please give that to me?" I stand barefoot on the icy sidewalk. The blanket pools at my ankles.

She hesitates, giggling. But I'm not playing. "Give it back," I say.

"Easy, Zell," Chief says. He stands and steps toward me, patting the air.

"Come on, Zell," says Dennis. "She's only teasing you. You need to put shoes on."

The bottoms of my feet burn on the ice, but I can't take my eyes off the warped cube in the small, honey brown hands of my girl neighbor.

Chief positions himself between me and her. He gives me a stern look and gently takes the cube from Ingrid, who gives it up easily. As bravely as she can without crying—I know she's swallowing tears because I recognize the effort—she whispers, "I like your dog." She stomps up her steps and slams the door behind her.

My feet are now totally numb. I kick the blanket.

And then EJ, from my kitchen, hollers, "I think we're all set, Chief."

I hear EJ walk around inside. I hear the legs of my kitchen table and chairs scrape the floor.

"There's nothing in it," I say.

"Okay," says Chief, handing me the oven present. "There's nothing in it. Whatever you say, Zell. Whatever you say."

"Of course there's nothing in it," says Dennis. "Now, cover up your feet before they get all frostbit."

I sit back down on the steps and wrap my feet in the blanket. I set the cube in my lap and finger the lid, melted and gnarled like a swollen lip. Ahab whines and steps toward me. I stroke his head and lower my face to kiss him. A tear sneaks from my eye and is absorbed in the dense, whiskered pucker of fur that is the equivalent of a dog eyebrow.

"Ay, Chief!" EJ calls from inside.

"Can you please get EJ out of my kitchen?" I say. "I just can't— I'm sorry, but—"

"Sure," Chief says. "Sure thing, Zell." He sighs and goes inside.

Dennis unclips his press pass and stuffs it into his pocket. He grips my shoulder in a fatherly gesture. "Be well," he says. A moment later, I watch his car bounce down the road.

Soon EJ and Chief emerge from my house and tromp down the steps.

"Zell?" Chief says—meaning, good-bye.

EJ doesn't speak to me, of course—he hasn't since The Trip. I think he's afraid of me. I can't blame him, because since Nick died, I haven't exactly been approachable, despite my efforts.

EJ stoops and softly tugs the blanket from my feet. Our eyes don't meet.

He and Chief join the other firefighters aboard Engine 1747. Russ drives, skinny, bare-armed Russ at the oversize steering wheel, bouncing down potholed High Street. Engine 1747 turns the corner. Puffs of gray, greasy exhaust hang over the street and fade, and the world is quiet again.

And save for Ahab, I'm alone. Just like that.

Ahab follows me into the kitchen, where I admit the new guy was right: There's no damage at all. The odors of smoke and fire extinguisher linger, but the room doesn't look any different than it did before the fire, except maybe a bit cleaner, somehow.

I smell something else. Coffee. Apparently, EJ brewed a half pot. Not for himself, I know, because I don't find any used mugs in the sink or dishwasher. He brewed it for me. I pour some and drink it black.

Ahab wants cookie dough. He cocks his head, dipping the eye-patch side of his face toward the floor. He doesn't really have an eye patch, but his fur's Holstein pattern makes it look so.

I pinch a dollop of dough and drop it into his elevated dish. He laps it up and nudges my hand for more, so I give him another peanut-buttery blob.

"Arr, Zell. I woulda chowed *all* yer treats. Cooked or uncooked. Every last bloody one. With or without a noggin o' rum. Yarr."

I think of Garrett Knox's daughter and her peanut allergy. She doesn't know what she's missing: peanut butter's salty-sweet creaminess. I'll bet she doesn't even have a memory of peanuts—no memory, no taste. A clean slate, a blank wall.

I put Nick's camo apron back where I found it, under the sink. And there I discover, in the trash can, heaps of soot-blackened paper towels. EJ, all that time, was cleaning my oven, cleaning my kitchen.

I notice the magnetic notepad on my refrigerator. The top sheet bears slanted, blocky man-handwriting: HEY, ZELL, TIME WE TALKED, COME DOWN TO THE MUFFINRY, ANYTIME, PLEASE.

EJ's business card is tucked under the magnet, as if I don't know where the Muffinry is. The card reads,

### EJ "The Muffin Man" Murtonen!
Come to Murtonen's Muffinry at 900 Main Street
in beautiful Wippamunk, Mass., for the best muffins
and coffee west of 495, or your money back!

FOR A COUPLE OF YEARS NOW, my heart does this weird thing, at weird times. Like now: four in the morning. The weird heart thing is sort of like being a widow—familiar by now, and yet completely foreign.

My heart thumps fast and hard. I sit up, gasping, and press my back against the headboard, which Nick trash picked and I painted midnight blue with silver stars of different sizes. Next to me, Ahab lifts his head. His eyes flash in the dark.

I count the seconds that pass during the spastic beats: six. Then the beats stop altogether, and I count the seconds that lapse during that weightless absence of internal thump: five.

My heart goes back to normal, plodding along steadily, calmly, unremarkably.

I turn on the light; I won't sleep. Ahab knows it, too, so he stands and eases himself down, daintily stepping on the footstool Nick trash picked for Ahab's exclusive use because, as he got older, jumping from our bed proved challenging, and a few times he slid right off the mattress and crashed to the floor, his legs splayed beneath him.

He follows me down the hall. I stand in the doorway of my office—I draw medical illustrations for a living—and inhale the scents of wood, wax, and eraser. I caress the slack jaw of the skeleton that hangs from a wheeled stand just inside the door. "Hi, Hank," I whisper.

Hank was Nick's name for the skeleton.

I'm hit with a Memory Smack; they plague me quite frequently. I was erasing something—an errant pencil mark alongside a tibia, or maybe I misspelled "brachiocephalic"—when Nick poked his head in my office door.

"You need a break," he said. He sang "Welcome to the Jungle." He took Hank down, held his wrists, and made him dance like Axl Rose: legs kicking out to the side, arms waving, hips swaying.

That was when we first moved in.

As so often happens when you're a widow, one Memory Smack leads to another, without regard to sequencing or time, and this second Memory Smack is from a trash night not so long ago: Nick beeped the horn and backed our crappy blue car into the driveway. Ahab and I watched from the door as he filled his arms with loot from the trunk. He smiled, took the porch steps two at a time, and planted a noisy kiss on my lips.

"Hope we like Gladys," he said.

"Who?"

That sharp autumnal smell clung to his dark hair. That smell of outside things receding into cold air. We in Wippamunk appreciate that process—it could be said we *worship* it—the annual beauty of fading, withering, and disappearing. That's our New England style.

Nick dropped his trash-night loot on the couch. We inspected it: a turntable, and a milk crate containing a complete collection of vinyl records by Gladys Knight and the Pips—in total, thirty-six albums.

The turntable and the albums were the very last things he trash picked.

The Memory Smack ends. Its edges turn black, and the scene shrinks until I can no longer see it, or smell it, or hear it.

Real time, real place.

Next to me, Ahab sniffs Hank's kneecap.

"Blimey, Hank!" I say softly, in Ahab Voice.

We continue downstairs, leaving Hank swaying slightly.

I Velcro Ahab into his gray fleece coat and tuck his ears into the elastic face hole. I tug a neoprene booty over each paw.

I zip my boots over my pajama pants, bundle my coat and scarf tight. I retrieve the warped, singed cube from a shelf in the living room, where I left it among Nick's dad's pottery. Even as the cube's contents knock around inside, I tell myself it's empty. The present feels heavy, though it probably weighs only a couple of pounds. I tuck it under one arm and clip on Ahab's leash.

We step outside, and the cold knifes through the thin cotton covering my legs. We slip and slide down High Street, past a uniform row of prefab colonial-style homes, all painted shades of tan, though in the dark they're a luminous, moonish color.

We pass Bedard's Orchard. Here Ahab sniffs expectantly for

Mr. B.'s fat orange cat, which he loves to try to chase, but the cat's not around tonight.

We pass the three-room police station and turn left onto Main Street. Ahab tries to cross because he thinks we're headed for the high school football field, where I let him off leash to run around. But we aren't headed for the high school tonight. Instead we climb Main Street, past the junction of Route 331. No cars. No traffic to speak of.

I feel the skin on my face tighten. I try to smile. I try to frown. It's so cold, I can't do either.

We pass the town hall and the town common and the cemetery, where gravestones from the eighteenth century tilt like bad teeth.

Ahab has no idea where we're going, but he takes the lead anyway, heading past the Congregational church, the Cumberland Farms, Wippamunk Gift Shoppe, Big Yum Donuts, and the gas station.

Main Street is dark, still, and lifeless—except ahead, where a traffic light blinks in front of Murtonen's Muffinry. Its windows are steamed. The smells of coffee, warm butter, and sugar waft into the empty gravel parking lot, and inside, yellow lights glow. From behind the building the butt end of the Muffinry van sticks out. I can just make out its edible-looking letters, the bite marks in the y.

EJ's massive shape moves inside the Muffinry's big bay window. He takes chairs down from tables.

Ahab and I continue on. But I stop abruptly when he growls. He never growls.

I scan my surroundings, trying to see what he sees—what makes him growl. But it's so dark, I can't see much, even with the blinking light. I realize I shouldn't have stopped, because now—standing in the parking lot with my breath hovering over me in icy puffs, stupidly gawping at Murtonen's Muffinry's gray-and-maroon-striped awning—I lose my nerve. Maybe I'm not ready to talk to EJ. Maybe I'm not ready to open Nick's present.

The air smells of gasoline, salt, and sand from the road, and EJ's muffins. EJ "The Muffin Man" Murtonen's delicious, cakey, moist, huge, Best of Wippamunk Award–winning muffins.

In my chest, the bottom drops out again, and my heart is suspended in beatless silence. Four frozen seconds. Five frozen seconds. Six. I really should call back Dr. Carrie Fung. But maybe if I don't, something bad—bad enough—will happen. After all, there's a lot for the human body to sabotage, so many gloriously fatal mistakes it can make. If I never return Dr. Fung's calls, some bad-enough heart episode might occur, and the event will lift me right off my feet, straight from this parking lot, straight up from Wippamunk, straight up from life. I'll float around beautifully—like dandelion fuzz spinning off a stem, like a tangle of Ahab's fur swept along the kitchen baseboard by cold wind when I open the back door to let him in. I'll be reunited with Nick. And we'll float around together, stunningly.

But the heartbeats return, as they always do: fast at first, then normal.

I'll walk home. I'll cue Gladys and the boys and fall asleep with my lips resting in the little indentation behind Ahab's ear.

"Ahab!" I whisper. "Come on, Cap'n."

He growls once more toward the parking lot, but he comes to me, because he always comes to me. And we head out again, back the way we came, toward High Street. Toward home.

"Harr, Zell, yer a yellow-bellied milksop," I say.

# EJ

Three and a half hours past midnight. Main Street is a black-and-blue ghost-town version of its daylight self. It's a strange time to know the world—firmly settled in neither night nor day. And just as the Muffinry van groans with protest when he turns the key, EJ himself needs a little coaxing. He rubs his face with both hands, allows a few body-shuddering yawns, and forces his palms to grip the numbingly cold steering wheel. (Finnish Americans are too tough for gloves, his dad always said.) He lets the engine idle for a few minutes, backs from his driveway into the bruised-looking world, and drives to the Muffinry.

Once there, he preheats the ovens. Turning the knobs—slippery with grease even after a good cleaning—he thinks of Zell's sooty oven. He'd known for years that Nick hid Zell's presents there. EJ knew she wasn't much of a cook, but he didn't know she *never* cooked. And the fact that it took her, presumably, at least a year and three months to discover this particular present, whatever it is—the fact that she hadn't touched the oven in that long—well, that fact makes him feel for her even more.

He mixes the blueberry muffin batter (sugar, flour, baking powder, salt, cinnamon, eggs, butter, vegetable oil, milk, and frozen blueberries that he picked himself in July at Wippamunk Farms). He pours the batter into extra-large muffin tins. At Murtonen's Muffinry, there are no bulk orders of premixed batter squeezed from plastic bags. He didn't graduate first in his class at Johnson and Wales for nothing.

He repeats the process for the corn muffins, then oat bran, chocolate, pancake, cinnamon apple, and zucchini tomato. He slides the trays into the ovens and sets the timers. A quick survey of supplies satisfies him that everything is stocked: cups, napkins, sugar packets. In an effort to impress Charlene—and she was impressed, because her last letter included a postscript that said, "Good boy for going green!!"—EJ recently switched to eighty percent recycled paper cups, unbleached napkins, and raw sugar. Organic ingredients are the next step, he thinks. Or maybe Fair Trade. He makes a mental note to learn the difference.

At the coffee station he tears open a bag of regular and takes a deep sniff as he dumps the grains into the filter. He repeats the process for decaf and all the winter flavors: eggnog spice, crème de menthe, butterscotch. Then he makes a pot of his own invention: New Orleans. He dumps regular grains into the filter and lays a few roots of chicory over the top.

He buys the chicory root from Charlene. Before he even stepped foot inside her café he knew she baked from scratch; he could tell by the aroma out front, on the sidewalk. The aroma of real butter, real flour. When the bells tinkled his arrival, she emerged from a back room. A taut apron accentuated her soft belly and ample hips. The body of a real woman, he thought; the body of a woman who takes her sweets seriously.

He ordered eight coffees. She laughed—eight coffees!—and set to pouring. He admired the exaggerated concavity of the small of her back, which made her round butt protrude invitingly. Black shiny hair curled around her pale ears and gave her the look of an imp.

She turned and smiled and handed him a tall cup of chicory-flavored coffee. "Yours is free," she said in a warm, slow drawl.

He took the cup from her small hand and thanked her. He noticed her diamond-shaped mouth.

She glanced outside at the Wippamunk interfaith van waiting in the street. "You from up north?"

"Uh, yes," EJ heard himself say.

"Drive all the way down here to help out with the Katrina damage?"

"Yep," his voice said again.

She smiled. "Some sort of volunteer group you're with?"

He didn't answer. Shadows smudged the skin under her eyes; batter streaked her wrists. We're made of the same stuff, EJ thought. She probably smells like coffee and sugar even after a shower. She probably relishes small talk with customers, and moments alone scraping silver bowls with white spatulas.

The bells jingled; Nick stood in the doorway. "Need a hand, Silo?" Nick asked. He always called EJ Silo, because that's his shape: tall and thick. Nick approached the counter, and Charlene handed him a tray that secured four cups of coffee.

"They're all on the house," she said. She screwed three more coffees into another tray and filled a paper bag with creamers, sugar packets, and stir sticks.

Nick spoke with Charlene in that genuine, friendly way of his. Told her all about The Trip, their work, where they were staying, what they were doing.

Charlene nodded, eyeing EJ. "Come back tomorrow, if you can," she said.

"Oh, we're only going to be in the touristy section today," EJ said. "Because—"

"We'll be back tomorrow," Nick said.

They finally left the café, each carrying a tray of coffee. Nick paused on the sidewalk. "Look at me," he said.

"What?" EJ stopped beside the van. His eyes met Nick's.

Nick laughed in that total-body way of his.

"What?"

"You know what." Nick jerked his head in the direction of the café. "You're totally macking on that cute Cajun coffee-shop chick. You've got the exact same look on your face as when you were twelve and France asked you to dance to 'Stairway to Heaven.'"

"Shh," EJ said. He glanced at France inside the van; Russ appeared to challenge her to a thumb fight, and she was ignoring him. It had been a very long time since EJ felt anything for France, and vice versa. It had been a very long time since EJ felt anything for anyone.

He sensed his cheeks reddening. "Don't say anything," he told Nick.

"I won't." Nick laughed again. "You dog."

Russ slid the van door open and took the tray from EJ. "What's funny? I always miss it."

"Nothing," EJ said. "Absolutely nothing." He took his seat next to Russ. But EJ smiled as he helped distribute coffee to everybody— Russ and France and Dennis, Chief and Father Chet and Pastor Sheila, who was driving—and he smiled the rest of the day.

Every three weeks since, each shipment of chicory root from New Orleans comes with a handwritten letter from Charlene. It usually starts with something like, "Thanks for your order. How's life in the Great White North?" as if Massachusetts is all impenetrable frozen tundra.

Charlene's never been to New England. He fantasizes about hosting her, showing her around town, all his favorite spots. The summit of Mount Wippamunk (though he'd probably have to drive her to the top because he's so out of shape); the second floor of the old fire station, with its antique brass pole and pool table from 1892; the bench in his own backyard, which looks out over Malden Pond. He'll show her his mother's name carved in the back of the bench. His father made it for his mother. His father always tinkered, always made things. The bench was the last thing he made before the divorce.

EJ can't believe it's been more than a year since he's talked to Charlene in person. He can't believe that all that time, she's continued to write, e-mail, text, and even, from time to time, call. When his cell phone beeps at four in the morning, he knows it's Charlene.

He was supposed to visit her once, in August. She invited him, and he made all the arrangements; he planned to take off two weeks and drive down. He even bought an extremely small diamond pendant at the Greendale Mall, but he returned it after she wrote, in her very next letter, about the atrocities of diamond mining, and some awareness rally she attended. He fretted about not having a gift and briefly felt sorry for himself that Nick wasn't around to give him advice.

But Charlene's mother died unexpectedly, and she called and tearfully said he shouldn't come. She kept apologizing, and he kept saying, "No, no, no need to apologize." That was half a year ago, and she hasn't re-invited him.

EJ pours himself a cup of New Orleans. He sips while flipping the chairs one-handed. Near the window, which is fogged from the ovens, he notices movement outside. He peers into the street and is startled to see a person there, a very bundled-up person. It could be anyone, and EJ squints before he notices Ahab. The Captain is unmistakable. He's the only greyhound in Wippamunk, and the town's only ninety-pound dog that wears a coat and boots six months of the year.

EJ recognizes Zell's yellow hat and mittens. The same Zell who caught lightning bugs in jars with him and Nick when they were seven or so. The same Zell—her bangs sprayed into an unmoving claw—who sat next to him freshman year in Ye Olde Home Ec Witch's class, sampled a blueberry muffin from the first batch he ever made, and said—even after Ye Olde Home Ec Witch gave her a detention for talking—"These're amazing, Eege. You should be a baker or something. Seriously."

So this is it, EJ thinks. Zell got his note, and now, finally, they're going to talk.

Something is under her arm—the present. The oven present from

Nick. Good God, EJ thinks; maybe she wants him with her when she opens it. He swallows hot coffee and stretches his free arm over his head. Good God. What the hell will he say to her?

Ahab leads Zell. They turn into the lot and approach the Muffinry. But they both stop short. They look at something, or *for* something— the source of an odd noise, maybe. EJ cranes his neck, but all he sees is blackness. Suddenly, Zell and Ahab turn around and practically run down the sidewalk, back down Main Street and out of view.

"Lost her nerve," EJ says. He sips some New Orleans and flips a chair. "Lost her nerve."

Moments later headlights sweep the parking lot. EJ checks the clock on the wall: The little wooden spoon is on the four and the big wooden spoon is on the six, which means Travis is late as usual. At least he's consistent.

The bells of the front door tinkle as Travis enters; the bristles of the mat make a scratching sound as he wipes his boots.

"Morning, hey," Travis calls.

"Morning." EJ opens the back door. He's about to toss a big empty butter tub into the recycling bin when a sort of silent command to be still grips him. His whole body seems infused with a wide-eyed and tingling awareness; if he had hackles, they'd be fully upright. It's the same skin-prickling, pupil-dilating readiness he experienced just before Nick's passage. That's how EJ thinks of it: not Nick's death, but his passage. Not something randomly, regrettably horrible, but something noble, like fate. Or at least like something Nick wouldn't protest, were he made to understand the events that would take his life.

EJ got the terminology—"the passage"—from Charlene. Early on he told her about his nightmares in which he witnesses, over and over, what happened to Nick. She wrote back that all survivors have nightmares; it's a symptom of post-traumatic stress disorder.

She wrote about "the passage" of Katrina victims: "They didn't die. They experienced a passage into somewhere else. That's what I truly believe."

EJ grips the empty butter tub. Goose bumps form along the nape of his neck. Something approaches—possibly the same creature that distracted Zell and Ahab moments ago. He takes a step back and thinks about black bears raiding trash barrels, then remembers it's winter, and bears are hibernating. Maybe it's a mountain lion, he thinks; they're rumored to roam the area.

Near the recycling bin, movement flashes—filmy, alien green eyes appear. The eyes are followed by a cat, lumpy and practically lop-sided with fur balls, a little potato sack with legs. It sits and meows. Old Man Bedard's cat. A true barn cat.

EJ laughs. "Bastard," he says. "You scared me." He tosses the butter tub into the bin, and the cat scampers toward the street.

# Nick

November 2, 2006
From: nicholas.roy@thewippamunker.com
To: rose-ellen@roymedicalillustration.com

Hello, Pants.

We are setting up our sleeping bags in the lunchroom of the school, which has already been rebuilt in the year-plus since the hurricane. It sort of sucks to be sleeping on a cafeteria floor, but I remind myself that it's better than being homeless like so many of these people were, and still are, in many cases, or so I'm told.

We finally rolled into town at night, so I couldn't see much because it was dark. But I guess tomorrow I'll get the lay of the

land. They'll be gutting one little house. By *they,* I mean everybody else but me and Dennis: Pastor Sheila, Father Chet, Chief
Kent, France, EJ, and Russ. I mean, technically Dennis and I are
supposed to remain unbiased outsiders as they work. He'll report
on the missionaries; I'll take pictures. We'll do a story and
photo-essay for *The Wippamunker* when we get back. Shouldn't
be too hard.

How was your cardiology appointment? I told Father Chet and
Pastor Sheila that you were having some heart issues, and now
they are praying for you. That sort of freaks me out, their praying,
but they are "people of the cloth," so I guess I should expect it.
They even had us all praying in the van at one point. The eight of
us holding hands with our eyes closed.

Anyway, I think you're going to be fine, Pants. I feel it. Seriously, Zell—when I get home I'll go to all your appointments with
you, every single one. But hopefully you won't have many more
appointments, because you're going to be all right.

When you write back tell me what the doctor said.

Take care of those perfect 34Cs. I will nuzzle them in my dreams.

I will write to you every day and call you when I can.

Nick

# 2

## Zell

*T*HE SUN'S UP, and the trash-picked stained-glass window overlooking my second-floor landing casts a reddish hue. I lean on my bedroom door, opposite the attic door. I hold Nick's nearly destroyed present. Gently, I shake it. The cube's contents knock softly. What makes that noise? Nothing, I tell myself. Nothing at all but dust, air, and melted ghost.

The doorknob opposite me is glass. It reflects a tiny me, still in coat and hat. I cover tiny me with my mittened hand. I turn the knob. I push open the attic door one inch. Two inches. I push hard, with my shoulder and arm, because the door scrapes the floor.

The smell of stale attic hits me.

Balls.

I can't do it. I can't open the door any farther. I tug it toward me until it latches and leave the cube in the hallway.

\* \* \*

MOMENTS LATER, I shiver on the back steps, watching Ahab pee like a girl dog next to the frozen hydrangea. As he pees he swivels his pointy ears—one black, one white—and sniffs the air, which still smells of burned plastic. It also smells of winter: old snow over dead grass over frozen earth.

One mile away Mount Wippamunk is a big bump on the horizon. It's a true monadnock—an isolated peak. Nick taught me the meaning of that word, a Native American word. The trails ribbon out and down like raindrop paths on a window. Already, even this early in the day, skiers and boarders look like fleas jumping side to side.

"I like your dog."

Ahab stops peeing and looks around.

The girl, my neighbor, leans out an upstairs window. Her hair is unbraided under the red ski hat.

"Hi," I say. "Sorry about yesterday. I was upset."

"It's okay. I get angry, too, sometimes. I'm Ingrid."

"I'm Zell."

"Five minutes," Garrett yells from inside their house.

"Your dog is the kind that runs really fast, right?" she asks.

"Yup."

"Your dog can't be faster than a cheetah, though, because cheetahs are the fastest land animals in the world."

"Really?" I say.

"Yeah."

I hear the rumble of Garrett's truck from the other side of the house; he's warming it up.

"My dad drops me off at school before he goes to work," she says. "He works for lawyers. He's going to be a lawyer someday, too, when he's all done with lawyer school. That's where he goes at night. And on Saturdays." She scratches at the windowsill and loosens a stuck acorn cap, which falls and lands in the yard without a sound.

"Hey. Want to know why I was baking yesterday?" I ask.

"Cuz baking is awesome?"

"Come on down here and I'll show you."

Ahab follows me as I retrieve *Meals in a Cinch with Polly Pinch* from the little powder room under the stairs. Back outside, Ingrid waits in her yard. Her backpack looks like it weighs as much as she does. She's dressed for school: tights, Uggs, denim skirt, snorkel coat with electric blue faux fur brimming the hood, and the big red hat. I pass her the magazine over the fence. She regards it at arm's length, as if to confirm it's really hers.

"The mailman put it in the wrong mailbox," I explain. "Anyway, there's a dessert contest. Check out page forty-eight."

She studies the pullout page, tracing Polly's face with a finger. "Whoa," she says. "Snap. Did you read this? The grand prize is that you get to meet her on *Pinch of Love Live*. The new, live version of *Pinch of Love*."

"And you win twenty thousand dollars," I say.

"Yeah, but you also get to *meet* her. Polly *Pinch*."

"Ingrid?" Garrett yells from inside. "Where are you?"

She flashes me a conspiratorial smile. One front tooth is bigger than the other. Instead of stuffing the magazine into her backpack, she chucks it at me. "Keep it. Just for today."

Somehow I manage to drop it. I grab after its slippery pages, but it flutters and slides down against my coat.

"See ya, wouldn't wanna be ya," she calls before darting up the steps.

I pick up the magazine, shake it to remove the snow, and find the contest details.

Win $20,000 and an all-expenses-paid trip for two to Scrump Studios in Boston! Be a special guest on the inaugural episode of Polly's new show, *Pinch of Love Live*!

Do you have an easy dessert that warms the soul? If so, Polly wants to bake it on her show! Show the world—and Polly Pinch—your kitchen creativity! Submit your word-processed recipes to the address below, or e-mail them via the online form at www.warmthesoulbakingcontest .com. Two lucky entrants will be deemed finalists by Polly's hand-selected expert baking staff. The two winning desserts will be baked on the first-ever episode of *Pinch of Love Live* on May 5. And one of those entrants will win an additional grand prize of $20,000!

Entries will be judged on originality, ease of preparation, and above all, scrumpness. Entries must be postmarked or e-mailed no later than March 10. No purchase necessary. See www.warmthesoul bakingcontest.com for details and full contest rules, regulations, and restrictions.

"WHAT DO YOU THINK, Cap'n?" I say. "Twenty thousand dollars. The exact amount Nick mentioned in his e-mail. The exact amount he wanted to raise for the Katrina survivors. It's got to mean something, right?"

Ahab sneezes, trots up the back steps, and whines. I let him inside. "Arr. Yer loony as a chigger in a rum barrel."

I'm on my way upstairs when, from the second-floor landing, through the nonstained-glass window, I spy Garrett and Ingrid leaving the house. He tosses a long wool dress coat and a briefcase into the passenger side of his pickup. Ingrid climbs into the second row of seats, and he buckles her seat belt. They make a game of kissing: She pretends she doesn't want to be kissed. He acts nonchalant, looking all around, apparently whistling, then swoops in for a kiss. He gets her twice on the forehead and once on the cheek. She giggles and giggles.

He gets in the driver's seat. Behind him Ingrid puts her head down; she's reading a book. Before he backs out his driveway, he adjusts his rearview mirror and looks right at me.

Balls.

I step away from the window, but he waves—a single flick of wrist, just like the other day—so I wave back.

His truck rumbles away, and I know there won't be any distractions for a few hours. So I transport the turntable and the milk crate of Gladys Knight and the Pips albums from the bedroom to my office, not far down the hall. I do not glance—not even once—at Nick's oven present on the floor.

Nick's g.d. present.

I set the turntable on a little chair next to skeletal Hank. Soon Gladys sings about being high on the wings of things and having a song in her heart.

I straddle my saddle stool and tilt my drafting table toward me. The sun shines on it, making it as white as a field of snow. I sketch on fresh paper, reaching every now and then for my eraser and for different pencils, which are organized by color and stored in little bins that slope upward like prayer candles in a church.

I draw for hours, getting up only to change the Gladys albums. At one point I ask Hank to switch the record, and I imagine him behind me, performing the task as agreeably as a butler. But when I turn around he's of course just hanging there, slack jawed.

Just like every other Friday, at quarter past one the mail truck parks in front of my driveway (not in it, of course, because I haven't shoveled). My bell rings—wheezes, really, in the sharp cold.

I let Russ in. He high-fives me with one hand, passes me my mail with the other. Ahab sniffs the envelopes, decides they're nothing special, and curls back up on the couch.

"Anything going out?" Russ asks.

"Not today."

His face is red and his fingertips are white, and a few minutes pass before he stops shivering. I make a pot of coffee. We split a large toasted tuna-fish grinder with extra cheese, which he brought from Orbit Pizza, and a bag of potato chips.

Russ eats without removing his fingerless gloves. He chews and talks simultaneously, listing every employee of the Wippamunk Post Office. "I like Paddy. Did you know he wears a toupee? Tammy is funny sometimes, but she thinks she's smarter than everybody else. Steve? Can't stand the guy. Never shuts up. Ever. Hey, this is off the subject, but did you know France got a kitten? She wants you to go over and meet it. Thing's cute as hell, but it made me sneeze twenty-two times in a row. France counted. . . ."

I let him do all the talking, as usual; it's easier to listen. I don't mention that it's hard to be around France because she reminds me, in particular, of Nick's last night in Wippamunk, when he went to photograph a gruesome car accident. France was at the accident scene, too, and when Nick got home he told me about the blood and shattered glass reflected in her flashlight beam. I don't like to think about all that.

When Russ finishes eating he unfolds a small bundle of butcher wrap and drops a hunk of roast beef into Ahab's elevated dish. He gallops into the kitchen at the sound and swallows all the meat in about two seconds. "Compliments of the great Greeks at Orbit Pizza," Russ says. He belches and gets up to leave. "Why do you think dogs dig me so much, Zell?"

"Must be the wifebeater undershirts."

"I bet you're right."

I walk him to the door. "Can I ask you something serious?" I say.

He shifts a little and glances out the window. The sunlight catches flecks of yellow in his blue eyes and accentuates his crow's feet. "Hit me," he says.

"Well, during The Trip, did Nick ever mention a present for me? I mean, a present he was maybe going to give to me when he got back?"

"No, babe. He never mentioned it." Russ puts a hand on the door. "Are you talking about the present in your oven?"

I nod.

"You mean you haven't opened it yet?"

"I can't."

"Do you need like a crowbar or something? I can bring one over and pry it—"

"No. I mean, I *can't* open it."

"Oh." He looks around the room a bit, avoiding my face. He doesn't know what to say; I can tell.

"Thanks for lunch," I say.

"You bet. Don't forget to feed Hank." He cuffs my shoulder like he's my Little League coach.

When he's settled in the mail truck, he calls, "You okay?" just like every Friday. "Right as rain?"

"Right as rain."

He grins and drives off.

I go back upstairs. I reset Gladys. I draw.


In the afternoon Ingrid rings my doorbell to retrieve *Meals in a Cinch with Polly Pinch*. Garrett waits in the truck.

"So," she says when I answer. "Come up with anything? For the Desserts That Warm the Soul contest?"

"Not yet. I mean, it's only been twenty-four hours since my last experiment, and—"

Garrett waves Ingrid toward the truck. "Come on, boo-boo," he says. "Don't make me late for class again."

"What about dinner?" she calls.

"We're stopping on the way. Let's go. You can read your magazine."

She rolls her eyes. "I've got to go."

"Thanks for lending me *Meals in a Cinch*," I say.

She nods and jumps down the steps, clearing all four.


BY LATE EVENING the cross section of my healthy artery is an eerie Martian landscape with gum pink walls. In my rendering, a small me could slip headfirst up the darkening arterial tunnel, right into the heart, which floats disembodied in the background. It's not some two-humped cartoon Valentine heart. It looks like a real human heart. Bulbous. Gelatinous. Impossible.

I sign my initials—RCR, for Rose-Ellen Carmichael Roy—in tight dark pencil in the bottom right corner. I spray the paper lightly with fixative and watch as it dries.


IT'S A DARK TUESDAY AFTERNOON, and I return from the grocery store armed with flour, baking soda, and baking powder.

Baking powder equals baking *power*.

Ye Olde Home Ec Witch be g.d.'d. I'll perk up my spirits, and I'll win this contest.

Gladys Knight and the Pips: check. Camouflage apron: check. *Empty* oven preheated: check. Ahab leaning against the legs of a kitchen stool, winking his eye-patch eye: check.

In the big bowl I combine sugar, egg, and vanilla extract. I add butter, a handful of flour, and three envelopes of instant cocoa. I mash a banana and four mini–Milky Way bars left over from Halloween and add those. I sprinkle in some baking soda and baking *power*.

Stir, stir, stir. Slap some grease on a baking sheet. Drop heavy dough in haphazard columns. Set timer.

Ye Olde Home Ec Witch would *not* approve. I picture her scowling over her bifocals at me as I take a seat on the floor, close my eyes, and snap my fingers like a Pip. Soon I feel Ahab's chin resting on my head, so I reach up and scratch his neck. I sing along: "Why don't you—make me the woman you go home to—and not the one that's left to cry, and die?"

Grunting, Ahab reclines next to me and drops his head on my thigh. I open a mini–Milky Way, take a bite, and offer the rest to him. Dogs aren't supposed to eat chocolate, but he loves it, and besides, a little won't kill him. He chews lying on his side. He doesn't even bother to lift his head.

The window above the sink frames Mount Wippamunk. As I gaze at it, a Memory Smack wallops me, and I submit, let it sweep me away: high school Nick on the chairlift. He swung his left boot freely over his snowboard and belted "Welcome to the Jungle," and my back hummed with the vibration of his voice. In the chair behind us, France—six or seven years before she would become Officer Frances—pelted the back of Nick's head with an ice ball she formed from the chunks clinging to her safety bar. "Shut up, *re*-tahd!" she yelled.

Nick turned and grinned his famous wide grin.

I slip into another, more recent ski-themed Memory Smack: Nick and I lounged in the Mount Wippamunk base lodge in front of the wood-burning stove. Our sopping-wet jackets and pants hung from hooks on the wall. Rain slashed the windows. But we didn't care about the foul weather; we got in some good runs.

He sipped steaming cider from a Styrofoam cup. He wore a battered wool sweater—one he had since high school.

"This is the life, right here," he whispered. His hot hand sank into my hat-head hair. His light brown eyelashes fluttered. His breath was sleepy, whistling waves. "Someday that'll be us," he said. He gestured with his cup to the wooden *Family of Skiers*: life-size statues of a mother and father, two little kids between them, heading off to the lift line. Their faces suggested that anticipatory thrill of the first run of the season.

"That'll be us," said Nick. He admired the strange, happy wooden family. "Soon we'll get started on our family. Except we'll have more than two. We'll have enough kids so that our whole family can be one big soccer team."

"How many would that be?" I asked.

"Nine, plus you and me makes eleven. There are eleven players on an official soccer team."

"Nine kids?"

"Sure."

"Yeah. Right."

The timer dings: real time, real place. Still on the floor, I reach over and open the oven. Zell's Banana Cocoa Milky Way Cookies form one giant gray spongy puff, like the brain of a large mammal. Some brain drips onto the floor of the oven and sizzles.

First my Flourless Peanut Butter Treats nearly burn the house down. Then I create this quavering, inedible lump. I think of Polly Pinch on the cover of *Meals in a Cinch*, those teens gathered around her, happy and unified, as if about to burst into a spontaneous, harmonized version of "Peace Train." Polly brings the whole world together with a smile and a Bundt cake, that cover seems to say.

And I bring no one together. Least of all myself. Nick wanted me to mother his children, yet I can't even operate an oven—or bake a single, normal cookie. A shameful loneliness carves into my chest, hollowing it out. I *am* the enormous lump I've created: a quivering, unidentifiable mess.

"Who goes through her whole life without cooking, Captain?" I ask. "Without cooking a thing?"

Ahab lifts his head and watches as I stand, wrap a dish towel around my hand, and grasp the heavy baking sheet. It clatters onto the stovetop.

"How did Nick stand it?" I howl. "How did he stand *me*?" A single tear splashes onto the half-cooked lump. And I spill over, big hot tears everywhere—my cheeks and chin, the ends of my hair, the apron. Even the top of Ahab's head, as he leans against my thigh.

The doorbell wheezes: w-h-e-e-z-e.

"Crap." I press an apron corner to my eyes and decide to ignore the doorbell until whoever is ringing it gives up and goes away.

W-h-e-e-e-e-e-z-e.

Balls.


Mr. Garrett Knox waits on the porch, loosening his tie. "Am I . . . interrupting you?" he asks.

I'm not sure what to say because technically he is.

"Smells great," he says.

"Really?" I say. "Thanks a lot. I was just baking some . . . cookies." I smooth the apron over my belly and stand a little straighter.

He peers at me, and I wonder whether he can tell I was just bawling my eyes out over the stove. I try to smile a little.

"You bake a lot?" he asks.

"Oh, every now and again. Sure."

"No wonder my daughter likes you so much." He laughs and

reaches for my hand. "Garrett," he says. His palm is soft, like that of a man who works at a desk. "Yeah, Ingrid sure is a fan of you."

"Really? Well, she seems like a great kid," I say.

"Thanks. She really is something else. Uh, you have . . ." He pretends to wipe the area under his left eye.

I mirror him; chocolaty butter comes off on my fingertips. "Oh. Nice." I force a smile. "My name's Rose-Ellen, but I go by Zell."

"Zell," he says. "Well, this is awkward."

"Yeah."

"No, I mean, what I'm about to say is awkward. Because I'm in a bit of a bind and I need to ask you a favor. A huge favor, actually."

Ahab comes to the door and leans against me. He eyes Garrett—that's actually pretty sociable for a greyhound, because typically they ignore strangers.

"Nice dog." Garrett scratches Ahab's head, then notices a streak of cinnamon on the nipple area of my apron and quickly looks back at my eyes, which I'm sure are puffy and bloodshot from crying.

"So what's up?" I ask, as Ahab licks my apron hem.

"Well, my nanny bailed on me," Garrett says. "She's been watching Ingrid while I'm in Boston Tuesday nights, and all day on some Saturdays. She got a real job, apparently. Left me in the lurch. I mean, I'm happy for her. But I really don't know what to do for child care now. And here we are, Tuesday night already, and I have to leave for class, like . . . twenty minutes ago. I've dragged Ingrid to class with me a couple times, but it's just awful for her."

"Why don't you send her to a friend's house for the night?" I say, trying to sound helpful.

"A friend's house?" he says. "I uh . . . I guess I didn't think of that option. That's a really good idea. For the next time, I mean.

But, well. I was wondering if *you* could watch her. Tonight. Like, right now."

I want to say, You're kidding me, right? I want to tell him about the me of just a few moments ago, when I sobbed into my failed dessert. Is it my moral obligation to inform Garrett that I'm so depressed as to be unfit to look after a child, even for a night?

Again I try to smile, but I'm sure I look just plain fearful.

Garrett stares at me. His mouth is grim, his eyes sincere. "I'm begging you. We just moved here from the other side of town. And it's been really hectic. I'm sorry to bother you. I am. But I'm begging, here."

Babysitting? At thirty-four years old? Well, maybe that's my widow style. My awesome widow style.

I shrug and say, "I guess so?"

"Oh, you're a lifesaver. Listen, Ingrid'll come right over to your house. She's on her way, actually. She'll do her homework, no problem. We already had dinner, so you don't have to worry about that either. And then she'll watch TV."

"What's okay for her to watch?"

"She only watches one show." He smirks. "I'll be home late. Like, *late.* How about you just let her fall asleep on your couch, and I'll scoop her up when I get home? She'll fall asleep anywhere, that one."

"I usually go to bed around ten thirty," I say.

"Shoot. Really? I'll be much later than that."

"I don't leave my door unlocked at night." Not a lie. Nick never locked the door; a lot of Munkers don't. But I do because I'm a widow.

Garrett bites his lower lip. "No, no. Of course not."

Ingrid comes out of their house. She drops her backpack over the porch railing and climbs over. "Well?" she says. "What's the plan?"

He glances at his watch. "I was thinking you'd be much more comfortable in your own house. Gosh, I hate imposing on people like this. Do you mind babysitting at our house?"

"Hold on?" I say. "Just a second."

I duck inside. Nick's Guns N' Roses key chain hangs on a little set of hooks just inside the door. I squeeze the cold keys and hold them to my lips.

Back on the porch, Ingrid hugs Garrett, and he strokes her head.

"Look," he says when he notices me standing there. "Never mind. I'm sorry to have bothered you. I'll take Ingrid with me to school tonight. So don't worry about it."

I hand him the keys. "Let yourself in when you get back."

"Yessss." Ingrid snatches her backpack and brushes past me; Ahab follows.

Garrett eyes the keys. "Are you sure?"

"It'll be fine."

"Guns N' Roses, huh?"

" 'Sweet Child O' Mine,' " I say, smiling.

He laughs through his nose at the reference and slides the keys into the pocket of his wool dress coat. "Oh," he says, extracting a little green box. "I almost forgot to give you this."

"What is it?" I take the box; it's labeled AUTO-INJECTOR.

"You shouldn't need it. But just in case." He turns and skips down the porch steps.

"Hey," I yell. "Garrett, I'm not qualified to give a kid an injection."

"Just keep her out of the peanut butter. She knows what she needs to stay away from. She's an old pro. And she's really a good kid, Zell."

He tosses his briefcase and coat on the passenger seat of his truck and gets in.

"But?" I shout.

"She likes you." He slams the door, salutes me, and rounds the corner.

I find Ingrid in the kitchen. She's studying my now-deflated dessert. "What's going on there?" she asks.

"Oh, nothing," I say. "Just trying to come up with something for the Warm the Soul contest."

"Does this have peanuts in it?" she asks, about to dip a finger. "Or peanut butter?"

"No. But it does have Milky Ways in it."

"Ooh. Better not risk it." She takes a step back. "Well, it looks weird, but I bet it doesn't taste half-bad."

I nod my thanks as she climbs on a stool and stacks her workbooks on the counter.

"Gonna do your homework?" I ask.

"Yep." She chews her lip and scratches out a few math problems. I can't remember the last time I babysat. Middle school, probably, when the Pierce twins down the street were six or seven. Now, as Ingrid makes herself at home in my kitchen, I feel an odd sense of displacement, as if *I'm* the one who's never been here before.

After a minute or so, she looks up. "You don't have to watch me, you know."

"Want me to show you around the house?"

"Well, it looks exactly like mine. So, I'm good." She goes back to her homework.

I don't know what to say, and I don't really want her here. But there's nothing I can do about that now. "Okay if I try to get some work done in my office?" I ask.

Ingrid giggles. "I'm not a baby. I'm nine."

"Right. I'll be upstairs if you need anything. Just yell."

She looks up from the paper and grins. "Okeydokey."

\* \* \*

WHEN I COME BACK DOWN A HALF HOUR LATER, the television's on.
Polly Pinch tosses silvery shrimp under a fine faucet spray. She winks
at the camera. "This is gonna . . . be . . . *scrump*!"

"Make yourself at home," I say, a little annoyed that Ingrid's
settled on my couch with her socked feet tucked underneath her.

"Thank you," she says, missing my sarcasm. She grins wide.
"Watch with me?"

I plop down on the other side of the couch.

Ingrid holds up a marker-stained hand. "Shhh."

The camera roves over Polly Pinch. Close-up of her rounded lips,
slightly parted. She drizzles her Secret Love Sauce Number 2™ on a
wok of sugar snap peas.

Close-up of her green eyes, as big as walnuts. She confesses her
obsession with a popular brand of potato chips.

Close-up of her diminutive fingers. She slices carrots on a damp
wood cutting board.

Close-up of her hip bones. She rolls out a Super Simp Flaky™
piecrust.

"Now what *this* baby needs . . . is a pinch!" Polly says. She
reaches into her potbellied ceramic canister labeled LOVE and flicks
her fingers over the now-sizzling wok.

After a few commercials, Polly sinks a fork into her special vari-
ation on Oriental stir-fry. A *super-simp* single-serving blackberry
torte waits at her elbow. "Until next time, don't forget that pinch!"
Her glossed lips enclose a forkful of shrimp. "Mmm! Scrump!"

Next time, it turns out, is now; the opening credits to *Pinch
of Love* roll. Big loopy letters swim across the screen, and Polly
sashays around her 1950s kitchen and lip-syncs the doo-wop theme
song.

"Back-to-back episodes?" I say.

"Yes." Ingrid laces her fingers behind her head. "Oh yes."

Ahab strolls into the room. He sprawls out on the couch between Ingrid and me. He rests his chin on her lap, and she rubs his snout with the tip of her finger. I can't believe how foreign it feels to look over at this small person I barely know sitting next to me, watching a cooking show.

"Is your homework done?" I ask.

Ingrid's eyes lock on the television screen. "Yes, homework is done. All of it. Every last bit."

Close-up of Polly's short, orange-painted nails. She massages a garlicky rub into a pork loin. "This rub'll really ratchet up the action," she says. "It's gonna—be—*scrrrrrump.*"

"Do you ever try to make any of these recipes?" I ask Ingrid.

"No," she whispers.

"Why not?" I whisper.

"Because she's going to teach me how to cook someday. In person, I mean."

"Who?"

"My mother."

"Oh," I say. "Well, that'll be nice." Until now, I assumed Ingrid's mother simply isn't in the picture. "So, where *is* your mother?" I ask, trying to sound casual and not nosy.

"Right there." She points at the TV.

"Polly Pinch?"

"Yup."

"Polly Pinch is your mother?"

Close-up of Polly's square white teeth. She introduces dessert: *super-simp* anisette mousse.

"Polly Pinch is your mother?" I repeat.

Ingrid looks at me. Her lips and nostrils quiver. "Nobody believes me."

"Sure I do. I believe you." But the truth is, I don't know what to believe. I suppose Polly Pinch *could* be Ingrid's mother, but then again, Ingrid could simply harbor some crazy little-girl fantasy.

Her jaw trembles as if she's holding back tears. As if she suspects I don't wholly buy her story.

"Now, what *this* baby needs . . . is a pinch!" says Polly, brandishing a bottle of whipped cream and striking a sort of *Charlie's Angels* pose.

"She's perfect," says Ingrid. "Look at her. She's beautiful, and talented, and funny, and smart."

"You must take right after her," I say.

"I know. I do. And I've never even met her." Ingrid covers her face with her hands. She emits a few squeaky sounds, and I'm pretty sure she's crying, or trying not to.

Balls.

I've never had a nine-year-old well up on my couch. I feel inadequate; I feel like crying myself. Nick would know what to say. Nick would know *exactly* what to say.

Polly dabs the corner of her mouth with a cloth napkin. "Mmmm."

I grab the remote and click off the television; Polly disappears in a silver blip.

"Ingrid?" I say.

She doesn't answer.

This is not good. The last thing I want is for my new neighbor to spend a teary night here because I thought her a liar. I have no idea what to do. I need to distract her.

"Want to play a game?" I ask.

She shakes her head. Her auburn braids swing alongside her face, and the beads click together.

I can't think of anything else to suggest. A bribe seems like a powerful option, maybe my only option.

"What would make you stop crying?" I ask. "What could I do *right now* to make you stop crying?"

Ingrid's shoulders slacken. She mutters something into her hands that sounds like "A blee bab run mass feelah."

"What? I can't understand you. Look at me."

Her hands slide from her face. Her cheeks are moist. She takes a deep breath. "To see Ahab run almost as fast as a cheetah."

"You want to take Ahab running? Like, now?"

She nods and backhands some snot off her chin. "Can he run really, really fast?"

"Your dad will be home soon."

"No, he won't. He doesn't come home until wicked late."

I glance at Ahab dozing with his head on Ingrid's lap. His whiskers twitch in his sleep. Is this how little girls are, I wonder, or is Ingrid a special case? A drama queen? Was *I* like this?

"Maybe some other time we can watch him run," I say. "When you don't have to go to school the next day."

Her eyes seem greener now. A single tear spills over and streams down her cheek.

"Okay?" I punch her shoulder the way Russ punches mine.

"No-kay. *No-kay.* You asked me what I wanted. And I told you." She coughs and snuffles.

She's right, of course. And for some reason I think of Nick's present. Nick's g.d. present. The human-head-size cube. It's sitting upstairs in my hallway, in front of my g.d. attic door.

"I'll make a deal with you." I slap my thighs. "You do something for me, and I'll take you to see Ahab run almost as fast as a cheetah."

Ahab lifts his head as Ingrid slides toward the edge of the couch. "What do you mean?" Her lips and nose are swollen from crying.

"Well, you know how you're allergic to peanuts?"

She nods.

"I'm allergic to my attic."

"For real?"

"For real. I have an attic allergy. It's severe."

She pats my arm. "I *love* attics. They're full of secrets and history, and sometimes even hidden treasure."

"They certainly are. You're a hundred percent right about that."

"Woman, I'm a *zillion* percent right about *that*."


"THAT THING?" SAYS INGRID, pointing to Nick's present.

I lean against my bedroom door.

"Last time I touched that thing, you sort of flipped on me," she says. "Remember?"

"I know. But I'm over it. Now I *want* you to pick it up. Don't shake it, though. Just carry it up to the top of the steps and set it down."

She notices the Magic Marker stains on her hands, licks a thumb, and rubs at them. "That's it?"

"That's it."

"Why?"

"Because that's where it belongs," I say.

"Everything has a place." She nods. "That's what my dad always says when he wants me to clean up my messes. He's a neat freak."

"That's right: Everything has a place. And that thing"—I point to the cube—"belongs in the attic. Which I'm severely allergic to."

"It was in your oven, wasn't it? You were trying to burn it up in your oven."

"I wasn't *trying* to burn it. It was an accident. I didn't know it was in my oven."

"How could you not know something was in your oven?"

"I don't bake much, okay?"

"Okay. But you're learning, right? For the contest."

"That's right."

"So, let's see this attic." She crosses her arms. "Probably looks just like mine."

"I doubt that, actually."

In the hallway the glass doorknob reflects tiny me and, beside me, tinier Ingrid. I put my hand over tiny me and tinier Ingrid. I shove the door with my elbow and hip. It opens one inch.

Shove. Two inches.

Shove. One foot.

She pokes her head inside and looks up the steps. "It's wicked dusty in here."

"I know."

"It smells totally weird."

"I know. Sorry about that."

"This is, like, wicked, wicked creepazoid, Zell."

I reach in. I feel the wall for the light switch. My heart does its crazy dance—thump-thump-thump-thu-thu-thu-thu—and as the light flickers on I crash back against my bedroom door.

"You okay?" she asks. "You really *are* allergic."

"I'm fine." I force a smile, and the beats stop altogether. Then my heart goes back to normal.

The extra light makes the doorknob twinkle. The floor in front of the first attic step looks not just rubbed raw but scraped away, scraped to the core.

Ingrid exhales mightily.

"Listen," I say. "You don't have to—"

"I do love me an adventure. Promise you're not going to flip on me if I pick that thing up?"

"Promise. No flipping."

"And you swear—pinkie swear—that all I have to do is carry it upstairs and leave it there, and we'll take Ahab running? Right now?"

"Pinkie swear."

"Even though it's sort of late?"

"Yup."

She stares into my eyes. She grabs my wrist, yanks my pinkie upright, and locks her own pinkie over it. Then she scoops up the present, cradles it, and pounds up the steps.

"What is all this stuff up here?" she calls. "What are all these—"

"Just put the cube next to that other box on the floor and come back down here. Don't touch anything."

"Okay, okay."

*Clunk.*

"Careful," I say.

"Sorry. I'm coming down."

I hear her place both feet on each step before she takes the next. "Hold the hand railing, okay?" I say.

"I am. Why are you so nervous?"

Because I'm the angry town widow? Because I'm a quivering mess who can't bake and who makes young children cry?

The attic door makes an awful screech as I pull it shut. Ingrid brushes invisible dust from her clothes before she takes my hand and leads me down the hall.

"Ahab time," she says. But she stops at my office door. It's open a crack, just enough to show Hank's fingertips and toes.

"Zell?" She approaches Hank.

"You might not want to go in there," I say, envisioning Garrett's horror when he learns that a model human skeleton hangs in my office. I reach to shut the door, but it's too late: She now stands opposite Hank. He seems to tower over her.

"Um, why is there a skeleton in front of me?" Ingrid flicks the light switch and looks all around—at the spinal column attached to the brain that hangs from the wall, at the scraped-up heart on my shelf. The sight of the heart sends me spinning into a Memory Smack: Nick gave it to me right after our graduation from Wippamunk High. As EJ and France posed for pictures, Nick grabbed me by the wrist and dragged me under the bleachers.

He produced a paper bag from his gown. "I didn't have time to wrap it. It came in the mail this morning."

I inspected the heart, holding it up in the crack of light that streamed between the bleachers. I welled up at his thoughtfulness; he knew I wanted to study medical illustration. In fact, we both knew from a very young age what we wanted to be when we grew up. That's probably why we grew so close in high school.

"You might be the only girl in the world who cries tears of joy when handling a model heart," he said.

I threw my arms around him and whispered, "I love you." It was the first time I said it. I remember the feel of his arms around my hips, his lips on my earlobe, as he said, "I know. I love you back."

The heart's pretty scuffed now, having traveled with me to college and graduate school and beyond.

Pointing, Ingrid marches to my desk. "Is that a big huge eyeball? Okay. That's an *eyeball*. Like, on your *desk*."

"Let's go," I say. "I don't want you to have nightmares about all this stuff."

She wags her head. "What kind of freakazoid are you?"

"I draw body parts. It's my job."

"First all that weirdness in your attic. Now all *this* weirdness. Show me?"

"Show you what?"

"Show me what you draw."

"Are you sure you want to see it? It's all sort of . . . graphic."

"I like graphic. I think." She straddles my stool and wheels it over to my desk. I take a seat at my laptop and show her my most recent scan: the cross section of the healthy artery. I explain that blood can flow freely through your arteries if you exercise and eat nutritious foods, but otherwise, all sorts of junk clogs them up, and that makes your heart sick.

She studies the illustration on the screen and recites the layers I labeled, sounding out the words: tunica intima, tunica media, tunica adventitia. "This is your job?" she asks.

"Yeah."

"That's pretty fly."

I close the file, and an e-mail remains open underneath it, one I started a while ago but never finished. Ingrid glimpses it before I minimize it. "Was that a letter?" she asks.

"Yeah. An e-mail."

"From who?"

"From me."

"To who?"

"To my husband."

"Why?" she asks.

"Because when people love each other, they write each other letters," I say.

"But I thought your husband was dead. That's what my dad told me when I asked him if you were married."

"That's right," I say. "He *is* dead." I'm not surprised Garrett knows the story. Nick was somewhat of a local legend, even before he died.

I reach for my big plastic eyeball and caress the nerves that run atop the choroid. I have to change the subject somehow, but I feel a knot forming in my throat, and I'm afraid to open my mouth.

Ingrid hops from the stool and climbs into my lap. Her arms ring my neck. I'm surprised by her familiarity, her seemingly instant trust of me. Was I so open as a child?

Her green eyes search my left eye, then my right. "You don't lie to me, do you?"

That stings a bit because I *have* lied to her—little white lies, about my attic allergy and liking to cook. I rub my thumb on the clear cornea. "Life's hard enough," I say.

"Trudy doesn't lie to me either. I can tell."

"Who's Trudy?"

"My step-grandmother." She sticks a finger into the plastic eye's pupil. "There's a hole in your eye? For real?"

"For real." I replace the eye and close my laptop. "Come on. Ahab's got some running to do."


Ingrid, Ahab, and I half trot, half slide down High Street. The blue faux fur on the hood of Ingrid's coat rings her round, freckled face. She laughs at Ahab's form-fitting fleece jacket and neoprene booties. I shush her as we slip and slide down the hill.

"What's his full name?" she asks.

"Captain Ahab's Midnight Delight."

"I don't get it."

"We didn't pick it."

"Who's we?"

"Me and Nick."

"Is Nick your dead husband?"

"Yeah. Look, just call him Ahab. Or the Captain. Or Cappy or Cap'n, for short." In Ahab Voice, I add, "Avast, me hearties!" which makes Ingrid laugh even harder. I don't even know what that phrase means, but Nick always said it, and it does sound piratey.

She asks me endless questions about Ahab.

What I don't tell her:

1. Nick was one of those guys who always knew he'd get married, buy a house, and get a dog. He accomplished all three tasks in exactly in that order.
2. We used to joke about "Captain Ahab's Midnight Delight" sounding like the title of a whaler-themed porno.
3. Nick took hundreds of black-and-white photographs of Ahab's first few years with us. Ahab chasing his tail, eyes wild. Ahab squinting in the sunlight. Ahab, Ahab, Ahab, as if he were our firstborn child.

What I tell her:

1. Ahab is a retired champion who came to live with me when he grew tired of racing other dogs around a track after a mechanical rabbit.
2. When he was a puppy, mean men tattooed his ears for identification purposes.

3. I brush his teeth every night with chicken-flavored toothpaste because greyhounds have horribly soft teeth.
4. He's supposed to be that skinny.
5. He doesn't catch Frisbees, fetch sticks, or sit.

Ingrid tests number 5. She stops him in the street and yells, "Sit!" and pushes his low back with both her hands.

He doesn't sit, just stands there.

"Arr, call this crazy lass off, me boy," I croak.

Ingrid giggles.

I hope Ahab feels like running tonight. I hope he'll put on a show for Ingrid. Because the truth is, sometimes he doesn't run. The mood doesn't strike him. Some nights I walk him to the field and unclip the leash, and he looks around, nose quivering. I give him a couple of minutes. He paws the ground or whines, and I clip the leash back on and he leads the way home. Greyhounds are like cats that way: moody, mysterious. Most of the time, you can't make them do what you want them to. And like a true Munker, Ahab keeps his reasons to himself.

Ingrid and Ahab and I sprint across traffic-less Main Street and trudge up the hill toward the high school. I huff from the exertion; my lungs hum with that weird cold metallic burn.

At the football field I close the gate behind us. For safety, the spotlights here shine all night, which is fortunate for Ahab, because he's going blind—his eyes seem milkier every day—and he can't see too well in the dark.

"You can only let greyhounds off leash in a completely enclosed area where they won't be able to run off," I say. "Like here. See?" I sweep my arm around the perimeter of the fence; it totally encloses the field. No gaps whatsoever.

"Why?" asks Ingrid.

I unclip Ahab's leash. He sniffs the night air. He is a solemn canine beatnik, composing a jazz poem in his head.

"Because he's likely to run after any furry, moving object," I say. "That's just the way he is. Once he locks on to a squirrel or a cat or whatever, there's no stopping him."

"Never off leash?"

"Never off leash. Unless it's completely enclosed." I strip off Ahab's booties and stuff them in my pockets. He gets very still. He even seems to stop breathing.

Memory Smack: As Ahab sprinted across this field, Nick, next to me on the bleachers, imitated the noise of a muscle car shifting gears.

Ingrid clutches my elbow. We anticipate the Captain's sudden motion, sudden speed. But he just stands there.

I peel his coat from his back; it crackles with static electricity. I bundle the coat under my arm, and he paws the snow.

"Run," I say.

He yawns.

"Ahab, run!"

He sneezes.

Behind us, car wheels crunch on ice. A police cruiser rolls up to the field, toward the gate. France sits behind the wheel. For a moment she watches us and talks into her radio. Slowly, she gets out of the cruiser, shuts the door, strolls over. She hangs her stick arms over the chain-link fence.

"Everything okay?" she asks. "Cold out tonight. Hey, Ingrid, right?"

Ingrid beams. "Hi, Officer Frances," she says.

France offers Ingrid a smile of crowded, yellowing teeth.

"Hey, France," I say through stiffened lips. It's so cold, my eyeballs sting.

She puts an arm around me and squeezes my shoulder against hers. "How's your kitchen?" she asks.

"Fine. No damage."

"So I hear. You doin' okay?"

Ahab trots to the fence and sniffs France's fingers. She tries to scratch his chin but can't quite reach. He walks a few paces away, squats, and pees. Steam rises around him like he's onstage at a rock concert or something. For some reason the three of us all watch him pee.

"I'm not exactly comfortable with you being up here alone at night, Zell," France says.

"I'm not alone."

"You know what I mean." She adjusts her neck warmer labeled WIPPAMUNK POLICE. "Be careful up here. You know? Watch for things. Be alert."

"Ahab's going to run for me," Ingrid says.

"Then we'll go," I say.

"It *is* quite a sight, seeing the Captain run," France says.

"So, can we hang out here a few more minutes?"

"Just a few more." She pounds her leather-gloved fists on the fence points.

"Cool. Thanks for not getting all Rosco P. Coltrane on us."

France laughs, because when we were little, our favorite show during Friday-night sleepovers was *The Dukes of Hazzard,* and our favorite character was Rosco. We always cracked up at his bumbling antics: getting tangled in the cord of his CB radio, chasing his sheriff's hat down a dusty road.

France won't ever get a pedicure with me, or take me to the mall to shop for a little black dress, or anything like that, but she's still my best girlfriend. My best girlfriend whose presence I have a hard time tolerating since The Trip, not only because she reminds me of Nick's last night in Wippamunk, but also because France was the one who convinced Nick and Dennis to go on The Trip in the first place, to shadow the group for a story in *The Wippamunker.* Nick returned all excited from that first informational meeting in the town hall basement. He wanted to go to New Orleans for the opportunity to photograph someplace—*any* place—other than Wippamunk. "I love it here," he said. "But sometimes it's just so . . . *here,* you know? Plus EJ's going, and France and Russ, and Dennis is totally sold on the idea. Could be cool."

Ahab lets out a long whine.

"He's cold, Zell," France says. "You took his coat off."

"He never runs with his coat on."

"Why won't he run?" asks Ingrid.

"Sometimes greyhounds just don't want to run," I say. "Ahab, run!"

"Sing," Ingrid says.

"What?"

"Maybe Ahab needs music to run to. My dad says *he* can't run without music."

"You sing, then."

"No. You sing. It's your dog."

"Nah."

"I think Ahab wants you to sing," Ingrid whispers. She tugs my arm. "He really, really wants you to sing."

France laughs. "Yeah, Zell. Sing for us. Let's hear it."

But I know Ahab doesn't like my singing. He only likes the singing of Gladys Knight and the Pips. And he loves the "Cookie Time" song, which Nick crooned whenever he gave Ahab a treat. He made it up to the tune of "A Pirate's Life for Me."

"Tell you what," France says. "I'll give you and the Captain and Ingrid a lift back home. In the croo-za." She lifts her chin at Ingrid, as if a ride home in the cruiser beats the hell out of seeing Ahab run. "Want a ride in the croo-za?" she asks.

Ingrid cinches her hood so that only her nose and eyes show. "Run, Ahab!"

He walks over to us and whines.

Ingrid sighs. She looks at her feet and kicks the snow.

Balls.

For some reason, the thought of disappointing Ingrid seems unbearable. So I take a big breath. I crow a wobbly version of the first thing that comes to mind. "Didn't you know you'd have to hurt sometime?" I even do the Pips' part, too—"Sometime, sometime." I blow mellow-pitched standup-bass sounds through tight, slightly parted lips.

Ahab cocks his head. He dips the eye-patch side of his face toward the ground. Then he explodes, lurching after imagined prey, tracing a huge infinity sign as snow spits behind him.

Ingrid throws back her hood and whoops, and her voice bounces off the towering white pines that edge the field. "I told you so!"

France rattles the fence. "Woo-hoo!"

I clap my mittened hands and warble the heartsick ballad, my face immobile with cold. "Didn't you know you'd have to cry sometime? Didn't anybody tell you love had another side?"

And the Captain—agape, with wild eyes—tears up the snow with abandon.

With g.d. abandon.


It's PAST TEN by the time France drops us off at home. She flies up High Street with the lights flashing. Ingrid asks to hear the siren, but

France says some other time because she doesn't want to startle the neighbors.

At home, Ingrid changes into pajamas without my asking her to. She begs me to fake body slam her onto the couch, so I do, and tuck my hairy afghan underneath her.

"Will you read to me?" she asks.

"What, like, a bedtime story?"

"Yeah."

"I don't have any kids' books."

"You must have something."

"I've got about a million old issues of *The Wippamunker* in the attic, and a wall full of anatomy textbooks. That's pretty much it."

"I know," says Ingrid. "*Meals in a Cinch with Polly Pinch.* I'll read it to you. I love to read."

"You've got to get some sleep." I go over to the turntable. I put my dry lips to the record and let them caress the tiny, cool ridges. As I cue Gladys, Ingrid says, "I like that sound." It takes me a second to realize she's talking about the crackly sound of the needle settling into the vinyl groove.

"I like it, too," I say.

Gladys sings about getting by okay, and learning not to cry away the day.

One paw at a time, Ahab heaves his old body onto the couch and gets comfortable. He sighs, nuzzles his nose under Ingrid's calves, and closes his eyes.

She tucks her feet under his rump. "I like how it looks like he's got an eye patch," she says.

"Good night. I'll be right upstairs."

"Zell? Your skeleton's sort of awesome."

"Hank? I'll tell him you said so. Sleep tight, okay?"

"Wait. I need to talk to you about something."

I stand by the coffee table, hands on hips. "Okay. Make it quick. Your dad won't be very happy with me if he finds out you were up this late."

"I think you need some help," she says. "With baking."

"You know how to bake?"

"Well, I do watch *Pinch of Love* several times a day. And I read the magazine cover to cover. Usually more than once. And since Polly Pinch *is* my mother, baking's in my blood. So maybe I could help you with your experiments. And we could win the contest *together*. As a team." She beams at me from the couch, my afghan wrapped around her little face like a bonnet.

I never anticipated sharing my baking endeavors, and I just don't think I can reveal my dysfunctional kitchen to anyone, let alone this little girl I hardly know.

"I'm not sure that's such a good idea, Ingrid."

She blinks, staring at me. Tears fill her eyes, just like before.

Balls.

"You know what?" I nod. "On second thought, two heads are better than one, right?"

She sits up, her eyes bright once again. "Right. Especially in a kitchen." Her arm protrudes from the afghan. "We have to pinkie swear it," she whispers.

We lock pinkies in the dim room. "We'll win the Warm the Soul baking contest together," she says. "And we'll get invited to *Pinch of Love Live* together. A team."

"A team," I repeat. "Sounds good."

I'm not really sure about this plan. But I'm locked in now; I pinkie swore. There's no turning back.

# EJ

EJ throws another log into the fire and returns to his bench. He removes his sweater; outside, before the fire in the February night, he wears a hat and a T-shirt, flannel-lined jeans, and boots.

A light goes on in Mr. Roy's workshop across Malden Pond. Nick's dad descends his basement steps. The three top steps are all EJ can see of the workshop because the windows are just above the ground, and most of the basement is underground.

Back in the day, Mr. Roy stored a six-person toboggan in his garage. The toboggan was old-fashioned, with polished wood and padded seats. Nick kept the bottom lubed with the waxy stuff he used on his snowboard.

As far as EJ's concerned, tobogganing—or the memory of it—makes living in "the Great White North," as Charlene says, worth the dark afternoons, the soggy socks, the staticky hair, skin so dry it feels sore, shoveling at five A.M., and having to warm up your car for ten minutes before you drive anywhere.

The Roys' side yard was the best in town for sledding. It was clear of obstacles, steep, long, and sloped right down to the pond. And so every snow day—from first grade through his senior year at Wippamunk High—EJ trudged across the ice to Mr. Roy's house. EJ and Nick built a little ramp by smoothing snow over a few logs. Before long, Zell arrived. She snowshoed through the woods from the north side of town, where her parents lived before they moved to Vermont. France came, too; her dad was a cop and dropped her off in his cruiser and gave the four of them—EJ, Nick, France, and Zell—a stern lecture about not driving anywhere today because the highway guys needed the roads to themselves while they plowed.

But the lecture was unnecessary because none of them had licenses yet, and besides, all they cared about was tobogganing.

EJ rode in front because he was heaviest. He straddled the sled and held it in place while the rest loaded on: first Nick, then Zell, then France, who was skin and bones. Still is. In a toboggan you can't hold on to the edge because there is no edge; you simply cling to the body in front of you. So they linked into each other, and if one person fell off, it caused a chain reaction. But none of them ever fell off.

EJ lifted his feet. They sailed down the hill, down, down, straight down, no need to turn, no need to steer. No way *to* steer, really, even if you had to. Mr. Roy's house whizzed by, and the wet, snow-splattered trees whizzed by.

Zell screamed the entire way down. France made no sound. Nick laughed his spurty, punchy laugh. EJ ducked behind the front of the toboggan, which scrolled like a wave over his knees. But his face was exposed, and snow and wind whipped his cheeks and forehead.

They sailed over the ice, fifty miles an hour, maybe more.

Good times, EJ thinks. Good times. He sips his beer. The night is bright thanks to the fire, the spotlight on the back of his house, and the moon, small and full and straight above.

He wonders whether Mr. Roy still has that toboggan. He imagines Charlene straddling him, her legs and arms wrapped around him tight, as they fly over the ice.

Then again, maybe she harbors no romantic inclinations toward him whatsoever. Maybe she wants friendship, nothing more. She's never mentioned a boyfriend, but that doesn't mean she doesn't have one. Or a girlfriend, EJ thinks. You never know. He chuckles and wills an arousing image out of his mind.

Across the pond the light in Mr. Roy's basement workshop flicks off.

EJ stands, stretches, and throws another log on the fire. Somewhere near, an owl calls: hoo-hoo, huh-hoooo. Hoo-hoo, huh-hoooo. It's the sound a barred owl makes, EJ knows, because Nick taught him that. Nick could identify every single type of bird in the encyclopedia, and imitate their calls, too. He was a frickin' genius that way. What was the barred owl's song? "Who cooks for you, who cooks for all?" Something like that.

EJ cups his hands, throws his head back, and hoots into the night: "Hoo-hoo, huh-hoooo. Who cooks for all."

He listens for a response, but the owl is silent.

"For Nick," EJ says. He draws out a belch and pours the remainder of his beer into the snow between his feet.

## Nick

November 3, 2006
From: nicholas.roy@thewippamunker.com
To: rose-ellen@roymedicalillustration.com

Hello, Pants.

So how big is this heart monitor you have to wear? Sounds stylish. And how long before they get the results back? Doesn't seem like Dr. Fung is too alarmed. That's a good sign, right? I told you you'd be okay. Keep me posted.

And don't let Dr. Fung fondle your gorgeous breasts too much.

So Day 1 is officially over.

Today, Dennis took notes and I took photos as everybody else— Pastor Sheila, Father Chet, Chief, Russ, France, and EJ—gutted this old woman, Verna's, house. You should have seen the g.d.

mold in her house. Or should I say, what *used* to be her house.
We gave her one small box of all we could salvage (in addition to
a bathroom sink which miraculously was in pretty good shape).
In the box were a few pots and pans and her son's bronzed baby
shoes. She cried when she found the shoes. She said her son
was her only baby and he died in 'Nam. She said after the storm
blew out, she waited on her roof for help. Just about everybody
around her left, but she stayed because she didn't think the storm
would be a big deal. And then the next morning, across the street
there was a dead, bloated body hooked onto the telephone pole,
caught somehow, floating there. Turns out it was her neighbor of
thirty-seven years. Can you even imagine that?

There I was taking pictures of this woman as she told Dennis
these awful memories: how she was waiting on her roof all alone,
sitting on a cooler full of bathtub water, squinting at this corpse,
trying to identify it—I felt so angry. How could that happen here, in
our country? But Verna, she seemed much more sad than angry.
She stood there on the sidewalk, in front of what used to be her
home, but is now a pile of rot, and she wept and talked about her
son and her neighbor. She was sad, but she was accepting, in a
wise sort of way. But I was just angry. Burning-up angry.

I don't know. It's hard to explain. Maybe Verna already went
through her anger. Used it all up.

Anyway, you would not believe the trash here, Zell. It's piled
along the street where people are gutting homes. It's at least
ten feet high and a half mile long. Mattresses, dressers, toilets,
refrigerators, shingles, siding. Nothing good for trash picking,
that's for sure. Everything is rotten or covered in mold.

I've attached some shots for you. Look very closely at that last one
of Russ, with the little boy sitting in his lap and hugging him. That
was taken at the church. They had an assembly earlier tonight, to

sort of thank the missionaries in advance, Catholics and Baptists together and even a couple Muslim dudes from the Islam place down the street. Yes, Russ's eyes are red. And it's not from all the dust and dirt and mold, if you catch my drift.

Father Chet said something to me today, as I was changing lenses during my conversation with Verna. He came up to me in his Tyvek suit and whispered in my ear, in his awesome African accent: "We are all connected."

But I'm not supposed to get involved, right? I'm down here with Dennis; he's the reporter, I'm the photographer. We're not supposed to be *with the mission.* We're supposed to record what our friends are doing and then publish a story on it in *The Wippamunker* when we get back. But I can't help it. I feel like I *am* a part of it, whether I like that or not. That's not very photojournalistic, is it? It's not very unbiased.

I wish you were here in this sleeping bag with me.

Have titillating dreams of me.

Your hunk,

Nick

# 3

## Zell

$\mathcal{M}$ORNING AGAIN. G.d. morning. I dress as Gladys sings about hating every morning that she opens her eyes and doesn't see her man.

Ahab sniffs around in the backyard, as Mount Wippamunk glistens. It's a freakishly warm Sunday, a weirdly melting world. Icicles drip, and somewhere a lone bird chirps.

Ingrid's in her backyard on the other side of the fence. She wears the huge red ski hat and a pink turtleneck. Mittens dangle from strings inside her sleeves. Her auburn hair hangs unbraided like frizzy curtains. "Come snowshoeing with us," she says.

I throw up my hands. "Wish I could. But I don't have any snowshoes." It's a lie. Thing is, snowshoeing with anyone besides Nick would be a betrayal, an admittance of some sort, like getting the car fixed or shoveling the driveway or cooking an occasional meal; things Nick used to do. Winter sports were something Nick and I did together.

"We have an extra pair of snowshoes that you can borrow," Ingrid says. "They belong to my step-grandmother."

Ahab trots to the fence. His tail wags once, twice. Ingrid's golden hand makes quick little circles on top of his head, so his ears flatten out to the sides.

"Please?" she says. "My dad really, really wants you to come."

"He does?"

"Yeah."

"Wish I could, but I have a lot of work to get done."

"On a *Sunday*? We're leaving now. Hurry up." She gives Ahab one last drawn-out scratch before she bounds inside.

Balls.

I think of some pamphlets Pastor Sheila handed me not too long ago, when she paid a house call. Pamphlets about grieving that stress the importance of exercise and a change in scenery, being social and making new friends.

"Okay," I say, even though Ingrid's already gone inside. Ahab cocks his head and whines.

I dig out my ski pants from the half-collapsed cardboard chest of drawers in the coat closet. I lace my hiking boots. I feel around for my fleece hat but decide against it because it's so freakishly warm out.

Nick's green aluminum snowshoes lean against the closet wall. They're dented and scratched. His ridiculous hat is stretched over the tips, a mid-1980s number with strings hanging down, a pom-pom on top.

I grip the soft hat and sniff its fibrous insides, which remind me of how I might draw stringy strands of muscle tissue.

"I'm going snowshoeing, Nick," I say. "I'm sorry."


GARRETT'S BACK IS TO ME. He tosses a big pair of snowshoes and a little pair of snowshoes into the bed of his pickup. He doesn't wear a coat, either, but red Under Armour, which accentuates his muscles.

Ingrid runs from the house with another medium-size pair of snowshoes. "Wait!" She hurls the extra pair over her head, and it clatters onto the others.

"What are you doing?" says Garrett. He closes the truck gate. "Trudy isn't coming."

"Zell's coming," she says.

He swings around. I'm standing on the sidewalk, water bottle in hand.

"Oh!" he says. "Hi."

He looks surprised, and it's clear to me now that Ingrid totally made up the part about Garrett wanting me to come with them.

I glance back at my porch, then stare at my water bottle. "Ingrid said—"

"Ingrid says a lot of things." He laughs. "Get in."


I PULL MY DOOR SHUT. "Nice ride," I say, admiring the tidy interior.

"Thank you."

As Garrett heads north on potholed Route 331, my insides churn with a crazy mixture of anxiety and guilt—as if I'm cheating on Nick or something. I stare intently out the window. We pass the stone foundation to an old farmhouse just a foot or two from the road. We pass Wippamunk Antiques, where the tips of a white picket fence poke from the snow like shark teeth. We pass Wippamunk Farms. My ears pop as we gain altitude.

"Beautiful day," Garrett says.

"Hmmm," I say.

At the stucco Prince of Peace Catholic Church, Father Chet—Wippamunk's first-ever Cameroonian resident—shovels slush from the sidewalk leading to the sacristy. He's been leading Prince of Peace for a few years now, and the general consensus among Wippamunk-ers is that he's sincere and kind, if a little kooky sometimes.

At a blinking red light looms the Tudor-style Wippamunk Free Public Library. And just past it, we catch a brown-gray-green view of central Massachusetts, the skyscrapers of Boston in the far distance.

Garrett cracks his window. He squints in the sunlight that glints off the snowbanks and the wet road. From an overhead compartment he extracts sunglasses and puts them on. "How's your kitchen?" he asks. "Any damage?"

"No," I say. "No damage at all, actually. Guess I was lucky."

"Anything we can do to help out?"

"Not really. But thanks."

"Anything at all, just say the word."

"Thanks."

"I was the one who called the fire department, you know," he says.

I realize I never even thought about who summoned the fire-fighters.

"I smelled smoke," he continues. "Then your alarm started going off, and I didn't know if you were in there, if you were dead or alive, or what."

Me neither, I think, as Ingrid adds, "It was really scary."

"Well, thank you. For calling the fire department," I say.

"Of course," he says. He drums his thumbs on the steering wheel. I can tell he's trying to think of something else to talk about. "So, life's hectic for me and Ingrid," he says after a while. "Between work and law school and Ingrid's school, the daily grind is pretty rough."

"Mine, too," I say. Which is a lie, because I work at home and have no kids, and don't really have a daily grind. I try to smile, but when I catch Garrett's eye, that anxious guilt roils inside my gut again. I look quickly out the window.

We drive a ways. Past an old cemetery, where, a few years back, Nick photographed elementary school students taking rubbings of the headstones. Past the abandoned orphanage where he and Dennis once spent the night for a feature on the legendary ghosts of Wippamunk. Past stone walls, scenic overlooks, gully streams, all of which make me ache, all of which cry out, Nick, Nick, Nick, even now.

"That's my step-grandmother's house!" Ingrid announces. She points to a big house with a barnlike side addition. Little plywood lean-tos protect the hedges in the yard. Stained-glass fairies decorate the windows. The fairies twirl slightly, catching the light. Near the front door a wooden sign reads, DON'T PISS OFF THE FAIRIES!!

"Dad, wave hi," says Ingrid. She waves like crazy to the brick red house.

Garrett waves.

"Dad," she says. "Why isn't Trudy my nanny?"

"Because I don't want you around all that heavy machinery. Besides, Trudy's a busy lady."

I raise an eyebrow. "Heavy machinery?"

"Don't ask. My stepmother is a . . . creative type. Crap, I missed the trailhead." He swings the truck around.

"Like me," I say. I realize too late how lame that sounds. "Where did you live before?" I ask. "In Wippamunk, right?"

"Just on the other side of town. My landlord raised the rent. That's why we moved."

"Do you have a mother?" Ingrid asks.

"She lives in Vermont with my sister," I say.

"My mother—"

"Here we are," Garrett says grandly, sort of like a circus announcer. He parks the truck at the mouth of a dirt road two-thirds of a mile from Trudy's house.

This road, I know, leads to a man-made lake. On its shores sits an old stone chimney. Nick and I pitched our tent there a million times and slept inside, cocooned in our sleeping bags, side by side.

WE STRAP ON OUR SNOWSHOES and trudge along the unplowed maintenance road, snaking up the undeveloped south side of Mount Wippamunk. Behind me Ingrid quietly sings the doo-wop *Pinch of Love* theme song. In front of me Garrett is silent except for steady, intent nose breathing.

In my head I frame the photographs Nick would take: sunlight shimmering; birches glistening; a bloodred cardinal cheep-cheep-cheeping; the spots where snow melted and refroze, distorting the impressions of everything that touched it—paws and pinecones and dripping icicles.

Snowshoeing is a trance. I lift one foot, then the other. My legs become heavy. The sun bakes my back. Sweat drips under my boobs, down into my bellybutton and waistband.

Twenty minutes up, Garrett veers off the road. Our legs sink deeper here, just above the knees. When you snowshoe, you're supposed to navigate these off-trail places where the snow seems forbiddingly deep.

To the left the ground pitches sharply, drops away into iced cliffs.

"Don't fall," Garrett calls.

I glance behind me; Ingrid's air drumming.

We enter a clearing. He stoops, unstraps his snowshoes, and scrambles up a six-foot-tall boulder. After kicking all the snow from the top, he turns, crouches, and offers a hand.

Ingrid kicks off her snowshoes. She throws herself at the boulder, and he pulls her up as if she's light as a bedsheet.

"Zell?" Garrett says. He grins down at me.

I shake my head vigorously. "I am not going up there."

"Oh, yes you are," Ingrid belts. "Doo-doo-doo, all you need—IS A PINCH!"

"It's a beautiful view." Garrett offers both hands. "Trust me."

Ingrid tosses her red hat high and catches it. She rummages through Garrett's backpack and pulls out a silver-wrapped cereal bar. She sings between bites: "Doo-doo-doo, all you need—IS A PINCH!"

I unstrap my snowshoes. "I'm heavier than I look," I say.

"I'm stronger than I look," he says. "Get a running start, and jump as high as you can."

I do, and he catches my forearms, leans back on the boulder, and hauls me up. I collapse onto his thighs.

"See? No sweat," he says.

"Yeah," I say, a little out of breath. "Thanks." I sit and help myself to a half-crushed cereal bar, which Garrett holds out to me.

The view is south and west, sunny and clear, deep and wide, a view that would bring Nick to his knees. Foothills and streams roll below us. They make me think of torn bits of tissue paper flattened into a collage. Turkey vultures soar, black Ws against the brilliant sky. The breeze blows—slight, then strong, then slight again.

Garrett smirks as Ingrid points out landmarks.

"Long Pond in Rutland," she says. "Wippamunk Reservoir. The city of Worcester. And way out there? Wicked way out? Mount Greylock. See it?"

"Yeah," I say. "I actually do."

In the western distance the ridge of Mount Greylock stretches long, like the back of a sperm whale—the sight that inspired Herman Melville to write *Moby-Dick*. Or so the legend tells us.

Ingrid pokes a straw into a juice box. "Aren't I a little old for juice boxes, Dad?" she asks.

"I don't know. How old is too old for a juice box? You're nine."

"Exactly." Her face glistens with sweat. She sucks down all the juice, until the cardboard becomes indented. "Here." She shows Garrett the empty box.

"Do I look like a trash can?" he says.

"Yes."

He yanks her hat down over her eyes, and she giggles. "Carry in, carry out, remember?" Garrett says.

"I know, I know." She puts the empty box in the backpack, then goes back to singing while tossing and catching her hat.

"Stop singing that, Ingrid," Garrett says. He's on his second cereal bar. "Sing anything but that. Please."

"Dad. Zell and I are going to enter the Warm the Soul baking contest together."

"You are, huh?"

"Uh—," I say. When I pinkie swore that she could help me, I didn't really think about Garrett's reaction, or whether he would even allow it. But he doesn't seem irritated. Actually, he seems amused.

"Yup," says Ingrid.

"I *am* thinking about entering it," I say. "The other day, with the fire truck? I was . . . baking."

"So I heard," he says. "I'm not much of a cook, either."

"You get twenty thousand dollars if you win," I say. "And an all-expenses-paid—"

"That's a lot of money," Ingrid says. "Right?"

She says it so quickly, I wonder if she doesn't want Garrett to know about getting to meet Polly on the set.

"What would you do with the money if you won?" he asks her.

"I would save it so that when I grow up I could go to France and study at the famous Cordon Blur cooking school."

Garrett leans back, rests his head on his backpack, and throws an arm over his eyes. "What would you do with the money, Zell?"

"I'd start a charity organization or something, for the people in New Orleans who are rebuilding their homes and communities in the wake of Hurricane Katrina, and the flood. That was Nick's last wish," I add.

"Dad?" says Ingrid. "I changed my mind. I would give my twenty thousand dollars to the people of New Orleans."

He sits up halfway and strokes her cheek. "You're a good girl," he says softly.

She sings some more: "All you need IS A PINCH. PINCH OF LOVE!"

"If you're going to keep singing, could you please do so quietly?"

"Sorry." She skips to the other end of the boulder and sits cross-legged. She slaps her thighs, humming the theme song.

"So you've got a bit of a Polly Pinch obsession yourself," he says. "No wonder Ingrid likes you so much."

"It's my new thing." The stupid truth is, I absolutely cannot wait to get home, watch *Pinch of Love,* and experiment with another batch of cookies. "Polly Pinch is pretty addicting," I say, "once you give her a chance."

"I don't encourage the Polly Pinch stuff. Believe me."

"About that contest. Ingrid offered to help me, so I said she could. I hope that's okay."

"Of course," he says. "I mean, as long as you realize that all she's going to want to do when you're around is bake, and bake, and bake some more."

I try to smile, and I think I succeed this time, because Garrett smiles back. I want to mention that Ingrid told me Polly Pinch is her mother but decide against it.

He hums a bar of the Polly Pinch song, then catches himself and clears his throat. "I remember reading about your husband in *The Wippamunker* last year. That was a nice article."

"Yeah. Dennis and my husband worked together at *The Wippamunker* for about ten years, so they knew each other pretty well."

"I'm sorry about your husband."

"Thanks." I scrape at some dead lichen on the boulder with my fingernail. "You married?"

"Nope. Never." He wipes his sweaty face on his sleeve. He takes my water bottle out of his backpack and offers it to me.

"Oh no, you first," I say. "You carried it."

He unscrews the lid, gulps almost half the water, and hands me the bottle.

Suddenly Ingrid runs up to us; tears dampen her cheeks. "Dad?"

"What is it, boo-boo? What's wrong?"

Ingrid points beyond the cliffs toward the sky. Her red hat is caught on the branch of an oak tree twenty feet out. Maybe thirty. A deep gulch and icy cliffs separate us from the oak, centuries old, a hundred feet tall, with peeling elephant-skin bark.

Garrett shades his eyes and studies Ingrid. "How did you manage that one?"

"I was trying to see how high I could throw it," she says. "And the wind came and took it."

"Looks like it's gone now."

"But it's not gone. It's right there."

High in the tree the red hat seems to shiver. Twigs poke it. It looks like some lanky-limbed creature is trying to rend the yarns and be born.

"Time to let it go, boo-boo." Garrett stands and shoulders into his backpack. "Maybe the wind will blow it down, and the next time we come here it will be on the ground, and we can get it then."

"But I want it now," she says. "I *need* it *now*."

"Let me try something," he says. He claps a snowball together. He cocks his arm back and hurls it forward, and the snowball shoots up—white dot against blue sky. It loses momentum six feet from the hat and plummets to the ground. He tries again, packing a smaller snowball. He flings his arm even harder this time but misses.

"I can't reach it, Ing." He sighs. "I tried. I'm sorry." He drops from the boulder and toes into his snowshoes. "Let's get moving. Time to head back to the truck. We'll get you another hat, okay?"

"Will you get it for me?" asks Ingrid, tugging my arm. A tearful hiccup escapes her mouth. "You have to get it for me. It belonged to my—"

"Time to head back," says Garrett, but not impatiently.

"Get it for me, Zell?"

The hat is impossible to reach, of course. She and I watch it for a moment. I will the wind to release it, but the hat stays fixed.

The cool breeze whips my hair across my mouth. I glance down at Garrett; I can't tell if he's looking at Ingrid or at me.

"I think it's gone for now," I tell Ingrid. I swig from my water bottle and offer some to her, but she shakes her head. "But like your dad said, maybe when you come back in the spring, it'll be on the ground."

"In the spring?"

"Yeah. In the spring."

I guide her toward the edge of the boulder. "And until then," I say, "you'll know exactly where it is."

NEXT TUESDAY AFTERNOON, Garrett stands on my porch again. The knot of his tie is loose, and a small oil stain—from salad dressing, maybe—dots his white shirt. The skin under his eyes looks droopy and pinched.

"I can't believe I'm asking you to do this again," he says.

Ingrid pushes past me and drops her backpack just inside the door. "Ahab!" she calls.

"I interviewed someone last night for a nanny position," Garrett says. "But she was . . . I mean, she was a nice girl and all, but she seemed . . ." He trails off. He glances at his watch.

I hand him Nick's keys. "Keep them this time."

He pockets the keys, looking overwhelmed. "I'll make it up to you. I swear." He hands me a big wad of bills.

"You don't need to pay me," I say. "Really."

He pauses for a second, like he's considering just stuffing the bills into my apron pocket and taking off. But instead, he nods. "Thanks, Zell."

IN MY KITCHEN Ingrid flips through *Meals in a Cinch with Polly Pinch*. "Finished my homework," she says before I even ask.

We brainstorm. Ingrid wants to make upside-down cake. I want to make oatmeal brownies. We draft a recipe for Oatmeal Brownie Upside-Down Cake, and I quickly realize that Ingrid is not the baking prodigy she hinted that she was. She suggests one cup of baking soda, but I convince her that's way too much. She suggests three cans of condensed evaporated milk and a dozen eggs, and I explain—gently—that we're not trying to feed an entire army. Finally, we negotiate a general plan of attack—adding oatmeal to the brownie batter, then creating alternating layers of brownie mix and cake mix.

"How do you know all this stuff about baking?" she asks. "What's too much, what's not enough? How do you know all that?"

How, indeed. From Ye Olde Home Ec Witch? Perhaps. Perhaps

I am the fallen soufflé in Room 8 of the basement of Wippamunk High School—Ye Olde Home Ec Witch's classroom. Or the soggy omelet in the beat-up frying pan with rusted handle in Room 8 of the basement of the high school. Perhaps I am shavings of carrot stuck in the sudsy sink drain, to which glaring Ye Olde Home Ec Witch points with a warty finger. (Did she really have warts, or was that detail simply part of the legend?)

It's inconceivable that Polly Pinch has warts. She is the santoku knife with forged-steel blade and slip-resistant polypropylene handle advertised on page eleven of *Meals in a Cinch*. She is the long-stemmed strawberry dipped in white chocolate fondue on page fifty-six. She is the porcelain cup of French-pressed Fair Trade organic shade-grown coffee on page ninety-nine.

And I am neither a kitchen Nazi nor a television chef with tight skin and perfect tanned boobs. I am Rose-Ellen Roy, née Carmichael, the soggy omelet trying to win a twenty-thousand-dollar baking contest. If not with Flourless Peanut Butter Treats, if not with Oatmeal Brownie Upside-Down Cake, then with Something Else Outstanding.

"You want to know how I know all this stuff?" I say. I hold the bowl. Ingrid stands on a chair and dumps the brownie mix. It mushroom clouds in our faces, and we both cough.

"Years and years of practice." I crack an egg with one hand.

She takes the eggshells and tosses them into the sink. "Practice?" she says. "But you said you don't cook. Like, not at all."

I grasp the wooden spoon and stir. "Let's not split hairs, hm'kay?"


FLOURY HANDPRINTS SMUDGE THE CABINETS. Sugar dots the counter. Brownish oatmeal sticks to the wall.

Ahab licks something next to the leg of a chair. He sniffs his way to the oven door, lapping flecks of batter here and there.

The Oatmeal Brownie Upside-Down Cake cools on the stovetop. It looks like black-brown volcanic mush.

"Last year?" Ingrid says. "I went to a Halloween party at my dad's work? And they had fake throw-up on the floor."

"Yeah?" I say.

She points to the Oatmeal Brownie Upside-Down Cake. "That looks like the fake throw-up."

"Mmm. How appetizing."

"So much for years and years of practice." Ingrid drums her fingers on the table. "Hey. I know someone who can help you."

"A fairy godmother?"

"Sort of. Grab your car keys, and let's go."

"I'm not going to drive us to someone's house I don't even know. Just tell me who it is."

"It'll be more fun if it's a surprise. Please?"

"Forget it."

"Well, I guess I'll just sit here and lick the batter off my arm." She drags her tongue from her elbow to her wrist. "Or maybe we should try to make a Right-Side-Up Cake."

Ahab sniffs Ingrid. She lets him lick her arm. "How much money do you win?" she asks.

"Twenty thousand dollars."

"That's a lot, right?"

"Yeah."

"You'd get all that money for the hurricane survivors. And I'd get to meet my mother. Finally."

Inside the pan, the oatmeal mass shifts. A wet spray plops onto the counter.

"That dessert is just bizarro," she says.

I sigh. "You win. Where are we going?"

Ahab licks Ingrid's arm completely clean. She fixes her sleeve and grins—widening her freckles, widening her eyes. Her smile reminds me of Garrett, and of Polly Pinch. She does resemble Polly, in the eyes mostly, and the mouth. Maybe Polly really is her mother.

"I want to surprise you." She skips through the living room to the front door. She waves at me to hurry up. Ahab gallops after her.

"Wait till you meet her," she says, tossing me my coat. "She's wicked awesome."

I LET INGRID SIT IN THE FRONT SEAT. She gives directions and seems so adultlike, I forget she's just a kid. Halfway up potholed Route 331, I wonder if she's big enough to sit legally in the front seat. Under the seat belt she looks so sunken, I almost pull over and make her get in the back. But she rolls down her window and howls into the icy wind. And so I roll down my window and crank up the heat as high as it will go.

We pass the library, lit up like a carnival. We pass the dark, abandoned orphanage; crumbling stone walls; the dirt road on the south slopes of Mount Wippamunk.

I pull into the driveway of the huge red house with stained-glass fairies in every window. A spotlight in the snow shines on the DON'T PISS OFF THE FAIRIES!! sign.

"So you think your step-grandmother is going to help us?" I ask.

"I *know* my step-grandmother is going to help us." Ingrid races from the car to the front door.

When I catch up to her, I lift the pewter fairy knocker and let it drop. A moment later the door swings open. A lanky woman stands before us. She wears protective goggles. Her jeans are duct taped to her construction boots, and the long sleeves of her T-shirt are duct taped to her bony wrists. A string attaching neon orange earplugs dangles around her neck.

"Well, hello there, Pumpkin Pie!" cries the old woman. She pushes back her goggles and stoops to embrace Ingrid.

I recognize, under the tight white curls, a square, craggy face.

Ye Olde Home Ec Witch.

If it's humanly possible, she looks even older than I remember.

Ye Olde Home Ec Witch is Ingrid's step-grandmother? Impossible.

Ingrid hops and hugs Ye Olde Home Ec Witch. "Hi, Trudy," she says.

Ye Olde Home Ec Witch pinches Ingrid's cheek. "How did you get here, Pumpkin Pie?"

"My best friend, Zell, drove us."

Ye Olde Home Ec Witch straightens to her full height, about five inches taller than me. She puts her hands on her hips and eyes me up and down. Years ago her beady eyes disdainfully sized up my half-raw pancakes. Her vinegary nose sniffed my not-gingery-enough gingersnaps. Her knobby hands swept naughty crumbs from my serving table.

She throws back her shoulders and seems to grow yet another inch. "Rose-Ellen Carmichael," she says. "As I live and breathe."

"It's Rose-Ellen Roy now," I say. "I can't believe you remember me. I graduated sixteen years ago."

"I never forget a face," she says. "Or a name."

"Mrs. Chaffin—"

"That's not what you're used to calling me, is it?"

"What?" I say, although I'm not really surprised she knows about her nickname. I feel a little uneasy, like I'm back in high school again, back in Room 8 in the basement. G.d. I stuff my hands in my pockets and pretend to study the bundled-up hedges under their protective lean-tos.

"I know what you called me," says Ye Olde Home Ec Witch. "And I know it wasn't always *witch*, either." She raises an eyebrow and glares.

Ingrid looks from her to me, and I wonder if "bitch" is in the vocabulary of a nine-year-old girl. Perhaps. But she doesn't seem to catch on, or maybe she's just unfazed. She grins and clings tighter, squeezing her waist.

Still glaring at me, Ye Olde Home Ec Witch pats the top of Ingrid's head. "You probably still call me that when you get together with your high school friends to reminisce," she says.

I hear a sound I've never heard before—a dry, scratching sound— and realize Ye Olde Home Ec Witch is laughing. Her face is soft now. It might even *glow* with something. Kindness? Understanding?

She reaches across the threshold and squeezes my hands in her cold claws. "I'm sorry for your loss, deary," she says. "Nicholas was a nice boy. A class act. That was a beautiful article Dennis wrote about him in *The Wippamunker*. I know my stepson moved next door to you. I was wondering when we'd bump into each other."

She gazes at me—lovingly?—and caresses my hands. "Come on." Ye Olde Home Ec Witch waves us inside.

Impossible.

Ingrid trots into the kitchen, climbs onto a swiveling stool at the breakfast bar, and spins away.

"Anyhoo," says Ye Olde Home Ec Witch. "Have a seat, and we'll put the past behind us. You're a different person now, living an adult life. And so am I. Call me Trudy."

Her boots make black marks on the linoleum. She strides to the stove, where a saucepan steams. "How about some hot chocolate?"

She pours it into two fairy-decorated mugs and sets them in front of us.

Ingrid slaps her palms on the counter. "Trudy, we need your help with a baking contest."

"I don't cook anymore, Pumpkin. You know that."

Ingrid waves a hand as if to say, She'll come around.

I take a sip; the hot chocolate tastes just as I remember in Ye Olde Home Ec Witch's class: grainy, buttery, not too bitter. Perfect.

"You're not at the high school anymore?" I ask.

"Honey, that place can kiss my crotchety old can," says Trudy.

"So what do you do in your retirement?"

"I run quite a lucrative business, actually. After Lew died—"

"Lew was my grandfather," says Ingrid, spinning on the stool so her hair flings out.

"After Lew died I needed something else to do," Trudy says. "Something different. Something more creative, for one. Cooking's creative, but not after you've taught the same recipes over and over to punk kids—no offense—for thirty years. I wanted something more creative. And also, what I wanted was something more . . . *aggressive.*"

"Aggressive?" I say.

"Aggressive." Trudy winks at Ingrid.

"Show her, Trudy," she says, slapping her own cheeks. "Show Zell the Barn."

Trudy leads the way to the Barn, an attached three-story side addition. Ingrid and I carry our fairy mugs through the kitchen and dining room, through a four-season sun porch. Fairies fill every available space. Ceramic fairies. Paper fairies. Glass fairies. Fairy plaques and fairy stationery. Fairy lamps and fairy wall hangings. Fairy salt-and-pepper shakers and fairy clocks.

We pause in a hallway, where Trudy opens a door. "You kids

have good timing," she says. "I'm just about to fire up my babies and start a new project."

She flips a few industrial-looking switches. Before us, the Barn lights up like a ball field. The cement-slab floor could fit eight cars easily, maybe ten. Push brooms and ladders of various heights lean against the walls. Wood shavings fill metal trash cans. Hundreds of cans of spray paint line shelves.

All around stand wide, tall tree stumps, stripped of bark. Some stumps are plain and smooth. Others resemble creatures. A dolphin juggling little red sticks. A coyote riding a skateboard. An eagle in green sneakers, reading a book.

Ingrid clasps her hands behind her back and strolls the aisles. She admires each wooden creature as if it was a priceless museum heirloom.

"The *Family of Skiers*?" I ask. I caress the beak of a giant cardinal fitting a baseball glove on the tip of its wing. "At the Mount Wippamunk base lodge? That's you? You're the wood sculptor? I heard a former teacher had done the *Family of Skiers,* but I didn't realize it was *you.*"

"The whole town's gonna realize it soon because Dennis is doing a big feature on me," Trudy says. "He's been hounding me for an interview for a while now, but I put him off. I guess I wasn't sure if my work is really worthy of *The Wippamunker.* But he talked me into it."

Trudy tightens her bootlaces. "That eagle is for the new grammar school they're building in Princeton. I like to keep them around for a week or two after they're complete, just so I can make finishing touches. I'm a perfectionist, as I'm sure you remember, Rose-Ellen. That's Johnny Appleseed." She points to the lanky likeness of a vagabondesque young man wearing patched clothing and cupping seeds in his palms. "I did that for the Leominster Historical Club. Johnny

Appleseed founded Leominster, you know. And that one's for the Worcester Aquarium." She points to an empire penguin waddling from an ocean wave carrying a beach ball.

"You certainly have quite a range," I say.

"I like to branch out. After all, the more you like, the happier you are. I do the paint jobs myself." She smoothes the duct tape against her wrists. "The outside sculptures are weather treated. The inside ones have just as much protective coating because of all the little loving hands that come caressing. And I use all found wood. I wouldn't want the environmentalists after me."

In a far corner, a blue tarp covers something that stands at least ten feet tall. Trudy notices me eyeing it.

"That's a work in progress," she says. "A very special and very important surprise commission that I'm working on. Top secret."

Ingrid slurps some hot chocolate and smacks her lips. "Tell us what it is, Trudy. The secret project."

"Can't, Pumpkin. You'll find out when the time comes. Tonight I happen to be working on something different. Something more time sensitive." She cracks open a glossy-paged library book to a photograph of a bobcat. "This was what I was about to do before you rang the bell. Got half an hour?"

"Yup," Ingrid says. I set our mugs on a shelf while she fishes around in a storage bin and pulls out two pairs of goggles. She slaps a pair on her head, then on mine, and leads me toward the Barn door, where we entered. We sit side by side on the concrete floor.

Trudy kneels next to another tarp, under which bulges a neat line of objects. Toreador style, she whips the tarp away.

Chain saws, lined from smallest to biggest. Twelve of them.

"The bigger saws are for the basic shapes: a head here, feet there," she says. She repositions her goggles and screws in her earplugs. "The smaller ones are for the detail work. Feathers, teeth, and so forth." She selects the biggest chain saw, stands, and cranks her elbow back. The saw whines and glugs. The smell of gasoline fills the Barn.

I adjust my goggles. "Wait a second," I yell. "You're going to carve that huge log"—I point to a smooth log standing upright on the floor—"to look like that bobcat"—I point to the book, now propped open on a table—"with *chain saws?*"

Trudy smiles, revealing yellowish dentures. She thrusts the growling chain saw overhead. "Honey," she yells, "does a bear crap in the woods?"

She dives at the smooth stump, and the blade's grinding notches sink into the wood. She circles the stump, plunging the blade in, pulling it out, and plunging it in again in a different spot. Chunks shoot up. Big chunks. Small chunks. More big chunks. More small chunks. They soar twenty, thirty feet in the air. One knocks against the ceiling rafters and lands near my feet. Ingrid scoops it up and waves it overhead. "Woo-hoo!"

One by one Trudy fires up the other chain saws until they all whine at her feet. She alternates from one to another. Sawdust collects around the stump. The bobcat takes shape just as she described: A head here, feet there. Half a tail. Long, low torso. Downward-pointing cheek fur. Tufted ears. Intelligent eyes. Fierce teeth. Thick claws on big paws. Then she creates one little ski underneath each paw, a skullcap-style helmet between its ears, and a flapping scarf. The bobcat looks like it's zooming fearlessly down a mountainside.

Finally Trudy turns to us. She looks a little sweaty now. She flashes a thumbs-up sign and one by one shuts down the chain saws. She selects ten cans from the shelves, cradles them in her arms, and deposits them on the floor. As she sprays, the scent in the air switches from gasoline to paint and aerosol. She waves her arms. Reddish brown fur appears. Black spots and streaks. A pink nose.

Black whiskers. Whitish teeth. Despite its accessories, the skiing bobcat appears so lifelike, I almost expect it to hiss, or purr, or lick its instep.

Ingrid erupts in applause and two woo-hoos. "Trudy, that is wicked, wicked mint."

"I'll say." She laughs and brushes the sawdust off her clothes with a big dust brush.

I drop the goggles back in the storage bin. "How did you—"

"How did I go from being Ye Olde Home Ec You-Know-What to all this malarkey?" She laughs again—this one coarse and hacking. She scrubs the sawdust from her curly white hair. "It's quite a story."

We follow her as she turns off the lights and shuts the Barn door. "I was cleaning out the shed the spring after Lew died," she says, "and I saw this Husqvarna chain saw hanging from the wall."

"Trudy, can I go to the bathroom?" Ingrid asks. She crosses her legs and hops. "Too much hot chocolate."

"You don't have to ask. Go, go." Trudy pretends to kick Ingrid's butt as she skips down the hall to the bathroom.

"Anyhoo, I almost set that old chain saw aside. I was going to sell it at the annual townwide yard sale. But—I don't know what came over me—I yanked the cord and fired up that Husqvarna. It was the first time I'd ever *held* a chain saw, let alone used one. The thing was a bad boy. It rattled my whole body, buzzed right into my bones."

Ingrid prances from the bathroom, but Trudy steers her around. "Wash your hands," she says. "With soap. For as long as it takes to sing 'Happy Birthday.'

"Anyhoo, behind the shed there was this tall old stump. I went up to it. I attacked it with the chain saw. And before I knew it— well, why don't I just *show* you."

Ingrid's back from the bathroom again. She wipes her hands on her jeans. "I didn't want to mess up the nice fairy towels."

"That's all right, Pumpkin," says Trudy. "Get your coat on. I want to show you two something outside."

We bundle up and follow the snowplowed path to the shed. Moonlight glimmers off the ice-coated trees. Ingrid hums "Happy Birthday."

Behind the shed Trudy shines a key-chain flashlight on the snow-covered tree stump. She brushes the snow away, revealing the likenesses of buildings that lean cartoonishly, still their natural wood color.

"Voilà," she says. "The Boston skyline, as studied from right here, through an old pair of bird-watching binoculars that Lew kept in the shed. I've been looking at those skyscrapers on clear days my whole darn life, as I'm sure you have, too. There I stood with this rumbling chain saw in my hand. I took a good long peek at the Prudential and carved it into the wood. Then I took a good long peek at the old John Hancock Building and carved *that* into the wood. 'Fore I knew it, I had chainsawed what any New Englander worth his salt—even a Mainer who can't remember the last time he left the state—would know as Boston. Into a damn tree stump."

"Wow." I run my mitten over the buildings. Trudy rattles off the names as I caress them. "One Financial. Custom House Tower. Yep. They're all there. Even the Citgo sign. See? They're crude, of course. Certainly not as fine-tuned as the work I produce now. But not bad for a first effort."

Ingrid wanders to a chicken-wire fence enclosing a low building with a small door. "Trudy, where are the goats?"

"They're all inside, Pumpkin. Keeping warm in the hay. Anyhoo." Trudy pockets her little flashlight, and we go back to the house under moonlight. Ingrid stays behind. She clicks her tongue and tries to coax the goats from their little house.

"That's how I discovered my . . . rather unusual, rather latent talent," Trudy says.

I catch my balance on a patch of ice. "No shit."

"Nope. No shit whatsoever. Weird thing is, I couldn't remember Lew ever using that chain saw. Ever. Now, maybe he used it as a younger man, before I knew him, when Garrett's mother was still around. But it was almost like that chain saw was hanging there all those years, just waiting for me to come along and put it to use. Hey, want to take home some goat cheese? I make it myself. It's delicious stuff. I just got my organic certification."

"Oh no. Thanks anyway."

"I'll put it in a little gift bag for you. Ingrid? Leave the goats be. Come on, now."

"Just one second," she calls.

Back in the kitchen Trudy wraps up some goat cheese.

"Trudy," I say, "I just can't believe you're—"

"So different from Ye Olde Home Ec Bitch?" She hands me a surprisingly heavy fairy-stamped paper bag. Piercing the bag is a little fairy—pointy chin, wistful expression, a beaded charm made from wire. I admire it for a moment, pluck it from the bag, and slip it into my pocket.

"I'm not that woman anymore, like I said," she says. "Time changes a person, Rose-Ellen. So does tragedy."

I think it's the first time anyone's said that word—"tragedy"—in my presence, since The Trip. I wait for her to say more—about how tragedy will change me—but instead she nods and says, "Keep it in the freezer. It'll last longer."

Ingrid comes inside, her eyes shining, her cheeks red. "I like goats," she says. "I like their beards, and the way they poop and eat at the same time."

"I like that about them, too," Trudy says, and I can tell by her face that she's holding back laughter. She kisses Ingrid's forehead. "Hey," she says. "Where's your old hat?"

"Oh." Ingrid holds her arms out as Trudy zips her coat to her chin. "I lost it."

"We'll get you another one, then."

"I don't want another one. I want the old one. It was my mother's."

Trudy glances at me. "Your mother's, huh?" she asks.

"Yes."

"So you're just gonna walk around without a hat?"

"Yeah."

"Suit yourself. Thanks for visiting."

"Trudy, what about the baking contest?" Ingrid says.

"I'll put on my thinking cap, Pumpkin Pie."

Ingrid buries her face in Trudy's sawdusty clothes. "Love ya 'n' like ya," she says.

"Love ya 'n' like ya," says Trudy, a sad sort of smile on her face.

I BACK OUT THE DRIVEWAY. Trudy waves from the living room behind a chorus line of stained-glass fairies.

Ingrid hangs her whole upper body out the passenger seat window and waves both arms. "Good luck with your top secret project!"

I roll down my window, too, and crank up the heat, and we howl as we sail down Route 331, back to the center of town. I take the road a little too fast, and my stomach spins into my throat, so I slow down. Ingrid begs me to speed, but I tell her it's not safe.

We pass the Prince of Peace Church, where I glimpse Father Chet in the second-floor sacristy window, his dark skin contrasting with the white wall behind him. My heart does its wild dance. Fast beats, then no beats.

Maybe it's sick, but I admit: I kind of like it, that feeling of suspension, that sense that something unknown—a force, a spirit—holds on to your heart, and won't let it beat, and won't let it go, at least for a little while.

# EJ

EJ's refilling a coffeemaker with decaf almond when France swings her cruiser behind the Muffinry van and parks. He knows she hates that joke about cops hanging out in the doughnut shop, and even though the Muffinry isn't a doughnut shop, it's close enough. Especially now that EJ serves beignets. So she always parks behind the building, out of view of Main Street.

"Hey, Eege," she says, stepping through the back door. She pours a cup of regular and sits on a sack of flour.

"France?" he says, which means, "Hi."

"Got any s'mores today?"

"Only in muffin tops."

"I'll take one."

"Comin' at ya, hey," says Travis from the register. He plucks a pastry tissue from a box, pinches the biggest muffin top, and Frisbee-flings it at France.

She catches it one-handed and takes a huge bite from the cakey disk. "Mmm. Delicious, Silo," she says, mouth full.

The nickname—Silo—makes EJ pause; it might be the first time anyone's called him that since The Trip. He flips the switch on the coffeemaker and savors its burbling sound.

"Hey," says France. She stands next to him. He can smell the marshmallows and graham crackers on her breath. "I want to talk to you about something," she says.

He surveys the Muffinry. Three old ladies sip coffee by the big bay window, but other than that, the place is empty. "What about?" He moves on to the butterscotch coffee—bangs the reservoir against the trash can, puts in a new filter.

She moves aside to give him elbow room. "Nick."

He's about to open the silver coffee bag when she says it. He pauses, the bag pinched in his fingers. "What about him?"

France hides her chapped lips behind her coffee cup. "I feel like there might be something we could do," she says. "Publicly."

He opens the bag, dumps the coffee, slides it into the machine.

"Because," she says. "You know. Nothing was ever done."

He turns on the coffeemaker. "What are you talking about?"

She glances at Travis; he's hunched over the counter, fiddling with his BlackBerry.

"Closure," she says.

"Closure?" EJ repeats.

"Yeah. Closure, fa crissake. Don't you get it?"

He opens his mouth to answer, but the Muffinry bells jingle and six people enter. Two moms ushering four kids. Travis pockets his BlackBerry. "EJ, please, hey," he says.

EJ sighs. He tops off France's cup, fits a lid on it, and hands it to her. "You on tonight?" he asks.

"No."

"Come over, then. And dress warm."

# Nick

November 4, 2006
From: nicholas.roy@thewippamunker.com
To: rose-ellen@roymedicalillustration.com

Hi, Hot-Pants.

Today I was taking pictures of Russ and Father Chet and a bunch of New Orleans guys as they rebuilt an altar in one of the churches down here. At one point I put down my camera to take a swig of water, and next thing I know, Father Chet is pressing a hammer into my hand. I told him I don't really know what I'm doing, but he showed me. I wasn't sure if I should be helping out. I mean, that isn't really my place. But when I looked over at Dennis, he smiled and shrugged. So I spent an hour or two learning from Father Chet. Some of these guys can hammer a nail in one or two swings. By the end of the day it was still taking me four or five swings, but I definitely got better as the day progressed. I never realized how satisfying it is to build stuff with your hands. Especially alongside other people. Also, I never really appreciated what a *skill* it is, this type of work. It's amazing the results you get, and how quickly you get them, when everyone is unified.

Chief Kent threw his back out early in the morning, so he went with Pastor Sheila to the library to help sort books. Pastor Sheila had thousands of books shipped down here in crates. (Dennis wrote about that book drive, remember?) The books were donated by people visiting the Wippamunk Library. The library down here was totally wiped out. They lost everything. There are actually no public libraries open in New Orleans, according to Pastor Sheila. But now this one library has a children's library that is bigger and better than it was before the hurricane, before the floods, thanks to the librarians and Pastor Sheila and the good people of Wippamunk. When Chief came back he was saying how cute all the kids were and how this one kid sat so still on his lap and listened to him read this one book over and over again, like thirty times.

EJ drives all the way into the touristy downtown to get coffee from this chick, Charlene. He is totally crushing on this girl. She's cute, too. I wonder if it will turn into a long-distance relationship or something. Seriously, he's that into her.

Anyway Charlene gives us coffee for free along with these Cajun doughnuts that they make down here that are seriously friggin' delicious. They would put Ye Olde Home Ec Witch to shame. Remember Mrs. Chaffin??!! Remember that story about Russ, how he took all that pink felt from some girl's sewing table and sewed a big old dick-and-balls together, and stuffed it with cotton and propped it upright on Mrs. Chaffin's desk? Remember how Ye Olde Home Ec Witch LOVED EJ??? Anyway, that's neither here nor there. . . .

France was planting flowers in front of the church's new sign and every car that passed beeped and waved and they yelled thank you out the windows. Everybody who beeped, France flashed them the peace sign, and that made them beep even more.

So right now I'm pretty tired, but it's a good kind of tired.

So have you heard back from Dr. Fung yet about your ultrasound? Maybe you shouldn't be worrying about Gail's mural right now because lifting your arms over your head to paint probably puts some strain on your heart, and maybe you shouldn't be doing extra stuff like that until you know what's going on with your ticker? Just a thought. Gail can wait, you know?

Sweet dreams from the Big Easy.

Nick

# 4

## Zell

"**S**HOULDA BEEN ME," Gladys sings. "You know that it shoulda been me."

I straddle my saddle stool and review my latest project: bones of the left hand, anterior view. I select the pencil labeled BONE WHITE, number 081, from the slopes of little bins.

My phone rings. I draw and hum along with Gladys as the machine picks up. A voice blares from all the way downstairs: "This message is for Rose-Ellen Roy. This is Joan from Dr. Carrie Fung's office at Worcester Cardiology. We've been trying to get in touch with you for some time now—*quite* some time now—and have left . . . *countless* messages over the past *year* stating that—"

I lean over, lift the phone off the receiver, and reset it. I return to my segmented phalanges. I half expect Joan to call again, but she doesn't.

I draw all morning and break for lunch with Russ. This Friday he brings a small cheese pizza from Orbit—the best and greasiest pizza in the whole state. My slice wilts and drips oil when I lift it from the box. Russ gives Ahab a wad of sliced turkey. He wolfs it down.

Before I return to my office, I tie on Nick's camo apron because it comforts me somehow. Back upstairs I recue Gladys. By late afternoon my finger bones stretch long and unadorned like a spiny desert plant, like a prehistoric insect. Finally I select SIMPLY BLACK—number 003—and sign my initials in the bottom right corner. I spray the paper and leave it to dry.

I approach the turntable, ready to lift the needle off Gladys, when the phone rings again. I consider hanging up on the caller before the machine even picks up, but instead I wait and listen. It's my sister.

"Yoo-hoo, Ze-ell, where've you been?" Gail asks. "Why don't you come up this weekend for a visit? It's been so long since you've been up here. We miss you. Tasha has been asking about Ahab. Tasha, come say hi to Ahab."

"Abe-abb!"

"Say hi to Auntie Zell, too."

"Abe-abb!"

"Anyway, come up anytime. And bring some Muffinry muffins. How 'bout a half dozen blueberry-brans for Mom and Dad's freezer? Blueberry because mom likes the antioxidants, and bran because Dad likes the fiber. And look, it doesn't matter if you finish the . . . listen. We just want to see you. Don't worry about the bathroom. Don't even *think* about the bath—" Beeeeeep. Gail talks so long, the machine cuts her off. I wait a second, but she doesn't call back.

I grasp Hank's plastic hand. I study the tips of his fingers, the knobby, pebblelike bones in his wrist. I imagine Gail's slope-side home—the gabled red-tin roof, the twelve-person hot tub on the wraparound deck. Her house is halfway up the Sachem trail on Okemo Mountain, in a thicket of pines. My parents live there, too.

Carefully, in my mind, I enter the house. I call "Cheerio!" to Gail's husband, Terry. He's short and British, and his breath always smells of asparagus. In my mind he lounges on the couch in front of the roaring fire in the fieldstone fireplace. On his chest, Tasha sleeps and drools.

I imagine Terry quietly calling "Cheerio!" back. Over Tasha's head he gives me the British version of the middle finger: index and third fingers in a narrow *V*, back side out, like a backward peace sign.

In my mind I pass Terry. I glide past the gleaming stainless-steel kitchen, down the hall. I open the French doors that lead to Gail's guest bathroom. I admire her three-thousand-dollar toilet, which looks like a tall hatbox.

Taped to the side of the vanity is an envelope. Inside the envelope is a photograph, one Nick took, of mountains in the first stages of thaw, of glistening boulders and evergreens. In front of the evergreens pose four people, as happily exhausted as sled dogs.

Who were they? When were they?

I snap back to real time, real place, as Ahab sidles up to me in that silent, ghostlike way of greyhounds. He licks Hank's heel.

I fold Hank's fingers down so just the middle one protrudes. "Heave ho," I say in Ahab Voice. I laugh at my joke. But just as easily as the laugh bubbles up, tears bulge. And a second later they roll down my cheeks, and then I just can't stop: I'm crying as hard as I did when I found out Nick was gone. I have no idea what prompts the sobs. They just *come.* And whoever says it takes one year to recover from the death of a spouse is crazier than I am.

Balls.

I clutch the turntable to my chest. Ahab follows me all over the house. I can't be in the office, where Hank hangs, where my big eyeball watches me from next to my old scuffed heart. I can't be in the bedroom, with Nick's trash-picked furniture. The kitchen doesn't do because I can see Mount Wippamunk framed in the window, all lit up, skiers and boarders little dots that jump side to side. The living room's out because Nick's dad's pottery—vases and bowls, decorative plates and teapots and teacups—crowds the shelves.

So I back into the little bathroom under the stairs. The powder room, Nick called it. I shoo Ahab because it's closet size, and the two of us don't fit inside. He blinks at me rather mournfully as I close the door between us.

I balance the turntable on the sink. I cue Gladys and the boys. I crash onto the toilet seat and slump against the wall.

The acoustics in here are fantastic. Violins swell, a woodblock knocks like a heartbeat, and Gladys pleads. All she needs is time. Maybe a thousand years.

Years ago I painted a mural in here. It's of Ahab, back when he was a strapping young captain. I captured him midstride, all four legs tucked under him. A furry torpedo. The photograph I painted from—one Nick took, of course—hangs in a frame above the sink.

Ahab was just two years old when we adopted him. The adoption place rescued him straight from a racetrack in Connecticut. Steroid injections made him muscle-bound, like a cartoon superhero dog. His butt and thighs were bald from lying around for extended periods on cement slabs. A scar made the base of his tail bald; handlers poke greyhounds with electric cattle prods for a faster start out of the gate, we learned. Scabs dotted Ahab's feet and legs, from other dogs nipping him as they raced to the food trough.

Memory Smack: The tan, plump woman in charge at the adoption place wore stained shorts covered with fur. "Remember," she said. "Never off leash. *Never.* If it's cold enough for *you* to wear a coat, then it's cold enough for your grey to wear a coat. You're gonna have to teach him everything. How to walk up and down stairs. How to play. How to be affectionate. He's never seen a vacuum before, or a mirror, or a washing machine, or a—"

"Abso-smurf-ly," Nick said. He knelt next to Ahab, and his arms made a wreath around Ahab's neck. He kissed the flat area between Ahab's eye and ear. "Let's get you to your new home, Cap'n," he said.

Ahab kissed him back, a dainty greyhound kiss, more twitchy nose than tongue.

"I think *that's* a good sign," the adoption woman said.

A door slams, snapping me back into real time, real place.

The door slams in the Knoxes' house, somewhere on the first floor. The needle skips on the turntable, and I twist the power knob to OFF. I hear whimpering. It's Ingrid. She makes a pathetic sound, like a pigeon cooing under a bridge.

I never hear Ingrid and Garrett make much noise through these walls. Then again, I never really listen. They probably have a powder room just like mine. Maybe Ingrid's right next to me, on the other side of the wall.

I hear Garrett's voice, more muffled than Ingrid's whimpering. I bet he's in the hallway, talking to her through their powder-room door.

"Listen, boo-boo," he says. "I'm trying to make our lives better by going to law school. And when I'm done, I'll get a better job and we'll have more money. A better life. But until then, life's gonna be *this* way."

"I don't want more money," Ingrid says. "I want my mother. I have a right to know my mother."

"Polly Pinch is for *women*. Not girls."

"I hate you."

The air seems to ring with her scream. After the ringing, a long empty pause.

"You can cook with Zell," he says.

"*Bake,*" she corrects.

"Bake, whatever. You can do all the *baking* you want as long as Zell's around, and as long as she *wants* to participate. Okay?" Garrett says something else, but I can't make out the words—they're a murmur. His footsteps fade.

Ingrid hiccups.

I don't know why—I don't even really think about it—but I rap my knuckles on the wall above the toilet tank, inside Ahab's torso.

A light, flat rap comes back in response. "Zell?" Ingrid says.

"Hey. Ingrid? You there?"

"Yeah."

I lean against the wall and press my cheek against Ahab's painted chest. "Are you okay?"

"No."

She doesn't say anything for so long that I wonder if she left. "Are *you* okay?" she finally asks.

"Right as rain," I say.

"Right as what?"

"Rain."

"I don't get it."

"Yeah. Me, neither."

Garrett's footsteps sound again. "Ingrid?" he says. "Are you ready to go to Zell's?"

She doesn't answer.

"Did you do your homework?" he asks.

"Yes. All of it."

"Good. Then grab your jammies and your toothbrush, and let's go. I'm late for my study group."

* * *

Moments later they're at my door. Garrett thanks me and hurries off. Ingrid doesn't say a word. She shuffles to the kitchen and slumps into a chair.

I have no experience navigating a little girl's moods. I'm not sure what to do or say. Should I leave her alone? Or is being alone the last thing she needs?

"Time to bake?" I ask.

She studies her hands, which rest in her lap, and nods once.

I sit opposite her. "What's your favorite treat?"

No response.

"Come on," I say. "Don't you have a favorite dessert?"

"Well, I do like peppermint ice cream."

"Hmm." I have neither peppermint nor ice cream. But I do have little candy canes left over from Christmas—Pastor Sheila gave them to me, along with the pamphlets on grieving. And I have half-and-half, which I sometimes stir into my coffee. Half-and-half's definitely not ice cream, but it's in the same family, right?

I grab twenty or so little candy canes from a cupboard and half-and-half from the fridge, and arrange it all on the table.

Ingrid observes the spread. "Peppermint Cream Dream," she says. "Do you think that's a good name for a dessert?"

"I do," I say. "It's got a fun ring to it. Whimsical, even."

"I don't know what that means. But I think we should make it."

"Cool. Ideas?"

She plucks a cellophane-wrapped candy cane from the pile, hurls it to the floor, and stomps on it. "Step one," she says. "Crush the candy canes."

A candy-cane-crushing frenzy ensues. She sweeps them all to the floor, and we dance, grasping each other's wrists and spinning. The kitchen fills with the sound of crunching and crinkling.

"This is awesome," Ingrid squeals, throwing her head back. "Aah! Come join us, Captain!" Ahab saunters in to observe us. He leans against the doorjamb, greyhound style.

"Step two," I say, bending over to scoop up the candy. "Open little wrappers and dump contents into saucepan."

"A saucepan?" She pulls up a footstool, and we shake the little powdery bits of candy from each wrapper into a small pan.

"We'll heat it up with the half-and-half," I say. "And when it cools, it'll be like, I don't know . . . eggless crème brûlée. Or something."

"All right, okay," Ingrid says. She sucks on a shard of candy cane. "I can dig it."

I pour a little half-and-half, slap a spoon into Ingrid's waiting hand, and turn on the burner. We lean over the stove for a while, not saying much, just watching flecks of red and white swirl around in the cream as the minty fragrance clears our sinuses. When the mixture starts to bubble, I turn the heat to low.

"It's too liquidy," I say. "We don't want a *drink*. It's gotta be thicker."

"Thicker?" Ingrid stirs with both hands on the spoon handle. "Add some flour."

"Ya think?"

"I dunno. You're the adult here, Zell."

A frightening thought. "Well, let's try it," I say, and dump in a little flour—and some sugar, too—as she stirs.

"Interesting," she says. And after several more minutes of stirring, we decide to pour the mixture and let it cool.

I grasp the pan handle and aim for two cereal bowls.

"You need ramekins," Ingrid says as I pour.

"What-y-kins?"

"They're like little round bowls."

"Really? I can't believe you know that."

"I may not know *everything* yet, but I do know a lot."

The mixture is thin and lumpy. I move the bowls to the table, and we sit and wait for the Peppermint Cream Dream to set up. Ahab rests his chin on my lap, and I stroke his ears.

"Want to taste test it?" I finally ask.

Ingrid lowers her nose to a bowl and inhales, wrinkling her nose. Then she dips her pinkie in the white-pink glop and sucks it. "Hmm," she says. "The texture's sort of like paste. *Tasty* paste. But definitely pasty."

"Tasty paste isn't going to cut it, Ingrid." I flick one of her braids and sigh.

"Back to the drawing board?"

"I'm afraid so." But I'm not really that disappointed in the failed experiment. I'm just glad Ingrid's no longer sulky and glum.

She pushes the bowl away. "Peppermint Cream Dream is too Christmasy anyway."

"Good point. We're not going for seasonal."

"We're going for . . . what, exactly?"

"Universal," I say.

"Exactly." She gets up and puts the bowls in the sink. "Universal."

"Wanna take Ahab to the field?"

His ears fling up at the sound of his name, and he peers expectantly at me, cocking his head.

"Aye, matie," says Ingrid, twirling around him. "Sail on!"

And later, at the field, Ahab prances and gallops, spins and sprints. It's almost like he's putting on a show for Ingrid. It's almost like he knows.

# EJ

France calls and says Dennis is coming over, too. So EJ drags two lawn chairs from the shed. The last time he used them was in summer, when he drove the Muffinry van to the town common to watch the fireworks. The first Fourth of July in a long time without Nick.

Now EJ puts one lawn chair on either side of the bench and drags a case of beer from the shed. His cell phone vibrates, and he fishes inside his coveralls, flips open his phone, and sees a text message from Charlene—"HEY HANSOME HOW R U."

"HELLO BEAUTIFUL, GOOD, BEAUTIFUL NITE HERE," EJ texts. He thinks it's a fine answer, somewhat romantic—flirtatious, even—but not too suggestive.

"SAME HERE, MITE GO 2 BAR W FRIENDS, TALK 2MORO" is her response.

"HAVE FUN," EJ punches. He wonders what her friends are like. He wonders if she's the type of woman who'd sit with him most nights of the week, most weeks of the year, in front of a fire pit, drinking beer and listening to night sounds and crackling logs.

Dennis arrives, pulling his clunker all the way into the driveway. EJ greets him with a one-armed hug.

"Do you have a copy of this week's paper?" asks EJ. "Mine wasn't delivered this week."

"Do I have a copy of this week's paper," Dennis repeats. "Please." He opens his passenger door, and several papers spill to the driveway. "How many you need?"

"Just one." EJ cracks open a beer and hands it to Dennis as Dennis hands him *The Wippamunker.*

"Hot off the press," Dennis says.

"Fresh from the igloo," EJ says of the beer, because most of the winter he stores it in the shed.

They clink cans and swig; EJ notes a few tiny ice chunks flecking his tongue as he swallows.

France pulls in, gets out of her car. "Beer me up, dudes," she says.

They all take a seat—EJ on the bench, France and Dennis flanking him in the lawn chairs.

"That Nick's dad's house?" France asks. She squints past the fire across the pond, where almost every window in Mr. Roy's little house shines yellow.

"Yeah," EJ says. "And there goes Mr. Roy, down into his basement." In the small square window just above the earth, Mr. Roy's body and head pass.

"He still got that workshop down there?" she asks. "For his pottery?"

"I'd imagine so," says EJ.

The fire snaps and fizzes. They're quiet for a while, watching the squares of yellow across the pond. EJ remembers being in Mr. Roy's basement workshop one afternoon, after tobogganing. Mr. Roy offered to teach him, Nick, Zell, and France how to center clay on the wheel. "Who wants to try?" he asked. "EJ?"

"I'm good." He felt intimidated by Mr. Roy's artistry, even though Nick's dad was pretty humble; for him this moment was about teaching, not showing off.

France looked away; she never volunteered for anything.

Zell raised her hand. She and Nick were always the artsy ones.

She sat at the wheel and dipped her hands in the little plastic water bucket.

Mr. Roy pulled up a chair. "Keep your hands perfectly still," he said, "and let the clay spin underneath them. Just keep letting it spin until it stops wobbling, stops struggling, and fits perfectly with your hands. That's how you center clay. You can't make anything until it's centered."

The clay shifted and lurched under Zell's hands, and her fingers kept spreading open, and little bits of clay flew out between them. She laughed at herself.

Nick watched, looking like he thought his dad was the coolest guy in the world. He pounded upstairs and returned with his camera, a big boxy contraption attached to a crazy-patterned old guitar strap. He took pictures of his dad teaching his girl how to center clay. Nick took pictures of EJ and France, too, their arms around each other.

Who knows where those photographs are now. Tossed out, probably, with so many other things tossed out over the years. Or maybe they're in a closet somewhere, piled inside a box. What would EJ see if he looked at them today? The same person, pretty much, except for the tattoos. Still EJ. Still Silo.

I'm more confident now, that's one difference, EJ thinks. Kinder, too. And hopefully more interesting. And smarter, definitely smarter.

France stands, crosses to the woodpile, and heaves a fresh log into the pit. She leans back to avoid the sparks that swirl up. She pulls the lawn chair closer to the warmth and sits down. "I'm gonna talk about Nick now."

Dennis clears his throat and digs his boots into the snow. "We're listening. Go ahead."

"Nothing was ever done for Nick, publicly," she says. "Mr. Roy had a memorial service, but it was private. Just for family. Which is totally his prerogative. But the rest of us, his friends—and Nick had so many friends—but we never had any . . . any—"

"Closure," EJ says.

"Right. Not to say that what you wrote about him in *The Wippamunker* wasn't closure, because it was, Dennis."

Dennis nods. He stares at the snow between his boots. "Yeah. But this sort of thing is different."

France describes in detail her plan to pay tribute to Nick's life. It's a good idea, EJ thinks. It's more than good. It's perfect. He's surprised at how much she's thought it out. It must have been hatching in her mind for a long time.

"It's just that I feel like we, the town, should bid him a proper good-bye," she says. "I don't want Nick's death hanging over us—" Her hand flies to her mouth. "That came out wrong, Eege. Sorry."

EJ ignores the slip. "What about Zell?"

"Have you talked to Zell?" asks Dennis.

"No," EJ says. "Not since . . . not in a long time."

"Pass me another beer, buddy?" Dennis says, and EJ tosses him a can.

"Zell should be a part of it," France says.

"She won't be a part of it," says EJ.

"I agree." Dennis cracks open his can. "She should be, but she won't."

"We'll do something anyway," says France. "And just ask her to be there."

"I'll help you organize," Dennis says. "I'll tell the others, too, and see if they want to get involved. Pastor Sheila and Father Chet and Russ and Chief. I'm sure they'd all dig it."

"I'll work on Zell," says EJ, even though he probably won't

because he's not sure he's able to face her yet. He left her that note in her kitchen, a brave move. But she didn't follow through.

"I wish you would talk to her," France says. "You haven't talked to her in so long. I miss the way it was. She should be here with us tonight. Hanging out. Having beers."

EJ's silent for a moment. Then he says, "I know."

"What about him?" France gazes across the pond at Nick's dad's house again. They watch as he mounts his basement steps carrying a box and descends again empty-handed.

"I'll talk to him, too," EJ says.

"I haven't seen him around town in a long time," Dennis says.

"He was always that way." France wipes her crooked-line mouth with the sleeve of her jacket. "Even before."

This is true, EJ thinks. Back before his parents divorced, Mr. Roy would go to dinner with them occasionally, and sometimes to bingo at the Blue Plate Lounge. He seldom visited Nick and Zell, though they stopped by his house from time to time. Other than that, Nick's dad was pretty much a recluse. So if his reclusiveness intensified after Nick's passage, it was hard to tell.

"What can you do?" EJ says. He belches, cracks open another beer, sips it, and holds the freezing can between his legs.

France hucks a looger through her curled tongue. It makes a high arch as she projects it into the fire.

"Nice," Dennis says.

She gives him the middle finger.

EJ reaches for *The Wippamunker* on the bench beside him. On the front page is a color photograph of a skinny white-haired woman. She wears safety goggles and sinks the blades of a chain saw into a huge stump of wood. "Teacher trades in cookie sheets for chain saws," the caption reads.

"Hey." EJ peers closer at the photograph. He tilts it toward the fire for more light. "That's Mrs. Chaffin. Ye Olde Home Ec Witch."

"She's still quite the character," Dennis says. "I just interviewed her."

"France, did you see this?" EJ shows her the paper. "She's got a chain saw. It's Ye Olde Home Ec Witch. With a *chain saw.*"

She grins. "I got a teeny confession to make. I was at her house a while back, on police business."

"Ye Olde Home Ec Witch's house?"

"Earlier this winter, someone living near the mountain reported seeing a mountain lion. I knocked on a few doors, just to lay any fears to rest. I mean, there hasn't been a mountain lion in Massachusetts for a century. Anyway, one of the houses was this big old beautiful red farmhouse, right on Route 331."

"I know the one." EJ nods. "With all the fairies in the windows. She lives there?"

"Yeah. Ye Olde Home Ec Witch answered the door. She actually remembered me. I couldn't believe it. She raises goats for cheese now, so naturally she was really worried about the mountain lion. She gave me some goat cheese. Have you ever had that? It's weird. Anyway, Trudy—"

"*Trudy?*" EJ says.

"Yeah. Trudy took me inside and showed me her sculptures."

"Sculptures?"

"Read my article, you illiterate," Dennis says.

"There's more pictures inside." France sits beside EJ and turns a few pages until she finds the new guy's photographic collage of Ye Olde Home Ec Witch's sculptures. "Check it out," she says.

"Holy . . ." EJ laughs. In the photographs, a wild turkey marches with a musket under its wing; a Boston terrier lights a stogie; a family of skiers approaches the lift line. "Chain-saw art business flourishes for retired home ec teacher Gertrude Chaffin," the caption reads.

"Let's just say," says France, returning to her lawn chair, "I brought her in."

"Brought her into what?" asks Dennis.

France's lopsided smile stretches wide.

# Nick

November 5, 2006
From: nicholas.roy@thewippamunker.com
To: rose-ellen@roymedicalillustration.com

To My Sweet Little Pants,

How's it hanging?

I have a bit of a cold. My throat's sore and I feel like I have a fever. Chief Kent got all paramedic on my sorry ass and made me take a couple aspirin and take a nap this afternoon. I felt like a wicked wuss, but when Chief Kent tells you to do something, you do it. I think I feel a little better now. Just a bit of a weird headache, that's all. It's probably all the mold, dust and toxins we are exposed to in our house gutting. I've been doing a little of that, too. So has Dennis. We didn't really think we'd be part of the effort when we got down here. But the weird thing is, it's hard to resist being part of the effort. Anyway, even though we wear masks and goggles and those protective suits, we are still exposed to some pretty funky stuff. But don't worry. I'll be fine.

Do you know what I didn't realize? Something like half the city of New Orleans still does not have water or electricity. They want people to come to the touristy sections, which are up and running. But you don't hear about all the devastation still here, in other parts of the city, because they don't want to scare away the tourists. So there's still this huge mess here that many people don't really know about.

Dennis is talking about making our story on this trip really big, like a two- or three- or even four-part series. He wants to do a couple huge spreads of my photographs. We want to spread the word about how much more help is needed down here. It makes me feel pretty cool to be a part of something so important.

But anyway, that's neither here nor there. . . .

How's your heart? You didn't mention anything about it when I called you yesterday, and I completely forgot to ask, but you've got to realize that it's on my mind a lot. I was so busy telling you about the tour we took of the Musicians Village. Oh, I can't believe I forgot to tell you about my Brad Pitt sighting. He was touring the village, riding a golf cart with his son sitting next to him in the front seat. He is seriously a good-looking dude. Even EJ was like, "Wow. I can't believe I'm saying this out loud, but Brad Pitt is pretty attractive."

This one guy invited Dennis and me into his FEMA trailer. He and his six kids and his brother and his brother's wife and their two kids live there. Like ten people in this little trailer. Unbelievable. He let me take all the shots I wanted because he said the worst part about a tragedy is thinking you have to go through it alone, and if we tell his story to the people back where we're from, the people in New Orleans will feel less alone. He said it much more eloquently than that, but that was the gist. When he said it, Dennis scribbled like mad, because he knew it was a great quote, maybe even the lead.

Anyway, did you get the results of the ultrasound?

I'll try to call you later today, okay?

Love ya.

Nick

# 5

## Zell

"TRUDY'S EXPECTING US," says Ingrid, buckling her seat belt. It's a dark afternoon, and as I drive up Route 331, I imagine mixing bowls lining Trudy's kitchen counter smallest to biggest, measuring cups neatly arranged alongside a stand-up electric mixer with its metal and plastic attachments. I imagine Trudy wearing a starched, freshly ironed apron. In my fantasy, we bake, but it's not like Ye Olde Home Ec Witch days. It's more like cooking with Polly Pinch—stress free, with an air of spontaneity and unconventionality. We stick our fingers in the bowl and lick them. We joke. We sing Gladys Knight and the Pips songs. We aren't graded, or tested, or even observed.

But when I clank the fairy knocker, no one answers. The door is unlocked, so we let ourselves in. The kitchen is stark. A tepid saucepan of liquid chocolate waits on a back burner.

"Truuu-deee?" Ingrid calls.

"Hello?" I call. "She must have forgotten we were coming over."

We hear a chain saw whine. Ingrid smiles—a mischievous expression, one I've seen on Garrett's face, too. She grabs my hand and pulls me through the rooms toward the Barn. Her beaded braids flop against her back.

In the hallway we smell gasoline fumes and wood shavings. When the whine of the chain saw halts, Ingrid raps on the door.

"Hello?" Trudy calls.

"It's me and Zell," calls Ingrid.

"Hang on just a sec. Don't come in yet. Wait *juuust* a sec."

We hear rustling.

"She must be covering up her secret project," Ingrid whispers.

"Okay," Trudy finally calls. "Come on in, Pumpkin Pie."

I push open the door and follow Ingrid into the Barn. Trudy cinches a cord over the blue tarps that hide the immense top secret project.

Ingrid runs but stops when Trudy commands, "No running!" just like Ye Olde Home Ec Witch.

"Sorry," says Ingrid.

"Come 'ere," Trudy says—once again Trudy. She kneels and spreads her arms. Her goggles restrain her poodlish curls, and her glasses slip toward the tip of her sweaty nose. "Come 'ere, Pumpkin Pie." Trudy smacks kisses all over Ingrid's little beautiful golden face.

"I told you we were coming over," Ingrid says. "To bake. Remember?"

"It doesn't do any good to make plans with me, Pump. I'm old!"

Trudy covers the chain saws, and I brush her from head to toe with the dust brush. We go to the kitchen and slurp reheated hot chocolate. Ingrid and I sit side by side on the stools; Trudy's opposite us, leaning against the counter.

"So," Trudy says. "What do we got?"

"We got a baking contest to win," I say.

"And time is ticking," Ingrid adds.

The deadline is March 10, I explain; you have to submit your entries by then, and judges choose winners after an unspecified waiting period.

Ingrid tears into her backpack and shows the magazine to Trudy, who holds the special foldout page at arm's length, tips her chin, and reads.

"Polly Pinch," she declares when she's done, sliding the magazine toward Ingrid. "She's the hot new thing, huh?"

"She's my mother," Ingrid says.

Trudy's eyes dart from Ingrid's face to mine. I pretend to take a long swallow. I want to ask Trudy who Ingrid's mother really is. Or was. She must know. But of course I don't ask.

Trudy shrugs. "Okay. And?"

"And Zell *needs* to win this contest," Ingrid says.

"And why is that?"

"Because her dead husband wanted to give the people of New Orleans twenty thousand dollars to rebuild their houses after they were destroyed in the Hurricane Katrina flooding. And if you win this contest"—she taps the magazine—"you get twenty thousand dollars. So it's fate. Plus, Zell would get to bring a guest onto the show to meet Polly Pinch, and that guest would be me. So it's like fate times two."

Trudy sucks her dentures. "Fate times two. Gotcha."

"Can you help us?" Ingrid puts her hands together as if she's praying.

"Would it be cheating if I helped you? I'm a retired professional, after all."

Ingrid chews her lip nervously, as if she hadn't thought of this. Two little wings of hot chocolate stain the corners of her mouth.

"Not cheating," I say. "We're just looking for a little guidance. A little inspiration."

"My baking days are over, of course," says Trudy. "But I suppose I can give you pointers. And I can supervise. I'm sure good at supervising." She winks.

"Our experiments haven't gone too well so far." I recap all our failures, starting with Oatmeal Brownie Upside-Down Cake and ending with our most recent disasters: Sin-namon Macaroon Yum-Yums, which proved way too complicated; Toffee Pudding Pound Cake, which was raw in the middle and which Russ deemed "too conventional" when I served it to him after lunch one Friday; and Mini Key Lime Custards, so tart they made Ingrid's face contort, and which Russ later refused to eat, proclaiming them "unmanly."

Trudy rubs her face with both hands. "Desserts that warm the soul," she muses; she pronounces it "wahm." "I just don't think I have that kind of thing in me, girls. Now, I can make snickerdoodles in my sleep. A cup of butter, one and a third cups of sugar, two eggs, two and a half cups of flour, two teaspoons—" She sighs. "Look. Retired home ec teachers don't *invent* things. They *follow* things. Recipes, sewing patterns. The likes of me just don't *lead*. Not when it comes to the kitchen, anyway."

"But Trudy," Ingrid says, "Zell and I suck."

Trudy tips her head back and laughs. Her narrow shoulders bob up and down before she composes herself and mildly scolds Ingrid for "foul language."

"I'll tell you what you're going to do," says Trudy. "You're going to do what any self-respecting, sensible, goal-oriented woman would do."

"Which is?" I say.

She flings the magazine over her shoulder. It flutters and lands in a tentlike heap in front of the sink. "Trail blaze," she says. "You're going to trail blaze."

Ingrid hangs her head. Her hands twist in her lap. "But that's what we've been doing. Trailblazing."

Trudy takes Ingrid's face in her gnarly hands. "Keep *on* trailblazing, Pumpkin Pie. Nobody ever cleared a path for themselves by giving up."

"What do you mean?" Ingrid asks.

"I mean, the only way out is through."

"I don't know what you're talking about."

"Zell does," Trudy says. "Zell understands."

Ingrid's gaze swings from Trudy to me. "You do, Zell?" she asks.

I think about Trudy's words—the only way out is through. The phrase sounds like something Yoda would say, or Mr. Miyagi. Nick might have said something like that, teasingly, when I complained about a common chore—vacuuming, taking out the recycling.

"We should go," I say. "I'm sorry we interrupted you, Trudy."

She shakes her head. "Nonsense. I've got some chain-saw art to work on. A commission for Rota Springs Creamery. And I love an appreciative audience. Interested?"

Ingrid hesitates, picking a hangnail. But soon her frown evolves into that mischievous grin, and she gives her stool one quick spin. Her braids fling up around her. And then I'm following her again as she skips through the rooms of the big old farmhouse.

In the Barn, Ingrid and I don goggles and earplugs. We sit side by side on the floor, watching as Trudy converts a towering hunk of wood into a glistening jimmy-studded six-scoop ice-cream cone.

* * *

A GLOOMY SATURDAY. Garrett hurries inside carrying Ingrid in one arm and a bag of groceries in the other. "I have a presentation this morning," he says. "Can't be late. Listen, Zell, we're going to be paying for all these baking experiments from now on."

Ingrid slides down his side and envelops Ahab in a hug.

"It's only right." Garrett sets groceries on the counter, fishes out a wad of bills, and stuffs them into my apron pocket. "This is extra, to cover your previous grocery bills. Ing told me about some of your experiments—buttermilk and lemons and oatmeal and cinnamon and on and on. I never really thought about how much money you were investing in this Polly Pinch contest."

"You don't have to pay for my—"

"Nonsense. You're the best babysitter in Wippamunk." He winks, then stoops to peck Ingrid. "Wish me luck," he says.

"Good luck!"

"Oh, Zell, I got you a present." From the grocery bag he pulls two oversize camouflage oven mitts. "Ingrid said you didn't own any, so."

"They match my apron," I say, slipping my hands into the mitts. "Thanks."

"Gotta love the dollar store." Garrett heads for the door. "Have a good time."

Mitts off, I rummage through the grocery bag and line the contents—gingerbread mix, licorice extract, eggs, condensed evaporated milk ("evap," Ingrid calls it, because that's what Polly Pinch calls it)—on the counter. "What are we making, Ing?"

She shows me a page torn from her notebook. *Gingerbread Women Cookie Samwitches with Licorish Filling*, it reads. *For the samwitches we need gingerbread, not the crunchy kind and not the cakey kind either but something in between and for the filling we need licorish and frosting to blend together to make licorish frosting.*

"Great idea," I say. "Where'd you come up with this one?"

She shrugs. "Made it up in math class the other day."

"What? You have to pay attention during school," I say. "You can't be playing Polly Pinch during math class."

She drags her toe across the floor, tracing an arc. "The contest isn't *play*. It's important."

"During math class, you should be doing *math*."

She sighs. "I know."

I imagine her doodling gingerbread women while her classmates dutifully scratch out long division, and I feel irresponsible, and unsure, and a little guilty. But soon Ingrid's bopping around the kitchen, singing an impromptu ditty about how she did all her homework, and outside it starts to sleet—fat silver slashes—and baking Gingerbread Women Cookie Samwitches seems like the perfect activity.

I start reading the instructions on the box of gingerbread mix.

"Don't bother," Ingrid says. "Remember what Trudy said? We're gonna trail blaze it, woman. The mix is just to get us started."

She insists that if we doctor up the mix just right, we'll strike the perfect consistency for gingerbread women cookies—halfway between crunchy and cakey. And she's so confident and enthusiastic that I start to believe we really can.

So, in the spirit of trailblazing, I add a little cornstarch to the mix, and fewer eggs than are called for, and milk. I fold over the ingredients with a spatula.

On a cookie sheet, Ingrid shapes the dough into two gingerbread women: a tall one for me, with wild hair, and a shorter one with braids and boots and a big hat.

While they bake, we make the licorice frosting, blending together sugar, butter, and a half teaspoon of licorice extract with an old-fashioned manual beater Nick used for his annual batch of eggnog from scratch. I hold the beater upright in the bowl while Ingrid cranks the wheel. "I wanted to buy licorice, but my dad said they probably have licorice *extract* instead, you know, like vanilla extract," she says. "And they did."

The frosting is successful—smooth and creamy, and actually pretty flavorful, if you like licorice. (I doubt licorice and ginger are two great tastes that go great together, but I keep this to myself.)

When the timer dings, I pull the cookie sheet from the oven. Gingerbread Cookie Me and Gingerbread Cookie Ingrid are indistinguishable blobs.

"Dang it," Ingrid says. She bangs a fist on the table as I set the sheet on a rack to cool.

"Nobody said this would be easy," I say. "No sense getting frustrated. We can always try again."

Ingrid drums her fingers on the table. "Can we have a food fight?"

"A food fight?" I say, wondering where she came up with that idea. "No way."

"Why not?"

"Because then we'd have to clean it all up."

"They're wasteful, too, right?"

"Yes, that's right. They're very wasteful."

She plops into a chair. "What are we going to do? We're never going to win the contest. At the rate we're going, we might not even *enter* it."

"We're getting closer."

"Well, we do seem to stink a little less lately."

I join her at the table. I dip my finger into the bowl of frosting and swipe it on her nose.

She giggles. "Oh no you didn't." She scoops three fingers into the frosting and smears it on my nose. Then I smear more under her nose, giving her a frosting mustache.

Her giggles escalate into peals of laughter. Ahab peeks around the corner, curious, sniffing the air, cocking his head.

Ingrid's face is covered in frosting now, almost like a beauty mask. "Can I let Ahab lick all this off me?"

"Whatever floats your boat, girl."

She kneels and calls for the Captain. He trots over, sniffing like crazy. She cracks up as he licks her nose clean and then searches her cheeks and chin and forehead and even her ears for more. He leans into her just a little too forcefully, and Ingrid crashes to the floor, squealing with laughter as Ahab stands over her, licking her face all over.

February 2, 2008
From: rose-ellen@roymedicalillustration.com
To: nicholas.roy@thewippamunker.com

Dear Nick,

That's right. I'm writing you an e-mail. I know most people would consider this "creepazoid," to quote Ingrid. She would also say it's "bizarro."

Who's Ingrid, you ask? My next-door neighbor.

I gave Garrett, her father, your Guns N' Roses key chain. The first night I babysat Ingrid, he gave the keys back. But when it became apparent that my babysitting was a regular routine, I told him to keep the keys. And he did.

It's Sunday night now, though, and Ingrid's not asleep on my couch. She's asleep in her own bed. She's supposed to be, anyway.

So I found your present hidden in the oven. Good one. I almost burned the house down.

I put your present in the attic. Actually Ingrid put it there. It's been about a year since I climbed those steps. I know I really should get rid of all those things up there. Maybe even donate them to the high school or something. Or has it all become obsolete? Useless junk? You were always a bit of a throwback that way. Maybe Wippamunk Antiques would take it all off my hands.

The other morning I went to the grocery store to stock up on sugar, butter, and flour, all of which, in the name of experimentation, I go through a lot of lately (long story). I wheeled my way to the checkout, when, surrounded by bottles of seltzer, I heard my name.

I stopped and turned. It was Pastor Sheila. She wore clogs, tights, and a red corduroy jumper dress. And all I could think about was that day—that day I found out about you, when I faced Pastor Sheila and Father Chet in Terry and Gail's driveway.

Anyway, in the grocery store, she asked me things. How are you, how's your kitchen, etc. I answered coherently enough. Then I asked her, "On The Trip, did Nick mention anything about a present he bought for me?" My theory, you see, is that it will be easier to open your present if I know beforehand what it is. Does that make sense in heaven? Because it sure as hell makes sense down here.

So, Pastor Sheila gave me the kindhearted Pastor Sheila smile. "No," she said. "I'm afraid not." She squeezed my arm, told me Wippamunk still prayed for me, Wippamunk will never forget. And she said, "Take good care."

Do you already know all this stuff, Nick? Do you know that I walk around all day without a bra on? And that I've taken to wearing your apron around the house, just for shits and giggles? Are you watching me? Hearing me? Knowing my heart? If so, then the following statement—hell, the whole e-mail—goes without saying: I miss you.

KNOCK-KNOCK-KNOCK, PAUSE. Knock-knock-knock, pause. A steady, unchanging rhythm. I'm in my office when I hear it, typing away to Nick. Ahab pads in and whines. Knock-knock-knock, pause.

We go downstairs and follow the source of the noise. It's loudest in the powder room. The knocking comes from the other side of the wall. Ahab stands in the doorway, tilting his head, as I call, "Hello?"

"Hi." Ingrid's voice sounds so distant. "I've been knocking for you."

"It's late. You have school tomorrow."

"I just wanted to wish you good night. I know we're going to win the Warm the Soul baking contest. I just know it."

"Where's your dad?"

"He's studying with his earbuds in."

"You should get into bed."

"I know."

"Get into bed and read a book until you fall asleep."

"Okay."

"Good night."

I get up and shut off the bathroom light.

Knock-knock-knock, pause. Knock-knock-knock, pause. Ahab whines.

"Ingrid?" I say. "You have to stop knocking now. You're driving the Captain nuts."

"Just one more thing," she says. "Love ya 'n' like ya."

Ahab leans into me, and I scratch his ear. I smile to myself. "Love ya 'n' like ya," I say.

4 23: True Burgundy.

399: Cherise.

314: Rainy-Day Blue.

My alveoli bulge from bronchial tubes like overripe purple grapes on a vine.

It's Friday, and Russ rings the doorbell precisely at one fifteen. A gust of wind sweeps through the house as I open the door. It's snowing outside, and frigid. He gives me his usual high five and mail delivery before clomping to the kitchen to dish out lunch: leftover chicken potpie, which his wife made for dinner last night.

I pour him a glass of milk as he shovels microwave-warmed food into his mouth. The phone rings, but I ignore it. The machine beeps, and my sister starts talking. "Yoo-hoo, Ze-ell. Why don't you return any of my calls? When are you coming up here?"

"That's Gail?" Russ asks, fork halfway to his mouth. He always had a crush on my sister. I think he still does.

"Yep, that's Gail." I scrape my plate.

"Well, I'm gonna answer it." He crosses the kitchen and picks up the phone. "Well, well, *well,* if it isn't the homecoming queen herself, Ms. Gail Carmichael-Dunbar," he says.

"Who's this?" my sister asks; I hear because the answering machine is recording.

"It's your trusty former sophomore chemistry lab partner *and* trusty former mail carrier."

"Oh." Gail sighs. "Hi, Russell. I'm still married, Russell."

"No funny business, now, Ms. Carmichael-Dunbar," he says. "I'm married, too. *And* I'm on the clock. The *government* clock. But it's good to speak with you. I can't believe you moved away. How's ski country, by the way?"

"Beats Mount Wippamunk."

"You can say that again."

"Beats Mount Wippamunk."

"Hello to your lovely parents," Russ says. "Here's your sister."

I roll my eyes as he hands me the phone. With his free hand he makes a fist and poses as if to sock me in the jaw. Then he cleans up the lunch plates.

"I've been so busy with work," I tell Gail. "But I'll come up. Tonight. For the weekend."

She squeals so loud, I hold the phone away from my face. When I put it to my ear again, she's saying, "What about the snow, though?"

"It's not supposed to be that bad here," I say. "What about up there?"

"It's always snowing up here anyway. Can't *wait* to see you."


MY CAR WON'T START. It hacks and chokes when I turn the key.
Fine snow falls, the flakes little slivers of ice, like fiberglass.
The car was Nick's domain. Nick's project.
Balls.

I bang on the steering wheel, the dashboard. I turn the key. Hack. Choke. Sputter.

In the passenger seat, Ahab whines.

I get out of the car and kick the door shut. Icy mud slides from the wheel well. The dislodged clump makes a slopping noise when it lands. I kick the front tire so hard, pain sears my big toe.

"Problems?" It's Garrett. He wears a fitted, stylish sweater. I can't make out his facial features because of the bright porch light behind him.

"Yeah. Car won't start."

With a grunt he lifts the hood and studies the tangle of hoses and black boxes.

I step back into the shadows, where I don't have to squint. "I didn't know you knew anything about cars."

"I don't, actually," he says. He lets the hood drop. "Where are you off to?

"My sister's. She lives in Vermont. On Okemo Mountain."

"Is it urgent?"

"No. Truthfully, it's not urgent. But it feels urgent, you know?" I think of the mural, the blank bodies with blank faces. Gail said not to worry about the bathroom, but of course, I *do* worry about it. Instead of skiing, I plan to lock myself in there until I finished what I started. It's time. "I have some work to do," I say. "Unfinished business, you could say."

The fiberglass snowflakes become thicker and fall faster. Polly Pinch would say the snowflakes are "really ratcheting up the action."

Garrett toes the snow with his left boot. "If you don't mind my asking, unfinished business related to what?"

"A bathroom."

"A bathroom?" He stuffs his hands into his pockets. "Will you explain it to me on the way up?"

"What? No. You are not driving me a hundred miles to Vermont in a snowstorm at ten o'clock at night." I meant to leave earlier, but I was working on a nasal cavity, and I couldn't resist frontal sinus, pharyngeal tonsil, anterior naris. All that space, all those labyrinthine chambers and passages, behind a face.

"This"—Garrett holds out his hand and catches a few flakes—"this is not a snowstorm. This is nothing. It's supposed to blow over anyway. It's no big deal."

"Famous last words," I say. "I can't let you drive me, Garrett."

He shivers and stamps his feet. "Why not? Why not let me drive you?"

"Because it's too much to ask."

He laughs—a deep belly laugh. "Oh please. You've been babysitting my crazy kid for weeks, indulging all her whims."

"That's different. I like babysitting your crazy kid."

"Well, I like driving. And you can pay me for gas."

"But it's so late. It's a two-hour drive normally, and in this snow—"

"I don't sleep anyway. You know that. I planned on studying all night, but I'm going cross-eyed. I need a break."

"What about Ingrid?"

"Oh, she sleeps anywhere. Besides, she'll go anywhere with you."

"What about the Captain?"

In the car, Ahab's ears point tall at the mention of his name.

"The Captain can keep Ingrid warm in the backseat." Garrett stands opposite me with his hands on my shoulders. "Please? Let me do this for you. I *want* to do this for you."

"Why?"

"I just do. Plus, all I ever do is drive to Boston and back. This'll be different. An adventure."

Fifteen minutes later we climb into Garrett's truck—Ingrid, Garrett, Ahab, and I—and haul ass up Route 331. The snow coats the road with shardlike flakes. Hannah Montana blares, and Ingrid sings along in the backseat. Ahab rests his head in her lap, and she holds his ear between her thumb and forefinger and caresses it. At her feet is the little suitcase I packed for him.

We pass Mount Wippamunk. The sight of it hulking in the snow triggers a Memory Smack: My wedding day, January 1, 1999. I wore a thirty-dollar bridal gown—a straight, beaded thrift-shop purchase two sizes too big—over my ski clothes. Nick donned two layers of long underwear under the powder blue tuxedo his dad wore to the senior prom in 1969.

At the mountain, Nick and I took the North Summit chairlift. In the chair behind us rode the best man and the maid of honor: Nick's dad, Arthur, and Gail, dressed for a normal day of skiing. My parents shared the third chair with Gail's husband, Terry, who wore a choir robe borrowed from Pastor Sheila. Under his robe, in the pocket of his purple one-piece, he carried a stamped slip of paper issued and signed by the governor, proclaiming him a justice of the peace for one day, and granting him the right to perform marriages in the glorious Commonwealth of Massachusetts.

At the top of the chairlift, near a cluster of hemlocks, we formed a semicircle and waited for Nick and Terry to unclip from their snowboards.

"Right," Terry shouted into the wind. "It's colder than a nun's you-know-what, so let's do this."

Curious skiers and boarders gathered around us as Arthur

produced the velvet bag from his leg pocket. Gail snapped pictures with her point-and-shoot, one mitten held between her teeth. Nick and I pulled off our mittens; he shoved a ring on my whitening finger, and I one on his. We kissed: a quick, cold peck. Laughing, teeth chattering, we put our mittens back on.

Terry said something like, "By the power vested in me by the Commonwealth of Massachusetts, I now pronounce you husband and wife."

The crowd of strangers hooped and hollered and banged their ski poles together. The lift operator in the booth raised his thermos in a toast. And our crazy little wedding party headed down my favorite trail—the double-diamond Look Ma, a curvy and steep narrow, with good-size bumps on the left-hand side. It leads right to the lodge, where, in the upstairs function hall, a fire roared, poinsettias decorated tables, and Russ and EJ's two-man band, the Massholes, warmed up.

With a new Hannah Montana song, Ingrid's singing gets a little louder, and the Memory Smack shrinks. Real time, real place. We're almost in New Hampshire now. Quietly, while Ingrid belts out tunes, I tell Garrett everything: about Gail's house, Nick's favorite place in the whole world. About the bathroom there, and the photograph Gail wants me to re-create on the bathroom wall, and the day I almost finished the project. I tell Garrett exactly how Nick died, including some details Dennis's article didn't divulge. It doesn't feel good to talk about all this, but amazingly, it doesn't feel horrible, either.

Ingrid's head pokes between the front seats. "Can we stay at Zell's sister's tonight?" she asks.

Garrett slows at a BLACK ICE warning sign. "I'm afraid not."

"Can we go skiing tomorrow?"

"No, baby. I have to study. You know that."

"You study all the time," Ingrid says. "Drop me off with Zell."

Garrett glances at me, as if to say, How about it?

"Could be fun," I say.

He laughs and shakes his head. "We're going to drop off Zell, and then we're going to turn around and go home, baby. Sorry. Some other time."

"Aww," Ingrid says. "That's no fun." She leans back and sings. After a while, just as we pass Allison's Orchard, she yawns through certain words. Before long she falls asleep with her head slumped against the window.

Garrett switches his iPod to John Legend. "That's a sad story, Zell," he says.

"I know."

"I'm sorry it's a *true* story."

"Everyone is."

He hums and drives. On Route 12 the snow thickens, and he slows even more. We gain elevation. The houses and gas stations along the side of the road grow sparse. We pass fewer cars.

"I really appreciate this, Garrett," I say. "Your driving me."

"It's all good," he says.

My eyelids droop and pop open. Droop and pop open. Droop . . .

I JOLT AWAKE. The truck swerves and fishtails—right, left, right. Garrett's palms slap the wheel as he tries to steady the truck and steer into the skid. We careen into the oncoming lane, which is empty—no headlights crest the hill.

My arms cover my face. My heart races. I don't breathe.

From the backseat Ingrid wails. "Daddy?"

And then we're completely spinning. 360. 720. 1080. Nonbeats: My chest seems to twirl with that empty, weightless wind.

Stillness.

Out the windshield all I see is the wide trunk of an old maple. We haven't hit it, I don't think. But we came close. The bed of the truck sticks out into the shoulder of the road, and the cabin plunges into the woods.

Garrett seems out of breath. "Everybody okay?" He twists around and caresses Ingrid's chin. She nods. Ahab whines, and she pulls him close and kisses his nose.

"Zell?" Garrett puts his hand on my knee. "You okay?"

"I'm fine," I say, despite the galloping in my chest. "You?"

He drops his head on the steering wheel—thud!—and mutters something.

"Garrett?" I say.

"Two-wheel drive." He sighs. "It only has two-wheel drive. It was thousands of dollars less than the four-wheel-drive option."

"Oh. Well, that's sensible, then."

"Yeah. It's sensible. If you live in Florida." He puts the truck in reverse, but the tires spin. An eighteen-wheeler hurtles past, spitting slush.

"You must slip and slide all the way to and from Boston," I say.

"Actually, I don't. That trip's relatively flat."

"True. Well, do you have any sand in the back? Or kitty litter?"

"You'd think," says Garrett. "But no." He throws it into reverse again and taps the gas pedal. The truck rocks a bit, but then the tires spin, and we slide a little farther into the ditch, on a steep incline. He yanks the emergency brake and sighs heavily. He's trembling, I realize—though barely perceptibly. He gets out of the truck, investigates the situation, climbs back in. "I don't think you're going to make it to your sister's house tonight," he says.

"That's okay. You have AAA or anything?"

He switches off John Legend and kills the engine. "Sorry."

"Nah," I say. "Don't worry about it. Not your fault." I glance at my cell phone: twelve thirty A.M.

"Should we call the police?" Ingrid says. "Call Officer Frances. She'll help us."

"I'm sure she would," Garrett says. "But Officer Frances is about fifty miles that way." He gestures behind us.

I peer out the window. The snow coats it so thickly now, it's hard to see. "Maybe someone will stop."

We wait for a few minutes, but no cars pass.

Garrett inspects his cell. "No bars."

I check my phone for a signal—none.

"Well," he says. "We just passed a place. We can walk there. It's not far. We'll get a couple rooms for the night? Figure out what to do in the morning?"

I shrug. "What else *can* we do?"

He exhales and shakes his head. He's frustrated, I can tell; maybe he's even embarrassed. But he doesn't want to show it. "How far are we from your sister's?" he asks.

"At least an hour. Probably more."

"Eff," he whispers.

We hop out of the truck, brace ourselves against the gusty snow-fall, and climb out of the ditch. In the shoulder of the road, I help Ahab into his coat.

"Isn't Ahab the cutest thing in the world?" Ingrid says as she helps me fasten his booties. She seems to be recovered from any fear she felt when the truck spun out, and she's not daunted by the snow whipping all around us. She's ready for another adventure. That's her Ingrid style.

Garrett's too tense to comment about Ahab. He looks down the road as I clip on the leash. I feel guilty; I never should have let him drive me. In truth, I wonder why he was so insistent on driving me in the first place, especially considering the weather, and the late hour, and the fact that his truck is only two-wheel drive.

We walk: Garrett first, then Ingrid, then me, Ahab leashed at my side. No vehicles pass. The wind blows so cold that the skin of my face tightens. We approach a clapboard farmhouse. Shingled cottages form a crescent around the house, and plastic sheets cover all the windows. By the walkway a spotlighted sign reads, TUNKAMOG LAKE SUMMER CABINS.

"Garrett," I call ahead.

"This is the place," he says. His steps quicken. "This is the place we passed."

"I think it's seasonal."

"Seasonal?"

"Only open in the summertime."

Garrett stops. He observes the cabins, the house, the sign. I join him on the walkway.

"Seasonal," he whispers.

Ingrid tugs his sleeve. "Daddy, will you carry me?"

He scoops her up in his arms. "Eff it," he whispers over her head. "We're knocking."

Just then the house's front door opens. A rotund, half-toothless woman in a kitten-patterned bathrobe steps outside. "Thought you were a ruh-*coon*," she says.

Garrett smiles.

She squints at us. "Cold enough for ya?"

"Do you have any vacancy?" he asks.

"We're a hundred percent vacant. But we're closed."

"We really need a place just for the night."

"There's a motor lodge ten miles back, in Walpole."

"My truck's stuck."

She squints at Ingrid, whose face is smooshed against Garrett's chest.

"Hi," Ingrid says.

This woman must think we're a family. I'm the mom; Garrett's the dad; Ingrid's our baby. Garrett smirks at me; the same thought's going through his mind, probably.

Finally the woman shakes her head. Her silver bangs swing across her forehead. "I'll call you a tow. But they usually take their sweet time getting here. In a storm like this, you're looking at a two-, three-hour wait."

"We really need to sleep," Garrett says.

"Me, too. I'll call the police. They can take you into protective custody for the night. They do it all the time for stranded motorists. 'Specially in the winter."

"And spend the night in a jail cell?" Ingrid says. She shivers and snuggles against Garrett.

"It's not like you're *in jail*," says the woman.

Ahab whines. I hear his teeth chatter.

"Zell, my wallet's in my back pocket," Garrett says. "Could you?"

I lift the hem of his ski coat and pull his wallet out. I try not to touch his butt, which I must admit is nicely shaped. I open the wallet—scuffed fake leather—and sift through a few twenty-dollar bills.

He eyes the woman. "Surely you have something for us."

She rubs her hands together and winks. "I suppose there is one cabin I could fix up for you. But there could be mice in it."

"Aww," Ingrid says. "Mice are so cute."

"Perfect," I say. "We'll take it."

"You sure?" Garrett whispers.

I nod because I can't think of any other realistic option.

With a wobbly hitch in her step, the woman leads us through the freezing three-season porch—plasticked over, like the cabin windows—into what serves as a reception area. It feels so good to be out of the freezing wind, and I feel my muscles relax.

Garrett drapes Ingrid in a brown plaid armchair with wooden armrests. But she doesn't sit still: She gets up and inspects her surroundings, standing on her tippy-toes to peer over the wood-paneled counter, which bears an enormous microwave and a television with a droopy rabbit-ear antenna.

The woman limps behind the counter and runs a finger under a row of keys. "I'll give you lucky number seven," she says. "It has the best atmosphere. The farthest from the house, and the closest to the lake." She turns and smiles at Garrett. Her gums look swollen.

"That's lovely, thanks." He takes the key from her hammy fist. "And your name is?"

She fishes around behind the counter and slaps a name tag on her left breast, which jiggles with aftershock. BOBBIE.

Bobbie produces a stack of woolen blankets. Dust poofs up around them as she pounds them into the counter. "Better take these," she says. "There's no heat. Pleasure doing business with you folks."

Garrett folds some bills in his palm and shakes her hand. "Pleasure's all mine, Bobbie," he says. "Pleasure's all mine."

I try my cell again: one bar. I call Gail, who coos in worry and disappointment. She offers to come get us, but I decline, because all we need is for her to get stuck, too.

Outside I hold the musty blankets as far from my nose as possible. Ingrid leads Ahab, who lifts his paws laboriously through the half foot of snow. He tries to step in Garrett's footprints. I watch his broad back as he leads the way.

When we reach Cabin 7, he wiggles the key into the lock. "Brace yourself," he says, tapping open the light-as-paper door.

Ahab steps inside and sniffs the cold air.

On a plastic table sits a little lamp. I flick it on; the lightbulb has somehow burned a hole into the duck-patterned lampshade. Two military-issue cots, with thin, stained mattresses, line the far wall. A deer head with small antlers tilts above a little fireplace. The flue must be open, or broken, because snow forms a pointy pile on the grate. A dresser in the corner seems fairly well crafted, and its varnish shines. I check the drawers: all empty except the bottom one, where mouse turds roll around like three-dimensional commas.

"Pretty much what I expected," Garrett says.

Ingrid leaps onto one of the cots. "Ahab, here, Cap'n. This is wicked cool. It's like we're totally camping out."

"You've got to calm yourself, boo-boo," says Garrett, scratching Ahab's neck. "It's late."

I set the blankets on the other cot and announce that I'm going to find the ladies' room.

"Good luck with that one," Garrett says. "Hey, want to take Ingrid while you're at it?"

She jumps up and grabs my hand. "I've seriously got to pee."

Outside, we duck into the spinning snow and investigate a few nearby outbuildings until we discover the bathhouse. At the sink, I inspect myself in the cracked mirror: choppy, fluffy hair all over the place. Eyebrows threatening to arch into a unibrow. Awesome.

I turn the faucet, but no water comes out. Ingrid shoots past me and darts into a stall.

"Um, Zell?" she calls. "The toilet water is frozen. Like, it's a block of ice."

"Well, there's nothing we can do about that," I say. "Just go."

"Okeydokey," she says. "Letting 'er rip. Hey. At least there's toilet paper."

Back in Cabin 7, the Captain heaves his old body onto Ingrid's cot and curls up at one end. It's so cold, I decide to leave his booties and coat on him.

Ingrid snuggles with Ahab, and Garrett tucks a blanket around her and tugs it to her chin. He tells her a bedtime story in hushed tones.

I try not to listen. It seems an intimate moment that I shouldn't be privy to, even though Ingrid and I have shared similar moments. I unfold a blanket and spread it on the floor.

"Zell, okay if I turn the light out?" Garrett asks.

"Go ahead."

We're plunged in darkness. In my head I say a quick prayer that the mice turds in the drawer are old, perhaps left over from last season, and that we'll remain unvisited by little critters.

Slowly my eyes adjust. I glance at Ingrid; the blanket rises and falls with her breath. Her face is old and young at the same time: about to become a woman's, but still very much a child's.

"Love ya 'n' like ya, Dad," she whispers.

"Love ya 'n' like ya," he whispers back.

"Can we toast marshmallows?" she asks.

"What?"

"Just kidding. G'night."

I kneel on the floor, about to lie down, when Garrett stands over me. It's so dark, I can't see him very well, but I can feel his body warmth, his breath.

"Hey," he whispers. "Don't even think about sleeping on the floor."

"I don't mind," I whisper. "You've been driving all this while. You take the cot."

He shakes his head. "Absolutely not. *You* take the cot."

I stifle a yawn. I imagine falling asleep in a mouse-infested shithole. Then I imagine falling asleep in a mouse-infested shithole while a warm strong human falls asleep against me.

"We could share the cot," I whisper.

He doesn't answer right away, and I can't read his face in the darkness. All I can see is his sharp-jawed silhouette. "To keep warm?" he says.

"Yeah. And I can protect you from the mice."

He laughs quietly. "It *is* pretty cold in here." He glances at Ingrid, then sighs. "I'll take the floor." He kneels next to me and elbows me. "Get outta my bed."

"Fine," I say, playfully nudging him back. I feel my way to the cot, crawl onto it, and curl up.

Just before sleep, I sense something like a tiny cold pinprick in the center of my chest, and I imagine Trudy's fairies twirling in the window, catching the light.


"Zell? Where's my dad?"

I wake with a start.

Ingrid stands over me. In the darkness I make out the zigzag cornrows on her scalp. A half-asleep thought flitters through my mind: Who braids her hair?

I turn on the light. Behind her the floor is empty; the blanket Garrett was using is gone.

Outside—close by—an owl hoo-hoo-hoos. A barred owl, I know, because Nick taught me the call they make: Who cooks for you, who cooks for all.

I sit up and rub my face. It occurs to me, in that dumbly sleepy way, that I'm still in my coat and boots. I march to the door. "Go back to sleep," I say.

Her mouth drops open. "Where are *you* going?"

"It's okay. Get back into bed. I'll go find your dad. I'm sure he just went to the bathroom or something."

She frowns but curls into a ball under the covers as Ahab repositions himself on her cot. "You can't leave me here by myself," she says. "I'm just a helpless little girl."

"Stay here. Stay with the Captain. Don't go anywhere, and don't open the door for anyone."

"Are you *expecting* someone?" She yawns and gazes sleepily at me.

"Just stay put." I don't want to leave her here, and I don't want to take her with me, and I'm freaked out that Garrett's not here. "Try to fall back asleep," I whisper. But she doesn't answer; she's asleep already. So I grab the key and quietly lock the door behind me.

OUTSIDE, THE AIR IS STILL, the sky clear except for black clouds that drift past the moon and remind me of twisted and waxed mustaches. It must be three in the morning.

I follow Garrett's big boot prints in the snow, down what seems to be an unshoveled path. The prints lead me into the trees, toward the lake. He hunkers on a fallen log a few feet from the edge of the ice. He doesn't move or say anything as I settle beside him. We sit shoulder to shoulder, outsides of thighs touching. We stare at the moon over frozen Tunkamog Lake. He smells good—warm, homey, like spicy drugstore cologne that he sprayed hours ago, that spent all day settling into his clothing, his hair, his pores. Just briefly, I allow myself to admire his attractive profile, his smooth skin.

"Couldn't sleep," Garrett finally offers. He pulls his blanket tighter around him. "Ingrid all right?"

"She's fine."

"Don't ever have kids, Zell," he says. "As soon as they come out, you love them so much, you're doomed. There's nothing you can do about it. You're just—doomed."

"Nick wanted a big family," I say. "He used to joke about having nine kids so our family would be an official soccer team. That was our little code word for our someday-family: the soccer team."

Garrett smiles. He strips a piece of bark off the log and skitters it across the ice. "I don't know what the hell I'm doing, as a father."

"You fake it pretty good."

"Ya think?"

"Yeah."

"Maybe this law school thing wasn't such a good idea after all. It's a lot to ask of Ingrid. Me not being there. Me studying all the time. It's hard enough on her, being the only black girl in her class. Pretty much the only black girl in the whitest county in the whole state, for that matter."

"I'm pretty sure Berkshire County is whiter," I say.

"You're probably right." He laughs through his nose.

"You could transfer your credits and take night classes somewhere else," I say. "Somewhere closer."

"I've thought of that."

"I'm sure Trudy would watch Ingrid if you asked. She's good people."

"I know." Garrett sighs. "I'm reluctant, though. Ingrid sure is a big fan of Trudy. But she's so busy all the time. I hate to burden her. Am I . . . am I burdening you?"

"Ingrid's not a burden," I say. Then, because I'm not sure what else to say, I add, "Well, kids are resilient."

"Are they, though? Are they resilient? Everyone says that, but . . ."

From far away—the other side of the lake, maybe—a coyote yips.

Garrett smiles. "Hear that?"

"Yeah."

"It really does make the hair on the back of your neck stand up. Zell? I'm glad you're doing that baking contest with Ingrid."

"Really?"

"She needs that. Maybe she'll get her obsession with Polly Pinch out of her system. It's good for her to be with a woman, and the time she spends with you is constructive. She likes to cook, and I *hate* to cook, so."

"I know it's a long shot—hell, it's crazy, but could you imagine if we actually win?" I say. "Imagine if Ingrid goes with me to meet Polly Pinch?"

He eyes me. "Goes to meet Polly Pinch?"

"That's the grand prize."

"I thought the grand prize was twenty thousand dollars."

"Right. *And* you get to be on the show."

His lips part slightly. "Oh. Wow. Really?"

"You get to bring a guest and cook alongside Polly Pinch. Ingrid's going to be my guest if I win. Didn't she tell you that?"

"She probably did. I'm just so preoccupied lately. And I hate to admit it, but I tend to tune her out when she goes on about Polly Pinch. But you really think you have a chance of winning?"

I shrug. "No. But I'm going to try anyway."

"Just because, right?"

"Yeah."

"Good for you," he says. "I like it."

He slides from the log and faces me, his back to the lake. "We'll cross that bridge if we come to it. In the meantime, I'm freezing my stones off."

"Likewise. Well, not actually."

"You're funny sometimes." Garrett laughs again, and for the first time it occurs to me that he laughs a lot.

"I'm sorry you won't get to finish your sister's mural this weekend," he says.

"I'll get up there soon enough. Gail's waited a long time already. She can wait a little bit more."

He sighs and resettles the blanket around him; in the breeze it flaps about his shoulders like wings. "Well, we tried," he says. "Let's go back to the cabin and get some sleep."

We face each other, and our breath hangs between us in short, white puffs. The moon glows high over the lake. He lowers his face, and I close my eyes as Garrett's fingers slide along my cheek and thread through the hair behind my ear. Electricity seems to flutter up my spine as he pulls me close and wraps me inside the blanket.

I slip my arms around his neck, and his mouth opens and closes against mine, surely, sweetly. I melt into his warmth. But then my head starts to swirl, and my heart gallops, and I break away, sidestepping until there's a few feet between us.

Balls.

"I'm sorry, Garrett; right now, I can't—"

"It's okay," he says, turning to gaze across the lake. "I understand. I just—"

"I know. Me, too. But, I think we need to just forget about this. For now."

He shivers and nods. "I got caught up in the moment. Sorry."

"Don't be." I pause, waiting for my heart to stop bucking. "Good night," I say, and turn and walk up the slope.

IN THE MORNING we're all pretty quiet, even Ingrid. Garrett smiles at me a little sheepishly as we fold the blankets between us. We trudge through the snow to the main house, where a cheery Bobbie invites us into her hot kitchen. She brews a pot of coffee, pours cranberry juice for Ingrid, and thaws waffles in the microwave. Then she calls a tow truck, and Garrett's able to drive us all home, back to Wippamunk, under a brilliant blue sky.

I try not to think about last night. I focus instead on the crisp new snow, so bright it hurts my eyes.

Near the Massachusetts border Garrett glances over at me. "Zell?" he says quietly, so as not to wake Ingrid, who's sleeping in the backseat, while Ahab rests his head in her lap. "I don't want things to be weird between us," says Garrett.

"Me, neither," I say. "No weirdness here."

"Good. You sure?"

"Definitely." I smile and nod.

"Good," he repeats. He hums along to John Legend, and I doze the rest of the way home.

I GET MY CAR FIXED. Something about the carburetor and the timing belt, and it costs me almost a thousand dollars.

Now, a week later, I drive to my sister's. I suppose I should feel cathartic. I got the car fixed, after all, even the broken turn signal. It's a huge step, right? But I feel nothing. No glee, no sense of accomplishment. No sadness or sentimentality. I feel the same: a continuous ache, a dull, steady, numb buzz.

I drive through New Hampshire and cross the Connecticut River into Vermont. My heart does its weird thing—it thumps fast and hard, then doesn't pump for five whole seconds. Should I call Dr. Fung's office, after all, and make an appointment?

I arrive at Gail and Terry's and park in their steep driveway, next to their many-windowed, pearl-colored SUV, which reminds me of an enormous snow globe on wheels. In the garage sits my parents' black 1983 Mercedes.

When I walk in, Gail, Terry, Mom, Dad, and little Tasha are snacking on cheese, crackers, and grapes. They wear thin wool sweaters and long underwear, as if they're just about to suit up for the slopes. They smother me in hugs and kisses. My mom hands me a glass of chilled chardonnay.

"It's not even ten in the morning, Mom," I say.

"I know," she says. "Isn't it wonderful?"

Ahab accepts strokes from everyone, even Tasha, who pounds his ribs. He lies down in front of the fireplace, which roars with freshly split logs. His legs stick straight out from his body. That's his greyhound style.

My dad carries Tasha to the kitchen table and bounces her on his knee. "Trot-trot to Boston," he sings, "trot-trot to Lynn, you betta be careful or ya might fall *in*!" He dips Tasha between his knees, suspending her upside down a couple of inches from the floor. She squeals and laughs. When he flips her upright, she claps her sticky hands.

"Again," she says.

"Trot-trot to Boston . . ."

"So *who* did you get stranded with the other night, trying to get up here?" Gail says. She spreads some soft cheddar onto a cracker and hands it to me. Terry stands behind her, his arms encircling her waist. He's four or five inches shorter than Gail.

"Your neighbor, was it?" Mom asks. She holds her wineglass up to the light and rubs a smudge off the stem. She pops a grape into her mouth and chews.

I tell them about Garrett, and how I watch Ingrid several nights a week and the occasional Saturday, while he's in Boston for part-time law school.

"Garrett, huh?" Gail says.

I nod.

"Is he hot?"

"Hey," says Terry, giving Gail a playful squeeze. "I'm standing right here, you know."

"Garrett's a good-looking man," I say.

"In what sort of way?" she presses. "Come on. Johnny Depp or Jude Law?"

"Well," I say. "More like Will Smith."

"*Really,*" Gail says.

"Who's Will Smith?" my mom asks.

Gail raises her eyebrows. "Sounds like I wouldn't kick him out of *my* Tunkamog Lake cabin."

"Stop," I say.

Maybe Terry and Mom and Dad sense the conversation's impending deterioration, because suddenly they pretend to do other things. My father resumes "Trot-Trot" with even more gusto. Terry steps over Ahab and throws another log onto the fire. Mom perches on a rattan bench in the foyer, opens up her compact, and applies under-eye concealer. She rumples her hair and mashes her lips together to spread her raisin-hued lipstick. "Christ on the cross," she mutters. "I look like a transvestite who fell asleep on a bus."

"So what's wrong with this Garrett?" Gail asks. "There's certainly nothing wrong with him physically, right?"

"It's only been a year," I sort of hiss at her.

"A whole year," she says, "and four whole months. And look: You're still not dead."

My eyes fill up.

She bites her bottom lip and puts her hands on my shoulders as if to brace me. For half a minute we face each other at arm's length. I stare at the reinforced toes of her neon yellow ski socks.

"I'm sorry," Gail says. "It's just that I've been reading all these books on grieving, to try to help you, to *understand* you. And they all say that the process—the really raw part of the process—is over after the first year. And here it's been *more* than a year, and you're still, well, raw."

I try not to cry. I really do. But before I can help it, tears spill over.

She's right, of course, and I suppose that's why the tears come now—because it *has* been a long time, and I *am* still raw. And Garrett's the most likely candidate for romance, and even with him, it felt too soon.

"Hey, hey, I love you," Gail says. She wells up, too. She gives me a Gail hug—a quick pump. She smoothes my bed-head hair, heavily, the way you pet a draft horse. "What I meant was, you're still *alive.*" She offers me a tissue box, but I wave it off.

"Listen," she says. "This Garrett seems like a nice guy. He loves his daughter, and so do you. Plus he has ambitions, and he's intelligent. And you like being around him. Maybe you should . . . think about him. He could bring you out of your shell a little bit. You know. Get you over the hump. Maybe a temporary arrangement?"

I come close to confessing last weekend's kiss and the confusion it stirred in me. But I know Terry and Mom and Dad are all listening, even though they're pretending not to. So I swipe my tears with my sleeve and say, "I—I'm fine. I'm sorry."

Gail pets my hair again. "For what?"

"I don't know."

"Stop apologizing. You apologize too much."

"Sorry."

We both giggle through our tears.

"Oy!" calls Terry, no doubt sensing the intensity lift. He claps his hands once and rubs them together. "Who fancies hitting the slopes, then?"

"You all go on ahead," Dad says. "I'll stay behind with Tasha."

And now Dad and Gail fake argue, because she wants him to stay behind but she won't admit it. Instead she insists that Dad ski, even though everyone knows Dad doesn't really enjoy skiing anymore because he's too old and creaky and his reactions are slow. But they finally agree that Gail and Mom will ski, Terry will snowboard, and Dad will watch Tasha, who's too young for Okemo's Little Stars ski school.

"Did you bring your gear up with you?" Terry asks me.

They're all silent. Since Nick died I haven't skied at all, not at Mount Wippamunk and certainly not here, at Okemo.

"I think I'll stay behind." I sip some wine. "I thought I'd finish the bathroom, actually."

"Are you sure?" Terry says.

"Oh, thank God," Mom mutters.

Gail shoots her a venomous look. "No one's rushing you to finish it, Zell," she says. "It can wait. It's only a bathroom."

"Yeah, I know," I say. "But I don't want it to wait. I want to finish it."

"In that case," she says, "everything is as you left it. I didn't move anything."

"Good. Great."

Terry steadies himself with one hand on the kitchen table and does a few deep knee bends to limber up. "You can borrow Gail's old gear if you want to come skiing instead."

"Nah," I say. "But thanks."

"Don't worry, Zell," Dad says from the table, in between "Trot-Trots" with Tasha. "I'll stay out of your hair." It's a funny thing for him to say because Dad's never in my hair anyway. He doesn't really talk to me to begin with, not since Nick died. And besides—these days, he has eyes for only Tasha.

"Well," Gail says. She collects all the wineglasses except mine and puts them in the practically bathtub-size sink. She goes into the foyer, gets two pairs of skis and poles from the closet, and leans them next to the front door.

"Zell, honey, did you notice Gail's new countertops?" Mom asks.

"They're Corian," Terry mutters. His inexplicable asparagus breath hits me as he steps into his purple one-piece snowsuit.

"They're Corian," Mom says. "Gail's designer chose green to suggest the out-of-doors. Aren't they just *amazing*?"

"I did notice them," I say, even though I didn't. "They're nice. Really nice."

Gail fastens the chinstrap of her glassy black helmet.

I hear my mother's back crack as she touches her toes a few times. "Your father's promised to stay out of your hair," she says. "Right, Dick?"

"Trot-trot to Boston," Dad coos, "trot-trot outside, stay outside all day so Auntie Zell can con-cen-*trate*!"

Tasha's upside down again. Her cropped black locks just clear the floor. She squeals and claps. "Again!"

Mom smoothes the Velcro band over the zipper of her jacket. "If my granddaughter cracks her head open on Gail's new ceramic tiles—"

"Let's go, Patty," Terry says. He gathers his snowboard and ushers Mom out the door.

"Keep Ahab off Gail's mohair couch, please," Mom says.

"Have a good time," Gail says. "Toodles!"

I watch out the window as Mom, Gail, and Terry clunk and waddle down the snowplowed walkway to the ski trail. There they put on the rest of their equipment and float away on Sachem, under lightly falling snow.

Dad does "Trot-Trot" a few more times; then he scoops Tasha in his arms and stuffs her into a fuchsia snowsuit. She screeches and flails her arms and legs. "We'll be outside in just one sec-*ond*!" he chants, putting his coat on and carrying her outside. I hear him clank around in the garage for sleds and shovels. I watch out the window as Dad, in his big duck boots, half drags the now-content Tasha down the driveway to the tallest snowbank.

I imagine what *our* kids would have looked like. Our soccer team. They would have had Nick's gray eyes and my unruly hair. They would have played so nicely with Tasha. They would have skied *and* snowboarded. I imagine our closet lined with little snow-shoes, little hiking boots. Little soggy mittens spread on the radiator to dry.

Balls.

I sit on the couch. Ahab curls into an oval in front of the fireplace. His tail and ears twitch in his sleep. As the logs pop, I mentally rehearse what will happen when I pull open the French doors to the guest bathroom and stand under the snow-covered skylights and vaulted ceiling. I'll peel the envelope from where it's taped to the vanity. My eyes will refamiliarize themselves with the photograph inside the envelope. The photograph Nick took after he set up his travel tripod in the snow.

I'll finish the g.d. mural. There's not that much left to do, if I remember correctly. Shouldn't take me longer than a weekend.

I approach the guest bathroom and swing the doors open. The

air in here still smells of acrylic paints and recent construction. Of new caulk and new pipes. Dust coats my box of tools, which sits on the floor between the toilet and the vanity.

I glance at the wall. I turn my whole body and look, full on. At the mountains, and the empty spots against the mountains.

I can't do it. I just can't.

Double balls.

I whirl around. I rush for the kitchen and grab my purse and Ahab's leash. Tears threaten to spill onto my cheeks, but this time they stay put and blur my vision.

"Let's roll, Ahab," I say.

He startles awake. We're out the door. Ahab vaults into the passenger seat, comes as close to sitting as his long, arthritic legs allow, and, with a horselike snuffle, thunks his face against the slobber-smudged window.

As I turn the key in the ignition, Tasha waves from the wall of a snow castle in progress. "Bye-bye, Auntie Zell."

She doesn't understand that I shouldn't leave. She hardly understands anything, because she's developed no g.d. understanding, no g.d. memories. She's a clean slate, pure, like the wall *before* I painted it.

Dad's head pokes up from behind the snow wall. He pulls back the furry flap that covers his left ear. "Zell?" he calls. "Everything all right?"

I back down the driveway. I roll down my window and cup a hand around my mouth, to lift my voice over the car's engine, over the buzz of the chairlift a hundred yards through the trees, over the plinking of falling snow. "Fine," I call, half choking on the tender bulge in my throat. "Just tell Gail to paint over it."

"Huh?" Dad says.

"Tell her to paint the bathroom a nice ecru or something."

"Bye-bye, Auntie Zell!"

"Where are you going?" Dad asks.

"Home."

"Zell, wait!"

February 17, 2008

From: rose-ellen@roymedicalillustration.com

To: nicholas.roy@thewippamunker.com

Dear Nick,

I went up to Gail and Terry's today. First time since you died, if you can believe that. Didn't go so well.

On the way home I took the shortcut behind the old Indian burial ground, over the Worcester Providence Railroad tracks. And who do I pass? Chief Kent, strolling behind his three-legged golden retriever.

And I thought about the attic, and the present that Ingrid carried up to the top of the steps. And I thought about how I asked both Russ and Pastor Sheila if they knew what it was. And I decided I'd stop and ask Chief Kent the same thing, find out if he had any inkling whatsoever about what the hell is knocking around inside that singed cube. Because maybe it will be easier—better somehow—if I know what it is, or think I know what it is. Maybe I won't even have to open it. I can give it away, give it to someone who'll appreciate it. Or put it out with the trash. No offense. But maybe someone will trash pick it. You loved trash picking.

So I pulled over and rolled down the window and watched Chief in the mirror as he trotted up to the driver's side. Ahab strained for the golden retriever, who hobbled around old Mrs. Dawson's lamppost and didn't pay Ahab any attention.

When Chief caught up to the car, we exchanged pleasantries. Then I said, "So what's in the cube, Chief?"

He looked at me blankly. "The cube? You mean the present in your oven?"

I nodded.

He whistled for his dog, who totally ignored Chief and kept on digging a hole by Mrs. Dawson's lamppost. I don't know if you've ever seen a three-legged dog dig a hole, but it's pretty freaking bizarre. Snow and eventually dirt flew up between her hind legs and piled in the street.

"I have no idea, Zell," Chief Kent said.

"Nick never mentioned it?" I said. "On The Trip?"

"No. Nick never mentioned it. Daisy! Stop! Sorry—hang on a second."

And he trotted over to his dog and yanked her collar until she stopped digging and sat, ducking her head. He scolded her, and Ahab started whining and panting, so I waved and drove off.

So.

So how's heaven? Hope you're having fun up there.

Love,

Pants

# EJ

Their last morning in New Orleans, Nick drove the interfaith van, and EJ rode shotgun. They picked up Charlene at her café. She approached the van slowly, carrying a tray of coffees and a bag of what turned out to be cheese Danishes.

"She's a keeper," Nick said as EJ watched her, admiring her hair, black and shiny in the sun.

"Help her open the door, dude," Nick said. "Southern chicks like that stuff."

EJ hopped out and slid open the door. Charlene pecked him on the cheek and climbed in.

"Good morning, Nick," she said, handing him a coffee. "I'm so glad you came. Keep going straight and turn left up there." She talked a bit about her new church and how it was being constructed to look like Noah's ark.

"Can't wait to see it," Nick said. "I'd like to learn more about carpentry and stuff. I'm thinking EJ and I should build something together when we get back to Massachusetts."

"Oh yeah?" EJ said. "Like what?"

Nick slurped his coffee. "Like a Man-Shed or something."

"A Man-Shed?

"Where we go to be men. You know. A place to drink beer and play poker."

"We don't play poker." EJ took a huge bite of Danish.

"Not yet we don't."

Charlene laughed. "Every man needs a Man-Shed."

Nick grinned into the rearview mirror. His plan, he said, was to erect a Man-Shed in EJ's backyard, by the pond, next to his tool shed. "Russ can help us," Nick said.

"Why my backyard?" asked EJ. "Why not *your* backyard?"

"Because my backyard's the size of a postage stamp. Whaddya think, Silo?"

EJ blew on his coffee. "I think that's the first good idea you've had since marrying Zell."

"Take a right here," Charlene said. "It's not far."

"These Danish are perfection," EJ said. They really were.

"Thank you, sugar."

Charlene listened, fascinated, as EJ told her about the freestanding sauna his great-uncle and grandfather built in the 1930s, on the shore of Malden Pond, not far from where his house is now. "The men of my family have a great tradition of sweating their balls off in a sauna for a half hour or so, then running to the icy lake and jumping in," he said.

She threw her head back and laughed—a laugh that made EJ think of clear, cool water. "Oh, I think I like this tradition very much," she said, and sipped her coffee. "Tell me more."

"My uncle and father and everybody, they all used to tease me that I couldn't be one hundred percent pure Finnish, because by the time I turned twelve, I was already thicker than any of the full-grown men in the Murtonen clan. I was brawny, in an un-Finnish way," EJ said. He recalled an indelible image: the naked silhouettes of old, lithe men as they galloped barefoot through the snow in the moonlight, tossing their towels aside, roaring with laughter, reeking of *sahti*, charging for the pond, and jumping in.

"When I was fourteen," EJ said, "a developer acquired that land in a shady business transaction, bulldozed the sauna, and built a McMansion."

"That's a shame," Charlene said. "A shame."

"And that's why we're going to build a *new* sauna," Nick said. "Adjacent to the Man-Shed."

"It'll be hard keeping ladies out of the new sauna," Charlene said. "Ladies like to get their sauna on."

"Well, maybe the *sauna* could be coed," Nick said.

"But not the Man-Shed." EJ hoisted his coffee cup and chugged.

"That's right," said Nick. "Not the Man-Shed."

"It's right here." Charlene leaned forward and pointed between the front seats. EJ liked the way her thin silver bracelets clinked. She smelled like confectioners' sugar. Her crystal earrings twinkled against her cheeks. "Pull over," she said. "You can park here."

"You know we're going to have to get building permits for the Man-Shed and the sauna," EJ said. "From the town."

Nick threw the van into park. "Screw building permits."

They all laughed and got out of the van. The skeleton of the new church rose from the flat ground like an enormous fossil. It was far from complete, but it already suggested a big ship. An ark.

Charlene introduced them to the construction manager, a guy named Pierre, her father's good friend.

EJ took a hard hat from Pierre and fastened the strap under his chin.

Nick grinned. "I don't think the big guy here needs that," he told Pierre. "Silo's skull's thick enough."

"After you, Nick," EJ said.

"Always the gentleman, Silo." Nick's hard hat didn't fit and looked comically small on his head. But they were only going to take a short walk-through. Ten minutes, tops.

EJ fell in step behind Nick, and Charlene walked behind EJ. As the corridor narrowed, he felt her hands on his shoulders. "Wait for me, sugar," she said. He slowed down.

They approached the framing of a big octagonal room, and Pierre pointed up and said eventually a skylight here would allow light to flood in.

"That'll be beautiful," said Nick, stepping into the octagon.

That's when EJ felt a tingling awareness zap his whole body.

From above, men's voices shouted.

Nick turned and locked his gray eyes on EJ.

\* \* \*

"Shit," EJ says. The sound of his voice sometimes stops the memory.

He flips open his phone and presses 2 until her number automatically dials. Charlene will reassure him that it wasn't his fault. That Zell will talk to him in her own good time, that she couldn't possibly hate him. Nick passed instantly, Charlene will say—in one instant. He felt absolutely no pain.

Her phone goes to voice mail. "Hey there," he says when it beeps. "I was just sitting here, thinking about you. I was just, well . . . I'd really like talk to you. If you're around. Later, maybe?" He snaps his phone shut to keep himself from saying more. "Shit."

A paper bag sits on his kitchen table: leftover chocolate muffins. He was going to put them in his freezer. Instead he zips the whole bag inside his jacket and walks across the pond in the dark. It's easy walking; the town recreation department cleared snow from much of the ice for the annual ice-fishing derby.

The Roys' house and EJ's parents' house—three-bedroom ranchers—were the first two on Malden Pond back in the seventies. Now scores of practically identical McMansions face the shoreline, on uniform lots completely devoid of trees.

EJ'd probably make a small fortune if he sold his waterfront property to a developer, who'd clear-cut the land, destroy the house, and erect yet another McMansion. But EJ's dad made the last mortgage payment just after the divorce, before he moved to California and before his mom moved to the Cape. It's nice not having a monthly mortgage. It's nice living in a small place that suits his needs, on a small pond whose sounds and smells make his surroundings feel wild and isolated.

Besides, as his father always said, Finnish Americans don't like excess.

EJ hikes up Mr. Roy's side yard. Memories flood him: sledding in winter, catching lightning bugs in jars in summer. Every fall, when EJ and Nick were so small that apple trees seemed climbable, Mr. Roy drove them to Bedard's Orchard. *If I tried to climb an apple tree now, I'd break the branches,* EJ thinks. *How is it possible that I'm the same person—the same being—as I was back then,* he wonders. *Or am I?*

He rings the doorbell. A minute later the door swings open, and he steps inside Mr. Roy's kitchen. The smell of this house—the dusty smells of electric heat and earth—are instantly familiar.

Mr. Roy wraps him in a two-armed hug. "There you are, Silo," he says. "I've been hoping you'd come pay me a visit."

EJ hands Mr. Roy the bag of muffins. "Hope they're not too squished."

They stand in the kitchen. Mr. Roy looks more or less the same: generic sweatshirt; Toughskin-style jeans; untrimmed salt-and-pepper beard and bushy hair, which gives his head a round, poufy appearance; deep-set gray eyes. The house looks the same, too—utilitarian kitchen with maroon backsplash; dark-paneled walls and heavy drapes in the living room, where an absolutely decrepit acoustic guitar leans against the couch.

"Want to go downstairs?" Mr. Roy asks. "It's warm down there. I don't run the heat much because the kilns take up so much electricity. I spend all my time down there anyway."

In the basement they sit on clay-stained benches. EJ rests one foot on the opposite knee and bounces that foot spastically: an old habit of which he's hardly aware. In the corner, three waist-high kilns radiate heat. They emit an oddly soothing clicking sound. Before long EJ starts sweating. We both depend on heat to forge our finished products, he thinks.

A corkboard displays Nick's photographs: Mr. Roy on a chairlift at Mount Wippamunk; Mr. Roy dipping the rim of a small planter into a bucket of glaze. Thumbtacks pin two patches, the kind you'd sew onto a sleeve, to the corner of the corkboard. The patches show a leafless tree on a green hill against a blue sky. A trail curls around the tree to the horizon.

Mr. Roy follows EJ's gaze. "Those patches are the official Midmass Footpath patches," he says. "Nick and I always talked about hiking it, section by section. You know about it, the Midmass?"

"It's that trail that stretches north to south across the state, right?" EJ asks.

Mr. Roy nods. "It's a footpath from Rhode Island to New Hampshire, about ninety miles total. It's divided into segments, so you can hike four or five miles at a time. Part of it runs right behind the Wippamunker Building."

The Wippamunker Building is on Reservoir Street, a huge converted factory, where, a century ago, they manufactured dyes. The brook flowed pink on Mondays and Tuesdays, yellow on Wednesdays and Thursdays, green on Fridays and Saturdays. *The Wippamunker* occupies the building now. EJ remembers Nick's darkroom, in the basement. The new guy probably uses it these days.

Mr. Roy untacks the patches and shows them to EJ. "The Midmass Footpath was something I always planned on doing with Ilene, originally," he says.

EJ straightens. He's surprised Mr. Roy mentioned that name. Growing up, Nick rarely discussed his mother. She died when he was very small. Somewhere in this house there probably exists a token to remember her by—a card she wrote, a coat she wore. But who knows where that token's stuffed away now.

"And then I planned on hiking the Midmass with Nick," Mr. Roy says. "But we never got around to it. You're supposed to order the patches when you've hiked the whole thing, but I went ahead and ordered them for us anyhow. Maybe I shouldn't have done that. Maybe I jinxed us." He eyes the patches in EJ's hand. "Sort of silly, I suppose. But those patches are the kind of thing Nick would have liked."

"He definitely would have liked them," EJ agrees.

"Take 'em. I'll never hike the whole Midmass. Who am I kidding."

EJ fingers the patches and puts them in his coat pocket. He feels suddenly depressed. He fights a vague urge to mourn missed opportunities, plans made and then forgotten. "I'll give them to Zell," he says.

"You do that," says Mr. Roy. "And give her my love."

"See her much?"

"No." He sighs. "Suppose I should pay her a call. But I haven't gotten around to it. She hasn't been to see me, either. How is she?"

EJ shrugs. "We haven't talked. Listen. I want you to know that we're planning a tribute for Nick. France is masterminding it."

He tells Mr. Roy about France's idea. "We'd love for you to be there. And if you'd like to participate in any way, you just let me know." He invites him to bring as many family members and friends as he likes.

Mr. Roy holds a hand over his brow, as if shading his eyes from bright sun. His pinkie trembles. "Does Zell know about it?" he asks.

"Not yet," EJ says. "I'm going to tell her soon, though. I think."

Mr. Roy stands and inspects the shelves behind him. Vases and plates line one shelf, mugs and goblets another. The objects are all in various stages of drying. "I'm not one for big productions, as you know, Silo," he says, his back to EJ. "I don't want to participate. But you have my blessing, whether you're asking for it or not. And you can bet your ass I'll be there. So will Nick's uncle Raymond." Mr. Roy glances at the kilns. "Nick was always blessed to have good friends."

As EJ leaves, Mr. Roy hands him the bag of muffins. "I appreciate the gesture, big guy, but I was never a fan of breakfast. Thanks all the same."

EJ zips the bag into his coat. "Do you still have the toboggan?"

"Want to see her?" Mr. Roy chuckles. He leads the way to the garage, where the long, heavy sled hangs on the wall, seat side out. EJ runs his palm along the pad, runs his fingertips along the wood edge.

"God, you kids used to go crazy for that thing," says Mr. Roy. "Good thing Ilene wasn't around for those days. She would never allow you to load up on that thing and get going as fast as you guys did."

EJ laughs. He remembers the rush of wind, the catch of breath in his throat as the sled reached top speed just before it leveled out and shot over the ice.

"Brings back memories, I'll bet," says Mr. Roy.

"Want to go for a ride?"

Nick's dad half sighs through pursed lips, as if to say, yeah, right. "I haven't been on that thing in thirty-five years."

"Well?"

"I'll pass. But you take her for a spin. And don't bring her back."

"What?"

"Take her."

"I can't take the toboggan, Mr. Roy. It's an antique. It's been in the Roy family for—"

"She's yours. I insist. What am I hanging on to her for? Nothing. It's not like I have any grandchildren to pass her on to." He whacks the seat cushion. "Nick would want you to have her. You know he would."

EJ shakes his head.

"Now, I insist," Mr. Roy says. He takes the sled from the wall and almost drops it, so EJ grabs the other end.

"I'll take good care of it; you know I will," he says. Together they carry the toboggan outside and set it in the snow so it points down the hill toward the pond. Across the ice, the backyard spotlight shines on EJ's fire pit, and the bench his father made looks miniature in the distance. He straddles the sled and lines up a path next to his footprints.

"Maybe you shouldn't do this in the dark," Mr. Roy says, the hint of a laugh in his voice. He squeezes EJ's shoulder. "Enjoy the ride."

His footsteps fade, and EJ hears the garage door rumbling shut. Alone, he considers the steep hill before him. There's not much moonlight or starlight. The snow and the pond form an indistinguishable mass of ghostly blueish white. He ducks behind the scroll of the toboggan. He's about to lift his feet when a beep sounds from somewhere in his coat. He fishes out his phone. The small rectangle of electric green illuminates the darkness. He retrieves a text message from Charlene: "JUST GOT YR VMAIL, STILL NEED 2 TALK? RU OK, WHAT RU UP 2???"

EJ punches his response: "SLEDDING IN THE DARK!!"

# Nick

November 6, 2006
From: nicholas.roy@thewippamunker.com
To: rose-ellen@roymedicalillustration.com


Hi, my sweet Honey-Pants.

Pastor Sheila is flying home tomorrow because she didn't want to leave her husband alone with the kids for more than a couple days. Father Chet is also flying home tomorrow because some old bishop or someone died, and he feels he should be there for the funeral. Anyway, Pastor Sheila is a really nice person. The past couple of days she is always talking about "construction versus destruction," which doesn't sound all that profound but when you're in a place like here you can really put it into context, if you see what I mean.

Anyway. Thanks again for letting me come on this trip. You're gonna be healthy and come with me on the next trip. You'll love it. I want to share all this with you. There is so much more to tell you than what I can convey in an e-mail or over the phone. We need to do this sort of thing together. Really share it and grow together. And then take the soccer team with us, when they're old enough. When I close my eyes at night in this stinky cafeteria I think of a little baby daughter who looks just like you. What do you think of the name Ilene, after my mother?

I hope I'm not scaring you with all this deep talk. It's still me, really!

Nick

# 6

## Zell

"WE'VE GOT SOME PROBLEMS," Garrett says. It's a Tuesday and he's at my door in jeans and a BU sweatshirt instead of his usual pin-striped suit. I was expecting Ingrid, and the television is tuned to the station that broadcasts *Pinch of Love,* which is about to start. I've just prepped ingredients for tonight's trailblazing experiment: a half cup of fresh basil, a tub of vanilla ice cream, and peeled, seedless tangerines.

"What's wrong?" I ask. "Where's Ingrid?"

"No Ingrid tonight," says Garrett. "I've involved you in our problems, Zell, and I shouldn't have. I'm sorry."

I pull him inside. "Give me a second and I'll make some coffee?"

"Lots of cream, no sugar."

"Got it." I make coffee, wondering if the kiss we shared somehow figures into the problems Garrett mentioned. I pour two mugs and bring them into the living room, where he's sitting on the couch, head in his hands.

"So what's up?" I set the mugs on the table.

"I got a phone call from Ingrid's teacher today. She said Ingrid hasn't been doing her homework. And she hasn't been doing it for a while."

"But she *does* do her homework," I say. "All the time. At least, when I ask, she tells me she finished it already."

"Do you check it?"

I never check it; it never occurs to me. "She doesn't pinkie swear on it," I say. "I don't make her."

"I haven't checked it in a long time," Garrett says. "I just trust her when she tells me she's done it. It's my job to check it. Not yours." He runs a hand over the top of his head. "Heck, it's my job to sit there and watch her and make sure she actually does it. She's only nine."

I feel like I should say something, but I don't know what, so I just sit and listen.

"I'm a zombie at work because I'm so tired all the time. It's a wonder I haven't been fired yet. Knock on wood." He raps twice on the coffee table. "And now I find out that I'm even a crappier father than I suspected. That my daughter's been lying to me for weeks."

"You're *so* not a crappy father—"

"It was wrong of me to put you in charge of my daughter, Zell. And I'm not going to class tonight. Ingrid and I need to sort things out."

"Where is she now?" I ask.

"She's home. Doing her homework. At least she'd better be."

"Where?"

"*Where?* In the kitchen. Why?"

"She might hear me from there."

"Huh?"

I go into the powder room and knock on the Ahab wall: knock-knock-knock, pause. Knock-knock-knock, pause.

After a second I hear Ingrid, on the other side of the wall, run into her bathroom. She knocks just as Garrett joins me. He looks perplexed.

"Are you doing your homework?" I ask Ingrid.

"Yeah." Her voice sounds far away.

"Pinkie swear?"

"Pinkie swear."

"Get back to it."

"Okay."

Garrett smirks and shakes his head. "Nice."

We return to the couch. "Can I ask you something?" I say.

"Sure." He gulps the steaming coffee.

"Is Polly Pinch Ingrid's mother?"

He sets his mug on the table. "To be honest, I can't believe you didn't ask me that a long time ago."

"I've wanted to ask you. But it's really none of my business."

"Can you turn that off?" He nods at the television; *Pinch of Love* has started. Polly discusses how her cat goes crazy when she cooks her "super-simp" Southern-style chicken à la king. The cat meows and rubs its cheeks on her shins and tries to jump up on the counter, Polly says. She blinks slowly, once, and smiles with her lips parted. "I guess my kitty thinks *just that much* of my chicken à la king."

"Christ," Garrett says.

I flick off the TV.

"So I dated this chick Anita during college," he says. "Anita looked a lot like Polly Pinch. As in, Anita could win a Polly Pinch look-alike contest. Ingrid found an old photograph of me and Anita together, and she's been hung up on the idea, ever since, that Polly Pinch and I were once an item. And that Polly Pinch is her mother."

"Is she?"

Garrett sighs. He rubs his face with both hands and then lets them drop into his lap. "Right after we graduated, Anita got pregnant with Ingrid. We decided to try and make it work. We got an apartment together, got jobs, saved money. But the whole time, I knew Anita was scared. I knew she wasn't into it. I had a feeling. . . . When Ingrid was four weeks old, Anita ran off to Atlanta with a jewelry salesman."

"Oh. Wow."

"Yeah," he says. "*Wow.* It sucked, to say the very least. But it was a long time ago and . . . I'm over it. I don't know if I can ever forgive her, but I can't blame her for running away. She wasn't ready for a baby. I mean, neither was I, but . . ."

"Do you ever hear from her?"

Garrett sort of snorts and scowls at the floor. "Not exactly."

He falls quiet for a while, so I get up, find the turntable in the kitchen, and bring it into the living room. Gladys sings about how she can't give it up no more, because she's much too strong. Garrett hums along. The popping sound of vinyl on a record player is soothing somehow, and it makes me think of dry kindling snapping away in Gail and Terry's fireplace.

"Nice mugs," says Garrett.

"Nick's dad made them. He made all this stuff," I say, gesturing to the pottery on the bookshelves.

"Zell? One other thing." Garrett pulls an envelope from his pocket. It's addressed, *To my mother, Polly Pinch, Boston, Mass,* in wobbly, little-kid handwriting. "I found this in the mailbox when I went to put some bills in there this morning. Have a look."

I sit and slide close to him, close enough to smell the coffee on his breath and his woodsy cologne. I worry that I'm *too* close, that I'm sending mixed signals. He shows me the envelope's contents: two five-dollar bills, eight one-dollar bills, nine quarters, seventeen dimes, a couple nickels, twenty pennies. Ingrid evidently found

Garrett's law-office letterhead lying around their house. She twisted and folded the papers into a little square, the way Nick, EJ, France, and I passed notes in middle school.

I unravel the square. Ingrid's handwriting emerges, in green ink.

*Dear Mom,*

*My neighbor and best friend Zell Roy says people who love each other write letters to each other, even when one of the people are dead. I agree and I also think people who love each other should spend time with each other. Here is some money for a bus ticket so that you can come visit me. If you come to the Wusster station my father or Zell will pick you up. I would pick you up myself but I am still too young to drive. Which you probably know. But maybe you forgot how old I am now. Or, if you mail my life savings back to me I will save it to come visit you in Boston. Maybe I can help behind the seens with your TV show. It is my faverit show. I am really good at mea-suring. Maybe I could measure stuff for you like flower and sugar. I am also really good with the pepper grinder. I love me a pepper grinder. Do you? I bet you do.*

*Love,*

*Ingrid Knox*

*P.S. Why do you have a different last name than me and my dad? Is it because famous people sometimes change their names to become more famous?*

* * *

AFTER I READ THE LETTER, I smooth it against the table. "Jeez," I say. "She saw an e-mail I wrote once. To Nick. That's probably what gave her this idea."

"To Nick?"

"I guess you could call it a . . . a coping mechanism."

"Maybe this letter is Ingrid's coping mechanism." He doesn't look up as he speaks. "Her teacher very gently implied that Ingrid doesn't appear to have many friends because all the kids at school think she's a nut-job, because all she ever talks about is Polly Pinch. She doesn't really ever mention friends, and she hasn't been invited to play after school at anybody's house in a while, or to birthday parties or stuff like that. I guess that's why I'd never thought about asking one of her friends' moms to watch her while I was in class. Her Polly obsession's only gotten more intense with this baking contest in her head. I thought for a while that it would be a good thing for her, but now I'm not so sure. Imagine her reaction when I tell her she can't cook at all anymore. Not even with you."

"You mean . . . ?"

"I've got to get through to her, Zell. I've got to get serious with this. She can't blow off school. I've got to just lay down the law. So no more Polly Pinch, period."

"No more baking experiments?"

"No. You're off the hook. And you're off the hook for babysitting, too."

I don't say anything. I imagine baking alone and fight off a surge of self-pity. Truth is, I don't want to bake alone. I don't want to be alone anymore, period.

"So what are you going to do with Ingrid?" I ask.

"Well, next week's not an issue because she's off to Nature's Classroom."

Nature's Classroom is the overnight hippy camp where pretty

much every public school fourth-grader in suburban Massachusetts spends a week hiking in the woods, singing Cat Stevens songs around campfires, and learning to distinguish raccoon poop from deer poop and coniferous trees from deciduous trees.

"After that I'm going to bring her with me to class," Garrett says.

"I thought that didn't work too well in the past," I say.

"It's *unfair* to expect other people to watch her. And I can't quit law school. I just can't. I'm so close. Just a few more classes. Maybe I'll take the summer semester off and we'll . . . reassess. Figure out a better situation."

"Have you ever thought about therapy?" The question blurts from my mouth—I don't know where it comes from, really.

Garrett laughs. "I probably do need a therapist."

"I meant for Ingrid."

He clears his throat.

"I mean, if she's really delusional about her mother," I add. "That's too much for any father to handle. Especially on his own."

He doesn't respond, and I suddenly feel ashamed, as if I stepped over some line. Who am I to give advice? *I'm* the one who should be in therapy. "I'm sorry," I say. I shake my head. "That was out of line."

He holds up a hand, shushing me. "I don't know. At this point, I don't want to make her feel like even more of a freak. She needs normalcy. She needs—I don't know. Who the hell knows."

"Maybe she just needs you."

"What's that noise?"

I turn down Gladys and the boys; we hear Ingrid knocking on the wall.

"I'll get that," says Garrett. He goes into the powder room, and I don't listen as they talk through the wall for a minute or so.

He comes back into the living room. "Thanks, Zell. She wants me to come check her homework. So I'm gonna go home now."

"Hey," I say. "I still have the EpiPen."

"Keep it. I have a million of them stashed all over. Oh." He pulls Nick's keys from his jeans pocket. "I guess I should give back these."

When I take the keys, his lips part, as if he's about to add something. But instead he nods and softly closes the front door behind him.

THREE FORTY A.M. It's just Ahab and me at the hilltop field, under spotlights so intense, they make it look like daytime. The snow here looks pockmarked, and the cold air catches my breath in little white clouds. I watch them disperse into the night.

On the far side of the field, snow flies after Ahab. He gallops half an arc, pauses, and strikes a beatnik-poet pose. He sneezes, and the sound echoes off the bleachers. Then he sprints ten feet in one direction, pivots, and sprints again, and I glimpse Mr. Bedard's cat on the other side of the fence. The cat swishes his tail and meows. Ahab gives up, paces toward the goalpost, and paws the snow.

I shiver and recall Garrett's lips on mine, his arms encircling me as he pulled me close and wrapped me inside the blanket. Kissing him was a mistake. It was too soon. It's still too soon.

My fingers find something small and metal in my coat pocket. The charm, Trudy's fairy, which pierced the paper bag of goat cheese she sent home with me, that first time I went to her house.

Finally, Ahab lopes back to me, panting. He's happy and spent, like those people meant for the mural in Gail's g.d. guest bathroom. I clip the fairy onto his collar, alongside his scratched, fire-hydrant-shaped dog license, which is proof that he is a Munker, embarrassed yet proud, like us all.

*February 2008*

*Dear Zell,*

*I am at Nature's Classroom. My dad told me to apologize to you. I am sorry for not doing my homework. I should not have lied to you about doing my homework. I hope you will keep teaching yourself how to bake and win the contest. Maybe if you win my dad will still let me be a guest on the show with you. That is my dream and yours, too.*

*Nature's Classroom is cool because we are outside a lot and I love to be outside. It is also cool because we learned about how the different tribes of Indians used to talk to each other with smoke signals and it reminds me of how we talk through the bathroom wall. I hope you are not mad at me for lying.*

*Love ya 'n'*
*like ya,*

*Ingrid Knox*

*P.S. There are mini courses here and my faverit one so far was the cooking one. It was better than Know Your Scat because we made cupcakes. But in Know Your Scat we just looked at poop from different animals and there were no cupcakes to eat.*

AHAB AND I SHARE A PILLOW. I breathe into his neck. I'm just about to fall asleep, hovering in that between-world, where sometimes Nick's voice sounds so close, I swear he's next to me in bed.

In my half dream—and in real life—Gladys and the boys sing about that midnight train. She'd rather live in his world than live without him in hers.

On the words "He's leavin'," the Pips skip. "He's leavin' "—scratch.

"He's leavin' "—scratch.

"He's leavin' "—scratch.

Ahab stirs, yawns, and rubs his face against the pillowcase. Nick's pillowcase.

I'm out of bed. I'm at the turntable, studying the record in my hands. The scratch is almost imperceptible.

"How, Cap'n? How'd it get scratched?"

I answer for him in croaking Captain Ahab Voice. "Peckered if I know, Rose-Ellen."

When I blow across the vinyl, a fleck of lint flies up. G.d. lint. Sometimes it's not big things that break me, that destroy me. Sometimes—maybe even most times—the small things are the most explosive. Something about that lint twisting around in the lamplight makes me feel lonely and fragile, hopeless and trapped and tiny. My hands shake; my lips tingle. I almost cry but stave the tears with a few deep, ragged breaths.

My heart doesn't thump for four whole seconds. I imagine it suspended in a dark cavity like a watch on a chain, like a sleeping bat in a wet cave. Then it beats again, crazily, like horses trapped and kicking in a fiery stable. Then nonbeats. Then fierce beats.

Nonbeats.

Fierce beats.

I need to get out of the g.d. house. Get away from the attic, the singed cube—and whatever is inside it.

I'll go to the Muffinry. And this time I'll enter the Muffinry. EJ and I will talk. It will be okay, and life will go on, because it has to. Because it should.

Trembling, I kiss Ahab above his furry eye patch and pull the covers to his chin. But he stands, shakes the covers off, and follows me downstairs. He'll never leave me, my Captain.

"Laugh, by Lucifer's teat, laugh!" I say. I yank on his booties, his coat. "'Tis a merry hour! Arr!" I zip my boots over my pajama pants. I zip my coat over my T-shirt—Nick's T-shirt from The Trip, one of the corny ones Russ made. It's red and says WIPPAMUNK LOVES NEW ORLEANS. Pastor Sheila gave me the T-shirt that morning in Gail's driveway. Paint covered both my arms, and a dead pine needle poked from Pastor Sheila's strawberry curls. Father Chet stood behind her, his hands on her shoulders, his cheeks wet. Mom and Dad, Terry with an arm around Gail, who pressed Tasha against her hip—the five of them watched from the deck, lined at the railing. In my memory they're perfectly still and sepia toned, like figures in an old-fashioned lithograph.

"Yo-ho-ho!" I clip on Ahab's leash.

We slip and slide down High Street, past prefab colonial homes, Bedard's Orchard, the police station. We turn left onto Main Street and head for the junction of Route 331.

The sky is a weird black-pink hue, no stars. Which means—as every Munker knows—snow. "Red sky at dawn," I mutter, "sailors be warned!"

My chest alternates between fierce thumps and nonthumps.

A police cruiser slows and stops in front of the cemetery gates, by the three-hundred-year-old maple, the oldest tree in Worcester County. Blue and red lights swirl as France stands in the open driver-side door.

"Hey," I say. "What's up?"

"Bit late for a walk, Zell."

I shade my eyes. "Or a bit early."

"Need anything?"

"Nah."

"Need a ride?"

"Just some fresh air."

Ahab whines; he hates stopping.

"France? Can I ask you something?"

"Of course."

"On The Trip, did Nick ever mention a present?"

"A present?"

"He was going to give it to me," I say. "When he got back."

"Is that what was in your oven?"

I nod.

"No. Not to me, anyway. Sorry."

"That's okay. Just thought I'd ask."

The tip of her nose is bright red; the rest of her face looks blanched. Major Memory Smack: At my wedding, toward the end of the night, I stepped out onto the balcony of the base lodge to clear my head. I gazed at Mount Wippamunk—the incredible spotlights, the skiers, the boarders, the chairs in their relentless ascents and descents. Next to me the roof sloped low, and a life-size Santa perched on a red sleigh. He gripped the reins, directing a team of little foam reindeer.

I heard a hiccup. "France?" I said.

Her bony arm—sheathed in navy crushed velvet—shot up from the back of the sleigh. Her speech was slurry. "Over here. That's Officer Frances Hogan to you." She kept her hand raised for the duration of our conversation; I spoke to brittle, hang-nailed fingers.

"You're not a cop yet, France," I said.

"Bummah," she said. "You mean I can't legally handcuff Santa?"

"Why don't you come down out of there?"

"I'm so happy for you, Zell. I'm so happy for you and Nick."

"Thanks."

Another hiccup gave way to sniffling.

"Beer tears?" I asked.

"Nick is a good man. And you are a lucky woman. You won, fair and square."

"Won what?"

"You won. You're a winner." Sniffles. Hiccup. "You're *the* winner. The winner of Nicholas Roy."

"Can I help you down out of there? It's not a real sleigh, France. It's probably only plywood or cardboard. And you're three stories up, on a slanted roof. And you've had *a lot* to drink."

"Ladies and gentlemen!" France shouted, like a bingo announcer. Her hand formed a thumbs-up sign. "We have a winnah!"

Real life. Real time. Four A.M. Main Street, Wippamunk.

"I said, do you want to come see my kitten?" France says. She tugs her head toward a little brick building nearby: Wippamunk Flowers. Her apartment's above the shop. "Come meet him. He's so cute."

"What about Ahab?" I say. "He likes to chase and eat cats."

France opens the back door of the cruiser, and Ahab climbs inside. He looks more like an heir stepping into a limo than a dog hopping into a car.

"We'll be right back, Captain," says France, shutting the door. "Good boy."

I follow her around the back of the flower shop and climb the slippery iron stairs, gripping the railing tight. She keys in, turns on a dull lamp, and makes a few kissing noises. The kitten skids across the kitchen floor, mewling the whole way. It's solid gray with a black nose, green eyes, and a scabby notch in its left ear.

"His name's Bergie," France says. She scoops him up. "It's short for Bergamot. I was going to name him Earl Grey—get it? Like the tea?—but I decided that was too obvious. So, Bergie it is."

"He's adorable," I say. "And the name suits him."

"Too bad Bergie and Ahab will never have playdates," she says.

Her apartment is hot, as if she turned up the heat full blast before she left for work. I undo my coat halfway. Little pebbles of kitty litter dot the kitchen floor.

She sits in an old wicker rocker next to the window. Bergie immediately settles in the seam where her legs touch. He tucks his front paws underneath his body. She scratches his chin and imitates his purring. "I got him at the shelter. The dog officer tipped me off that he had a kitten. A cute little sweet gray kitten who'd been abandoned. Want some soup?"

"Nah," I say. Soup's an odd thing to offer someone at four in the morning, but that's France.

"I could open a can and heat some up."

"I should get back to the Captain soon."

I look around. Besides the kitchen, there are only three rooms: a closet-size bathroom; a little sitting room with a stained, sagging couch and milk crates for bookshelves; and a tiny bedroom. Through the bedroom door I see the corner of an old cedar chest, and a bedpost, which Bergie apparently uses as a scratch post.

"Are you okay?" France asks.

"Sure." I unzip my coat all the way and take off my hat. "What do you mean?"

"I mean, we haven't hung out in a while. We should go out for a beer or something sometime. At the Blue Plate. Talk about things. You know. Girls' night."

I try to look enthusiastic about girls' night—I appreciate the thought—but my face falls.

Balls.

"I'm sorry, France," I say. "It's just that, a lot of times when you're around, I think about Nick's last night in Wippamunk. It's not your fault, of course. But . . ."

She gives Bergie's back one long, slow stroke. "You mean, the accident on Old Rutland Road?"

I nod. "I just wish his last experience with Wippamunk was a positive one. Instead of a horrible one."

A Memory Smack nearly sends me reeling, and I steady myself on the back of a kitchen chair. I awoke at 12:02 A.M. to find a note on Nick's pillow.

*Hon,*

*Hopefully you won't wake up until you're supposed to, but just in case you wake up, I wanted you to know that I had to go take some photos. France called me—bad, bad accident off Route 331.*
*Shouldn't be too late. Don't worry.*

*Nick*

HE CAME HOME an hour later, maybe more. He took off his boots. They thunked on the floor. I heard him undressing, and I kept my eyes closed, my back to him, as he told me what happened.

On Old Rutland Road his headlights illuminated a flattened tangle of metal and rubber, glass and tree bark. What used to be a black car was upside down. Blood washed the pavement and the dashboard, which rested against the base of a tree. Fragments of guts and brain and skull dotted the pavement.

France walked around the car and shined her flashlight here and there. Dennis followed Chief Kent around the scene and took notes. Nick photographed the tow-truck operator, who struggled trying to hook the wreck onto a big chain.

"It was horrible," said Nick, fluffing his pillow and sinking into it with a sigh. He caressed my butt cheek over the blanket. "Horrible and sad. France said the driver was just a kid. He was flying down Old Rutland Road. It's a curvy road, slick with wet leaves this time of year. Kid wasn't wearing a seat belt. He struck a tree head-on. First responders searched for his body for twenty minutes because it had flown fifty yards into the woods and landed ten feet up, in the trees. Zell?"

"Yeah?"

"I'm sorry. I shouldn't be telling you all that. Filling your head with all that."

"It's okay," I said. He snuggled against me, and somehow I fell asleep, feeling almost guilty for my comforts: my husband's arm around me in our warm bed, Ahab stretched across my feet.

And just a few hours after that, I awoke to Nick kissing me good-bye. "Don't get up," he said. "Keep sleeping."

He thunked his suitcase down the stairs. "I'll be back before you know it," he called. "We'll have epic reunion sex."

"I love you," I called from bed. "Be safe."

I watched out the window as Nick shook Chief Kent's hand and plucked a Big Yum Donuts doughnut hole from the carton Russ offered, as EJ shook his head in mock disgust. It's the last time I saw Nick alive: He loaded the suitcase into the interfaith van, popped a doughnut hole into his mouth, and blew a powdery kiss to the house.

Without warning, Bergie leaps to the floor and bolts under the table. Real time, real place. France gets up and stands next to me so our shoulders touch. She crosses her arms. "In a way, it *was* beautiful," she says. "Nick's last night in Wippamunk."

[175]

I think about what Nick told me, about the carnage and the car parts strewn everywhere. France saw all that. How could she say that?

"Beautiful?" I say, trying not to sound angry. "How do you figure?"

"Well. Nick came home. To you."

I never thought of it that way. But she's right, of course: Technically, Nick's last memory of Wippamunk *wasn't* what happened on Old Rutland Road. It was coming home.

"Right?" says France.

I nod and try to smile. "Right as rain."

On top of the radiator, I spy something that confuses and startles me: Nick's handwriting. His message of congratulations fills the cardboard backing of a picture frame turned to face the wall.

"Is that the photograph Nick took of you?" I ask. "On your academy graduation?"

France passes me the frame. I study the close-up of her face— slanted smile, scarred skin. The stiff brim of her cop hat tilts above asymmetrical, unplucked eyebrows.

"Why'd you have this backwards?" I ask.

"Why would I want to look at a picture of myself?" She studies her chewed fingernails. "Why was Nick always so nice to me, Zell?"

I return the frame to the radiator, so Nick's handwriting faces the wall. "Because Nick was a nice guy," I say. "Because he was a good friend."

France glances at her portrait. She hasn't changed much since that day. Not physically, anyway.

"Because it was an important day," I add. "You realized a life-long goal, and Nick wanted to mark the occasion."

"I miss him," France says.

"I know." The familiar heat gathers behind my eyes, but I don't want to cry, so I quickly excuse myself and go to the bathroom, even though I don't really have to pee. I rest for a while on France's cushiony blue toilet seat, which always struck me as very un-France. But then, that's France. The litter box is in here, on the floor in the narrow linen closet, which doesn't have a door.

When I go back into the kitchen, France offers me the sleepy, purring Bergie. I take him in my arms. He licks and nibbles my neck, then closes his eyes.

"Where were you walking to, anyway?" she asks. "You usually just walk up to the high school. I never see you this far up Main Street."

"The Muffinry." I kiss Bergie's incredibly soft head.

"Wow." She knows EJ and I haven't spoken since The Trip. I'm sure she's thought of orchestrating a meeting—an intervention of sorts—but she's not one to meddle.

"Well," she says. "Why don't you let me drive you the rest of the way?"

"It's only a block and a half down the street. But thanks for the offer."

"You shouldn't be out walking around this time of day."

"The only other person I ever see on Main Street at four in the morning is you, France." I place Bergie on the kitchen chair. He doesn't wake up.

"It would make me feel a lot better if I drove you," she says.

I smile. "Okay, Rosco."

She throws an arm around me and walks me to the door, doing her best impression of the famous Rosco P. Coltrane laugh: a guttural yet high-pitched chortle.

A moment later I'm hopping into the back of the cruiser. Ahab wags his tail once, greyhound style. His nose twitches a few times against my ear, his version of a kiss.

France drives slowly up Main Street, past the Congregational church, the Cumberland Farms, the Wippamunk Gift Shoppe. The cruiser hums along smoothly, and before long we swing into the gravel parking lot of Murtonen's Muffinry.

"Thanks for the ride," I say.

"My plezs," says France.

"I loved meeting Bergie."

In the rearview mirror France's eyes smile. "He's a keeper, isn't he?"

"I hope the rest of your shift is uneventful."

"I hope you have a good talk with EJ. I'm really glad you're going to talk to him. You know?"

"I know." I follow Ahab as he steps from the car and makes his way over the pointy stones in the lot. Around us drift the smells of warm butter and sugar. We approach the striped awning, and when we're standing underneath it, France pulls onto Main Street and turns left.

I press my face to the window, but I can't make out much through the steam. Inside, music plays; a Nirvana song ends and a Guns N' Roses song starts. Everybody listened to that stuff in high school. Nick played it in our attic for hours. For years. EJ Murtonen still spins it.

Ahab whines.

"Go on, ya yellow-bellied tick sucker," I say in Ahab Voice. "Or I'll stove in yer old woodblock."

I try the door. It's locked.

Inside, a rounded six-foot-three shadow approaches. A muscular, tattooed forearm swipes the condensation, and EJ's close-set blue eyes peer through the glass. He looks older; his blond eyebrows seem bushier than I remember.

"Zell?" he says.

My teeth chatter, but it's not because I'm cold. It's because I'm nervous.

The door opens. Sweet, delicious smells engulf me. It's painful to look at him.

A Bruins bandana covers his scalp. A grease-smeared apron stretches tight across his belly. Flour dots his clogs and black-and-white houndstooth pants; his goatee looks like it's been dipped in flour.

He looks me up and down. "You okay? It's four in the morning."

"I know. I'm fine."

"Hi, Ahab. I smell good, don't I? Good boy."

Ahab closes his eyes and leans against EJ's legs. "How's your kitchen?" he asks.

"Oh, fine. Thanks."

He unclips the leash, and we watch Ahab dart inside. He sniffs all twenty-four table legs in Murtonen's Muffinry, then curls up in a corner behind the cash register.

"Jeez," EJ says. "We haven't talked since well before your fire. Not since—"

I hold up my mittened hand. "Let's not."

He nods.

"Listen," I say. "I need your help."

For a moment he doesn't move, just stands there watching Ahab. Eventually he crosses the floor, lifts two chairs from a table, and sets them upright. "Sit."

He goes behind the counter and returns with two plates, each holding a steaming, sugar-sprinkled doughnut-pouf. "It's a beignet," he says. He takes a seat and sighs. "Southerners know how to make a goddamn doughnut; I'll tell ya that much. I think I've perfected them. Almost, anyway."

We eat our beignets in silence. I realize I'm tasting the delicious Cajun doughnuts Nick described, the ones the café owner—Charlene—taught EJ to make.

We slurp coffee from paper cups. It's strong, toasty, and nutty. That's how he makes it since The Trip, he explains. "It's got chicory in it."

I try not to look at him.

Ahab gets up. He whines and pants and puts his head in my lap; he's telling me I forgot to take off his coat and booties. I strip them off and place them under the table, and he curls back up in the corner. His tail rests over his snout, covering his eyes.

EJ glances at the wooden-spoon clock. "Travis is late," he says. "Again."

"Travis?"

"My newest indentured servant."

We watch out the window as snow falls. It covers the parking lot with white.

EJ checks his ovens and returns with a carafe. He refills our cups.

"Did he mention anything to you about a present?" I ask. I don't say Nick's name, because with EJ, I don't need to.

"A present?" EJ asks.

"A present that he bought for me." I blow on my coffee. "That maybe he was going to give to me when he got back from The Trip."

He lifts his cup to his nose and holds it there, breathing in. "You're wondering what almost burned your house down."

I can't see EJ's mouth, but I know he's smiling, because the outside corners of his eyes crinkle. "He hid stuff for you in the oven all the time," he says. "I knew that." He takes a long drink. "Fairly hilarious, when you think about it."

"Yeah." I smile. I almost even laugh.

"As for a specific present? No. No, I'm sure I would have remembered, had he told me about anything specific. And if I knew there was a present waiting for you all that time, in your oven, I would have said something."

I sigh. "I was hoping you'd be able to tell me what the present was. But I kind of knew you didn't know."

"That's what you came here to ask me?"

"No, actually. That was just sort of a bonus question."

"There's something else?"

I force myself to look at his face. "There's something else."

He cracks his knuckles. His eyes dart all over the place. I know he doesn't want me here, and for a second I consider leaving, just getting up and walking out the door.

But it spills out of me. Everything. And as soon as I speak, relief seems to wash over EJ. He watches me the whole time I talk. He strokes his goatee and sips his coffee.

I confess my adult life of frozen meals and take-out dinners, and the contest I feel destined to win because the prize is twenty thousand dollars, the same amount Nick specified in his e-mail. When I mention the dollar amount, EJ nods slowly.

I recount Flourless Peanut Butter Treats, Banana Cocoa Milky Way Cookies, Oatmeal Brownie Upside-Down Cake, and on and on. How every baking disaster made the lips purse, the tongue prickle, or the eyes water; left the mouth oversaturated or dry as dust, left the stomach too empty or too full, left the soul decidedly unwarm.

I tell him about Trudy and the Barn, the chainsawed bobcat, the Boston skyline. I describe Ingrid. How she thinks Polly Pinch is her mother, but Garrett says she isn't. How she resembles Polly Pinch, in the eyes mostly, and the mouth, and how the hue of Ingrid's skin seems a perfect fifty-fifty blend of Garrett's and Polly's together. Garrett doesn't want Ingrid to bake anymore, I say, because she's been slacking off in school and doesn't have friends her age, and the baking incites her Polly Pinch fixation, which Garrett thinks is unhealthy, although I'm not quite convinced it is.

I talk so long, my throat actually hurts, but it's a good hurt, as if I opened a little valve somewhere and let out some stale air. I probably haven't spoken that much since Nick died. I push my cup across the table, and EJ refills it again, wrinkling his brow. "I'm still stuck on the part where Ye Olde Home Ec Witch fires up twelve chain saws and carves a bobcat out of wood." He laughs, and the laugh seems to surprise him. "Did you see the article about her in *The Wippamunker?*" he asks.

"I don't read it anymore."

"Yeah. I figured that."

Outside, headlights sweep the parking lot, but it's not Travis, just some guy turning around.

Usually I don't sweeten my coffee, but I shake three packets of sugar and stir them into my cup. "The Polly Pinch contest is for amateurs," I say. "I'm one hell of an amateur; that's for shit sure."

"But I'm a professional," says EJ. "If I help you, we would be breaking the rules."

"I know." I sip my coffee. "I don't want you to *help me*, help me. I just need a little inspiration."

He nods. "How much time do you have until the deadline?"

"A few weeks."

He clears his throat and crosses his arms. "I'll speak plainly, Zell: You're never going to win over Polly Pinch with Milky Way bars, brownie mix, and instant oatmeal. You ever watch her show?"

"All the time, lately."

"She likes balance. Flavor. No heavy stuff. And nothing you can buy in a box or in a wrapper. She likes *food*. She's class. All the way." He swipes his bandana from his head, revealing thinning blond waves. "I'm not so sure you've come to the right person for inspiration. I mean . . ." His voice gets soft, and he twists the bandana in his lap. "I'd do anything for you; you know that. It's just that my skills are pretty limited in this area."

"In what area?"

"The *foodie* area."

"EJ, you're the only student ever—*ever*—to receive an A-plus in Ye Olde Home Ec Witch's class. That's got to mean something."

He blushes and waves his hand. "That was high school. Small-time stuff."

"But you went to Johnson and Wales," I say. "You're the Muffin Man. You're *the* Muffin Man."

"In Worcester County, I can't be beat. Probably in all of Central Mass., I can't be beat. That much is true. But next to Polly Pinch? *Polly effin Pinch?*" He frowns and leans back in his chair, balancing it on two legs. "Next to Polly Pinch, I'm a ham-and-egger. Hang on a second."

He gets up, pats a rack of muffins to make sure they're cool, and arranges them in the display case. On his way back, he stoops to scratch Ahab, who sighs, content.

As EJ takes his seat again, I swallow more coffee. "Can I ask you something?" I say.

"Anything."

"Where do you get your inspiration from?"

He grins. "Charlene and I were just discussing that. And the truth is—as flaky as this sounds, I'll admit it to you—dreams."

"Dreams?"

"I dream of ingredients. So does Charlene. How weird is that?"

I roll my finger in the sugar on my beignet plate and suck it. "It's pretty weird, Eege."

"I dream of ingredients that seem to have no logical relationship to one another. Like . . . I don't know, like cashews and—lemon zest or something. And then in the morning I write those two things down. And in the days and weeks that follow, out of the blue, I realize why I dreamed about them. I realize where they fit in. How they fit in. They don't always go together, but sometimes they do. So maybe you just need to pay attention to your dreams."

"I don't think that's gonna work for me." I rest my head on the table, and a tear slides across the bridge of my nose.

EJ's floury hand grips my forearm. "Zell?"

I don't answer.

"So I'm Finnish American," he says.

I lift my head and nod. "I know. Everybody knows that."

"Third generation. Both sides. My mother's last name was Haapajarvi. Her mother's last name was Hakkarainen. My grandfather and his brother built a sauna with their bare hands, on the shores of Malden Pond. Why am I telling you this?"

I sniff and shrug.

"Because you can learn some very important life lessons from a Finn," he says.

"Like how to make glögg?"

"Glögg is Swedish."

"Oh. Sorry."

"Listen. A Finn never balks from a challenge." He claps his hands, sending a puff of flour into the air.

I inhale the dust and cough.

"And you know what else a Finn never balks from?" He jabs a finger in my face. "Home Ec Bitches, the likes of Polly Pinch."

I almost laugh through my tears—almost. EJ smiles and nods

[184]

into his coffee cup. He raises a finger midswallow. "Before I forget, I wanted to give you these." He pulls two patches, green and blue and yellow, from his cargo pocket.

They're official Midmass Footpath patches. I recognize them right away. "Did Arthur give you those?" I ask. Nick's dad always wanted to hike the Midmass with Nick. They talked about it for years, in fact. But they never got around to it.

I slide the patches into the back pocket of my pajama pants, even though I don't want them. "Thanks."

"Mr. Roy says hello," EJ says. "Maybe you should call him."

I start to say no, because I haven't seen Arthur since the memorial service, and I just can't imagine talking to him now, but outside a car grinds into the parking lot.

"That'll be Travis, punctual as usual," says EJ.

A moment later the moon-faced Travis appears in the doorway. An old-school winter Patriots hat bearing an angry minuteman in a three-point stance sits askew on his head. "Come check out this cat fight, hey," he says.

EJ and I meet him at the door. EJ flicks on a spotlight that floods the parking lot, where Bedard's cat faces a sleek, black animal that appears half cat, half weasel. They don't react at all to the light or to us; they're consumed with each other.

"Weird-looking thing," says Travis.

"It's a fisher," I say. I know because Nick came home all excited once with photographs of a fisher. They're hard to photograph because they're reclusive, he said.

This fisher is lean and powerful, with a squarish head, a tail as thick as nautical rope, and claws so long I can make them out from here.

Bedard's cat hisses and yowls. The fisher swipes at the cat but misses.

"Damn," says Travis. "That thing's nasty." He sticks his fingers in his mouth and whistles. Both animals crouch and look at us. Cold air swirls inside the open door.

Ahab shoots from his dozing spot and gallops for the door, mouth open, eyes blazing.

"Ahab, *no*!" I grapple after him. I leap and grab for his hind legs but hit the floor hard, arms empty.

Ahab is a black-and-white torpedo. He knocks aside Travis and EJ.

"What the—," says Travis, catching his balance. "Where'd the racin' dog come from? That dog's got *balls*."

Ahab yelps when he hits the lot's jagged, frozen gravel. But he doesn't slow down. He's got two targets now and gallops full speed for them. Stones kick up behind him.

The fisher bolts, a black blur. It darts for the trees and scampers down the ravine at the end of the lot.

Bedard's cat ducks low. It cries and spits and swipes a paw. Then it, too, springs into the woods and disappears down the slope.

Ahab gathers speed.

"Cappy!" I sprint across the gravel. Footsteps sound behind me—EJ gives chase, too.

"I'm staying right the fuck here is what I'm doin'," Travis shouts. "Haven't you ever heard of cat scratch fever? That's a real thing, hey."

Ahab pauses at the edge of the woods. He sniffs the air where, seconds ago, the cat stood. Cap'n's ears point tall. He's as still as one of Trudy's statues.

I slow to a walk, not wanting to startle him. EJ creeps up next to me, breathing hard.

"Ahab, cookie time!" I sing. I hope he'll turn to me, looking for a dog biscuit. "Cookie time; cookie time for you!"

The snow thickens. It looks like a thousand white-beaded curtains.

I'm five feet from Ahab. Four feet. I hear his teeth chatter. I see muscles quiver under his fur as snowflakes land there.

Three feet. I reach out my arm. "Cookie time, Cappy," I whisper. My fingers are one foot from his rump. "Please."

He looks over his shoulder and blinks his big brown eyes.

"Sorry, Zell," I whisper. "But I'm a braver beast than that milksop, and I'll prove it. By the Almighty's balls, I'll prove it! Yarr!"

"Gotcha!" EJ leaps for Ahab but slips. He thuds to the ground with a groan. "Shit."

Ahab scampers down the slope. I trot to the edge, but I can't see much. The crashing of frozen leaves and twigs fades away, fades to silence.

"I'm sorry," Travis says as I follow EJ to the Muffinry van. "I didn't even know that thing was in here."

"Just stay here and man the shop 'til I get back, Trav," EJ says.

We drive all around town as the sun comes up. EJ leaves his window rolled down and calls for the Captain. His voice is pretty loud, even without his meaty hand cupped around his mouth.

He trolls slowly down Main Street a few times, which isn't a problem this time of day, because there aren't any cars. When he turns onto a side street, the glove compartment pops open, and an almost-empty bottle of cologne tumbles to the floor. The cologne was a Christmas present from me and Nick a few years ago; EJ always complained about the smell of muffins that seemed a permanent part of him. I shove the bottle in the glove compartment and slam it shut.

"I'm sorry, Zell," EJ says. "I'm so sorry. Ahab's just so quiet. I totally forgot he was there."

I start to say it's okay but stop when I feel my eyes well up.

Ahab will come back to me. Ahab will come back.

EJ returns to Main Street. We scan the trees between the nail salon and the video store, where a GOING OUT OF BUSINESS sign dominates the window.

"Nick sure did love that dog," he says quietly.

Balls.

I take a few jagged breaths as the tears spill over. I turn to the passenger window and press my forehead on the cold glass.

"Shit." EJ rubs my back a little, but when I don't respond, he stops. "That was the wrong thing to say," he says.

"It's just that I thought for sure we'd find him by now," I say.

"Well, it's only been twenty minutes or so since we started driving around."

"I know. But I thought we'd hop in the van and cruise around a little bit, and see him walking up the road. And he'd run up to us."

"That could still happen. Let's give it a few more minutes."

I wipe my eyes with the sleeve of my coat and notice Bedard's cat strolling down the sidewalk in front of Big Yum Donuts. "There's the cat," I say.

"If I ever get my hands on that thing," says EJ, which makes me smile just a little, in spite of everything, because EJ wouldn't hurt a flea in that cat's mangy fur. He pulls over, and the cat takes off down the sidewalk. EJ hops from the van and chases it, shaking his fist. "A-hole!" he yells.

I get out and walk in the opposite direction, calling, "Ahab! Ahab!" My nose is numb; my voice is hoarse. I trot down a side street, where little Cape Cod houses are closely set. I jog past a few driveways. I look all around, and my tear-stained face stings in the cold.

In one driveway a car runs. In another house the kitchen lights flick on, and I hear a radio announcer give a weather report. At the next driveway a man wearing a ski coat over his bathrobe stoops to pick up the daily. Old lift tickets flutter from his zipper as cold wind blows.

"Excuse me, have you seen a dog?" I ask. "Tall, skinny, black-and-white?"

"Sorry," he says, his voice scratchy with sleep. He goes inside.

The Muffinry van creeps along beside me. The passenger door swings open. "Get in, Zell." EJ pats the seat. "You'll find him, but just not right now. Come on. I'll take you home."

I HAVE TO PEE SO BAD, I zip straight to the powder room. When all the coffee's out of me, I wash my hands, gazing at Ahab's likeness on the wall. Young, speeding Ahab. I blow my nose on a length of toilet paper and shudder a few teary sobs; I think I'm done crying, at least for now.

"Zell?" Garrett says through the wall. "Everything all right?"

"Ahab's gone."

"*Gone?*"

There's a pause. Then he says, "I'll be right over."

I meet him on the porch. He wears fake shearling slippers, and the hood of his BU sweatshirt is pulled up over his head. "What happened?" he asks.

And after I tell him, he offers to drive me around, just like EJ did.

I hesitate, feeling needy and pathetic. "Oh, don't worry about it," I say. "I'll drive around by myself."

"Two pairs of eyes are better than one," he says. "I don't mind. Really."

"It *would* make me feel better," I say. "But what about Ingrid?"

"She's still at Nature's Classroom."

"Oh. Right." I'd forgotten.

And a minute later I'm hopping into Garrett's truck. "I told work I'd be late," he says.

We drive Ingrid style: heat cranked, windows down. At my suggestion we scour the high school campus first. We drive around all the buildings. We peruse every parking lot and circle the bleachers a couple of times. Next we troll the outskirts of town. We hang out the windows and call for Ahab every ten seconds or so. I sing the "Cookie Time" song; Garrett picks it up and belts it as he drives.

He takes Route 331 past Trudy's house. At the mountain he turns around and heads down Old Rutland Road, and we zigzag slowly along the turns. At the site of the accident Nick photographed on his last night in Wippamunk, someone erected a makeshift shrine: a white wooden cross that bears the name Dylan Mead and the date he died, the letters and numbers formed in black electrical tape. A small wreath of plastic flowers leans against the cross.

After about an hour and a half of searching, we head back. It's prime commuting time now, and the traffic is steady—dirty cars and trucks speed along in slushy, sandy snow. We take our spot in the stream of traffic. Something is different about Main Street, something about the telephone poles.

"Can you stop a sec?" I say. Garrett puts his hazard lights on and pulls over, and I step onto the snowplowed sidewalk and approach a pole. At eye level is a sheet of paper featuring Ahab's likeness. I instantly recognize the photo: Ahab leans against the dented back bumper of Dennis's rattletrap of a car. Nick took the shot a few years ago, on a brilliant September day when I walked Ahab to the Wippamunker Building to meet Nick for lunch.

Garrett's at my side now. I smooth the paper against the splintering wood of the pole and read.

*Missing greyhound. A black-and-white male answering to the names Captain Ahab and Ahab. The beloved pet of longtime Wippamunker photographer Nicholas Roy, who died last year during an interfaith mission trip comprised of local churchgoers helping rebuild homes and churches in New Orleans. Anyone with information as to Captain Ahab's whereabouts should contact Ms. Rose-Ellen Roy of 111 High Street, Wippamunk, or Officer Frances Hogan at the station.*

I glance up and down Main Street. Every third telephone pole sports eye-level pinups of Ahab.

"That was fast," Garrett says. "That was *really* fast."

"Would you mind stopping at the police station?" I ask.


FRANCE SITS AT THE DISPATCHER'S DESK. Her black boots are propped up, her hands laced behind her head. A cup of yogurt waits next to a big olive green panel with all sorts of knobs and dials. She smiles sadly when I enter. "You like?" she yells through the bulletproof glass that separates the dispatcher's desk from the lobby. "Did you see them?"

"I like," I say. "Thanks."

"EJ called me, so I called Dennis. He has some of Nick's old photographs on file at *The Wippamunker.* He doctored up a flyer and photocopied it. He and the new guy drove around town and put them up all over the place."

"But it's only been, like, not even three hours since he went missing."

France gives a little shrug. "What can I say? When Munkers get behind something, they get behind something."

"He was wearing a fairy charm."

She twists up her face. "Huh?"

"Ahab. On his collar. You know. It's silver. Handmade. Little different-colored beads. Looks like a little fairy. With wings."

France scribbles the detail onto a notepad. "Little silver and glass fairy with wings. Got it." She spoons some purple yogurt into her mouth. "Was he microchipped?"

"Yes. All the greyhounds at the adoption place were micro-chipped before being placed in homes."

She nods. "That's really good. The dog officer was just here, and he said dogs with microchips have a really high chance of returning. It's a proven statistic." She stands and presses her palm to the glass. "We'll find him, Zell."

GARRETT DRIVES ME HOME. I thank him the whole way and beg him to let me pay for gas, but he refuses. "This was for the Captain," he says.

He walks me up the porch steps. At the door he embraces me, a real hug, long and full, and I let myself sink into his body, his warmth.

"You'll get him back, Zell," he says into my hair.

I want to say that I believe this. That in a few hours Ahab will get bored of the hunt and start making his way back here. But the truth is, I'm not sure. I'm just not.

"Breakfast?" asks Garrett, smiling gently.

"Breakfast."

I SHOWER AND BREW MORE COFFEE. I go to draw a hip socket—femur head rotating smoothly inside pelvis's ridgelike acetabulum—but I sketch, instead, Nick. He guards an icy outcropping, and his soldier-angel wings are azure and orange, like the flames that unfurled from the present in my oven. And at his side, Ahab, in full dog-battle regalia, peers over the ledge.

# EJ

Every morning before work EJ cruises the streets of Wippamunk, searching for Ahab. He shines his high beams into dense patches of underbrush. Some days he even hikes a little into the woods, which makes him realize how out of shape he is.

He searches in the daylight, too, leaving Travis in charge of the Muffinry. Travis is capable. Punctual, no, but capable.

It's two in the afternoon, and there's the usual lull in traffic, after the lunch rush and before the end-of-the-school-day rush. Past the Blue Plate Lounge, EJ catches a whiff of French fries, which reminds him of the old-grease smell in the cafeteria where they slept in New Orleans. Pastor Sheila sequestered herself in a corner, out of courtesy, because she snored, but EJ thought her snoring actually was kind of cute. Father Chet took over another corner, and Chief Kent was by himself, too. Dennis and Nick put their sleeping bags close to each other toward the middle of the room, so they could talk about *Wippamunker* stuff, and mull over ideas for their story and photo spread. Nick showed Dennis the days' shots on his camera; it was sort of their before-bed ritual. And the remaining three—EJ, France, and Russ—hunkered together. Some nights they giggled and whispered like kids at a slumber party.

One night, toward the end of the trip, after Pastor Sheila and Father Chet flew home early, EJ couldn't stop thinking about the woman they met the first day, Verna, who told them about her neighbor's corpse caught on a telephone pole. He thought about the bronzed baby shoes of Verna's only son, who died in Vietnam. He laid awake and imagined random scenes from her life. Verna carrying a big tub of potato salad to a backyard barbecue. Verna draping tinsel on a Christmas tree. He supposed about an hour had passed since everyone turned off their flashlights. Then he heard his name whispered. It was Nick.

"I'm awake." EJ clicked on his flashlight to see Nick, in his sleeping bag, worm toward him.

"How about that church today," Nick said. They'd worked all day, rebuilding a parish hall next to a Baptist church. They swung hammers alongside a local imam, and a rabbi, and a Catholic priest.

"Yeah," EJ said.

"I wish I was handier," Nick said. "I'd like to learn more about carpentry and stuff."

"You should come with Charlene and me."

"Where?"

"She wants to show me her new church. They're building it now. It's gonna be really big, and they're making the outside look like Noah's ark."

"That's pretty cool," Nick said. "I *would* like to see it." He paused, then said, "I miss my woman, Silo. I miss her a lot."

"How is she? How's her heart?"

"I guess the tests so far are inconclusive. They still haven't figured out what's going on. But I have a feeling everything's gonna be just fine."


EJ's PHONE RINGS. Real time, real place. It's Charlene.

He blinks the water from his eyes, pulls over to the side of the road, and clears his throat. "Hello, sweetness," he answers.

"Hey, big guy. Find the dog yet?"

"Oh, man." He switches hands and turns down the radio. "Ahab's chances aren't looking too good. So many things could have happened to that dog. What if that fisher bit him and gave him rabies? Or what if the fisher scratched him, and he got a blood infection, and crawled under a bush somewhere and died of a fever? Or what if he froze? Zell makes him wear a coat and boots even when the thermometer reads fifty degrees. And it's in the twenties lately."

"You're torturing yourself with these thoughts," Charlene says.

EJ closes his eyes at the sound of her warm-honey voice. He feels washed with sudden gratitude: Dogs go missing; people fight, divorce, and die; but he can call Charlene any time, day or night, and she consoles him.

"It does you no good to think about these things," she says.

"Nick loved that dog. Zell, too. I mean, they *loved* that dog."

"It's not your fault. It's nobody's fault. Dogs chase cats. That's the nature of things."

He sighs. He taps his phone on his forehead a few times, then returns it to his ear. "Would you hate me, Charlene? I'm pretty sure *I* would hate me. But I'm a man. You're a woman. Would *you* hate me?"

"She'll come around, EJ."

"I miss Nick."

"*I* miss him, and I only met him a few times." Her breath sounds funny—drawn out and deliberate.

"Where are you?" he asks.

"Out back, doing a little yoga."

He chuckles. He doesn't even really know what yoga is, but he pictures her stretching her arms overhead, her eyes closed, a soft smile on her face. "I'd bet you look pretty cute doing yoga," he says.

"Well, then, you'd stand to win a lot of money, sugar." She inhales slowly, exhales slowly. "Listen. Life isn't simple. But the beauty of it is, you can always start over. It'll get easier."

"Oh yeah?" He rolls down his window and waves, urging a car to pass. "When?"

# Nick

November 7, 2006
From: nicholas.roy@thewippamunker.com
To: rose-ellen@roymedicalillustration.com

Hiya, Rose-Ellen. Russ here, your friendly neighborhood mailman, or to be politically correct, your friendly neighborhood "mail carrier." Just wanted to write hello, we are working hard and having a lot of fun, too. I'm handing your husband's laptop back to him now cuz he's looking at me like he wants to kick my scrawny butt, never get in the way of a man and his woman, ha ha, see ya, over and out, Russ #1 Mailman in Central Mass, or as EJ would say, #1 Mailman West of 495, ha ha.

Hey, Pants. Nick here.

I'm still feeling pretty run down. Head cold. Bleck. But that's neither here nor there. . . .

The reverend of this church down here got all choked up when he saw that we had rebuilt a couple walls in the parish hall. He put his palms on the wall and put his cheek in between his hands and he said, "We're coming back, aren't we?" It was pretty touching. Pretty affecting to see how affected he was. I got a couple good shots of him—see attached.

And I've attached other shots, too. One is of a building that crashed into a pier and has been sitting there since the hurricane. And check out the one of all the old abandoned cars. It's been a little more than a year after the hurricane and there are something like 200,000 cars that have been abandoned in the streets of New Orleans. It's like, "What do you do with that kind of trash??" You know?? Insane. Verna—the sweet old woman whose house we gutted—said that there are still 5,000 more houses that need to be gutted. 5,000!!! It's an unfathomable amount of work.

I want to start making muffalettas when I come home. They're these insane and ginormous ham sandwiches they make in New Orleans. But they're not just your ordinary ham sandwich. They've got hard-boiled eggs, some sort of relish made with olives, and capicola and provolone. I get one every day for lunch. EJ brings them from the café where he has been going—he is totally in love with that café owner, Charlene.

Charlene also makes these French doughnuts called beignets. EJ is thinking about making and selling them at Murtonen's Muffinry, and all the proceeds will go to a charity he and I are hoping to start. It'll take a hell of a lot of doughnuts, but our goal is $20,000. I know, sounds a little steep, a little overambitious, but why not? Why the hell not? On the ride home we are going to hash out some fund-raising ideas and sort out how we're going to spend the money. Pretty cool, huh?

I have been thinking about our "soccer team." Wink, wink. I feel ready. I know you do. But more on that later. That's a conversation we have to have in person, right?!

Love ya.

Nick

# 7

## Zell

FEW DAYS AFTER AHAB'S DEPARTURE, Gail drives down from Okemo and helps me search the town. We drive around for two hours in her SUV. But we don't see the Captain.

Now we sit at the Muffinry's most coveted table—the one by the front bay window—at noontime. Gail wears a belted cashmere sweater and peanut-size diamond earrings. She picks up her chocolate-marshmallow muffin and holds it next to her face. "Look at this," she says. "It's bigger than my head. Last night I did an hour on the elliptical and an hour on the rowing machine just so I could come here with you and eat this whole thing. Otherwise, I might as well rub it directly onto my ass. Murtonen's Muffinry is the only place I miss—actively *miss*—since I moved to Vermont."

Gail peels off the top of the muffin. Steam licks her chin. "But that's beside the point," she says. "I want to talk to you about something." She pops a bite of muffin top into her mouth and throws her head back. "Jesus H. Christ, that tastes good."

I know she's thinking about her guest bathroom and the mural. "I told Dad to tell you to paint it a nice ecru," I say.

"Look. I'll *pay* you."

"Can't you hire a college student to finish it?"

"Hmm." She rips open five sugar packets, dumps their contents into her coffee, and stirs slowly. "That's not a half-bad idea. A college student."

"Put an ad on Craigslist," I say. "Offer a couple hundred bucks. You'll have a dozen starving art students lined up at your door faster than you can say—"

"No. I want you to finish that bathroom, Zell." She looks at me hard. "Not some college student who doesn't know me, who doesn't know *us*."

"Then you're going to have to wait. Because I can't do it right now."

She clears her throat and sets her spoon carefully on the table. "Because of Ahab?"

"I don't know. I just can't."

"You know, Terry says Ahab just 'went off on a toot.' It's what the British say when dogs decide to leave home for a bit. Isn't that adorable? His parents' beagle goes off on toots all the time. And he *always* comes back unscathed. Listen, I'm *sorry* about Ahab. I know what he meant to you. But it's too early to give up hope. And I don't mean to rush you into finishing the bathroom. I just think you ought to follow it through. Isn't it time? Besides, maybe it will help take your mind off things."

The bell jingles then, and I look up from my coffee to see Father Chet striding through the door. I don't think I've talked to him since the memorial service. He catches my eye, smiles, and approaches our table. My heart stops beating. Five seconds. Six seconds. It beats again, furiously at first.

"Father Chet," I say. "What are you doing here?"

"I thought Murtonen's Muffinry could use some color," he says. He tips back his head and laughs. "Hello, Row-sel-*len*. I have not seen you in a long while."

I try to give him a little smile. "Likewise. Nice to see you."

He nods at Gail, then bends forward a little and whispers something in French. It sounds like *noose um blah blah blah*.

"I don't know what that means, Father," I say.

He wags a long finger in the air and moves toward the counter to order a coffee. "Babel Fish, Row-sel-*len*. And if you eat that whole muffin? Ten Hail Marys."

Gail beams at Father Chet, and when he's out of earshot, she smacks her hands on the table. "Who was *that*?"

"Father Chet. You saw him before. In your driveway. Remember?"

"Ahh. Right," she says. She sighs and looks askance a moment, no doubt remembering that awful day. Then her face brightens. "Well, anyway, *he's* not ugly, is he? In a Seal kind of way?"

"For shit's sake, Gail. He's a Catholic priest."

"That could change." She digs a pen from her purse and scribbles something on a napkin.

"What are you doing?" I'm not hungry, but I nibble my strawberry-wheat muffin.

"I had a semester of French in college," Gail says. "I can sound it out well enough. I'm gonna look up what he just said on Babel Fish. When a sexy man talks, Gail Carmichael-Dunbar listens. And takes notes."

"Gail Carmichael-Dunbar, who is married. Happily. And raising a child. Happily."

"I'm taking notes for *you*, sweetie."

"You're disturbing."

"Cheers." She hoists her coffee, touches it to mine, and chugs.

\* \* \*

I CAN'T SLEEP. My impulse is to take Ahab to the field. But I can't, of course. So I tote the turntable to my office and cue Gladys, who asks what good her eyes are, if she can no longer see her man's tender, tender smile?

I draw a newborn skull. Its squiggly lines suggest the spot where the skull plates eventually shift, fuse together, and harden. The sutures make the newborn skull malleable. They allow the bones to move during birth and, later, during growth.

The anterior fontanelle is the technical term for the soft spot. When Tasha was born, Nick and I drove up to the hospital near Okemo, and I held little Tasha in my arms and found myself sniffing—instinctively, unconsciously—the soft spot, the most vulnerable spot.

I take a break from the skull and go downstairs, wrap up in my hairy afghan, and sit on the back steps for a while. I stare at the gate and imagine Ahab walking through it.

Pangs of guilt tear up my chest. I try not to think about all the things I could have done to prevent Ahab from taking off, but it's no use. Could have kept him leashed at my side. Could have told Travis to shut the door as soon as he came in. Could have grabbed Ahab's tail and yanked it with all my strength until he slid back to me.

I try not to think about the many ways a skinny old half-blind dog can die in the winter woods, but that's no use, either. He had no coat, no booties, and milky, failing eyes. I envision charging moose and packs of coyotes, black bears that wake from hibernation ravenous. I remember Ahab's ribs, their outlines visible under his fur; his grayish teeth chattering; the bloody scabs that form on his paws in colder months. How, on his back legs, the skin between his tendons and his bones is so thin you can see through it, the tiny crisscrossing veins.

I hear a crunching noise beyond the gate. An animal noise.

"Ahab?" I whisper to the dark. "Cappy?"

An orange pouf leaps from the shadows to the gatepost. It's the orchard cat. It settles on the post, watching as I tighten the afghan around my shoulders. I stamp my foot and hiss. The cat leaps from the post and gallops off.

An achy bulge forms in my throat. I try to swallow, but it won't budge.

"Anytime you want to come home, Cappy," I whisper. "Anytime is okay with me."

TRUDY LENDS ME HER HANDHELD MIXER, and I use it frequently because I want to fill up the house with noise so I'm not constantly reminded of Ahab's absence. One night I blend a loose concoction of strawberry yogurt and Nutella. I watch as the pink turns rosy tan, and think about how Ahab would hate the mixer, because it's pretty loud.

"Sorry, Captain," I say, even though he's not there to be bothered by it.

I try to be neat, but batter flings from the bowl and flecks the counter and cupboards.

Knock-knock-knock, pause. Knock-knock-knock, pause.

I head for the powder room, wiping my hands on my apron. "Ing?" I say to the wall.

"I'm back from Nature's Classroom," she says. "I just got back. I wanted to come over but my dad said it was too late and not to bother you."

"How was it?"

"I really like hiking. More than I used to, I mean. My dad says we should hike more, the three of us."

"Where's your dad?"

"Guess."

"Studying with his earbuds in?"

"You always ask where my dad is. Do you *like* him or something?"

"Yeah, I like him." I hear Ingrid giggle. "You're laughing at me," I say.

"Yeah," she gasps. "I totally am."

"Why?"

She doesn't answer.

"Listen, do you know about the Midmass Footpath?" I ask.

"No."

"I'll tell you about it tomorrow. We should hike some of it." I've been thinking about the Midmass, about those nerdy patches EJ gave me, which Nick would love. We never hiked the Midmass much; Mount Wippamunk offers much more in the way of a view, whereas the Midmass, while pretty, meanders through woods and rarely rewards its travelers with vistas where you can look out over land for miles. Nick was a sucker for a vista.

"Okay," says Ingrid. "Whatev."

"I'll come, too." It's Garrett's voice.

"Hey!" I shout. Ingrid giggles again. "I thought this was supposed to be a little thing between Ingrid and me."

I hear Garrett's deep laugh. He says, "There are no secrets in the Knox household."

# EJ

"Mail for the big guy." Over the counter, Russ passes Travis a stack of envelopes secured with a rubber band.

"Mail for the big guy," Travis repeats. He tosses the stack to EJ, who straddles a stool by the back door.

EJ taste tests a pomegranate scone. He lets the mail fall to the floor at his feet. "Thanks," he says, and brushes a crumb from his goatee.

"Package for the big guy," says Russ. "Package from New Orleans." He hands a small brown box to Travis, who carries it to EJ.

"Hey, Russ," EJ says.

"You *still* hearing from that chick with the . . . ?" Russ spreads hands in front of his chest as if cradling melons. "When are you gonna make a move? You're not getting any younger."

EJ swallows a bite of scone and glares.

"I'm not getting in the middle of this, hey." Travis grabs a bottle of cleaner and a rag and walks over to the tables.

"I'm workin' on it," says EJ. "Okay?"

"Easy, Silo," says Russ. "I'm just sayin.'"

EJ stands and presses the half-eaten scone into Russ's hand. "Eat this," he says. He grabs a plastic knife from a cup on the display case and slices through the tape on the package. He knows what's inside: his monthly shipment of chicory root, in perfect condition, as always. He takes the sealed plastic bag, tears it open, and inhales.

"This—whatever this is—is seriously freakin' delicious, Silo," says Russ, smacking his lips. "But it's a bit dry."

"It's a scone," EJ says. "Dunk it in coffee or something."

Russ pours a cup and soaks what's left of the scone.

EJ notices, inside the box, a folded slip of lined purple paper. A handwritten letter from Charlene.

"What's that?" Russ asks. "Get a little bonus this month?"

EJ ignores him. He takes Charlene's letter over to the stool, sits with his back to Russ, and reads.

*Dear EJ,*

*I feel the time has come to ask you a very important question, and that question is, What are we? What I*

*mean by that is, I am very much enjoying our relation-
ship the way it is, but I would like to know if it is going
to progress into anything more serious. I like hearing
from you several times a day—the text messages, the
e-mails, the occasional phone conversation. Truth be
told, I care for you deeply, as if you were a very close
friend that I see every day, maybe because in my head,
I do see you every day. I have never met anyone who
seems as compatible to me as you. And yet you are hundreds of miles away, and I've only met you a handful
of times, those mornings you came in to the café, more
than a year ago now. Why have you kept in touch with
me? Is it just to be my friend? If so, that is fine. Is it
because I was there when your friend passed, and you
feel some sort of connection to me, because of that? If
so, that is fine, too.*

*Please don't take this letter as a threat or a complaint.
We can continue being friends, because as I wrote above,
I treasure your friendship. But I sense that there is more
between us. This would be easier to figure out, of course,
if we were seeing each other every day. I don't know if
I'm asking for a committed relationship. I don't even
know if you're attracted to me in that way at all. I guess
I'm just asking for a little clarification. Whenever you're
ready (no pressure). I hope this letter doesn't make things
weird between us. You can be perfectly honest with me.*

*Love your friend
ALWAYS!! ~*

*Charlene*

Alicia Bessette

# Nick

November 8, 2006
From: nicholas.roy@thewippamunker.com
To: rose-ellen@roymedicalillustration.com

Hi, Pants.

Today this guy, William, let me photograph him while he sanded spindles for a new hand railing near the checkout desk of the library. He had his granddaughter strapped to his back while he worked. She's this tiny little gorgeous thing. She slept the whole time. William told Dennis about the day after the hurricane. How the water in his kitchen got up to three feet from the ceiling, and he and his wife tried paddling down the street in those big Rubbermaid storage bins, but they kept capsizing. So they just swam around for a bit and climbed up onto the roof of a neighbor's house. The water was almost bottle green, he said, and they saw a couple fish flash by. Finally a couple of guys with two rowboats lashed together took them to this bridge somewhere, and under the bridge it was dry, and fifty people or so had set up camp. They were under that bridge for two days until rescue came. The water got dirtier each day, he remembered, and by the time they left, it was murky and oily, and empty soda cans and dirty diapers bobbed in it.

Now William and his wife and daughter and the little baby live here in this new neighborhood. He said his old neighborhood is pretty much a ghost town now. He said back when school started they stood out on the lawn and applauded as a yellow bus rounded the corner. They were so happy to see that bus because it meant "a return to normalcy," that's how he put it.

Dennis asked him, "Why didn't you leave?"

And William looked at him like he had six heads and said, "Because this is home."

And I can understand that. I have been thinking this crazy corny stuff, like, to have the love that we have, you and me—the roof over our head—Ahab, our little happy family—jobs that we love— beautiful Mount Wippamunk practically in our backyard—we are so lucky, Zell. Luckier than most. Also I think it's the simple things that make a person lucky. Sorry, but there has been a lot of cheesy but important talk like that among the guys down here. We all feel really fortunate. I'm still not really down with the whole three-times-a-day group-prayer thing, but you do get used to it, and well, it's interesting and it makes you think. I'm not saying I want to start going to church when I get home, but I'm just saying, maybe I'm becoming more serious about what I can offer my fellow man. Plus a few nights in a row sleeping on a concrete floor in a school cafeteria can be humbling. (We have gotten a lot of offers from people wanting us to stay with them, but Father Chet and Pastor Sheila always turn them down. So cafeteria it has been.)

Well, I was going to write more but I'm absolutely exhausted. The attached photos will have to suffice! I'll call you tomorrow at some point.

I hope your heart is being less weird!

Love,

Nick

# *8*

# Zell

March 5, 2008

From: rose-ellen@roymedicalillustration.com

To: nicholas.roy@thewippamunker.com

Hi, Hon.

Ahab got loose and ran after Old Mr. Bedard's cat. I just can't
believe it. Every night I sit on the back steps just like we used to, and
I look at the mountain. Every night I open the gate and wait for Ahab
to come walking through. I want him to walk up to me and rest his
long nose between my knees while I scratch his neck. If that happened, I would cry so hard. But he's been gone for two weeks.

I'm sorry. I'm so sorry. It's probably good that we never got around
to making ourselves a soccer team, because I would be a pretty
shitty mother. I can't even keep a dog from chasing a cat.

I hope they let you check e-mail in heaven. Or wherever you are. I
try to picture you in a fairy-tale-like place where you can snowshoe
and take photographs of birds and bobcats and deer all day long.

A perennial snowy mountainside near your own private cabin, where a perennial fire roars in a fireplace. An angel army protects you, and you always have hot chocolate, the way you like it, with a dollop of marshmallow fluff floating on the top. And whenever you want a foot rub, the heavenly version of me gives you one. That's what I wish for you.

I love you.

I miss you.

I wicked miss you.

Love,

Your Zell


IT's NOT FAR, but Garrett drives Ingrid and me to the Midmass Footpath trailhead behind the Wippamunker Building. Ingrid seems older, and taller, even though she was gone only a week. I try to remember if I felt different when *I* got back from Nature's Classroom—more curious about my surroundings, maybe? Braver? More mature?—but I can't really recall.

Garrett tells Ingrid about Ahab—that he ran away, and even though we searched long and hard, we didn't find him. She doesn't say anything, just weeps quietly in the backseat and looks out the window. After a minute she wipes the tears from her face. As we pull into the lot she asks, "When's he coming back?"

"He might not, boo-boo," says Garrett. He reaches into the backseat and strokes her chin.

She pushes his hand away. "Maybe we'll see him today, on the trail."

"We might," he says. "We certainly might."

"This one girl in my class?" says Ingrid, absently kicking the back of my seat. "Her uncle's dog went missing one day? And three months later, they found him in Kentucky. The dog walked all the way from Wippamunk to *Kentucky*."

"So maybe Ahab just felt like a road trip," I say—even though Ahab was the laziest dog in the world, and the chances of him embarking on an extended cross-country jaunt are as slim as he is.

"Exactly," she says.

We put on our snowshoes in the parking lot. It's been a while since I stood this close to the big old converted factory. Nick's dark-room was in a corner of the basement, where the walls were half dirt, half brick. But in the darkroom the walls were plastered over, of course.

Memory Smack: The day I sold my first freelance illustration I walked to the Wippamunker Building from the apartment Nick and I shared, which was right down the street. With a five-dollar bottle of champagne zipped under my fleece, I snuck unnoticed past the reception desk and descended the steep stairs. I ducked away from the cobwebs and rapped on the darkroom door.

Nick turned down Guns N' Roses and opened the door a crack. "Pay the toll," he said.

I slipped him the bottle.

"You sold something?" he asked.

"The inner ear."

"Good money?"

"Great money."

"You think you can do this? I mean, you think this is gonna work? Freelance?"

"Totally."

He opened the door. I entered and closed it behind me, savoring the darkroom's chemical smell.

We whispered. We always whispered in the darkroom. Something about it was intimate.

"That's awesome, Zell." Nick pinched the bottle between his knees and popped the cork. "Congratulations."

We passed the champagne back and forth. We laughed and kissed. He showed me, through the enlarger, some photographs he was developing for that week's sports section: the Wippamunk High School girls' soccer semifinal.

He told me how earlier that day, his dad met him for lunch and they drove to Bedard's Orchard to pick apples. And on the way there, they drove past an old house, white with orange-red shutters. Half a house, really—a twin—but a big old Victorian with new siding and a wide front porch, nonetheless.

"So?" I said. I swallowed some champagne and passed the bottle.

"So, it's for sale," said Nick. "And it's affordable."

"I'll have to make a few more sales first."

"Maybe we could get a dog."

"Maybe we could convert one of the rooms into a darkroom."

"Maybe we could have a bunch of babies."

"One thing at a time." I sidled up to him, between him and the enlarger, and wrapped my arms around his neck.

He pushed my hair back from my face. "Hello, Pants."

"Pants?"

"That's your new nickname. Cuz you wear the pants."

We laughed and made out in the red shadows. The cold tip of his nose mashed into my cheek. Behind Nick, the photograph of the ponytailed center forward heading the ball into the goal floated too long in the developer bath—so long it turned completely black.

* * *

REAL TIME, REAL PLACE. Ingrid, Garrett, and I hike past the Wip-pamunker Building, alongside the brook. Eventually the trail peels away from the water and heads north, toward the turbines of the defunct wind farm—the towers' giant white blades glint above our heads. Every now and then Ingrid calls for Ahab. But other than that, there's no sound besides the swish and crunch of aluminum in snow, and our panting breath.

After a while, Ingrid stops for a water break. "That's the rule," she says, passing me a bottle. "Hike for twenty-five minutes, break for five. I learned that in Nature's Classroom." She fishes around in her coat and holds up an empty, clear plastic baggie. "Ta-da."

"What's that for?" I ask.

"In case I see any animal scat, I can collect it."

"Always be prepared," I say.

Garrett smirks. "She never struck me as a girl who would be into that sort of thing, but hey." He crosses all his fingers on both hands, and I know he hopes Nature's Classroom somehow cured Ingrid's Polly Pinch obsession.

But his face falls when Ingrid says, "Hey, Zell, remember when we went snowshoeing and I lost my red hat? The hat that belonged to my mother? Well, my dad and I went back there the other day, and it was still there, high up in the tree."

I don't comment, just half smile.

Ingrid stuffs the little baggie into her pocket. "Are you still baking?"

"Yeah. But it's not the same without you."

"Dad says the Polly Pinch ban is still in effect. Right, Dad?"

"You have to prove yourself, Ing. You have to do your homework. All of it. For a long time. Then you can bake with Zell again."

"I know, I know." She consults her pink Hannah Montana watch. "We've got two more minutes of break time. So tell us about this trail, Zell."

I tell them about the Midmass. It's a footpath, built and maintained by volunteers, scenic despite being so close to cities and suburbs. I show Ingrid the patches EJ gave me. "Nick's dad got these for him and Nick," I say. "They were gonna hike the Midmass together, but they never got around to it."

"Can I have one?" she asks.

"Ingrid," Garrett scolds.

"It's okay." I hand her one. "Here."

"Cool, Zell. Thanks. Break time's up," she says. "Let's go. Another twenty-five." She snowshoes ahead, studying her patch and shouting for Ahab every few paces.

Garrett and I trudge behind her. "Nick's dad live around here?" he asks.

What I tell him:

1. His name is Arthur Roy, and he lives right across town in a little house on Malden Pond.
2. I haven't seen Arthur in more than a year. The memorial service he planned for Nick—because I was too distraught to plan it myself—was held a week before Christmas, at the Collins-Parks Funeral Home in town. Father Chet recited a few generic words about death and heaven and Jesus before a small gathering of Nick's mostly dark-haired, gray-eyed family, and me and my parents (Gail and Terry were in England, visiting Terry's family). Afterward, as I was getting into the back of my parents' car, Arthur approached me and thrust a heavy box into my arms. "Here," he said. In the box were ashes.

[213]

3. Arthur called me that first Christmas Eve, but I didn't pick up. He left a slurred, rambling message, something about sending me a fruit basket. I never got one.

What I don't tell Garrett:

1. I put the ashes in the attic and felt so walloped by Nick's absence that I haven't been up there since.
2. One time in high school, Nick told me his only memory of his mother, Ilene. He was on his back on a brown-and-yellow carpet and looked up through a glass table. It was someone else's house, he said, because they never had a glass table, or a two-tone carpet. His mother smiled down at him through the glass. She pressed her nose against it, and her breath fogged it up and obscured her face. That was the only time he ever talked about her.
3. Arthur left our wedding early, right after he finished his dinner.
4. He came to Okemo with Nick and me for a weekend, when Gail and Terry first moved. Nick was irritated because his dad read a book the whole time. He sat at the kitchen table in his holey socks and didn't join conversations or the Saturday night game of Trivial Pursuit. The book he read was about gardening; I remember because of the irony: Arthur doesn't garden—he didn't then, either—and his yard's always looked unruly and overgrown, like his beard.

Garrett and I snowshoe next to each other, not really talking much, for a good while. Ingrid's fifty feet ahead. Whenever the trail curves, we lose sight of her, but we hear her call, "Ahab!"

"So the contest deadline's coming up, right?" asks Garrett. He's obviously changing the subject, and I wonder if I went on too long about Nick's dad.

"In a couple days," I say. "Yeah."

"Have you got anything?"

I explain my recipe involving strawberry yogurt and Nutella. It's totally not what EJ recommended, but I just can't come up with anything fresh and *foodie,* as he says. I guess I'm in a rut.

"I know I won't win," I say. "But I have to finish what I started, right?"

"Right."

I ask him about the babysitting situation, and he says Ingrid's going to spend a lot more time with Trudy. It's hard for him to ask for help, but she seems to love having Ingrid around, he says, and he's glad for her involvement, because a girl should know her family, and Trudy's the only family around, really.

"She cried her heart out when I told her she couldn't bake with you," he says. "Cried her heart out."

I look up the trail. A man stands a few feet from Ingrid, a fellow hiker. I hear her ask him if he's seen a dog.

"Ingrid!" shouts Garrett, hands cupped around his mouth.

The man has a roundish head of black-and-white hair. A beard grows close to his eyes and almost completely covers his cheeks. He doesn't wear snowshoes. Red gaiters cinch just below his knees and cover all but the toes of his boots.

For a second—even less than a second—I don't recognize him. Then I think, it's what Nick would look like in thirty years, if he stopped shaving.

Arthur. I run to him, a bouncy, slow-motion run, because of my snowshoes, which slap my heels with each stride.

I stop when I'm a foot from him, and then I don't know what to do. Arthur doesn't say anything, just squeezes his eyes shut and hugs me tight. I can't remember the last time he hugged me. My wedding, maybe?

I let myself be hugged. Finally I stand back as Garrett catches up to us.

"This is Arthur Roy," I say. "Nick's dad. These are my neighbors, Ingrid and Garrett."

"We're gonna turn around now and head back," says Garrett. He squeezes Ingrid's hand. "We'll wait for you in the parking lot."

After they turn, she says, "Daddy, is Zell okay with that man?"

"She's fine," Garrett says. "She's going to be fine."

Arthur hears the exchange and smiles sadly after them. He clears snow from a nearby fallen log and gestures for me to sit with him.

"I haven't been hiking in so long," he says.

I look at the ground. I realize he's probably had those gaiters since the 1970s.

"It feels good to be out here," he goes on. "Isn't it a shame that all these years this old trail's been here, so close by, and Nick and I never took advantage of it?"

"It isn't so surprising to me," I say. "I bet there are a lot of people around here who intend to take advantage of it but never do."

"Maybe I *will* hike the Midmass after all. Maybe you and I can do it together." Without looking at me, he grips my knee.

"I'd like that," I say, even though I know we'll never hike it together. We just won't.

"I lost Ilene. Nick was so small when that happened. He couldn't even talk yet." He sighs. "And then I lost Nick. Our boy."

He holds his hand over his eyes, like he's shading them. He sits like this for a while, and soon his pinkie trembles. "I'm sorry I haven't been around at all, Zell," he says.

"Me, too."

"I just can't."

"I understand."

"I know you do," says Arthur.

A twitchy squirrel crosses the path a few feet away. It hops over the upturned snow, then skitters up a tree, and soon after, we hear hikers approach, and our heads turn in the direction of crunching snow. An older couple tramps past, the man huffing heavily, the wife searching the bare branches for songbirds. She smiles and says, "Beautiful day." Arthur nods and waves in response.

When they're out of view, when we can't hear the scrunch of their snowshoes, Arthur turns and looks me straight in the eye. "Spread his ashes?"

"Not yet," I say, swallowing a lump in my throat.

He nods.

"Not yet," I repeat, a little louder this time. He grips my shoulder and pulls me tight, and we sit locked in a sideways hug for a long time, until my toes and nose turn numb.

A FEW EVENINGS AFTER THE MIDMASS HIKE, I wake slumped at my drafting table. Before me is the outline of a spleen I started. I drooled on it, apparently. So I tear the paper from the clips and ball it up and hurl it at Hank.

My heart hammers wildly, then slows, as Gladys sings about neither one of us wanting to be the first to say good-bye.

I realize I'm hungry. Ravenously, deliriously hungry. So I go downstairs. I root around in the refrigerator, knocking over a pickle jar, a jelly jar, a tub of butter. I open the freezer door, and behind a stack of frozen Polly Pinch meals, I notice the small white package labeled FAIRY GOAT MOTHER FARM. 100% ORGANIC. MADE WITH

LOVE BY TRUDY KNOX. It's the goat cheese that Trudy gave me that first time I visited her house and saw the Barn.

I lean against the counter. "All this time," I say in Ahab Voice, "and you've been settin' on buried treasure."

First, I thaw the goat cheese in the microwave. Next, I preheat the oven. An image leaps to mind: Nick's mystery present, blazing away on the top rack.

They say fire is therapeutic. Cleansing.

"Ha!" I shout.

My fridge has one of those old-fashioned egg savers—a dozen roundish indentations on a built-in tray. In one of the little indentations sits not an egg, but a lime. I pluck it; greenish gray mold clings to the very bottom. I slice off the moldy part and grind it up in the garbage disposal. "Mere jetsam, lads!" I say. "Cast it to the gray water. Arr." I juice the remainder of the lime, unsure of the role it will play.

Next, I survey the cans in my cupboard. Great Northern beans? No. Artichoke hearts? Pass. Pineapple rings?

Hmm. Pineapple rings.

I open the dusty can and drain the juice. I arrange the rings in a casserole dish and smear goat cheese on top. I pour the lime juice over it. Next I reach into the cupboard and pull out honey and drizzle it on, long and slow and thick.

"Into the fire it goes! Yarr!" I put it in the oven.

Minutes later, I slide my hands into my dollar-store camo oven mitts, courtesy of Garrett, and watch the timer tick off the few remaining seconds until—ding!

I reach into the oven. I lift the lid off the casserole dish. The pores of my skin open as fragrant limey steam rises.

After it cools, I taste it. It's not quite a winner yet. And besides, it lacks Ingrid's special touches, her contributions.

But it's a start.

It's a g.d. start.

WINDOWS DOWN. Icy wind whipping. Heat blasting. I fly up Main Street. In the passenger seat sits the casserole dish.

I stick my head out the window and howl into the flying-by night. I howl all the way to Trudy's house.

INGRID'S AT THE KITCHEN COUNTER doing homework when I walk in, and she slides off the stool and runs to me and smashes her bony little body into mine. I hold the heavy dish out to keep my balance.

"Hold on," I say. "I don't want to break Garrett's rules."

"What do you mean?" Trudy says.

"I have a baking question." I set the dessert on the counter.

Ingrid pushes her books and papers aside. "For the Warm the Soul contest? You got something?"

I nod. "I need your opinion, Ing."

Trudy peers over her glasses at the dessert. "I hereby declare that I am making an executive decision to temporarily lift the ban on baking, so that Ingrid and I can direct our friend in her endeavors."

Ingrid claps.

"Now, mind you." Trudy turns the dial on her gas stove until flames lick the pan of hot chocolate. "I'm no longer the authority on such things. I'm old. I've passed the torch."

"What torch?" wonders Ingrid.

"To who?" I ask.

"To *whom,*" Trudy says. "The Muffin Man, of course. He's more of a success than I ever was. After all, as the saying goes, 'Those who can't do, teach.'"

"I'll take it to him." I lift the lid off the dish. "But right now I want you guys to test it out."

Ingrid licks her lips. "Smells scrumpy."

"I don't think it's quite there yet," I say. "But almost."

Trudy hands me a butter knife. It sinks through the layers of goat cheese, pineapple, and gooey, hot honey. I transfer a small portion to a red glass plate, which Trudy extends to me.

Elbow sharply raised, pinkie extended, Ingrid carves out a small bite with a fork. She lets her lips close around the tines.

"Well?" I say.

She swallows and folds her hands in her lap. "Assertive. Tangy. Creamy. The goat cheese balances the acidity of the pineapple quite nicely."

I stare at Ingrid. Trudy throws her head back and cackles, witchlike.

Ingrid shrugs. "What?"

"Nothing," I say. "So do I have something?"

"Oh yeah," she says. "You have something. Your turn, Trudy." She pushes the plate toward her.

"Be brutally honest," I say.

Trudy raises a wiry gray eyebrow as Ingrid offers her the fork.

She takes a bite, nods enthusiastically, and crosses the kitchen to pour hot chocolate into three fairy mugs. "It's delicious," she says. "Now, you see? All those experiments you thought were failures weren't really failures at all. It's because of those quote-unquote failures that you were able to create *this*. You understand?"

There she goes again, getting all Master Yoda on me. "I do understand, Trudy," I say.

She sucks her dentures. "I think—and this is only my opinion—I think it lacks presentation. First of all, it needs a crust. As it is, it's way too messy looking. A crust would hold it all together. And also, you need to fem it up a little bit."

"Fem it up?" Ingrid takes a slurp of hot chocolate. "What does that mean?"

"It means, make it girly," Trudy says. "Make it your own."

"Right," I say. "Make it my own. Got a big cookie sheet or something, Trudy?"

"Please," she says. "You've come to the right place."

She sets a cookie sheet on the counter, and I dump the contents of the casserole dish onto it. It slowly spreads to the edges.

"Uh, I'm not quite sure where you're going with this, Zell," says Trudy, mug paused halfway to her chin.

"Color," I say. "It needs color. It needs . . ."

Ingrid and Trudy search each other's faces for ideas.

"Berries?" Ingrid suggests.

Trudy snaps her fingers and pulls a bowl of raspberries from her fridge. "I just thawed these babies this morning. Picked 'em over the summer and froze 'em. Want 'em warmed up?"

"Nope. Chilled. Just like that." My fingers sink into the cold berries, which stain my fingers. I sprinkle them on the dessert.

"Now, how about brown sugar?" I say. "Just a dusting."

Trudy pulls a box of brown sugar from a cupboard and hands it to me. The crystals fall from my fingers and catch the light.

"Don't forget Polly Pinch's most important rule," Ingrid says. " 'Give it something unexpected.' "

I reach for the pepper grinder by Trudy's stove, next to the fairy trivet.

"Ooh," Ingrid says as I grind away. "I love me a pepper grinder."

"Knife me," I finally say.

Trudy slaps the blunt butter knife into my palm, and I shape what's left of the warm, peppery, limey, honey-smothered, raspberries-and-brown-sugar-topped, pineapple, goat cheese mélange into a two-humped cartoon Valentine heart.

"Now, that's what I call femming it up," Trudy says.

Ingrid claps. "Don't forget that pinch!" She mimics Polly's slowly batted eyelids, her slowly parting lips.

As if playing charades, Trudy takes the lid off an imaginary canister and offers it to me. I dip my fingers into it and flick them over the dessert, sprinkling it with a pinch of love.

"What do you call it?" Trudy asks.

"I haven't thought of a name, actually," I say. "The real question is, What *is* it?"

"I got an idea," says Ingrid. She clears her throat. "Why don't you use the word 'scrumpy' in the title? 'Scrumpy' is my favorite adjective. I made it up. It means, 'scrump, but better.' "

"I like it," says Trudy. "Scrumpy Pineapple Pie?"

"It's not really a pie, though," I say.

"Throw a crust on it and it will be," says Trudy.

"It's more like a pudding," I say. "Ish. 'Scrumpy Pineapple Puddingish Pie'?"

Trudy shakes her head. "Who the hell would eat that?"

Ingrid gets somber. "How about we name it after Ahab? What's his full name again, Zell?"

"Captain Ahab's Midnight Delight."

She mulls this over, drumming her fingers on the counter. "So we could call it 'Scrumpy Delight.' For Ahab."

"Scrumpy Delight," I repeat. "And so it is." I flick a little more love to christen the lopsided concoction. It's lost its heart shape and now looks as pitiful and lumpy as Old Man Bedard's cat. "A dessert only a mother could love," I say.

Trudy sighs. "Let's hope not."

* * *

WE POLISH OFF THE REST OF THE SCRUMPY DELIGHt. It really does taste pretty good, but I make a mental note to include less lime juice, to cut back on the wateriness.

Ingrid finishes her homework and goes to bed. But she's reading, I know, because when I go to the bathroom, I see the light on in the spare bedroom.

Trudy and I drink hot chocolate. She spikes hers with two thimbles of Dr. McGillicuddy's Peppermint Schnapps, which she keeps locked in a liquor cabinet she made when she first became interested in working with wood. She offers me some schnapps, but I decline because I've got to drive home.

Trudy, in the rocker next to the wood-burning stove, grows tipsier with each sip. She becomes philosophical, which even a little schnapps is bound to do to a person who doesn't drink often. She talks about how grateful she is, every day, that she's able to be a Renaissance woman and pursue her various "blisses," as she says: chain saws, goats, fairies. She wonders aloud whether it's chance, or fate, or somehow both, that bring people where they are in life.

Trudy and I don't talk for a good long while—we just sit, sip, and listen to the mantel clock tick.

As I get up to leave, she throws both arms around me, rests her chin on my head, and steers me to the door. "Well, Zell, there's only one thing I know that's harder than death," she says. She helps me into my coat. "And it seems to me like you're doing a pretty decent job at it."

"What's that?" I say, yanking on my mittens.

"Life."

* * *

W-H-E-E-E-E-E-Z-E.

Eight o'clock Saturday morning. I rub the sleep from my eyes, stumble downstairs, and answer the door yawning. Garrett's on my porch. Ingrid sleeps in his arms; she's still in her pajamas.

"She got up early to watch cooking shows," he whispers. "But then she fell asleep on the couch. She looked so cute, I just couldn't wake her. I need you, Zell. I'm really in a bind, here. Trudy fell repairing the goat fence. She tripped on the ice."

"Oh no," I say. "That's horrible. Is she okay?"

"She's fine. Just needs a couple stitches; that's all. A friend's with her at the emergency room. I have an exam this morning."

Ingrid murmurs in her sleep.

"You're my only backup," he says.

"I'll take her," I say. "I'll watch her. But I'm baking. I mean, I'm doing Polly Pinch stuff. Today's the deadline. I'm perfecting."

Garrett nods. "Consider the ban lifted." Gently he drapes Ingrid on my couch. I take her backpack from him.

"You're a goddess, Zell. Anyone ever tell you that?"

"You're the first," I say, smiling. "But you won't be the last."

He chuckles, and Ingrid stirs and looks around. "Dad?"

"The ban's lifted, boo-boo," he says. He kisses her forehead.

"The ban's lifted?"

"Yes. Now I gotta run."

She stands and grins sleepily. They do a quick version of their kissing game; he looks around nonchalantly, then suddenly swoops down to kiss her. She giggles and tries to avoid him, but he smacks her once on the nose and once on the neck.

"Wait." Ingrid yawns. "Does this mean you'll definitely let me go on *Pinch of Love Live* with Zell, if we win?"

Garrett smirks. "Sure. If you're a finalist, you can be a special guest on the show."

"Pinkie swear?"

"Pinkie swear. Gotta go. Love ya 'n' like ya."

"Love ya 'n' *love* ya," Ingrid says.

S HE CHANGES INTO CLOTHES, and we hop into the car. I drive to the grocery store with a deep sheet print still slicing my cheek. In the produce aisle, Ingrid and I sniff seven different pineapples before selecting the most fragrant one.

"Better get two," she says as I load the heavy fruit into the shopping basket.

"Why?"

"Because you're Zell; that's why. You need backup. In case something crazy happens with the first pineapple."

"Crazy?"

"Like smoke. Or flames. Or explosions."

I hesitate, wondering whether I should be insulted. But when she nods and grins, I grab another pineapple and hand it to her. "You're absolutely right, Ing."

We stock up on raspberries and honey, limes and pepper, too. In the checkout aisle, Ingrid tosses two chocolate bars onto the conveyer belt. "This brand's safe for kids with peanut allergies," she says.

"Is that your breakfast?"

"Breakfast? No, it's for the Scrumpy Delight. Don't you know what my mother always says? 'Just about every dessert is improved by chocolate.' "

At home, we set about creating Scrumpy Delight, Prototype II. I grumble about making a crust, but Ingrid bats her hand. "Just whip up a Super Simp Flaky."

I steady a cutting board and slice the top off the pineapple. "I forgot Polly Pinch has a piecrust recipe."

"I'll go find it online." She pounds upstairs to use the laptop in my office and minutes later skips back into the kitchen waving a printout. "Found it."

"I have an idea," I say. "We're going to grill the pineapple." That trash-picked old grill was Nick's domain, but I don't think he'd mind if I used it now.

"Grill it?" Ingrid says. "*Love* it."

Out back, I'm amazed the coals ignite. I scrape some flaky black gunk off the metal and lay fresh pineapple rings across it. Before long, juice drips and sizzles, and brown grooves form in the fruit.

Back inside, I chop the pineapple into small chunks and stir it with softened goat cheese, honey, and a little lime juice. Ingrid grinds pepper into the mixture, singing a little ditty about how she loves pepper grinders. We prepare a Super Simp Flaky—which lives up to its name—put an entire chocolate bar in the center, and spoon the pineapple mixture on top. I attempt to fold it into a heart shape. But the crust rips, and the baking sheet just isn't big enough, and the pineapple mixture oozes everywhere. I try to salvage some, but a big blob slips to the floor and splatters.

"Aren't you glad I made you get a second pineapple?" Ingrid says.

Round two. I slice the second pineapple into spears and grill them. When we've got another Super Simp Flaky ready to go, I whip up more pineapple-cheese mixture and spoon it on top of the chocolate bar.

"Now what?" I wonder. "Should I try making a heart again?"

"Try something different," says Ingrid.

I drag the edges of the crust toward one another, forming a sort of rectangular shape. The baking tray accommodates it perfectly, and the dough stays intact.

"Perf!" says Ingrid. "It looks like an envelope."

"An envelope of deliciousness."

"Right."

Twenty-five minutes later, as I pull the tray from the oven, she gasps. "It smells so good," she says. We wait for the quasi tart to cool a bit. Ingrid stands on a footstool and edges the crust with raspberries. Then she sprinkles the whole thing with brown sugar and love.

"I wish Ahab were here to sample this," she says.

"Do you think he would be proud of us?"

"I do." She nods. "I do."

"Me, too. Well, time to write all this down."

"Aren't we going to taste test it?"

"We are, but not just yet."

We march upstairs. Following a traditional recipe format as best I can, I type exactly what we did into a Word document. She watches over my shoulder, saying, "Good job, Zell," every few minutes.

"Now for the true test," I say when I'm done. "The Muffin Man."

Ingrid does a few pliés. "Awesome. I can't wait."

"I'll let him know we're coming."

Travis answers the phone: "Thanks for calling the Muffinry for the best coffee and muffins west of 495," he says. He pronounces it "faw-niney-fy." "Can you hold?"

"Travis, it's Rose-Ellen. EJ's friend. Is he there?"

"He's wicked busy. Saturday morning and all."

"Tell him I think I've got something."

"Huh?"

"Just please tell him I think I've got something."

There's some muffled noises.

"Zell?" It's EJ. "You got something?"

"I got something."

"Well, what the hell are you waiting for? Get over here and let me sample it."

Ingrid sits in the backseat as I drive to Murtonen's Muffinry. Under my thigh I tuck an envelope addressed to the contest judges at Scrump Studios in Boston. The envelope is unsealed, so we can show EJ the recipe before we mail it.

I watch Ingrid in the rearview mirror. She's holding the platter of Scrumpy Delight on her lap.

"Don't breathe on it," I say.

"I'm not breathing on it," she says. "I'm not even breathing."

"Don't touch it."

"Just drive, woman."

The Muffinry bustles. The bell jingles almost constantly as customers come and go. The only available table is the one in the corner, near the register. Here EJ waits. He's dressed in his usual garb: clogs, checkered pants, Bruins bandana. He stands when he spots us and grandly gestures for Ingrid to set the platter on the table.

Travis emerges from the kitchen and hands EJ a dessert fork and a small, sharp knife.

"Wow," Travis says. He raises his eyebrows and nods at the platter. "Nice presentation."

EJ points to the register, where a line of customers waits.

"I'm going, hey," Travis says. "I'm going."

"Now, then," EJ says. He carves out a piece of Scrumpy Delight, sniffs it, and pops it into his mouth. He chews slowly, tipping his chin and exhaling heavily through his nose. He strokes his goatee and swallows.

"The raspberries are a nice touch," he says.

Ingrid punches the air. "Yessss! The raspberries were Zell's call. For color."

He places another piece of Scrumpy Delight on the center of his tongue and closes his lips around it. He runs his tongue along the insides of his cheeks. He swallows and smacks his lips, tasting his mouth. "Goat cheese?"

"Yesss!" Ingrid punches the air again.

"Organic." I nod. "Made right here in town."

"By my step-grandmother." Ingrid shadowboxes EJ's stomach.

He laughs and waves her away. "That?" he says, pointing to the dessert. "Whatever that is? It makes me silent."

"Silent?" says Ingrid. She's unsure whether that's good.

EJ swipes off his bandana and holds it over his heart. "Silent out of respect."

"It's good?" I say.

"It's excellent." He refits his bandana. "I think you've turned a corner with this dessert, Zell. And, as we used to say at Johnson and Wales"—he covers Ingrid's ears with his hands—"this dessert is going to put asses in seats."

"I heard you," Ingrid says.

EJ feeds her a bite, and her eyes grow huge. "Mmm," she says, nodding.

"Now, tell me," says EJ. "What do you call it?"

I show him the recipe. He scans it, underlining words with his pinkie. "Pineapple and goat cheese and chocolate and brown sugar. Genius. Absolutely brilliant."

Ingrid bursts into a sort of hula dance. She waves her arms and chants, "Uh-*huh*, uh-*huh*, Zell's brilliant, she's genius."

EJ high-fives me. "Did it come from a dream?" he asks.

"Indirectly. I made it right under the wire, too. This sucker's got to be postmarked today." I reach for the fork, but EJ's staring at me. "What?"

"Well—then what are you doing here?" he says.

Ingrid stops hula dancing. "What do you mean?"

He points to the clock. "The post office closes at *noontime* on Saturdays."

I push my chair back from the table. Am I that out of touch with Wippamunk—with the world—that I don't even know this basic fact of weekly life?

"It does not," I say. "Please tell me the post office doesn't close at twelve."

"Yyyyeah. It does. And it's—eleven fifty-four."

"What if I drop it in a collection box somewhere in town? Would it get postmarked today?"

"In theory, I suppose," EJ says. "But you never know."

Balls.

Ingrid snatches the recipe from EJ. She and I quick step to my car. The post office isn't far. Sixty, maybe ninety seconds up the street.

In the backseat she licks the envelope and seals it. A space in the traffic opens, and I jerk the wheel left and swing into the first parking spot. Her head whacks against the window with the sudden momentum.

"Ouch?" she says.

"Sorry."

It's eleven fifty-eight.

She sprints to the post office doors, but they're locked. She pounds on the glass as I join her at the door. Inside a bald man in a gray uniform glances at her and quickly ducks into a back room.

"Hey!" she yells. She pounds on the glass some more. "Hey, you in there!"

The inside lights turn off. "Are you kidding me, sir?" I yell. "It's not twelve yet. It's eleven fifty-eight. Okay. It's eleven fifty-nine. But it's not twelve."

Ingrid rests a cheek on the glass and looks at me with the face of a pitiful puppy. "We could drive our entry to Boston and hand deliver it," she says.

I bang my head. "Balls, balls, balls."

The door Ingrid's leaning on swings open. She stumbles over the threshold, nearly into the bald man in gray, who now wears a windbreaker. He zips it to his chin and frowns. "Do you know what today is?"

I grab the envelope and thrust it at him. "I know very well what today is. It's March tenth, and it's the same date that needs to be postmarked on this envelope. *Please*."

The man reaches his arm out the door, aims his car keys down the parking lot, where several other cars are parked, and pushes a button. In the back of the building an engine rumbles.

"Today, young lady, is my first golf outing of the season. I've got a two twenty-five tee time on the Cape, and I've been fantasizing about it since last fall, the last time I golfed. And I'm not gonna miss my tee time. So if you'll kindly excuse me."

"But it's not twelve yet," Ingrid says. She makes an exaggerated sad face.

The man looks at his watch. "Wulp, it is now. It's 12:01, in fact." He steps outside between us, relocks the door, and marches toward his car.

I glance inside; a light remains on in the back room, where a few workers chat and sort mail.

I grab Ingrid's hand and follow the man up the sidewalk. I'm not really sure what I'm going to do or say. But from behind the building a rusty Jeep careens around the corner. Russ. He skids to a stop, rolls down his window, and toots the horn. "Hiya, Zell. Ingrid."

"A little help here, Russ?"

He slaps the steering wheel. "Come on, Phil," he says to the man. "Why don't you let the lovely ladies here inside? Lick their stamps and give 'em a thrill."

"Because I've got a two twenty-five tee time—"

"I know, I know," Russ says. "And you've been dreaming about it since last fall. Listen, I'll take care of them."

Phil bats a hand at Russ, as if to say good riddance, and continues to his car.

Russ parks, and we follow him to the door. He pretends not to notice as I wipe tears from my face with my sleeve. I don't know why, but I'm crying.

"It's okay, Zell," whispers Ingrid. She squeezes my hand. "We made it."

Russ puts a key into the lock. "Now, zen," he says, in an exaggerated French accent, because he always finds a way to dork up a situation. "You have a spess-yee-ale some-sing to mail?"

Ingrid tells him how we pulled into the post office parking lot at eleven fifty-eight, but the grumpy man wanted to go golfing and wouldn't let us in, which was very, very unfair.

Russ acts as if her story is the most fascinating he's heard in a long while. As she talks, he takes a spot behind the first window, pushes a few buttons on the computer, and folds his hands on top of the scale. "Let's do this," he says.

I hand Ingrid the envelope, and she rolls onto her tiptoes and hands it to Russ.

"Anything liquid, fragile, perishable, or potentially hazardous?" he asks.

"Huh?" says Ingrid.

"I'll take that as a no."

"Of course," she says, "I don't know why we didn't just *e-mail* our entry. Wouldn't that have been easier, Zell?"

"From the mouths of babes." Russ tosses the postmarked envelope into a dingy bin.

G.d.

I cover my face with both hands. "I forgot about that option, Ing. But you're certainly right. It would have been easier."

"No matter," she says. "We made it. Thank you, Mr. Russ."

# EJ

It's a good thing Charlene has free long distance, because EJ talks to her tonight for almost two hours. She calls and asks right away if her latest delivery of chicory arrived, and for the first time, he lies to her.

"Not yet," he says. "It'll probably come tomorrow." He doesn't want to talk about her letter that was packed with the chicory; he'd get too nervous. He wants to write his response.

They talk, and somehow they get onto the subject of childhood summers, and she tells him about the sleepaway camp in Mississippi where she was a camper and later a counselor. He tells her about his closest equivalent: Nature's Classroom. How one night after dinner, a camp counselor was going to teach the song "Moon Shadow." Nick raised his hand and said he knew it, because his dad taught him. And he got up there next to the counselor on the little platform, and the counselor strummed her guitar, and Nick sang. At first a couple of kids snickered, but eventually everyone grew still and listened. Nick was a ten-year-old folk star. He led sixty-five kids and fifteen adults in his own squeaky-voiced version of Cat Stevens.

EJ talks and talks, and Charlene laughs at all the right moments. After they finally say good night, EJ finds, in a bottom drawer of his mother's buffet—stuffed away with taper candles that have never been lit and a brocade runner for the dining room table—stationery. Thick, cream-colored paper with shimmery gold trim and matching envelopes. The buffet was among several pieces of furniture his mother left behind when she moved, because she thought the moist ocean air of Truro would ruin them somehow.

The stationery smells like candles. He spreads it on the dining room table, thinking that his mother would yell at him for writing there because the pen might make marks in the wood. But he doesn't worry about this now.

It's been a while since he's written a real letter, with pen and paper. He feels silly, self-conscious. His handwriting is blocky and slanted and ugly. But he writes because Charlene will like it.

*Dear Charlene,*

*I'm not much of a writer, so this is going to be a short letter. I don't think I've written a letter since middle school when me and my friends used to pass notes in class all the time, my spelling is bad so I apologize in advance for any stupid mistakes. I want you to know that I'm coming down to see you. I don't know when, exactly, but it'll be soon. Aside from the Muffinry I have no real attachments here. I know you know this already but my parents are divorced and I never see them anymore, I live in the house I grew up in, and a lot of times it's lonely. I don't know why I'm writing about all this right now. Anyway, I'll come down. We'll spend some time together. We'll talk and figure things out. I am glad you feel the way you feel, I feel that way too, like we are good friends—great friends—who could probably be something much more.*

*Love (and I do mean that),*

*EJ*

*P.S. To answer your question, I am very attracted to you.*

*2nd P.S. I'm bringing you a surprise. Two surprises, actually. You'll see.*

# Nick

November 9, 2006
From: nicholas.roy@thewippamunker.com
To: rose-ellen@roymedicalillustration.com

Hey. It's late. Everybody's asleep but I can't sleep. I would call you but I don't want to wake you up. I'm typing this in my sleeping bag.

I could get mad—very mad—about the government's response to Hurricane Katrina. I could come away disillusioned, defeated, deflated, dispirited, ashamed of my country. I bet a lot of volunteers leave feeling that way. I'm sure the people who live here feel that way, too, sometimes. And I don't blame them. Not at all. And I won't deny that there is some of that in me. There is disappointment. And at times, disgust.

But there is also hope. The hope is bigger than the disappointment. Maybe that's easy for me to say. I'm sure if I'd been living down here after Katrina hit, I'd feel very different.

I wouldn't quite say I feel proud or patriotic, but when I look around down here, I see so many people united. Coming together to build a better world. To help each other heal.

I hope these e-mails don't freak you out. I know I probably don't sound like the Nick you're used to. But don't worry, Pants. I'm still the same old Nick. I'm not about to join an ashram or take a vow of silence or something.

But I think you'll like the new me. Because I want my life—our lives—to have meaning. I want the work I do to affect other people in a good way. I want to touch others' lives and improve them, without condescending to them. That's a fine line to walk, but I think I know how to do it. And I think I can teach our soccer team how to do it, too.

This trip is giving me confidence. I know I never really talk about this, but a lot of times I feel sort of stupid for never having gone to college. (At least not a regular four-year college.) Sometimes I feel less than an intellectual, because I am, I guess. But being down here, I know that even just doing little things—even when I just show up and smile at someone—I am making a difference and I am doing enough. And you don't need to have a bachelor's degree to do that. Also there is no job too small or unimportant and you don't need to be a master carpenter to come down here and help. All you need is love, to quote John Lennon. Sounds cheesy, maybe even cliché. But I guess there is a reason cheesy clichés become cheesy clichés, if you catch my drift. But that's neither here nor there. . . .

Lately I've been thinking a lot about the injustices in life. Why are there people in the world whose every possession is wiped out, whose world is crushed, whose family is scattered about, and then there are people like us, so lucky, so happy, with (knock on wood— knock on my head!) no major catastrophes to speak of? I wonder why that is. Who is in charge of all that? Do you ever wonder about stuff like this? You probably do. You're "deeper" than me. That's one of the things I love about you.

I can't wait to see you and kiss you all over and just hold you in my arms for a while. I keep imagining our reunion in the driveway. You'll come running out to meet me. Ahab will be waiting at the door. Do you realize that we've been married eight years, and we've never spent any time apart? Ever, until now?

We're leaving tomorrow afternoon. In the morning EJ wants me to go with him and Charlene to tour a construction site—some big new church they're building on the outskirts of town. I still don't feel tiptop, but I'll go. Why not? I might get ideas for the Man-Shed EJ and I are going to build in his backyard. A Man-Shed with an attached sauna. More on that later.

Then we're hitting the road. And I'll see you day after tomorrow!!! DAY AFTER TOMORROW!

I love you.

Nick

# 9

## Zell

GLADYS SINGS OF SITTING ALONE with no love to call her own.
I wear Nick's apron. I drink coffee like a pro. So what if it makes my hands shake? So what if I risk spilling on my anterior view of digestion? I live on the g.d. edge.

My digestion is front on, no hiding. It's heavy on 242: PEACH FUZZ and 276: NAVEL ORANGE. I've been at it for days, and now all the big players shine up at me: esophagus and stomach, transverse colon and intestines. They make an odd combination of organs, delicate yet diligent. Mouth is there, too, and oral cavity, and glottis; few people realize digestion begins here, with the first bite.

I'm about to sign my initials when—wheeze. W-h-e-e-e-e-e-z-e.

France stands on my porch. She's dressed off duty, as she dressed in high school: hiking boots, jeans, fleece vest. Her brown hair is pulled back into a stunted ponytail, like always. Loose short wisps float above her ears.

"Hey, girlfriend," she says.

I lean in and give her a hug. "Hey."

"I was out hiking just now."

"Beautiful day for it," I say, because it's one of those early spring days when the sun's so bright, it's almost painful. But in a good way.

"I was looking for Captain Ahab," she says. "I hiked along the power lines for a while, behind the Muffinry. Then I headed north about a mile, toward the mountain." She reaches into her pocket. "Anyway. I found this."

In her palm is the fairy charm. The beaded wings are scuffed and chipped, and one foot is missing.

"It's Ahab's, isn't it?" she says, handing it to me.

I fold my fingers over it and nod. The damaged wires poke my skin.

"Maybe it means he's near," she says. "He's trying to get back to you by following the power lines to Main Street. Or maybe he felt like an adventure and followed the power lines in the opposite direction and walked all the way to New Hampshire. Or maybe it means nothing, other than the fairy came loose or got snagged on something and fell off."

"Did you look around for him?" I ask. "I mean, in the place where you found this?"

"I looked all around. I called for him. I even sang that dumb 'Cookie Time' song Nick used to sing." She purses her lips into a half smile, remembering.

Guilt creeps in—guilt and regret for letting Ahab get away—and I hang my head. "Oh, I'm sorry, Captain," I say. I step onto the porch, wondering how Nick would react if he were here. Would he be angry with me for letting Ahab escape? Or would he understand, and forgive me?

Next to me, France leans on the railing. "It's not your fault, Zell."

The mail truck careens around the corner now. Metallica blares. Russ screeches to a stop in front of the house, snaps off the radio—which is attached with a bungee cord to the dashboard—and mounts the steps. He stuffs mail in the Knoxes' box, then hands me mine: a paycheck, a credit card offer, and the newest issue of *Meals in a Cinch*, which I now subscribe to. As always, Polly adorns the cover. This month she straddles a hot pink motorized scooter, and her shiny locks flow from underneath a matching helmet. I glance at the headline and notice it somehow combines the words "vroom vroom" and "chili."

I sigh and try to put Ahab out of my mind. "Nothing from Scrump Studios, huh?" I say.

"It's only been a couple weeks," Russ says. "Patience, my child." He jabs my arm, then France's, and skips down the steps and drives off.

"Hey," France says. "Want to go get that beer now?"

"Not just now," I say. "But soon."

She gives me a quick hug and takes the porch steps and walks backward a few paces toward the street, squinting in the sunlight. "You'll be okay, Zell."

She pivots and strides down High Street toward the apple orchard.

"Thank you," I call after her, and she waves without turning around.

SATURDAY MORNING. Gladys sings about how life is so crazy, how love is unkind.

The spleen I'm drawing looks like a lax, mottled fist, gray and purplish, tucked under the ribs, under the dome of the diaphragm. My spleen is a warrior—it destroys and recycles red blood cells. But it's also a reservoir, saving the blood until it's most needed.

The doorbell wheezes. I go downstairs and see Russ's outline through the gauzy curtain. I open the door. Ingrid's next to him. Her hair is swept into a side ponytail above her right ear. Garrett waits behind her, hands on her shoulders.

"What's up?" I say.

"Open it," says Ingrid, as Russ hands me a big pink envelope. He raises his eyebrows a couple of times, like a vaudevillian. He switches his mailbag from one shoulder to the other.

I study the envelope. It was postmarked in Boston, and the return address reads "Scrump Studios."

I tear it open and unfold official Desserts That Warm the Soul! letterhead.

"Is it from my mother?" Ingrid says. "Read it out loud."

Garrett pulls her against him as I read.

" 'Dear Ms. Rose-Ellen Roy, Congratulations! You are one of two contest entrants chosen to appear on the first-ever episode of *Pinch of Love Live*, the live version of Polly Pinch's original hit show, *Pinch of Love*. Polly is excited to bake your Scrumpy Delight live in front of a studio audience—alongside you and a guest of your choosing—on May fifth!' "

Russ flaps his elbows like chicken wings and screams, "Cock-a-doodle-doo!" Ingrid shushes him. "Sorry," he says. "Please continue."

I keep reading. " 'The winner of twenty thousand dollars will be announced at the conclusion of the taping. Please call Scrump Studios at the number below as soon as possible so that we can make further arrangements. I look forward to discussing with you what will happen on May fifth. You should feel proud of your accomplishment. More than two thousand entries—from all over the world—were received.' "

"Is it signed Polly Pinch?" asks Ingrid.

I scan the letter. "No. It's from Polly Pinch's personal and executive assistant, Mr. Spike Miller."

Ingrid pulls the page away from my face and peers at me. "What does this mean, exactly?"

"It means our dessert—"

"Our *genius* dessert."

"Scrumpy Delight might win twenty thousand dollars. We'll find out on May fifth."

"And?" she says.

"And, it means I get to go to Boston and be on *Pinch of Love Live.*"

Her bottom lip quivers. "Does it mean I get to meet Polly Pinch?"

Garrett chews his lip.

"I've been good." Ingrid tugs his arm as if she's ringing a huge heavy bell. "I've been doing my homework. And extra credit. And plus, you lifted the ban."

"Are you *sure* you're a finalist?" Garrett says.

I show him the letter.

He glances it over, scraping his bottom lip with his front teeth as he reads. He looks unsure, as if he's wondering if it's a good idea, after all, to let his Polly-obsessed daughter meet her idol on live television.

"All right," he says.

"Yes?" she says.

"On the condition that you say absolutely nothing—zero—to Polly Pinch about her being your mother. Not a single word. Is that understood?"

"Why not?" she says.

"Because it wouldn't be appropriate."

"Okay. I promise. But I'll get to cook with her?"

"You get to cook with Polly Pinch," I say. "On live television."

Russ leaps and touches his heels together.

"Snap!" Ingrid throws her arms up and wags her head from side to side. "Bring it in. Group hug. Come on. Let's hug it out."

Russ and Garrett each put an arm around Ingrid, but I step back.

"Zell?" Russ says.

My nostrils quiver and my heart pounds as I hold back tears.

"Zell, what's wrong?" Ingrid says. "We *won*!"

Nobody says anything for what seems like a long while.

I drop my head into my hands.

Balls.

The tears spill, and my body jerks with ragged breaths. "How can I go on television? I write e-mails to my dead husband." I peek through my fingers from Ingrid to Garrett to Russ. "I talk to my dog, who isn't around anymore. I listen to vinyl records. I'm crazy and depressed. I cry all the time. I go for days without wearing a bra—"

"Okay, TMI there, Zell," Russ says. "TMI—"

"—and this stupid apron. I wear it constantly, even when I'm not baking."

"The sign of a true kitchen goddess." Ingrid breaks free of Garrett and Russ and wraps her arms around my waist and smashes her cheek into my apron. She looks up at me and whispers, "You did it."

I heave one last teary snuffle. "When no one's around, I talk like a pirate. Like a g.d. *pirate*."

Russ grins. "That's why we love you, Zell." Then he's hugging me, too, and I'm smiling in spite of my tears. Garrett laughs, and Ingrid calls, "Ahoy, maties! Shiver me timbers!"

\* \* \*

Tree branches smash against my bedroom window. The needles squeak against the glass.

I sleep. I wake. I think of Ahab. I drift and stir and sleep some more.

Wheeze. Wheeze. Wheeeeeeeeeze.

I open my eyes, half expecting Ahab to groggily press a paw into my arm.

Wheeze. Bang, bang, bang.

Bang, bang, bang. Wheeeeeeeeeze. The red numbers on the clock read 6:18.

Garrett's on the porch. He wears flannel pajama pants and a North Face jacket unzipped over a white undershirt. Red rims his eyes. He grits his teeth as the wind whirls.

"Is Ingrid here?" he asks.

"What? No. What are you talking about?"

"She slept over at Trudy's last night."

"What happened?"

Trudy just called, he says. Ingrid wasn't in her bed this morning. Trudy couldn't find her anywhere in the house—not in the kitchen, or the Barn, or the basement, or the attic. She looked outside, too, behind the shed, in the goat pen. No sign of her.

I glance outside at the gray sky. Snowflakes swirl everywhere, a freak spring storm. "She's not here, Garrett."

He closes his eyes. "Come with me to Trudy's?"

"Of course."

I tuck my pajama pants into my boots and zip my coat over Nick's T-shirt from The Trip. I ride shotgun in Garrett's pickup.

He steers with one hand up Route 331. With the other hand he holds his cell phone and speaks calmly to the 911 operator. "Yes.—No.—I'm not sure.—No.—No.—Her step-grandmother. My father's second wife.—There's no way in hell.—I'm on my way there now.—Yes.—Thank you." He gives Trudy's address and hangs up.

Past Wippamunk Farms. Past Wippamunk Antiques and its picket fence. New snow whitewashes dirty old snow.

We gain elevation. My ears pop. Past Prince of Peace Church and the gap in the tree line where central and eastern Mass meet is a green and white lumpy carpet below us. Here the wind heaves like a supernatural force against the windshield. The truck veers over the center line.

"Did you *feel* that?" says Garrett as he corrects the wheel. He snaps off the radio when a disc jockey announces sudden and localized blizzardlike conditions west of 495.

"It's *April*," I say, as if to scold the weather.

The truck fishtails a couple of times. Garrett grits his teeth and bangs on the steering wheel. "Come on, two-wheel drive," he mutters. "Come on."

Above the road the blinking red light swings from its pole. Sirens blast behind us; two Wippamunk police cruisers pass and continue up the hill.

Garrett crawls through the intersection. "I bet they're going where we're going."

I help myself to a piece of hardened gum stashed in the glove compartment. I unwrap a piece for Garrett and hand it to him. His mouth works around the gum.

"I'll kill him," he says.

"Who?"

"Any sick—"

"We'll find her. She probably just wandered off. There's no reason to believe anyone's—" I trail off. I chew my gum and look absently out the window. The smell of spearmint fills my nose. Where the hell could she be?

"There won't be any footprints," Garrett says.

"What do you mean?"

"Because of the snow. Her footprints will be all filled in."

"We'll find her."

At the abandoned orphanage more sirens blare behind us. This time a cherry red Bronco that says WIPPAMUNK FIRE passes. The striped Muffinry van follows. A single yellow beacon swirls from the van roof.

"The Muffin Man?" says Garrett.

"The whole town's gonna get up for this, Garrett," I say. "You'll see."

CHIEF KENT ORGANIZES SIXTY-THREE GRIM-FACED VOLUNTEERS on Trudy's front lawn. Some volunteers adjust walkie-talkies; others test batteries in flashlights. Some strap on snowshoes; others shoulder backpacks. One woman wears tan Carhartt coveralls. One man assembles collapsible hiking poles. Their cars and SUVs are tilted in muddy ditches along Route 331.

EJ distributes color photocopies of a picture of Ingrid. The photograph shows her in her big hat. The red yarns skim her eyebrows and accentuate her green eyes. She smiles. One front tooth is bigger than the other.

Garrett and Trudy hug on the front porch. The edges of a butterfly bandage on Trudy's brow ruffle in the breeze.

Officer Frances approaches them. "The house appears secure," she says. "There are no signs of forced entry." She asks questions while another officer scribbles Trudy's mostly monosyllabic answers into a notebook.

"What about the mountain lion?" asks Trudy. "The neighbors said they saw one."

France puts a hand on her shoulder and says the last mountain lion in the state of Massachusetts was extirpated—she actually uses that word—in the 1800s. "They're probably seeing a bobcat," says France. "Bobcats're a lot bigger than you'd think."

Dennis, in his threadbare jacket, weaves among the crowd, taking notes. I remember Nick's e-mails—he wrote that he should remain unbiased in New Orleans, an observer, but he couldn't help feeling like he *belonged,* somehow, to the scenes he photographed. I wonder if Dennis feels this way now. Inextricable from his surroundings, from these people. Connected.

Chief Kent mounts the front-porch steps, half a body length above the crowd. "Ingrid Knox is four feet, five inches tall and weighs sixty-eight pounds," he says.

"We can't hear you," a volunteer shouts from the back of the crowd.

EJ trots to the Bronco and retrieves a megaphone, which he passes to Chief Kent. Chief studies it, clicks it on, and holds it to his mouth. The megaphone amplifies the wail of the wind as well as his gravelly old voice.

I shrug my shoulders against the cold. I feel an odd little pinprick sensation, deep in my chest—the same one I felt the night Ingrid, Garrett, and I got stranded at Tunkamog Lake Cabins. After a few seconds, the sensation fades, and I listen as Chief Kent addresses the crowd.

"Ingrid Knox is four feet, five inches tall and weighs sixty-eight pounds. She has long auburn hair and light brown skin and green eyes and freckles. She was last seen around nine P.M. last night in this house and was wearing pink pajamas, and her hair was in two French braids. Like many of us, she knows these woods well. But snow and wind can be disorienting and frightening, especially for a nine-year-old child."

A volunteer asks about setting up an incident command center.

"That'll be up to the state police," says Chief. And just then two Massachusetts police cars pull up Trudy's driveway. The troopers immediately start discussing business with some of the local cops.

Another volunteer asks about an Amber Alert, and another yells, "What about the K-9 unit?"

"Look, these are reasonable questions. But let's not get ahead of ourselves," says Chief. "Let's not panic. Munkers aren't panickers. Am I right?"

"Right," the crowd murmurs.

Chief passes the megaphone to the local police chief, a compact, muscular man with a trim white beard. The police chief gives more instructions—don't touch anything that looks like it could be important, don't wander off alone, and so on.

The volunteers disband in groups of two and three. Dennis and a Wippamunk police officer pair off and enter the woods behind the shed. France and Chief take a route diagonal from the house, across the road. EJ and the police chief head for the north side of the mountain. The state troopers stay behind.

I stand alone on the frozen lawn, where the snow falls thickly. After a while I approach Garrett, still on the porch.

"They made me stay behind," he says. "How am I supposed to stay here and wait?"

Trudy opens the front door. "Come inside and warm up," she says. "Both of you."

He and I sit in the living room, and eventually Trudy joins us, her arms full of wood. She piles some logs into the stove, and soon the wood is snapping and the room is warm and the smell of wood fire fills the house.

She goes into the kitchen and returns with a tray of fairy mugs. We each take a mug and blow on our hot chocolate. Nobody really says much.

After a while the door knocker clanks.

"Thank you for coming, Father," Trudy says as Father Chet steps inside. He shakes the snow off his jacket. He perches on the edge of the rocking chair next to the stove.

A minute after Father Chet arrives, Pastor Sheila knocks. She enters without saying a word and envelops Trudy in a giant hug. Pastor Sheila's glasses fog up immediately in the stove-warmed living room. Her crazy frizzy red-to-silver hair glistens with snowflakes.

She and Father Chet conduct a sort of group prayer. Next to me on the couch, Garrett bows his head and interlaces his fingers at his heart; Trudy, eyes closed, nods occasionally.

I hold my mug on my lap and stare into my warped reflection in the hot chocolate. Their words are about thankfulness and being shown the way, gathering together and community, the beauty and curse of nature and wildness, and children as God's creations. The words make me feel good, like I belong. Like this will all end okay. And I think about Nick's e-mails, and how he grew accustomed to the group prayers on The Trip. I see what he meant. There's some comfort in the idea of every person in a room concentrating on the same thoughts, connected by the same meditations. I find myself trying to remember the last time I was in a church. Gail and Terry's wedding, maybe.

As the prayer winds down, my heart does its weird thing. It gallops, stops. Gallops, stops. Gallops, then—just as Father Chet crosses himself, and Pastor Sheila takes both Garrett's hands in hers—my heart resumes its regular beats.

I take my photocopied flyer of Ingrid from my pocket, unfold it, and study it. The hat nearly topples from her head. I think of that time we went snowshoeing, how warm it was that day. I think of

Ingrid dancing on top of the boulder and tossing her hat, catching it.

Red hat against blue, blue sky.

I know where she is. My head pops up. "Garrett," I whisper. I intend for only him to hear, but everyone's eyes are on me. I thrust the flyer at arm's length.

"What?" he says.

"Look at it. Look at the photograph."

He stares at it. "Zell, what?" he says, frustrated. Then recognition creeps over his face. "Oh my God. Of course."

We stand and head for the door, hurrying into coats and boots.

"Garr?" says Trudy, following. "What is it?"

"We know where she went." He kisses her cheek. "Stay put."


GARRETT'S SO MUCH FASTER THAN ME; he's many paces ahead by the time I reach the end of the driveway. I follow him, turning left and sprinting for the dirt road. He slips on the ice but catches his balance, passing the cemetery and the haunted orphanage, whose gabled, forbidden-looking attic reminds me of my own.

He waits for me at the yellow gate that blocks the dirt road from vehicles. He catches his breath as I circumvent the gate and get tangled in a patch of pricker bushes. Small thorns snag my pajama pants and slice my skin. A cold metallic fire burns in my lungs.

The wind lashes, and white swirls spin in tall columns. Branches dip and weave, stretch and circle. Deeper in the woods a dead branch crashes, breaking other branches as it falls.

I stand next to Garrett now.

"Stop." He spits the word, the way he scolds Ingrid.

"Stop *what*?" I say. And I realize I'm crying. Again. I cry because I can't stand loss anymore. First Nick. Then Ahab. And now Ingrid.

Garrett needs me to be strong right now, but I'm not strong. Maybe I've never been strong.

He takes off again. I follow him, and we both run hard. I search the ground for little Ugg footprints until I remember his prediction that the snow will fill them in. The wind whips away my voice. "Ingrid? *In*grid!"

The lake comes into view. On its shores a gray lump takes shape, and I think it's Ingrid, but as Garrett passes it, I realize it's only the old stone chimney. He turns right and takes the road up the mountain. The same road we snowshoed on that weirdly warm Saturday, just a few months ago.

"Stay here," he yells. "In case she takes a different trail down."

I cup my hands around my mouth and shout, "Okay," as loudly as I can. I remain where I'm standing, my feet planted on the shore of the lake, next to the beaver dam, a crazy mess that looks like a timber shed destroyed in a storm, frozen on the ice.

The snow falls like a singular, solid mass. It pelts my face and stings my eyes. I watch Garrett for as long as I can. I don't want to let him out of my sight. But eventually the snow swallows him, and I'm alone, and before long a whiteout surrounds me. White is all there is, white everywhere.


I STAND IN PLACE until the snow thins a bit. A few minutes go by, maybe five. If it was hard to imagine Ahab wandering alone in conditions like these, it's unbearable to imagine Ingrid doing the same. The snow makes me think of thousands and thousands of nerves, glistening like silken threads.

I can't stand it any longer, this waiting in the wind and not knowing, so I take the road after Garrett. The stones underfoot are icy, and I slip and crash to the ground. But I hike on, up, up, haul myself over a huge felled tree. And on the other side, I see a smudge of red.

Ingrid's soggy hat. Mud and ice cake it; dead leaves and pine needles poke from it.

The hat, I realize, is on Ingrid's head. It covers most of her smiling face.

Garrett's kneeling, and his arms are wrapped tight around her. The dead tree shields them from the wind.

I don't know if I belong to this embrace, but I join it. I kneel, throw my arms around Garrett's shoulders, and nuzzle my face against Ingrid's. When she speaks, I can almost feel the relief washing over Garrett. He squeezes her; I squeeze him. Gratitude emanates from us like shockwaves.

Ingrid's breath is hot in my ear. "I thought maybe all that wind would knock it down out of that tree. Zell, remember? You said in the spring I could go back and look for it on the ground. And, well, it's spring. And you were right. It was on the ground."

I open my mouth to respond, but my throat feels empty, a hollow tunnel. I feel an internal collision, like my insides are all smashing up against each other. I can't tell whether I'm trembling from cold or nerves.

"I can't believe I got my hat back," says Ingrid, her teeth chattering. "I woke up and it was so windy, and—"

"All that matters is you're okay," I say. "We're all okay."


THE POLICE CHIEF QUICKLY GATHERS THE VOLUNTEERS, thanks them, and dismisses them. EJ invites everyone back to the Muffinry for free coffee, and they applaud before they disperse and get into their cars and SUVs and head back to town.

In the kitchen, Chief Kent checks Ingrid's vital signs and makes sure she's not hypothermic or dehydrated. "Everybody out," he says, "except Ingrid and the chiefs."

We all file out—Garrett, Dennis, Trudy, France, and I—and gather in the living room, where I catch snippets of Chief Kent's stern voice. "It's dangerous to hike in the woods alone, especially in snow and cold, without telling an adult," he says. "You gave the whole town a scare."

I hear Ingrid say, "Sorry, Mr. Chief," very quietly.

The police chief leaves, and Chief Kent escorts Ingrid from the kitchen. He picks her up, puts her on the couch, and bundles her in a knitted afghan so that only her eyes and nose show.

Garrett gives Chief a one-armed guy hug–handshake; they thump each other on the back, and neither of them speaks.

ONE BY ONE, after the hot chocolate turns cold, we disband. I follow Garrett to his truck and think of asking him for a ride but decide to give him and Ingrid their time together.

"See you later?" I say, as he buckles Ingrid, still bundled in the afghan, into the backseat of his pickup.

He shuts the passenger door. He looks even more tired than he did earlier this morning, when he picked me up. "Thanks, Zell," he says, extending his hand. When I shake it, he pulls me in for a quick hug.

"You bet," I say. "Drive safe."

Pastor Sheila putt-putts away in her teal sedan, France takes the "croo-za" back to the station, and Dennis returns to the Wippamunker Building.

It's just me and Father Chet, so he offers to drive me home. Sitting in the passenger seat, I realize I still feel shaky. Like I had too much coffee or something. At first we don't really say much, Father

Chet and I. He turns onto the road, flicks the windshield wipers to hyperspeed, and accelerates just a little. The snow thickens and flies toward us.

Eventually we make small talk about the weather forecast, and the rumored mountain lion, and how lucky Garrett was to find Ingrid. And finally, I ask whether Nick ever told Father Chet about a present for me.

"A present?" Father Chet says. "Nooo, Row-sel-*len*. No present."

We drive a ways, not speaking. He stops at the Main Street intersection, and the turn signal ticks and ticks. I look around at the gas station and the cemetery, the almost-three-hundred-year-old town hall and the Congregational church's cross-topped steeple, barely discernable against steel-colored clouds.

Father Chet hums. The light turns green. He takes the corner slowly, saying the same thing in French that he said that day in the Muffinry, when I was there with Gail a while back. "*Noose um blah blah blah.*"

"You said that before, Father."

"*Ouai.*"

"I still don't know what it means."

He pulls into my driveway. I grasp the car door handle, waiting for an explanation.

Finally he stops humming. He rolls his bald head against the headrest and winks. "I think you'll figure it out when you're ready to hear it."

I FLOP ONTO THE COUCH—still in my coat and boots—and drift to sleep almost immediately. I don't wake up until after the sun's gone down. I wander around the first floor of my house, turning on lights, feeling lonely, before I decide to make Scrumpy Delight and bring it next door. A small offering of sweetness and warmth might be just the right thing to make everybody feel better.

"Ingrid's asleep," says Garrett, leading me to the bright yellow kitchen. "She had a big, long bubble bath, and she's been asleep since four thirty."

We sit opposite each other. Garrett eats nearly half of the Scrumpy Delight, thanking me between bites. "This is freakishly tasty," he says.

"I know," I say. "Pretty weird, right?"

He laughs and pushes away the plate. "Don't take this the wrong way, but I'm sort of shocked that you're a finalist. I mean, what are the chances?"

"A few thousand to one, apparently."

"It's almost like fate."

"I'd like to believe that," I say.

"I can't believe I'm letting Ingrid go on *Pinch of Love Live*. But how can I *not* let her go, at this point?" Garrett shrugs. "I mean, I promised. I pinkie swore."

"Maybe she'll get the Polly Pinch stuff out of her system. Like you said."

"Somehow I doubt that."

I smile.

Garrett shakes his head, loads his fork with limey goat cheese and peppery, chocolaty grilled pineapple, and offers it to me. It's about to slide right off the tines, onto the table. I hesitate, unsure if I should take the fork or let him feed me.

"Quick," he says. "Eat it."

So I lean forward and open my mouth, and he giggles and pops the fork in. Chewing, I catch a few crumbs of crust in my cupped hand.

It's the first time I've tried the finished product, I realize. And it's delicious. It really is.

He pulls two beers from the fridge, pops the tops with a bottle opener, and offers me one. "I'm torn between grounding her until she turns eighteen," he says, sitting back down, "and giving her anything and everything she wants. I mean, really, what's the responsible parent's reaction, here? After your daughter runs away in a blizzard?"

I take a swig of beer. "I think she learned her lesson."

"When am I gonna learn mine?" He laughs, and I try to laugh along with him, even though I don't really understand what he means.

An awkward silence follows, and neither of us knows where to look. I sip my beer. Garrett clears his throat and fingers a groove in the wood table.

Finally I gesture to the plate, where the remaining Scrumpy Delight forms a crescent shape. "Well, maybe we should save the rest for Ingrid," I say.

"Definitely," he says, stifling a yawn. "She'd like that."

HOURS LATER, I can't sleep. I switch on the lamp over my drafting table, but the glare hurts my eyes, and the pituitary gland I start sketching looks too square, too flat. And then . . . knock-knock-knock, pause. Knock-knock-knock, pause.

I head downstairs, into the powder room. "Ing?" I say to the Ahab wall.

"No," says Garrett from the other side.

"Oh. Hi."

"Were you asleep?" he asks.

"I was drawing."

"I'm sorry I snapped at you. You know. Earlier. In the woods."

"I'm sorry about the hat," I say.

"Why are you sorry about the hat?"

"Because that day, when it got stuck in the tree, I told Ingrid she could get it later."

"It's not your fault, Zell. I told her the same thing. Believe me. I don't blame you for a thing."

"Good night," I say.

"Love ya 'n' like ya," he says, chuckling.

"Love ya 'n' like ya," I say, and smile.

April 18, 2008

From: rose-ellen@roymedicalillustration.com

To: nicholas.roy@thewippamunker.com

Hey.

Ingrid went missing in a snowstorm (we found her) and I feel responsible. Never mind; it's a long story. Point is, I can't seem to do anything right since you died.

Except one thing: I'm a finalist in an extremely high-profile international baking contest (laugh here) and I'm going on *Pinch of Love Live,* the new live version of Polly Pinch's original show. And if I win, I'm going to donate the prize money to the people of New Orleans. Because that's what you would have wanted.

What should I wear for my debut television appearance? I tried on a few nice tops hanging in my closet, including the black scoop-neck I paired with black slacks for your memorial service. But no tops fit me; they seem just squeeze-y enough to make me feel uncomfortable and self-conscious. Or maybe I'm just not used to wearing nice clothes, because for the past year and a half, I've sort of let myself go, as the saying goes.

Spike Miller, Polly Pinch's assistant, whom I called in response to my notification letter, said "wardrobe specialists" will dress me if they're unhappy with my own outfit. He recommended I wear red, because red is a universally flattering color, especially on camera. But I have nothing red except an old Red Sox sweatshirt and, of course, your T-shirt from The Trip, which I am actually considering wearing.

It's rather random, how I came to possess the shirt. The day you died, I was painting Gail's g.d. guest bathroom. I was mixing colors and testing them on my arms, because I'd run out of room on the wall. The mountains, trees, granite, and snow were all painted, and I was about to incorporate new colors, for clothing and skin. I wanted to get them right. Plus, I was feeling loopy, probably from reading all your e-mails, especially your last one, about how inspired you felt, about how you couldn't wait to get home and show me the slideshow of your photographs, and make plans for the soccer team. I was really looking forward to meeting the new you and entering a new phase in our life, a new phase in our love.

There is something sensual about stroking the bristles of a wet paintbrush across your forearm. Using your own body as a palette, a testing ground. Both my forearms were striped with different colors when my mom knocked on the door.

"There's someone here," she said. "They're calling for you. In the driveway."

"What?"

"Come outside." She sounded a bit frantic. "I think there might be a problem or something. Come now."

I lifted a corner of the drop cloth, found my cell phone, turned it on. Ten missed calls from Kent Powers—Chief Kent. Four missed calls from Chester Claude Mbo—Father Chet. Three missed calls from Sheila White. I never did listen to those messages.

Mom, Dad, Terry, Gail holding Tasha, they all followed me and gathered on the deck. Pastor Sheila and Father Chet were in the driveway. They stood in front of Sheila's teal sedan. I ran to them.

It's weird the details you remember. Pastor Sheila wore a tunic-length patchwork shirt. She came right up to me. In one hand she held the T-shirt. With the other hand she gripped my arm.

"We've been trying to reach you," she said. "The Ludlow police offered to come, but we wanted to tell you ourselves. We tracked you down, tracked down your sister's address, and drove—"

"Tell me what?" I said.

"There's been an accident." Pastor Sheila's voice quavered. She pressed the shirt into my hand.

That's how I found out you were dead.

I sank my face into the shirt. I wanted it to smell like you. But it didn't. It didn't smell like anything at all.

And it still doesn't really smell like anything, even though I've worn it so much since that day. To bed, to the grocery store.

Sheila said later that the shirt got mixed up in the wash somehow; an old lady from a church down there offered to do everyone's laundry, and Sheila found your shirt in her suitcase when she got home.

Anyway, at least the "Wippamunk Loves New Orleans" message is a good cause to advertise on *Pinch of Love Live.*

And, it will be appropriate for the tribute afterward.

What tribute, you ask? See the e-mail from EJ, pasted below. . . .

Hi, Zell. EJ here.

I've been meaning to tell you about something. I was hoping you would hear it through the grapevine by now, or see it in *The Wippamunker,* and I wouldn't have to tell you, but neither of those things happened, and the time is approaching, so.

I don't know why I haven't told you face-to-face. We didn't talk for so long, and then it just seemed like a difficult thing to bring up with you. And then Ahab. Anyway, e-mail is easier. So here goes.

We're planning a tribute to Nick. France came up with the idea. So we can have closure, she says. A lot of people are involved. There are going to be some nice surprises. It's really important that you come.

Problem is, the tribute is the same day as the *Pinch of Love Live* show: May 5. You see, Russ was there when you found out you were a winner, and he realized the show and the tribute were scheduled for the same day. But we couldn't reschedule the tribute, because we'd advertised for weeks in *The Wippamunker*, and we're expecting a lot of people.

So anyway, I talked to Garrett and he will take you back to the town common right after *Pinch of Love Live.* (Or if it rains, the town hall.)

If you want to come, that is.

Please come. We want you there. Invite your family, too.

Okay.

Love,

EJ

# 10

## Zell

*I*T'S A RAINY, RAW MAY 5. By the time I hop into Garrett's pickup, Ingrid's already air drumming and belting along to Hannah Montana tunes. The plan is that Garrett will drop us off at Scrump Studios and park, and then join the *Pinch of Love Live* audience; Spike Miller was nice enough to send him a ticket.

We drive to Boston. Garrett seems to glance at Ingrid in the rearview more often than usual. When he catches her eye, he winks at her.

"Nervous?" he asks me, as we cruise along the Mass Pike.

"Yeah," I say. "I have to admit, I kind of am."

"Me, too," he says.

When we reach Boston, we pull over to the Scrump Studios building, near Quincy Market. "Remember, Ingrid," Garrett says to the rearview mirror. "Not a word to Polly about her being your mother."

Ingrid salutes him.

Outside, a slight, spiky-haired man hurries to the truck. He clutches a clipboard to his chest. A Bluetooth earpiece hugs his ear.

I roll down my window. "I'm Rose-Ellen Roy. Am I in the right spot for—"

"I've been waiting for you. You're late," he says. He jabs his hand inside the truck to shake my hand. "Spike Miller. Let's go."

Ingrid hops out the back. "Bye, Dad!"

"Don't I get a kiss?" Garrett says.

"We're late." She stands next to Spike and grasps his hand.

"Break a leg," Garrett says. I'm about to hop out when he says, "Wait. Shut the door? I think I should tell you something. Roll up the window, too."

"What?" I say. "What's wrong?"

Garrett sighs. "Fact is, *you've* been a better mother to her, Zell. You." He opens the glove compartment and extracts an envelope decorated with stickers. I recognize it: the letter Ingrid wrote to Polly Pinch, which he intercepted.

"Give this to her?" he says. "Make sure she gets it, okay? I'll explain it all to you later. I promise."

"Give it to who?"

He grips the steering wheel and stares at it.

"Oh no," I say. "Don't do this to me now, Garrett. You've got to be kidding me." I glance at the sidewalk, where Ingrid is telling Spike some animated story. He nods absently and examines his clipboard, looking mildly dyspeptic.

I lower my voice. "Is Polly Pinch Ingrid's—"

"I'm not kidding you," Garrett says. "That story I told you before, about the look-alike? It was—just don't tell her anything, okay? Just let it unfold."

"Don't tell who what-ything?" I want to ask more; I feel like I might bubble over with questions. "Let *what* unfold?"

Spike taps my window. "Let's go, people!"

"You'll be great, Zell," Garrett says. He looks at me, his eyes a mix of anxiousness, regret, and need. "I'll be watching. You'll be great. You'll both be great." He squeezes my thigh.

"Why?" I say. "What are you hoping to accomplish by letting this happen?"

He shrugs. "It's time Anita saw her daughter."

"Anita?"

"Polly. Her real name's Anita."

"You drop this on me *now*?" I stare at him; my mouth hangs open. Not only do I have to worry about appearing on live television, and making it back to Wippamunk on time for this mysterious tribute to my dead husband that apparently the whole town knew about before I did, but I also have to worry about a celebrity chef's unrehearsed reaction to meeting the daughter she apparently gave up on almost nine years ago.

"Don't worry," says Garrett. "I'm sure it will all go smoothly."

"Right. I'm sure it will all be super simp." I tuck the envelope in my bag—a huge fairy-patterned bag, courtesy of Trudy.

"I'm sorry I lied," he says. "This is all so complicated, and I guess I just wasn't ready to face the truth. But Ingrid *is* ready. I think she's been ready for a long time."

I take a deep breath. "I understand," I say. And it's true; I understand what it's like to lie, in order to get through just one day; what it's like to not want to face the truth.

"I didn't expect things would get this far, Zell. Television and everything."

"It's okay. Neither did I." I squeeze his hand. I get out of the truck, and he pulls away from the curb.

Balls.

* * *

"Nice to meet you," I say to Spike.

He forces a tight smile. "Follow me."

He leads Ingrid and me into the lobby of the skyscraper, through a shiny hall where the hard-soled shoes of serious women and men echo off tiled walls and floors. No one looks at us. We pass a big gleaming reception/security desk and ride an elevator. Spike's beady eyes rove my outfit—"Wippamunk Loves New Orleans" shirt, jeans, big shoulder bag. The beady eyes move to Ingrid, whose red hat swallows her forehead.

Ingrid offers Spike a wide grin. "If Zell here wins the contest," she says, "she's going to donate all the money to New Orleans so they can rebuild the city."

Spike says nothing.

She keeps talking: about hundreds of thousands of abandoned cars in New Orleans, and thousands of houses that need gutting, and overcrowded "femur" trailers and nonexistent libraries, all of which she knows because I've told her about Nick's e-mails.

"Ingrid." I hold a finger to my lips. "Shh."

"But it's important," she says.

I smile at Spike. He clears his throat and inspects papers on his clipboard.

We exit the elevator, cross a hall, and step into another elevator. Ingrid chews her thumbnail the whole time.

The second elevator ride ends. We follow Spike down more halls. These halls are somewhat dingy. Closed doors are labeled CONTROL ROOM, BOOTH, DO NOT ENTER, DO NOT ENTER—EVER, GREEN ROOM, MAKEUP, and WARDROBE.

Finally we pass a short row of doors all labeled GUEST, and in one of these small rooms, Spike deposits us.

"Sit." He points to a threadbare upholstered couch against the wall. "Wait."

Ingrid and I exchange glances.

"Mr. Spike?" Ingrid says. She plops onto the couch. "What's happening?"

"Makeup's coming to you. So's Wardrobe." He's in such a hurry, he slams the door.

HALF AN HOUR LATER I wear knee-high leather boots, a pencil skirt, and a collared, sleeveless shirt. My lips are painted a deep brick red. Wet black outlines my eyes. Fake glasses rest on my nose, and my hair is shellacked into unmoving waves.

Ingrid inspects me. She lifts my arms and circles under them. "You look—"

"—like a freak?" I say.

"No. Like a cool librarian."

"Thanks. I think."

"How do I look?" Ingrid, in royal blue, does a little tap dance. She wears ballet flats, leggings, a tunic cinched low around her pre-hips with a thick plastic belt. Two basketball-size Afro-puffs dominate either side of the zigzag part in her scalp. Her lips and eyelids shimmer with sparkles.

"You look like you could perform alongside Hannah Montana," I say.

"Oh my God. Are you even serious?"

"No. Wait. You look like Hannah Montana would be your two-bit *opening act.*"

"OMG."

Spike pokes his head in the door and claps crisply. "Ladies, Ms. Pinch regrets that she's unable to introduce herself to you before the show, so she's going to have to do it later."

I don't have time to worry about what that exchange will be

like, because Spike keeps talking. "Here's what'll happen. You'll do everything I say. After that, if Ms. Pinch asks you a question, answer it, but don't talk too much." He looks directly at Ingrid. "Get that?"

She nods.

"When you're seated onstage you'll be fitted with a microphone," Spike says. "Once that microphone's on, don't fidget, and don't frown.

"And remember," he adds. "We're *live*, so mind your language." He turns on his heel and zips down the hall. "Follow me."

We speed walk to the set. "Stay," he orders, seating us in metal folding chairs against a wall.

Ingrid points at a white ON THE AIR sign. We squint at the stage until our eyes make sense of the bright, bright lights: We have a side view of Polly Pinch, who wears a frilly apron and addresses a huge camera labeled CAMERA 1. She appears to occupy an old boxcar diner. Stools ring a chrome counter lined with malted milkshakes; glass jars of gumdrops, striped straws, coconut shavings, and licorice laces; and the infamous LOVE canister. Beyond the boxcar a luminous kitchen awaits: black-and-white tile floor, chrome table, six-burner gas stove, bulbous-looking refrigerator.

The audience watches, enraptured, from sleek seats that slope up thirty rows.

Men in black shirts operate cameras that slide around like robotic limbs. Polly takes turns addressing each camera. She talks about the two prize-winning desserts and about the meal she'll cook later: her own special twist on traditional chicken and waffles.

Ingrid cups her hand around my ear and whispers, "Chicken and *waffles*?"

"I think it's a Southern thing," I whisper, just as Polly says, ". . . and boy, is this dish *scrrrrump*! So don't go away. We'll be right back."

A green APPLAUSE! sign flashes. The audience claps.

The white ON THE AIR sign fades.

Three women surround Polly. One adjusts the frills of her apron. Another spritzes her hair. The third attacks her forehead with a makeup sponge.

"What's soul food?" Ingrid says. "Is Scrumpy Delight soul food?"

"Hell yeah," I say.

"You said a bad word."

"I know. Sorry. I'm a little nervous."

"I'm not."

"Good. You shouldn't be."

"I can't find my dad." She shades her eyes and searches the audience.

"He's there," I say. "He's somewhere. We just can't see him because of the lights."

Spike reappears and crouches next to me. He wears a headset now. "Go time," he says. "Ready?"

Ingrid nods. Her Afro-puffs bounce all around.

Onstage, Spike's wordless minions swarm us. They position us on the diner stools. After they disband and disappear backstage, Ingrid and I have wires down our backs and pea-size microphones clipped to our collars.

Spike taps my mic, then Ingrid's. "Remember my four rules?" he says.

Ingrid counts them on her fingers. "Don't talk too much, don't fidget, don't frown, and mind your language."

"Good girl." He darts away.

"Remember the other rule?" I ask Ingrid. "Your dad's rule?"

"Don't worry. I'm not gonna say anything." She elbows me as Polly Pinch approaches the stools.

"Play it cool," I whisper.

Ingrid makes a ring with her thumb and index finger. "Playin' it cool," she mouths.

Polly stops at the stool next to Ingrid. On it slumps a scraggly, barrel-chested guy in a cowboy shirt—the other contest winner. A few inches of white hair ring his otherwise bald scalp. His spine straightens when Polly Pinch stands before him and offers her perfect hand.

The lights are so bright that the tiny hairs on the back of my hands look as dark and defined as pencil marks. My underboobs are sweating. A lot. My knees feel drafty and too exposed.

Nonbeats. Fierce beats. Balls.

"Hi." That familiar, inviting voice, warm and thick, like maple syrup. Before me, the famously sharp jaw accentuates famously sharp collarbones. Perfectly round boobs bust from the frilly apron. Green eyes electrify smooth tan skin. Freckles dot her nose, cheeks, and cleavage, like sprays of ground cinnamon.

"Hi. Polly Pinch." She pumps my hand. "Congratulations on your Hidden Cranberry Spice-eez."

"Oh, thanks," I say. "Pleasure to meet you. I'm . . . uh . . . I'm Scrumpy Delight, though."

"Oh, right. Right. You're Rose-Ellen. And who's your little helper here?" Polly shines her gorgeous face at Ingrid.

Ingrid's jaw quivers. She mutters something, but it's inaudible.

I hold Ingrid's hand in my lap and squeeze it. "This is Ingrid," I say.

Polly scrunches up her eyebrows.

Ingrid lifts her head and stares at Polly. And then, on Polly, I see a face that television land never sees: one totally void of expression, like an open-eyed sleepwalker.

Spike waves his clipboard. "People!" he yells. "We are live in five, four, three—" He mouths, "Two, one," jabbing the air with his fingers. He sweeps his closed fist toward Polly and scoots offstage like a villain in a musical.

A doo-wop theme song plays, and Polly pinches her cheeks and bustles to her diner booth. The green APPLAUSE! sign flashes. The audience erupts: clapping, whistling, woo-hooing.

Polly smiles, showing her teeth. Her voice sounds shaky. "Welcome back to *Pinch of Love Live*. I'm your host, Polly Pinch."

## EJ

Much of Wippamunk watches *Pinch of Love Live* in the town hall. Chief Kent won't allow more than three hundred people inside—that's the maximum number the fire code permits. So he sends the overflow to the Blue Plate Lounge, Orbit Pizza, and Murtonen's Muffinry.

People occupy every available space in the Muffinry. EJ's modest little shop is standing room only, with many more patrons than chairs. It's the best day of business he can remember.

Travis brings a big television from his house and sets it up in the bay window. He sits next to EJ behind the cash register. They survey the crowd, and Travis blathers about how hot Polly Pinch is. Finally the credits roll and the theme song starts playing, and the Muffinry goes from loud chatter to total silence.

On the screen, Polly moistens her lips. Her eyes follow the trolling camera. EJ thinks she looks rather like a deer in the headlights; maybe live television just isn't her bag.

"I have some guests here with me onstage," TV-Polly says. "And *one* of them is the winner of twenty thousand dollars, and my first-ever international baking contest, Desserts That Warm the Soul."

The camera trains on a bouffanted woman dressed like a 1950s diner waitress. She displays an issue of *Meals in a Cinch with Polly Pinch* magazine and vogues it with her hands. The television audience claps.

"Let's taste one of our winners," Polly says.

Laughter murmurs through the television audience. In the Muffinry, an old guy shouts, "She can taste *me* if she wants."

"Oh, excuse me," says Polly. She giggles and touches her fingertips to her lips. "I meant, of course, let's taste one of our winning *recipes*. Ladies and gentlemen, I give you Hamill Harding of San Diego, California, whose delectable cookies were deemed by the expert panel of judges as—and I quote—irresistible, and light as a cloud, yet boldly flavorful."

The camera shows Hamill Harding, an old cowboy-looking guy. He does a little seated bow and rolls an imaginary top hat down his arm and off his fingers. "Thanks, Polly," he says.

The bouffanted diner waitress now vogues Hamill's cookies. They're square and arranged on a silver tray.

"Little Miss Ingrid? Honey?" Polly shoots a frozen glance at Ingrid, whom the camera shows for the first time. The Muffinry explodes in applause and whistles. Zell sits next to her. She looks good, EJ thinks. She looks good.

"Would you do us the honor of having the first delectable bite of Hamill Harding's Hidden Cranberry Spice-eez?" Polly's gaze trains on the camera again. "Ingrid is . . . the . . . special helper of our *other* guest, whom I'll introduce to the world in just a second."

Ingrid winks at Polly, then at the camera, as it zooms in on her face.

"That little girl's a natural!" says the old-timer in the Muffinry.

Ingrid selects a thick cookie from the tray on Hamill's knees. She lets her lips linger on the cookie, Polly Pinch style. She swallows and takes another bite. "Mmm," she says. "Scrump." She licks her lips and gazes at the camera.

The television audience laughs, and the Muffinry erupts in whistles and laughter, too.

Ingrid finishes the cookie. Polly addresses Hamill Harding with another frozen smile. "Now, Hamill. Before we move into the kitchen and get baking these bee'yoots, care to share your inspiration for your Hidden Cranberry Spice-eez?"

Hamill rubs the knees of his khakis and clears his phlegmy throat. "Well, I was inspired by the cranberry bogs in New Jersey, where I spent my summers as a kid, visiting my second cousins. I love cranberries, and I always cook with them. Most people are used to dried and sugared cranberries, but I cook with fresh cranberries whenever possible."

"Mmm. Fresh cranberries," says Polly. "They're so crisp and tart, and their color is just bee'yootiful. What else do you want to tell us, Hamill?"

"Well, in my Hidden Cranberry Spice-eez, the binding ingredient—and this might come as a surprise, because it doesn't seem to quite go with cranberries, and plus, you can't even really *taste* it—but the binding ingredient is actually peanut butter, Polly."

The camera shows Ingrid bite another cookie. She coughs mid-swallow and covers her mouth with her arm. She seems to blush.

"Just a pinch, Polly." Hamill grins and goes "heh-heh-heh" at his little joke. Polite laughter ripples through the television audience; one person claps four times. In the Muffinry, someone groans.

The camera shows Ingrid again. Her eyes grow wide. And a little wider, until they're bulging.

"Something's wrong here," EJ says.

"Yeah, hey," says Travis.

Raised welts form on Ingrid's neck. She slides from her stool. She gasps and presses her head spastically against the counter.

"What's going on?" people in the Muffinry ask. "What's wrong with the little girl?"

The camera shows Zell, who slaps her forehead. "Balls!"

"Dude," Travis says in EJ's ear. "I think your friend just said 'balls' on live television."

Zell's microphone thumps as she rips it from her shirt. "Did you say there's peanut butter in those cookies?"

A little metropolitan-looking man with spiky hair—obviously someone who's supposed to be backstage—runs onto the set. He makes an urgent throat-slicing signal at Polly.

Polly turns to the camera. "We'll be right back. Don't go away."

# Zell

The white ON THE AIR sign fades.

I kneel and fan Ingrid with my hands. "There's a thing in my fairy bag," I shout. "A pen."

"A *pen*?" Polly says, her face blanched.

"An EpiPen! A friggin' EpiPen! Where's my fairy bag? Someone get my g.d. bag!"

Two of Spike's minions dash backstage.

"Garrett?" I scream. I see him dart from the back row, down the steps. He trips up onto the stage and joins me at Ingrid's side.

"What's wrong with her?" Hamill says.

"She's got a peanut allergy." I tear off my fake glasses and fling them to the front row.

Hamill's and Polly's mouths drop open.

Ingrid appears to stop breathing.

AT THE HOSPITAL EMERGENCY ROOM, they wheel Ingrid away on a gurney. She looks so small, swamped by the oxygen mask. I wonder what she hears of the commotion around her—nurses and doctors bustling and yelling.

Now the backs of my knees stick to the waiting-room chair. Garrett's next to me. His elbows rest on his knees, and his head hangs low.

"I'm sorry," I say. "It's my—"

"She left me."

"What?"

"She left me," Garrett says. "She left *us.*"

"Who?"

"Anita. Anita Pinchelman was her name. She changed her name to Polly Pinch."

A man in scrubs enters the waiting room. Garrett and I both stand, but the man approaches a young couple seated across from us. They listen solemnly as he explains something.

Garrett and I sit back down.

"We tried to make it work," he says. "But Anita—*Polly*—decided she just didn't want to be a mother. She didn't want any of it. She really did leave me when Ingrid was a month old, for a traveling jewelry salesman. He took her down to Atlanta with him. I guess that's where she learned something about cooking. Ever notice how much Polly relies on traditional Southern flavors in her recipes? All that 'ratchet up the action' nonsense? Polly's taken all these soul-food classics and lightened them up a little. Made them healthier. You know, with spices instead of lard or whatever. That kind of thing."

Garrett rests his chin on his fists. "She didn't cook jack-crap when we were together, Zell. Not even a tray of frickin' brownies. She was as hopeless as I was in the kitchen."

The man in scrubs leaves the waiting area, and the couple across from us collapses in the chairs. I glance out the window, where a pair of sparrows flits to and from a nest under a nearby window ledge.

Garrett stares at his shoes. "When things in Atlanta didn't work out, Anita moved back to Boston, but not with me. She moved in with friends and changed her name to what she thought would work well for an actress—something with alliteration, that sounded like she could go from angel to go-go dancer, depending on the circumstances. She went to every audition she heard of, trying to find acting work. Her roommate told me Anita was about to move to Los Angeles when she tried out for some cooking show. She didn't even know what the audition was *for*. And just like that"—Garrett snaps his fingers—"she's teaching all the English-speaking world how to cook. She's got the most famous clavicles in North America. She's on cracker boxes, billboards, Big Yum Donuts commercials."

"You mean, she doesn't really know how to cook?"

"She does now, apparently," Garrett says. "But when I knew her? Like I said. Not even a tray of frickin' brownies."

"Damn," I say, a little too loudly.

"I tried to get in touch with her when I found out she was back in town. Before she got famous. I missed her, sure. But I also wanted Ingrid to have a mother."

"What happened?"

"Anita wouldn't see me. She wouldn't return my calls. Finally one day I got a letter saying that if I didn't stop calling her, she'd take out a restraining order against me. Hardly a good thing if I wanted to be a lawyer someday. So I stopped calling her. I just stopped calling her. And that was that.

"A good while later," he says, "when I was moving to Worcester to save money on rent, I found a box of her old stuff in the attic. Old CDs she never listened to, a couple sweaters, photographs. I moved that box with me from Boston to Worcester to all the different apartments we had in Wippamunk before we moved in next door to you. I don't know why I hung on to the box for so long. Maybe I was hoping she would come back to us. That we would work it out. Someday. Eventually. In that box of Anita's old stuff? That's where Ingrid found that old picture of us. And Anita's old ski hat. Her old, ratty, ugly, red ski hat."

I remember the first time I babysat Ingrid, and how I bribed her to move Nick's present to the top of the stairs. She said she loved attics, because they're full of secrets, history, and hidden treasure.

And truth, I think; they're often full of truth.

"So Ingrid found the box," I say, "and those old photographs of you and Anita, and she just . . . knew?"

"How could she not know? Ingrid looks just like her. She's the little black Afro'd version of Polly Pinch. We watch *Pinch of Love* together, you know, just flipping through the channels on a Saturday night or something. I subscribe to the magazine, just to keep up with Anita, with her career."

"It's a pretty good magazine," I say. "I mean, it's pretty educational."

"Yeah. Even a dummy like me can follow those recipes. Anyway, Ingrid put that hat on her beautiful little head, and it was all over."

"You ever hear from her?"

"She sends me checks every six months or so, starting when Ingrid turned two," says Garrett. "Pretty sizable ones, too. I put them all in a savings account for Ingrid. You know, for later in her life. In case she really does decide, someday, that she wants to move to France and study the culinary arts."

"How much does Trudy know about all this?"

"She knows everything. She's as tight-lipped as they come about family business."

"A true Munker," I say.

"Trudy loves my daughter; that's for sure."

A woman's voice comes over the intercom: *Paging Dr. Flores. Paging Dr. Flores. Line three, please. Line three.*

"Am I a bad parent?" Garrett bites his lip. "Am I a terrible father?"

"What? God, no. Are you kidding me?"

"I just didn't want Ingrid to get hurt. I didn't know what to do. What does a twenty-three-year-old kid do with a little baby? A beautiful little baby girl?" His head's back in his hands, elbows on knees.

"She hasn't had a peanut reaction in so long," he says. "I've never even had to use the EpiPen on her. Nobody has, ever. Everywhere she goes, I warn whoever's in charge that she has a peanut allergy. And I give them an EpiPen. And of all the places I *forget* to give this warning? The set of her own mother's cooking show. *Cooking show.*"

"You do the best you can, Garrett," I say. "I think you're a great dad."

"I almost killed her with a teaspoon of peanut butter when she was eleven months old. I was making myself PB and J, and she reached for the knife, so I dipped a spoon in the jar and handed it to her. Twenty seconds later I turn around and she's sitting there in her highchair, red as a tomato, eyes bulging, grabbing her throat.

How was I supposed to know? Nowadays everybody knows about peanut allergies. But back then?"

I rest my hand on the dip between his shoulder blades. "You *weren't* supposed to know," I say. "Sometimes I think none of us are supposed to know much of anything, in the grand scheme of things. Know what I mean?"

Garrett's deep sigh seems to warm my palm. A different man in scrubs enters the waiting room and approaches him. "Mr. Knox?"

"Is she okay?" says Garrett.

"Ingrid's going to be just fine," the man in scrubs says. "We gave her an adrenaline shot, and she's recovering. We're running some tests, and after she rests a bit, we'll let you in to see her."

Garrett opens his mouth, but no words come out. He covers his face with his hands.

The man in scrubs shoots me a kind smile before turning and leaving the waiting room.

"Garrett?" I say. I think he might be crying.

I sit with him for what feels like a long time. He doesn't move or make a sound, just hunches over in the chair. Finally his hands drop to his lap. "Wanna hear something ironic?" he says. "I didn't tell her the truth about her mother because I didn't want her to become distracted by it." We both laugh, but softly, so as not to disturb the others in the waiting room, whose problems might be bigger than ours.

"Anyway," he says. "I'm sorry I lied to you about all this."

"I understand," I say. "I really do. Hey, there's a vending machine out near the restrooms. You want anything?"

"A coffee'd be great. Get yourself one, too." He takes a few dollar bills from the wallet in his back pocket and waves them at me.

"Keep your money," I say, standing and straightening my skirt.

I'm about to push through the door when he says, "Zell?"

"Yeah?"

He's watching me now, his eyes brimmed red. "Nice boots."

"Thanks. Not mine."

He sighs again and blubbers his lips. "Well, you looked pretty slammin' on that set today, Zell. If you don't mind me saying so."

"I don't mind." I smile. A real smile, teeth showing and everything.

I PASS THE VENDING MACHINES, trying not to inhale the scents of urine and disinfectant, dirty sheets and Jell-O. I pause at the bubbler and slurp the cold, metallic-tasting water. Water from the Wippamunk Reservoir, I think, as I wipe the back of my hand across my mouth.

Someone rushes toward me—a lurching, high-heeled run. Polly Pinch, née Anita Pinchelman. Rivulets forged by tears stain her foundation. "Rose-Ellen," she says.

"Ingrid's fine," I say. "But they don't want anyone to see her just yet. They're running some tests."

"I came as soon as we finished taping. *That* shouldn't have happened. I reprimanded my staff. We will have EpiPens on the premises from now on. I'm so sorry. She's all right?"

"She's all right."

Polly bends at the waist, drops her head between her knees, and breathes once, twice, through her nostrils. When she flips upright, her face is composed and attractively blushed. She smiles the TV smile I'm used to—vaguely prim yet vaguely seductive. "Good, good," she says. "And how do you know Ingrid?"

"She's my neighbor."

"Really?"

"Really."

Polly chews her top lip. "Really."

"He's in the waiting room." I point down the hall.

She tilts her head. "Really?"

I nod.

Again she bends at the waist, breathing loudly. She flips back up. Smiles.

"Before you go in there." I fish around in my bag. "Ingrid was going to give you this." I find the envelope—the one containing Ingrid's letter to Polly, and Ingrid's life's savings.

Polly fingers it.

"Careful," I say. "There's money in there."

She nods and stuffs it in her leather handbag. "Thank you," she says, clicking off down the hall. Before she enters the waiting room she turns. "By the way. You didn't win after all."

"What?"

"The Hamill guy from San Diego won. Despite the . . . interruption, it was a successful episode. Even though I was a complete train wreck. Even though Spike teamed up with a camera operator to physically prevent me from following the EMTs to the ambulance. The bastards. But they were right. It would have been career suicide to leave. So I pulled myself together. You have to when you're live.

"Hamill took your place as my kitchen helper when I baked Scrumpy Delight. What a dessert, Rose-Ellen. I mean, it's not your ordinary tart. Chocolate? And goat cheese? And a citrus fruit? And *pepper*? Now, that's original."

"So you really liked it?" I say.

"Of course I liked it. But, well, the judges didn't choose it. I'm sorry." Her arms fly out and drop to her sides.

I nod. "It's okay. I'm just glad Ingrid's all right."

She smiles wanly and continues to the waiting room.

I get two coffees from the vending machine and fix Garrett's the way he likes it: lots of cream, no sugar. I'm about to push through the door when I hear his and Polly's voices.

"So what kind of a stunt was that?" Polly says.

"I thought it was time you had some contact with her," he says.

"I send money. In fact, I've been very consistent with sending checks. And you've been very consistent in depositing them."

"Money isn't contact. She wants you, Anita. She needs you."

"It's not that I don't want anything at all to do with her. In fact, recently, I've thought quite a bit about getting back in touch. But honestly, I didn't think you'd welcome that. And the *timing* of all this—"

"When would be a good time for you? Sometime in the *next* decade?"

There's a pause, and I hear a deep exhalation, but I'm not sure who exhales.

"This is a lot for me to take in right now," Polly finally says. "I'm sorry."

"You're goddamn right you're sorry."

"I was so young. I was so scared."

"You were scared? *You* were scared?"

"I was very wrong. A coward, even. But I can't change the past."

"A restraining order, Anita? *Really?*"

"I wanted a clean break. But I'm a different person now."

"How so?"

"I'm—I don't know. I'm different. I'm sure you are, too. I just can't believe you let her come on my show."

"You'd believe it if you knew how much she adored you," Garrett says. "Besides, I promised her she could go, if Zell was a finalist. And I want my daughter to know me as a man of my word. I've lied to her long enough."

*Paging Dr. Turner,* comes a voice over the intercom. *Dr. Turner, line two.*

"Do you really think you were acting in Ingrid's best interest?" says Polly.

"I don't believe you know the first thing about acting in a child's best interest, Anita."

Neither of them speaks for a while. I hear Polly stand and clear her throat. "Listen," she says. "I've got to run. But here's my card. When she's ready—when *you're* ready—call me. We'll hang out or something, the three of us. Or maybe just me and Ingrid, or whatever. We'll see how it goes. How would that be?"

Garrett doesn't reply.

"I mean, maybe you're right. Maybe it's time," Polly says. "Maybe it's not too late to . . . I don't know. Is that what you *want*?"

He still doesn't say anything.

Polly's clicky footsteps approach the door.

I dash away a few steps, then turn around and stroll, as if I'm just now coming up on the waiting area.

In the hallway Polly eyes me, sniffles, and strides toward the exit. "Keep those clothes, Rose-Ellen," she calls over her shoulder. "You look good. And keep up with your baking, too. You never know where things will lead."


MORE PEOPLE SIT IN THE WAITING ROOM NOW: two women in saris with perfect posture; a flat-haired teenager in tight jeans, her legs draped over an armrest; a smelly man with no front teeth stooped at the window.

Garrett leafs through a magazine and sips his coffee. "I see a lot of long conversations with Ingrid in my future," he says. "How do you explain to a nine-year-old that you've been lying to her? That she was right all along?"

"You'll figure out a way," I say. "Don't worry."

"Crap. I hope so." He shakes his head.

"So did you get what you want?" I ask. "I mean, from Polly?"

"Who knows. I don't even know what I wanted, really. I guess I just wanted Ingrid to feel less . . . restless or something. But Anita seems as unreachable as ever." He shrugs. "I'll call her eventually— once I explain things to Ingrid."

The waiting room door bursts open. It's Dennis. "She okay?" He looks around and tucks his press pass under his lapel. The other people in the waiting room stare at him.

"She's fine," says Garrett.

I stand and air kiss Dennis. "What are you doing here?"

"You appeared on live television," he says, out of breath, "with the most recognizable celebrity chef in the world. This is the biggest news to hit Wippamunk since Cornelius Grambling fertilized his hay-fields with clam bellies and stunk up the whole town for weeks. And right now I've got another big story to cover, back at the town hall."

"The tribute for Nick," I say. I completely forgot. Judging by the look on Garrett's face, he forgot, too.

"I came looking for you here because I figured you'd need a ride," Dennis says.

"I wish Ingrid and I could be there," says Garrett, standing. "We were supposed to drive you back, of course, but—"

A nurse enters and bids the two sari-clad women to follow him.

"You have other things to worry about right now," I say. I roll on my tiptoes and kiss Garrett's cheek.

He looks surprised and sad, touched and exhausted, all at the same time. He squeezes my biceps. "Thanks."

"Say good-bye to Ingrid for me?" I say. "Let her know I was here?"

He nods.

I link my arm through Dennis's, and he speed walks through the door and down the hall. His urgency makes me laugh a little, and laughing feels good. Dennis laughs, too, and then we're running through the hospital arm in arm. Running and laughing.

PAPERS AND NOTEBOOKS occupy the passenger seat of Dennis's car. I open the door, and three old steno books and a yellowed issue of *The Wippamunker* slide out onto the wet pavement. The pages flap and pucker in the rain.

"Oh. Sorry," Dennis says. He reaches in through the driver's side and tosses the mess into the backseat. "Just give me a second here."

His car smells like old spilled soda. It's not long before we're cruising along on the Mass Pike. I listen to the rain and the squeaky windshield wipers.

"Dennis?" I say after a while, breaking the silence. "Thanks for the flyers. For Ahab."

"It was nothing," he says, not taking his eyes from the highway. His chin is prominent, his face long, almost concave, like a crescent moon. "He'll come back, don't you think? Happens all the time."

"I hope so," I say. "I do hope so."

"The new guy helped me get those flyers up all over town, you know."

"What's his name? The new guy?"

The rain kicks up, and Dennis taps on the brakes. "Allen," he says. "He won a regional press award for his photos of the ice-fishing derby."

"You like him? Allen?"

"I like him." He glances at me. "But it's not the same, Zell. It'll never be the same."

I gaze out the passenger window. "Did Nick tell you what the present was?" I ask. "The one that was in my oven?"

"Sorry," he says, glancing over at me. "I'm afraid he didn't."

So that's it. I've asked everyone from The Trip—Russ, Pastor Sheila, Chief Kent, France, EJ, Father Chet, and finally Dennis. And none of them know the contents of the singed cube. I could ask others. Arthur, perhaps. Maybe even Terry or Gail.

But no, I decide. I'm going to confront this thing head-on.

"Haven't you opened it yet?" asks Dennis.

"I'm going to," I say. "Soon."

SOMEWHERE AROUND FRAMINGHAM I recline the seat and close my eyes. When I open them again, almost forty minutes have passed. It's still raining. Dennis pulls into the town hall parking lot in Wippamunk.

"You awake?" he asks. The lot is full, so he parks illegally on Main Street. "All the cops are probably inside, anyway."

We weave through the lot to the yellow colonial-era building. Inside, rain smashes against the small wavy squares of window glass.

"After you?" he says when we reach the auditorium doors.

"I'm going to take just a little time, I think. I'll be right in."

He nods and enters. Before the doors fall closed, I glimpse Russ, in a navy suit and soft-soled black shoes, onstage with a microphone in his hand, standing between the American flag and the Massachusetts flag.

I can't go in there. I just can't. Instead I open a little door in the corner labeled BALCONY. I feel my way up the narrow steps.

The small musty balcony is empty save for a little two-seater bench that pinches my butt when I sit on it. I'm behind the crowd. It's bigger than a hundred people. Much bigger. I pick out the usual suspects: EJ, France, Father Chet, Pastor Sheila and her family, my parents, Gail and Terry, Arthur. I recognize a few other faces. Most of these people are strangers. But not strangers to Nick, evidently; or at least, not strangers to his work.

Dennis steps onto the stage and whispers something to Chief, who wears a sweater vest and wingtips. Chief nods as Russ passes him the microphone. Behind them a black cape covers a ten-foot-tall object. I recognize the shape of the object. It's from Trudy's Barn. Only when I saw it, blue tarps covered it. Trudy's top secret commission.

"I've received word that our VIP has arrived, so I'm going to kick things off," Chief says. He glances up into the balcony and catches my eye. I look away.

"I'm not much for making speeches," says Chief. "But I've been asked to say a few words on this solemn occasion, even though we all know why we're here. So, Russ? Thanks for warming up the crowd. I'm going to be brief, because we're definitely violating the fire code here." A dozen people laugh good-naturedly.

"I got to know Nick pretty well on the mission trip we were both on last fall, in New Orleans, to help rebuild homes there," Chief continues. "Nick was a fun guy, but there was a seriousness to him, too, a sensitivity. He was very observant, and a good listener and hard worker. He helped keep the mood light, despite all the devastation around us.

"And all you have to do is look at Nick's photographs to know he was a humanitarian, in the truest sense of that word. Nick's photographs are his legacy, and that's why we've put together, here to my right, a sort of walk-through installation of his most gripping work from our mission trip last fall. I hope you'll all take the time to enjoy the photographs. Police Officer Frances Hogan and reporter Dennis Jolette, of Nick's former employer, *The Wippamunker,* both had a big hand in putting the exhibit together. Let's give them a round of applause—beautiful job, guys."

Applause ripples the crowd. The photographs are several feet wide and tall and mounted on easels. I wonder where France and Dennis got the money to put all this together. Their own paychecks, probably.

Some shots I recognize from Nick's e-mails; most are new to me. The photos of New Orleans—and there are so many—show construction, as opposed to destruction, which I'm sure was Nick's thematic intention. My eyes go to the photographs of people I know. Russ, a tool belt cinching his hips, points to a ceiling joist. Little Pastor Sheila from the back: She wears a Tyvek suit, and she stands before a towering pile of rubbish. Father Chet in his sleeping bag and collared pajama top. He shows the cover of his book, titled *With Every Step, Peace.*

One shot is of Nick, riding in the interfaith van. The shot is slightly out of focus, and I wonder who took it. He wears the "Wippamunk Loves New Orleans" T-shirt—the very shirt now balled up in my bag. I reach into the bag, next to me on the bench, and gather the fabric in my fist.

"Now," Chief says. "Local artist and one-of-a-kind original Gertrude Chaffin was commissioned to create something to remember our boy Nick Roy by. And I think you'll all agree that what she came up with is exactly how we'll remember Nick: *by* his craft. *Of* his craft. *Doing* his craft.

"So, Trudy? Thank you from the bottom of our hearts. I want everyone to know that Trudy donated this work. She wouldn't accept any remuneration for her efforts. We're still undecided about where this statue will be permanently kept. There's talk about raising funds for a park in town, in his name. If anyone is interested in heading that up or helping out with it, please speak with me afterwards."

Trudy takes the stage and speaks softly into the microphone. "Many of the people responsible for today—Frances Hogan, Russell Stapleton, Emmett Murtonen, and so on—are my former students. How marvelous it's been to sit back as the years unfold, and watch them become whatever they are to become in this world. How wonderful, the people who have emerged from this place, this town. Nicholas was my student, too." She replaces the microphone in its stand and bows her head. So does everyone in the hall.

A minute of silence passes.

"Well," Chief finally says, and people lift their heads. "Without further ado—I've always wanted to say that—let's unveil what's under here. Mr. Stapleton? Will you do the honors?"

A camera flash bursts; the new guy—Allen—snaps shots as Russ reemerges from the front row. He somberly grips the edges of the black cloth and sweeps it away. The crowd seems to hold its breath collectively. Then, as one, the crowd moves up a foot or two, closer to Nick.

He's larger than life. He wears faded jeans, a down vest, and rectangular tortoiseshell glasses. Even from way up here I can see that Trudy got the minutest details right: a small gold paperclip binds the broken left stem of his glasses. A diamond-shaped pockmark is etched on his chin, where his grandmother's Maine coon cat bit him when he was seven. He wears his tan Timberlands. The sleeves of his red flannel shirt are rolled to his calloused elbows. The lens protrudes from the camera in his hands. He looks like he's just spotted something he wants to photograph.

A subdued applause circulates, then fades. The room returns to silence, except for the sound of one person weeping. And for once, the weeping is not coming from me. It's coming from Arthur. Someone—Nick's uncle Raymond?—bear-hugs him.

My hands fly to my mouth. I stand and knock over the little bench, and it clatters to the floor.

Everyone turns and looks up. No one speaks, but the faces are kind. So kind and raw that I can't look at them. I can't look at anyone or anything.

I run down the dark balcony steps and out to the parking lot, and among the neatly arranged rows of wet cars and trucks, I hang my head between my knees, Polly Pinch style. I take deep breaths.

Deep, deep breaths.

"Zell?"

It's EJ. I recognize his chef clogs. He wears them with wrinkly black slacks, a more-wrinkled button-down shirt, and a cheap tie that hangs two inches above his waistband—the same exact getup he wore to France's academy graduation, years ago.

I'm still bent over. Blood buzzes to my head, and snot drips to the slick pavement. My neck feels stretchy and my lips tingle. But I don't cry. I don't g.d. cry.

"I can't look at you right now, EJ," I say. "You of all people."

"I know. I know. It's okay. You don't have to look at me."

## EJ

Zell's doubled over in the parking lot, still in the fancy clothes she wore on television. She's soaking wet; they both are. He watches her a moment, wondering what to say, wondering whether this whole thing— this *closure*—was a mistake, after all. Maybe closure is a myth.

The town hall's front doors swing open, and people stream out, pulling on lightweight raincoats and popping open umbrellas. At the sound of their voices, Zell straightens but still doesn't look in EJ's direction.

"Let's go sit in the van," he says. "Come on."

She nods, and they hurry to the Muffinry van. He climbs into the driver's seat and unlocks the passenger door for her. Once inside, she stares through the rain-blurred windshield at the people, in bunches of twos, threes, and fours, zigzagging through the lot. Droplets cling to the ends of her hair.

This is not an uncomfortable silence, EJ thinks, sitting there, as rain plinks off the van roof. It's a patient one. He strokes his goatee, which he trimmed for the occasion. It has a tendency to grow in uneven points if he's not careful. He gets a whiff of Zell's hairspray, then his own sweet and earthy smell, like chopped almonds.

"Did we do the wrong thing?" he finally asks. "With the statue and all?"

"Of course not. It's amazing," she says. "It's perfect."

"Want to see something else cool?" says EJ.

Zell half laughs, raising her eyebrows, studying her fingernails. "What?"

"Turn around."

In the back of the van sits an enormous wooden sandwich half. The bread is thick and white, and lunchmeats are layered along with cheese, hard-boiled egg slices, and a greenish paste. Olive paste, EJ knows. He remembers the salty tang of it, and how Charlene called it tapenade.

He whistles admiringly, to lighten the mood a bit. "It's a muffaletta," he says.

Zell half laughs again, crouches, and makes her way toward the back of the van. She touches her fingertips to the wondrous, ridiculous muffaletta. She presses her lips to it, just for a moment, then kneels next to it.

EJ joins her, resting his hand on the top slice of bread. If only the statue were real, he thinks. If only he could take a bite, feel that many-textured comfort.

He tells Zell about his visit with Ye Olde Home Ec Witch, to commission the muffaletta. Mrs. Chaffin—he had a hard time calling her Trudy, even though she insisted—gave him a tour of her woodshop. He strolled among the creatures—an otter sunning on a beach chair, raccoons square-dancing atop a garbage pail. She showed him her latest school mascot, hopelessly un-PC: the Wippamunk High School Mountaineer, a barefoot, toothless old man waving a shotgun, with torn pants, knobby ankles, and a long, scraggly beard.

"Was Mrs. Chaffin really as mean as we made her out to be, back in high school?" EJ asks. "Or were we the mean ones, all along?"

"I know what you mean," says Zell, eyeing the huge toothpick protruding from the top of the sandwich. She still can't look at him, he knows.

"Anyway," he says. "It's for my friend in New Orleans. This baby, I mean." He slaps the muffaletta twice.

"Charlene?" asks Zell.

"Yeah. Charlene."

Zell points to EJ's left, at an old amplifier left over from his and Russ's The Massholes days. "What's that?" she asks.

From atop the amp, EJ retrieves a shallow tub of ice. Inside the tub is a Bundt pan filled with snow.

"I'm going back down to New Orleans," he says. "I'm staying down there for a while, until I figure some things out. This snow is for Charlene, too. She says she hasn't seen snow in years. Can you imagine that? I've been keeping this snow in my freezer. And I just thought I would test it out, drive around with it in this little tub of ice, to see if it melts. And so far, so good. I figure I can stop on the way and replace the ice, as needed."

He hands Zell the Bundt pan. "Travis'll run ship while I'm away," he says. "You shoulda seen the Muffinry today. A ton of people came to watch you on TV. Is Ingrid okay?"

"She'll be fine." Zell's fingertips brush the snow inside the pan. "You love her? Charlene?"

"That's what I'm going to find out, I guess," EJ says.

"She's the one whose new church you were going to see." She sets the pan of snow next to her.

EJ grips Zell's shoulder, which feels as hard as wood. She hiccups and sucks in her bottom lip, just like a little kid who fell off a bike and skinned her knee. But she doesn't cry. The rain drums harder against the van, slashes sideways past the little round window above her head.

"Life used to seem so simple," she says. "Me, Nick, Ahab. Nothing else really mattered." She breathes hard through her nose. Her face is all scrunched up, but her cheeks remain dry.

EJ doesn't know what to do, and he's run out of things to say. So he kneels and leans into her, wraps his arms around her, and squeezes. His goateed chin scrapes her scalp as she returns the embrace.

"I've got to start from scratch now," says Zell, her voice quiet and steady. "Every day. Every minute, it seems."

"There was nothing I could do," he says into her damp hair.

"I know."

"It should have been me."

"No."

"It could have been me. Easily."

"But it wasn't."

He feels it break over him like a windy gust: hot breath and tears, for all they've lost. "Don't hate me anymore," he pleads, weeping. "Don't hate me because it wasn't me."

Zell buries her face in his chest. Her fingertips are freezing-cold points on the nape of his neck.

"I could never hate you, Silo."

# 11

## Zell

*A* DAY AFTER THE POLLY PINCH INCIDENT, Ingrid's peppy as ever. She even goes to school that Monday, and she and Garrett come over later to tell me about the party her teacher threw, and how she read Dennis's article on the Warm the Soul contest to the class, and afterward they talked about cooking and food allergies and being on TV.

And the next day, just an ordinary Tuesday, I wake up, throw back the curtains, and enter the attic.

I'm not sure why. Maybe it's simply the notion that overtakes me—the notion that it's time.

I'm surprised how dusty the steps are. I mean, you think of furniture getting dusty, and shelves, but not really stairs. But my feet leave prints on each step, as if in snow.

I tote the turntable with me. At the top of the steps—before I even look around—I plug it in and set it on the floor. Soon Gladys sings—in every beat of my heart, there's a beat for you.

I stand straight and tall, throw my shoulders back, and face the unfinished room. I half expect Nick to be there, edged in red light, his back to me as he clips a photograph up to dry. I imagine slipping my arms around him, smelling his smell—coppery sweat, woods, Old Spice—over the pungent odor of darkroom chemicals.

But the red lights aren't on, of course. The sun shines through loose slats in the boarded-up window.

I run my fingers over his equipment. It's all pretty dusty: the enlarger, the copy stand, the developing tank, the print washer. The sink, the tongs, the film reels. The sponges and gloves. Dust coats the jugs of chemicals on the floor. I caress his beat-up old camera bag, the one he never used anymore but couldn't bear to throw away. I page through an old notebook in which he scribbled the names of people he encountered around town, for captions. I finger that little brush-thing that puffs air to clean the lenses. The bristles are so soft.

Other than the dust, everything is as Nick left it, even that shot he took of Ahab and me in the backyard, the day before The Trip. Ahab's tongue is wagging, and it looks like he's smiling. That photo hangs from the cord, totally dry, of course. It's curled stiff, in fact. I might do something with it. Flatten it out and put it in a frame, maybe.

I sit on the attic floor and open the cardboard box Arthur gave me after the memorial service. I undo the twist tie on the plastic bag inside—a twist tie, like on a loaf of bread!—and sink my hand right in. And I pull out a fistful of Nick. He's whitish gray and chunky now, more like gravel than dust.

Then I move on to the singed cube. Part of me expects the oven present to be a joke. Like a jack-in-the-box. Or a can of peanut brittle that isn't peanut brittle at all, but a fake snake, all coiled up, that springs and wriggles like crazy when you open it.

I bang the cube on the floor a couple of times to crack open the lid, because it melted shut in the fire. Finally the lid breaks off. And inside is an authentic potbellied ceramic Polly Pinch LOVE canister, in perfect condition, which is uncanny, really, when you think about it. When you consider that half of Wippamunk's volunteer fire squad tromped through my kitchen that day. When you consider all that wild black smoke rolling from the oven.

Is this gift intentionally ironic, I wonder? Was Nick trying to say something smart-ass about how I never cook? Maybe. Or maybe he had no idea it was a Polly Pinch accessory. Maybe he thought I could sweep my eraser pellets into it. Maybe he just saw it in a shop somewhere and said, "Hey, Zell can keep her coffee fresh in this thing." Maybe he simply thought I'd like it.

At first I think the LOVE canister is it, but I realize there's something *inside*. So I pry off the big cork lid.

I look inside and find a new heart. A new model heart, to replace the old one he gave me for our high school graduation.

I sit there at the top of the attic steps for some time, my feet planted between the box of ashes and the LOVE canister, and I hold the heart, which amazingly still smells like new plastic. I remember our graduation day, how Nick dragged me under the bleachers. How I kissed him as the sun streamed through the wood. He said I was the only woman in the world who sheds tears of joy over a model heart.

This new model is dissectible, so I remove the atrium walls and the front heart wall to check out the inside. I inspect the ventricles, the arteries, the upper section of the esophagus, the upper bronchi. I hold a valve up to my eye and peer through it, down the steps, and it's like looking through a red-ringed lens.

Smiling, I blink the tears away, tuck the heart under my chin, and hug my knees. The pulse in my neck throbs against the plastic, and it's as if I could absorb this new heart, make Nick's gift a living, beating part of me.

Then I realize, it always has been. It always will be.

In June, I head to Okemo for a week or two; there are things there that I need do. But I don't tell Gail and Terry about these things. I just ask them if I can visit for a while. And of course they say yes.

The drive to Vermont is positively verdant. I pull up the driveway, and Terry comes to the door. A pink boa circles his neck.

"Playing Princesses?" I ask.

Tasha wobbles behind him in too-big high-heels. "Auntie Zell! Abe-abb?"

"Welcome," says Terry, waving me inside. "We're so glad you decided to come up."

"Did Gail hire a college student?" I ask. "To finish the bathroom mural?"

"A college student?" Terry says. "No."

"Did she paint over it?"

He laughs his theatrically British "What the hell" laugh. "No, no, of course not. The mural's waiting for you, whenever you're ready."

"I'm ready."

"Brilliant. Now?"

"Now."

G.d. now.

I breeze past my parents, who hunch over a chessboard in the living room. My mother half stands. "Rose-Ellen, you're here. Can I pour you some wine?"

"I'm all set, Mom," I say. "I just need to do this."

In the bathroom, I hold the envelope, grainy with dust and brittle with age. I pinch the edge of the photograph and slide it out. Mountains in the first stages of thaw, boulders and evergreens shimmering. We stand in a row. Our faces are sunburned and exhilarated. Terry, head to toe in purple, wraps his arm around the much-taller Gail, who poses with angled elbows and a lowered chin, as if she's a model on a photo shoot. I'm next to Gail, and Nick holds me close. He wears the same A-shaped, pom-pommed ski hat he's worn since eighth grade, the one that's stretched over the tip of his snowshoes in my closet.

The morning of the photograph, when we had snowshoed about three-quarters up Okemo, Terry announced that he had to drain the main vein. He asked Gail to lend him some assistance, because he didn't want to injure his back hefting heavy objects.

"Ha, ha," Gail said. She unzipped her pocket and reapplied lip balm.

"Cheerio," Nick called after Terry, who entered a thicket of spruces.

Seconds later Terry hollered for us, so we followed his prints, past his still-steaming yellow hole. We found him standing in a small clearing that looked out over peaks to the north. Killington, probably, and beyond it, Mount Ellen and Mount Abraham. To the east towered Ascutney.

Terry had discovered a hidden vista. No sign pointed to it; no tracks led to it. We enjoyed our own private viewing of blue-gray peaks and puffy clouds.

Nick fished around in his camera bag. "This deserves to be recorded for prosperity."

Terry chuckled. "Posterity, you dim-witted colonist." He slurped water from his bottle.

"Posterity," Nick said. "Whatever. Do you mind hanging out here for a second while I get the shot set up?"

"Hell, no," Gail said. She held her cell phone out, and when she got a bar she called our parents. They put Tasha on, and Gail cooed, "Love you, doodle-bums. Be a good baay-beee."

We stayed there the whole morning—talking, laughing, snacking on raisins and granola bars. We made chairs out of snow.

After an hour, Nick rubbed a stick of sunscreen all over his face and said, "Trivia time: What does 'Okemo' mean in Abenaki?"

"Stupid colonist?" Terry said. He rested his head on Gail's lap.

"Nope," Nick said. "Gail? Guesses?"

Gail rolled her eyes. "Zell, got'ny trail mix?"

Nick threw an arm around me, pecked my forehead, and sighed. "'Okemo' means 'All Come Home.'"

R EAL TIME. REAL SPACE. On the bathroom wall, against the mountains, are four empty spots where Terry, Gail, Nick, and I, as happy and exhausted as sled dogs, will finally appear.

"Hi," I whisper. My hand fills the white space for Nick's face. My forehead touches the spot where his forehead—damp, wrinkled from squinting—belongs.

I hear my sister clear her throat. She pokes her head in and talks softly. "Before you get started, and before I forget, I just wanted to show you something. Remember that hot priest in the Muffinry?"

"Father Chet?"

"Sweet Father Chet." She slides into the bathroom. "Remember he whispered something sexy to you in French? And I wrote it down and said I would translate it on Babel Fish? Well, I finally got around to it, and here's what I came up with." She shows me the wrinkled, coffee-stained napkin.

Underneath the phonetically spelled French words is Gail's translation—a statement I remember from one of Nick's e-mails, a statement that frustrated him, because Father Chet never offered a concrete explanation:

*WE ARE ALL CONNECTED.*

I PAINT ALL DAY. The next morning—after my parents leave to take in the annual polo tournament—I work for another two hours or so. Until the mural is complete.

That's it. I feel no sense of ceremony, not even a real sense of accomplishment. The mural was something that needed doing—an unfinished project. And I finished it, and . . . that's it.

Nick looks just as he does in the photograph: sweaty, eager. Except he's life-size, and shinier, and somehow seems touchable.

After I wash up, I summon Gail and Terry, who hold hands and observe my art with wistful expressions on their faces. Tasha totters in and points. "Uncle Nick?"

Terry crouches and tucks an unruly curl behind her little ear. "That's right, love," he says. "Uncle Nick."

I LACE UP MY HIKING BOOKS. I zip Ahab's fairy charm into the pocket of my shorts. And in the passenger seat of my car, I buckle the seat belt over the LOVE canister.

It's the best kind of summer day in Vermont: cloudless and dazzling and almost warm, and I head toward Mount Holly, where you can access that old overgrown trail that goes practically straight up the back of Okemo. Okemo's butt crack, Nick used to say. The same overgrown trail we snowshoed that winter day, he and Gail and Terry and I.

But this time I hike alone, the LOVE canister tucked under one arm. Its contents are surprisingly heavy.

It's a beautiful hike. Everything around and underneath me—trees, leaves, dirt—is damp, warm/cold, and becoming new. There is practically no breeze whatsoever—the air seems so still. And I meet no other people as I climb, which is fine with me.

Huffing and puffing, I hike straight up. No stopping. Briefly I search for the hidden vista Terry discovered on our winter hike, but I don't find it.

At the summit I expect to see some other hikers, but it seems I've got the place to myself. I approach the rickety, defunct fire tower, where a NO TRESPASSING sign is chained across the first step. But I say, "No trespassing? Whatev" (I actually say this aloud), and vault right over the chain.

Up, up, up the tower. Twisting, winding up. The higher I get, the more the tower sways and groans, and I think maybe I shouldn't have trespassed. But I keep going: five stories up.

When I reach the top, I catch my breath a moment and wish I'd carried some water with me. I suck fresh mountain air through my nose to clear it of the residual smell of paint and closed-up bathroom.

I fish in my pocket for the busted charm, pull it out, and finger it. Its fairy wings and one remaining foot flash in the sunlight. I cock back my arm and I'm about to fling the charm into the woods—but I hear something. An animal? A person? It approaches the tower. Twigs snap, leaves crunch. I search the ground far below, but can't detect the source of the noises.

Ahab? I wonder, and my chest leaps at the thought. I imagine him appearing at the edge of the trees, sniffing the air. In my fantasy,

Ahab's collar is gone, porcupine needles protrude from his side, and his eye-patch eye is swollen shut. He's suffered, but he's survived, and he's as self-possessed as an old sea captain. That's his greyhound style. I imagine climbing all the way down the tower steps to bury my nose in his neck, where the fur smells like spring; like dried sylvan blood; like indelible, unknowable adventure.

"Yarr!" I whisper, watching the trees where the twigs and leaves continue to crunch. "A noggin o' rum's what I need!"

Finally the creature appears—a fox. It's still for a moment, just long enough for me to admire its daintiness. Its white cheeks and chest blaze in the bright sun. It continues past the tower, unaware of my presence.

I remember Terry's prediction that Ahab simply "went off on a toot" and is sure to return, and Ingrid's classmate's uncle, whose dog walked to Kentucky.

I pocket the charm—I'll hang on to it for a bit more. Just a little while longer. What was it that Nick wrote? *There is disappointment, but there is also hope.* Something like that.

I give the LOVE canister a big old two-handed shake. I don't say anything, and I don't even really *think* anything. No prayer, no song, no reflective good-bye pause. I simply whip the LOVE lid off and, as if splashing a bucket of water on a soapy car, I toss Nick's ashes to the blue sky—try to coat the sun, the tips of the pines, the peaks of the mountains, with him. He is in this spot forever now, and yet, at the same time, gone.

Neither here nor there.

Tears rise, and somehow a laugh, too. That old pinprick sensation plucks my chest. But it's not one tiny, distant puncture; it's a thousand of them, making me feel like I'm contained and bursting, hot and cold, happy and sad, all at once.

June 29, 2008

From: rose-ellen@roymedicalillustration.com

To: nicholas.roy@thewippamunker.com

Dear Nick,

Thank you for my Polly Pinch canister and my new heart. It's a beautiful heart. A wonderful replacement.

Speaking of hearts, I have finally discovered what is wrong with mine.

Since you died, my cardiologist's office left about a million messages on my answering machine. I never called back. I didn't want to know what was wrong with me. I didn't care. Or maybe I was afraid *nothing* was wrong with me. I wanted my heart to be fubar, and I wanted it to kill me, so that I would be reunited with you in heaven. Yeah. That's how pathetic I've felt.

Then just a few days ago, after I got home from Vermont, my doorbell rang. I figured it was Ingrid or Garrett or Russ or Gail. But it was Dr. Fung, with her silky chin-length hair and dewy black eyes.

She told me one of her office assistants somehow knows Pastor Sheila. Via that social chain, Dr. Fung learned that you died on a mission trip in New Orleans, and that ever since, I've been hopelessly depressed. And so, when it became apparent that I would never answer the phone, Dr. Fung took it upon herself to call on me personally.

I thought she was going to tell me that I suffered broken heart syndrome. That's a real thing, you know. Something about the stress hormones released when you get shocking news—the stress hormones stay in your system indefinitely, straining the heart. But then

I remembered that I've had my weird heart thing since *before* you died, so it couldn't be broken heart syndrome.

"How many cups of coffee do you drink a day?" asked Dr. Fung.

"Three. Sometimes more."

"Like how much more?"

"Like three," I said. "Or seven or eight."

"Drink less coffee, Rose-Ellen," Dr. Fung said. She smiled.

Drink less g.d. coffee.

"That's it?" I said.

"That's it."

"You're saying jack-crap is wrong with my heart?"

"Yes. I believe you're just overcaffeinated. Some people are extremely sensitive, so knock off the caffeine, and we'll see what happens."

So, that's the story of my heart. How do you like that one? All that drama, all that worry, for nothing. I could have come on The Trip with you after all.

Imagine if I did. Imagine how different our lives would be.

Maybe that morning you wouldn't have agreed to tour the construction site of the big new church they were building on the outskirts of town. Maybe EJ and you and me, the three of us, would have taken a morning to ourselves, gone to Charlene's café to hang out and discuss things. The people, the projects, the work we did in New Orleans, and the work that still must be done.

Or, imagine if EJ wasn't so courteous. What if *he* walked first, directly behind the construction manager, instead of letting you go first? Or, imagine if I toured the site with you, and *I* went first. Imagine if that scaffolding collapsed on *me.* Imagine if that beam landed on me. Crushed *my* hard hat, and underneath it, *my* skull, *my* brain, *my* spine.

I know all about the spine, how it's constructed. Winged vertebrae protect the spinal column, and spongy disks between the vertebrae allow the spine to flex. Inside the sheath hum all those nerves. Thousands and thousands of nerves, fine as hair, alive with electricity, vibrating their messages, their commands.

When were you going to give me the presents? When you got back from The Trip? For Christmas? Were you going to call me from the road that afternoon, and tell me to open the oven?

As you always used to say, these questions are "neither here nor there." They are inconsequential. With time, I suspect, they will simply blow away.

Anyway, here's another e-mail I'd like you to see. I got it this morning. I think it'll make you happy. It's pasted below.

I don't know when I'll e-mail you again. This might be the last one for a while. But I still love you.

I'll always love you.

~Zell


Dear Ms. Roy,

You might remember me: Hamill Harding from San Diego. I was glad to hear, through Polly Pinch's assistant, Spike Miller, that the little girl made it through her horrible ordeal okay. I sure am sorry about that. If I had known about her peanut allergy, I would never have allowed her to eat a Hidden Cranberry Spice-eez.

I've been thinking a lot about what Spike told me when I was backstage, getting ready. The little girl told him that you planned on donating the prize money to a New Orleans charity, if you won.

That you were inspired by the e-mails your husband wrote while he was on a mission trip.

I did some research and found a couple articles online from this little newspaper, The Wippamunker, where, I gather, your husband used to work. I saw an archived article about how he died during the mission, and another more recent article about a public tribute his friends put together, displaying his photographs. And how that chain-saw artist donated a statue of him. My wife and I were very touched by the way your community came together, and by the impact one man seemed to have on so many people.

I found a link for making online donations to the interfaith group your husband traveled with. I understand that all donations help the people of New Orleans rebuild their city—their churches, schools, and libraries—and in turn, their lives, in the wake of the hurricane. My wife and I decided to donate half of the prize money I won in the Warm the Soul contest to the interfaith group. Mind you, money doesn't solve all the world's problems. But in this case, I think, it'll go a long way.

Yours truly,

Hamill

BACK IN WIPPAMUNK, I don't see Ingrid and Garrett for a few days. The truck's gone, and their side of the house remains inactive. I'm a little lonely without them, but it's probably good for me to spend a few days by myself, to catch up on work and even do a little spring cleaning. I find myself performing chores I haven't done in years, like laundering the curtains in the living room and rotating the mattress. I even wash Hank head to toe with Windex and paper towels. And I take my little woven rugs out back and shake them. I swear when I reposition them on the floor, they look brand-new.

Then one late afternoon, as I'm upstairs putting finishing strokes on a patella, and Gladys is crooning away about peaceful waters and gentle breezes, I hear Garrett's truck rumbling up the road. I skip downstairs to greet them on their side of the porch.

Ingrid runs to me and hugs me so tight, I have to take a couple of steps backward to keep my balance.

"Whoa," I say. "Hi there."

"I haven't seen you in, like, forever," she says. "Were you drawing? You smell like pencils."

"It's my new perfume."

She giggles. "We spent three days in Boston."

Carrying a little suitcase in one hand and Ingrid's backpack in the other, Garrett pauses on the steps. I glance at him and smile. He mouths "Hi," not wanting to interrupt Ingrid's story.

"Trudy came out one day, and we rode the swan boats in the Public Gardens," she says. "And another day when it rained, we met my mother at the science museum. They have a lightning show there, and my mother screamed because she was really scared by the crazy loud lightning noises. It was funny. But I wasn't scared. And at Fenway Park I ate vanilla ice cream from a little plastic batting helmet. And there's a red line painted on the sidewalk that leads you to Paul Revere's house. Did you know that? It's called the Trail to Freedom."

"She means the Freedom Trail," says Garrett, laughing. "Come on in."

He leaves their things by the stairs and follows Ingrid into the kitchen, where she roots around in the fridge. "What's for dinner, Dad?"

"I don't know yet, boo-boo." He opens the curtains over the sink and pushes up the window, grunting a little when it gets stuck. And I realize, I'm not just watching him trying to get the window unstuck.

I'm *admiring* him. I admire the muscles in his back, working under his T-shirt, and the fact that he thinks to open a window, first thing, after a few days away.

"OMG." Ingrid whirls around and slaps the side of her head. "Zell's present! How could we forget?"

"It's in the front pocket of my suitcase," says Garrett. "Why don't you go get it?"

She twirls away toward the stairs, and I sit at the kitchen table. "You got me a present?" I ask.

"Oh, just something small," he says, and winks. He sorts through the mail, separating envelopes into two piles on the table. A warm breeze lifts the curtains and stirs my hair.

"While you took a little vacation in Vermont," he says, "we decided we'd take one, too, in Boston. And we ended up hanging out with Ingrid's mom for a bit."

"How was it?" I ask quietly.

"It was . . ." He trails off and crashes into the chair opposite me. "Awkward. But awkward's better than nothing, I guess. Right?"

"Right. It's a start."

"A start," he repeats, and I remember that night at Tunkamog Lake, the feeling of his fingertips threading through my hair, the warmth that enveloped me when he pulled me close. I flash him a half smile over the piles of envelopes. "Yeah," I say. "A start."

Ingrid sashays grandly into the kitchen, and Garrett and I share one last glance before giving her our attention. She hoists a flat object wrapped in a plastic bag. "Ta-da. For you."

"For *me*?" I say, feigning surprise. Inside the bag is *Scrumpy Every Time*, Polly Pinch's brand-new, debut cookbook. I flip through the glossy pages and see that she signed it, *To Zell, who warmed my soul.*

"Thanks so much, you guys," I say. "I'll definitely get a lot of use out of this."

Ingrid claps and jumps around a little. "Isn't that cool? I got one, too. *Signed.* Anyway, Dad, *dinner*?" She hops next to his chair and throws an arm around his neck. "I'm starving."

"You shouldn't say that," he says, kissing her palm with a loud smack. "You're not *starving.* You just feel really hungry."

"Okay then, I feel really, really hungry."

He gestures to the cookbook with Ingrid's hand, which makes her giggle. "What should we have for dinner, Zell?" he asks.

"You're asking the wrong person," I say with a laugh. "But, okay." I open to a random page, where Polly is shown barefoot in a sun-flooded kitchen, wearing faded denim clam diggers and fitting a lid on a lobster pot. "How about this?" I suggest. "Grilled Lemon-Pepper Lobster Rolls with Super Simp Caesar?"

"Mmm." Ingrid nods.

"Sure," says Garrett. "I'll just go on out back and fish some lobster out of the ocean."

"*Dad.*" She rolls her eyes, Ingrid style.

"Seriously," he says, "I think I can probably find something in the freezer to throw on the grill. Zell? Join us?"

"Yeah," says Ingrid. "We can cook dinner, the three of us. Like a *family.*" Her eyes are big and bright, and Garrett eyes me expectantly.

"Why not?" I say. "I'll go grab my apron."

"Yessss!" she says. "Don't forget your matching oven mitts."

"Great." Garrett heads for the freezer. "And what about Gladys?" he asks. "Can she join us for dinner?"

"Of course," I say, getting up from the table. "She's quite portable."

"I'll come with you." Ingrid grasps my hand and pulls me to the door.

I skip beside her, and my throat makes a sound, and a second goes by before I realize—I'm giggling.

I'm skipping, and I'm g.d. giggling.

Maybe it's my new Zell style.

# Scrumpy Delight (For Ahab)

Yield: One Scrumpy Delight. Serves two to four.

For best flavor, use fresh pineapple, and grill slices before chopping. If using
canned chopped pineapple, drain juice well.

1 heaping cup well-chopped pineapple (if substituting fresh
   strawberries, apples, or peaches, wash and dry fruit
   completely)
2 ounces spreadable goat cheese, softened slightly in microwave
   (substitute other soft cheeses, such as cream cheese, if desired)
1 tablespoon honey
1 teaspoon fresh lime juice
Scant ½ teaspoon freshly ground black pepper (sounds like a lot,
   but trust us)
Polly Pinch's Super Simp Flaky™ piecrust (substitute store-
   bought crust, or make your own from scratch using a favorite
   recipe, if desired)
1 (1½-ounce) dark or milk chocolate bar
2 teaspoons whole milk or cream

## Garnish

Brown sugar
Chilled fresh raspberries (substitute blueberries, if desired)
Freshly ground pepper to taste

Preheat the oven to 425°F. Lightly grease a baking sheet.

Combine the pineapple, cheese, honey, lime juice, and pepper in
a large mixing bowl.

Carefully lay the piecrust flat on the baking sheet. Repair any
tears in the dough with moistened fingertips.

Place the chocolate bar in the center of the piecrust.

Pour the pineapple mixture onto the chocolate bar. Using a spatula, spread the mixture out toward the edge of the dough, leaving about a 1-inch margin.

Using your fingertips, drag two opposite sides of the piecrust to meet in the center, forming a rectangle. Brush the top of the crust with milk.

Cook for 20 to 25 minutes or until crust is golden brown.

Remove from the oven. Sprinkle with brown sugar and pepper, if desired. Garnish with berries.

Using a sharp knife, divide into segments.

Best served warm.

# Acknowledgments

I extend my deep appreciation to the following individuals, who brought this book to life: my agent Laney Katz Becker; Celeste Fine; my editor Erika Imranyi and the team at Dutton; kind authors Amy MacKinnon, Roland Merullo, and Rachel Simon, for generous advice; relatives, friends, teachers, and colleagues who support and inspire me, especially the Adamses, my parents Barbara and Robert Bessette, my brother Rob, my sister Ann-Marie Hanlon, Scott Humfeld, Jim Keogh and the Landmark crew, Benj Lipchak and Jessica Sands, Lori Litchman and Dave Tavani, Joe Molis, Bob Moran, the Quick family, the Rayworths, Susan O'Keefe, Sue Rubenstein, the Shagenskys, Jay Sommer, Jan Trembley; those who read my early work, especially Shelly Halloran; volunteers who helped in and around New Orleans and the people from that area who shared their trials, fears, successes, and hopes; and most of all Matt—my love, my breath, my heart.

# About the Author

Alicia Bessette was born and raised in Massachusetts. A freelance writer and pianist, Alicia and her husband, novelist Matthew Quick, live near Philadelphia with their adopted racing greyhound. *Simply from Scratch* is her first novel.